REDNECK™

CREATED BY

Donny Cates & Lisandro Estherren

DONNY CATES
CREATOR, WRITER

LISANDRO ESTHERREN
CREATOR, ARTIST

DEE CUNNIFFE
COLORIST

REDNECK VOLUME 1. FIRST PRINTING. OCTOBER 2017. PUBLISHED BY IMAGE COMICS, INC. OFFICE OF PUBLICATION: 2701 NW VAUGHN ST., STE. 780, PORTLAND, OR 97210. ORIGINALLY PUBLISHED IN SINGLE MAGAZINE FORM AS REDNECK #1-6. REDNECK™ (INCLUDING ALL PROMINENT CHARACTERS FEATURED HEREIN), ITS LOGO AND ALL CHARACTER LIKENESSES ARE TRADEMARKS OF SKYBOUND, LLC, UNLESS OTHERWISE NOTED. IMAGE COMICS® AND ITS LOGOS ARE REGISTERED TRADEMARKS AND COPYRIGHTS OF IMAGE COMICS, INC. ALL RIGHTS RESERVED. NO PART OF THIS PUBLICATION MAY BE REPRODUCED OR TRANSMITTED IN ANY FORM OR BY ANY MEANS (EXCEPT FOR SHORT EXCERPTS FOR REVIEW PURPOSES) WITHOUT THE EXPRESS WRITTEN PERMISSION OF IMAGE COMICS, INC. ALL NAMES, CHARACTERS, EVENTS AND LOCALES IN THIS PUBLICATION ARE ENTIRELY FICTIONAL. ANY RESEMBLANCE TO ACTUAL PERSONS (LIVING OR DEAD), EVENTS OR PLACES, WITHOUT SATIRIC INTENT, IS COINCIDENTAL. PRINTED IN THE U.S.A. FOR INFORMATION REGARDING THE CPSIA ON THIS PRINTED MATERIAL CALL: 203-595-3636 AND PROVIDE REFERENCE # RICH – 764760. ISBN: 978-1-5343-0331-7 ISBN BBFP: 978-1-5343-0626-4 ISBN IJ: 978-1-5343-0627-1 ISBN DCBS: 978-1-5343-0628-8 ISBN NB: 978-1-5343-0629-5

SKYBOUND™
FOR SKYBOUND ENTERTAINMENT

ROBERT KIRKMAN CHAIRMAN
DAVID ALPERT CEO
SEAN MACKIEWICZ SVP, EDITOR-IN-CHIEF
SHAWN KIRKHAM SVP, BUSINESS DEVELOPMENT
BRIAN HUNTINGTON ONLINE EDITORIAL DIRECTOR
JUNE ALIAN PUBLICITY DIRECTOR
ANDRES JUAREZ ART DIRECTOR
JON MOISAN EDITOR
ARIELLE BASICH ASSISTANT EDITOR
CARINA TAYLOR PRODUCTION ARTIST

PAUL SHIN BUSINESS DEVELOPMENT ASSISTANT
JOHNNY O'DELL ONLINE EDITORIAL ASSISTANT
SALLY JACKA ONLINE EDITORIAL ASSISTANT
DAN PETERSEN DIRECTOR OF OPERATIONS & EVENTS
NICK PALMER OPERATIONS COORDINATOR

INTERNATIONAL INQUIRIES: AG@SEQUENTIALRIGHTS.COM
LICENSING INQUIRIES: CONTACT@SKYBOUND.COM

WWW.SKYBOUND.COM

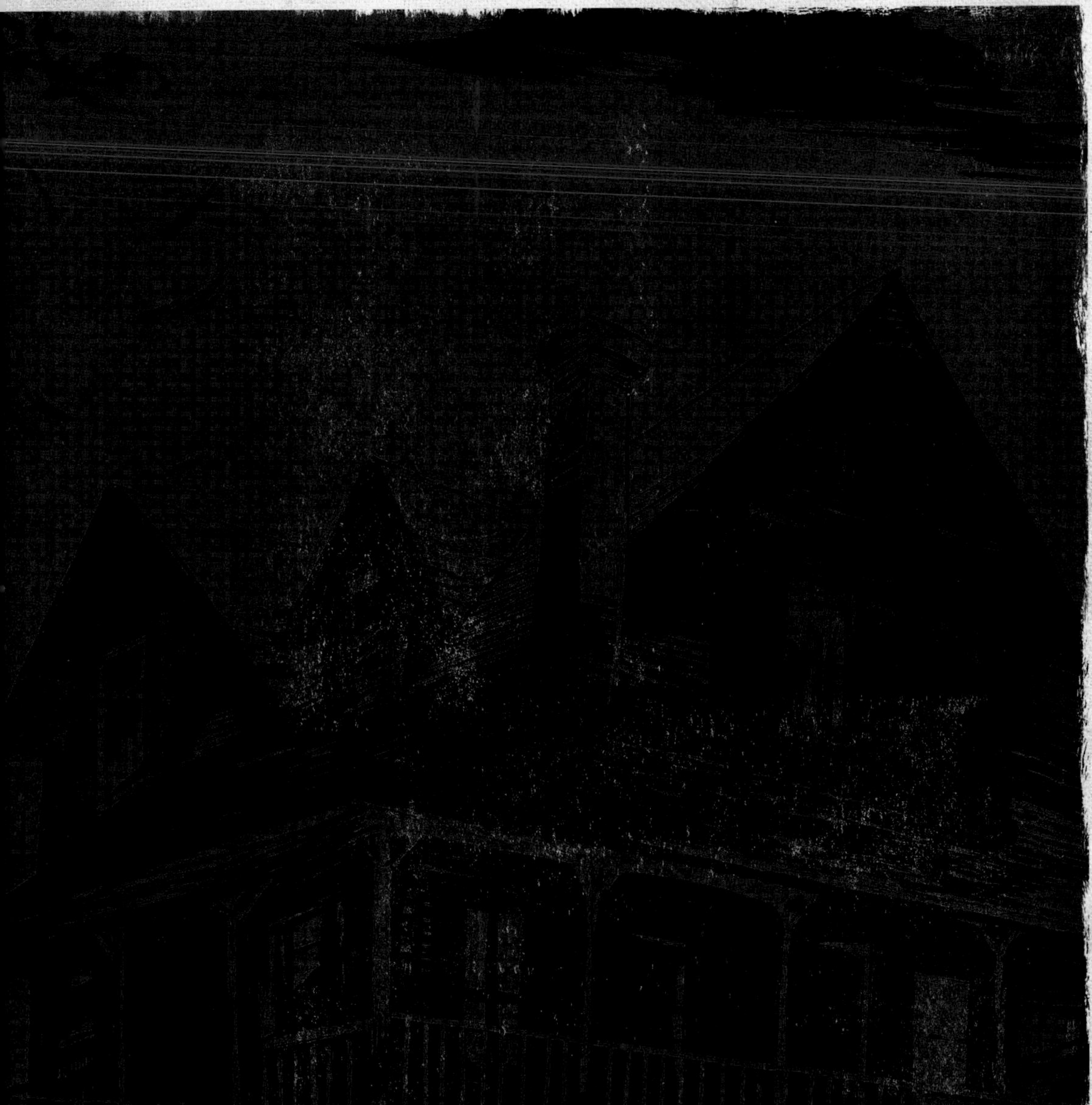

JOE SABINO
LETTERER

ARIELLE BASICH
ASSISTANT EDITOR

JON MOISAN
EDITOR

® IMAGE COMICS, INC.

ROBERT KIRKMAN CHIEF OPERATING OFFICER
ERIK LARSEN CHIEF FINANCIAL OFFICER
TODD MCFARLANE PRESIDENT
MARC SILVESTRI CHIEF EXECUTIVE OFFICER
JIM VALENTINO VICE PRESIDENT

ERIC STEPHENSON PUBLISHER
COREY MURPHY DIRECTOR OF SALES
JEFF BOISON DIRECTOR OF PUBLISHING PLANNING & BOOK TRADE SALES
CHRIS ROSS DIRECTOR OF DIGITAL SALES
JEFF STANG DIRECTOR OF SPECIALTY SALES
KAT SALAZAR DIRECTOR OF PR & MARKETING
BRANWYN BIGGLESTONE CONTROLLER

KALI DUGAN ACCOUNTING & HR MANAGER
SUE KORPELA SENIOR ACCOUNTING MANAGER
DREW GILL ART DIRECTOR
HEATHER DOORNINK PRODUCTION DIRECTOR
LEIGH THOMAS PRINT MANAGER
TRICIA RAMOS TRAFFIC MANAGER
BRIAH SKELLY PUBLICIST
ALY HOFFMAN EVENTS & CONVENTIONS COORDINATOR
SASHA HEAD SALES & MARKETING PRODUCTION DESIGNER
DAVID BROTHERS BRANDING MANAGER
MELISSA GIFFORD CONTENT MANAGER
DREW FITZGERALD PUBLICITY ASSISTANT
VINCENT KUKUA PRODUCTION ARTIST

ERIKA SCHNATZ PRODUCTION ARTIST
RYAN BREWER PRODUCTION ARTIST
SHANNA MATUSZAK PRODUCTION ARTIST
CAREY HALL PRODUCTION ARTIST
ESTHER KIM DIRECT MARKET SALES REPRESENTATIVE
EMILIO BAUTISTA DIGITAL SALES REPRESENTATIVE
LEANNA CAUNTER ACCOUNTING ANALYST
CHLOE RAMOS-PETERSON LIBRARY MARKET SALES REPRESENTATIVE
MARLA EIZIK ADMINISTRATIVE ASSISTANT

WWW.IMAGECOMICS.COM

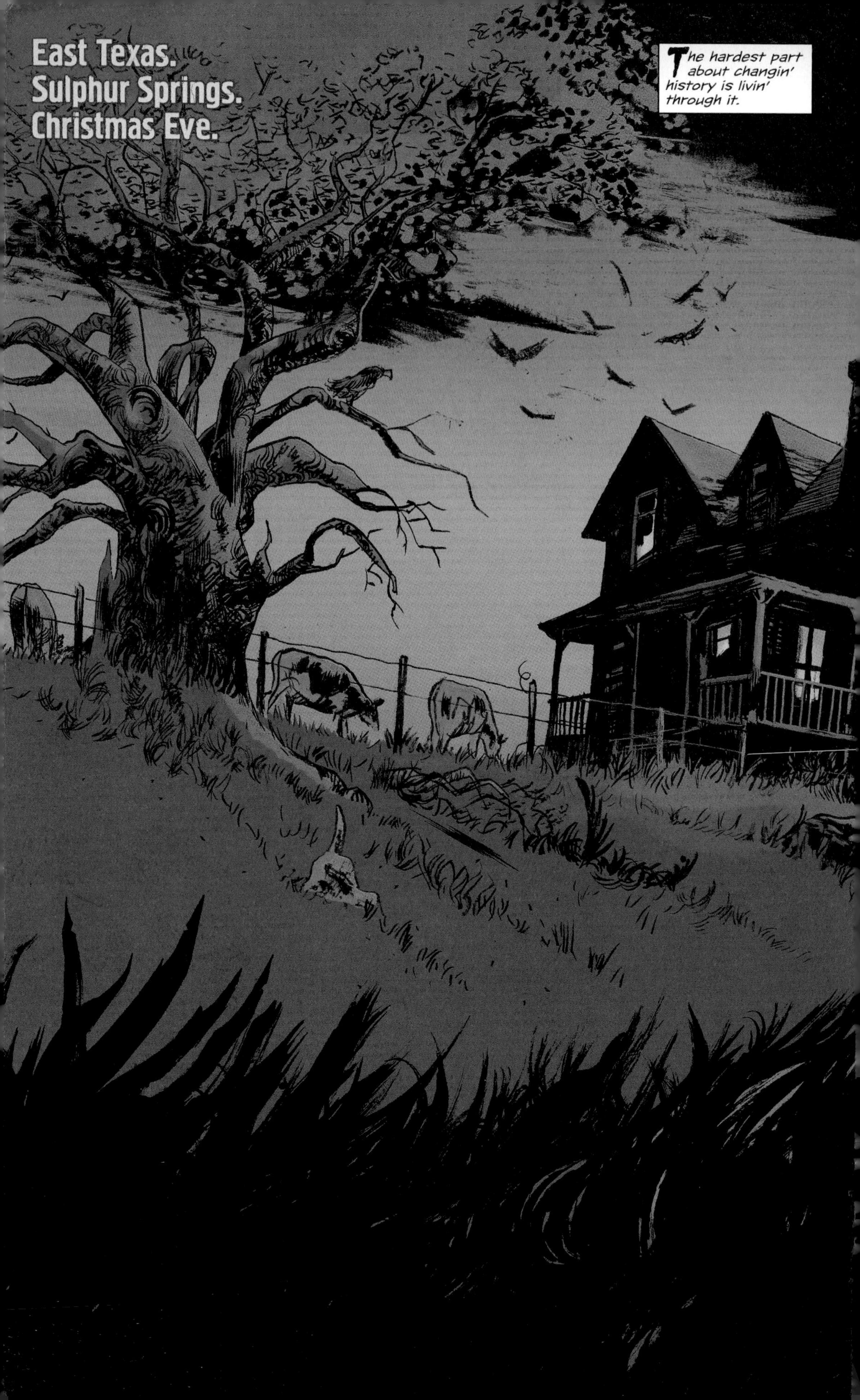
East Texas.
Sulphur Springs.
Christmas Eve.
The hardest part about changin' history is livin' through it.

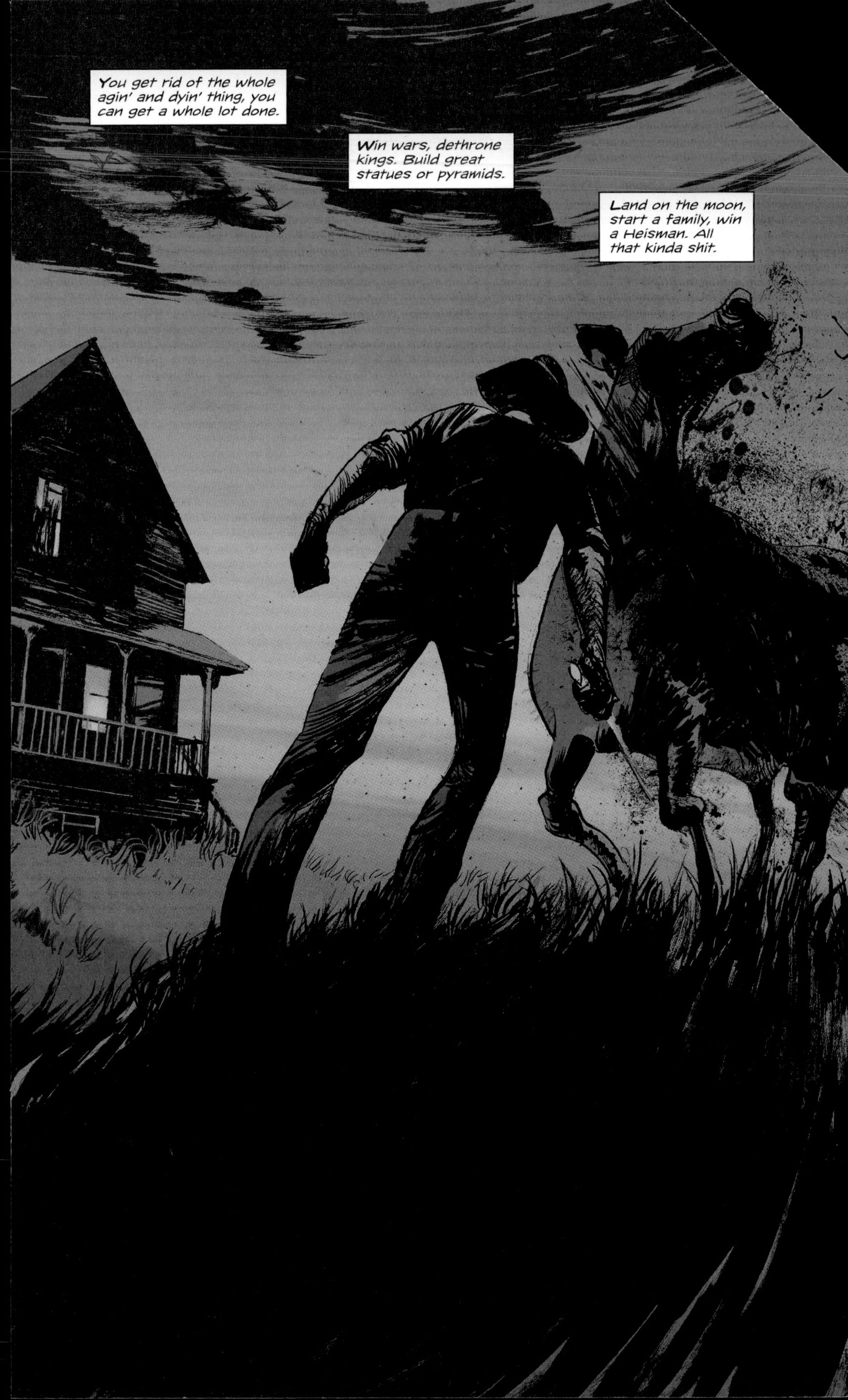
You get rid of the whole agin' and dyin' thing, you can get a whole lot done.
Win wars, dethrone kings. Build great statues or pyramids.
Land on the moon, start a family, win a Heisman. All that kinda shit.

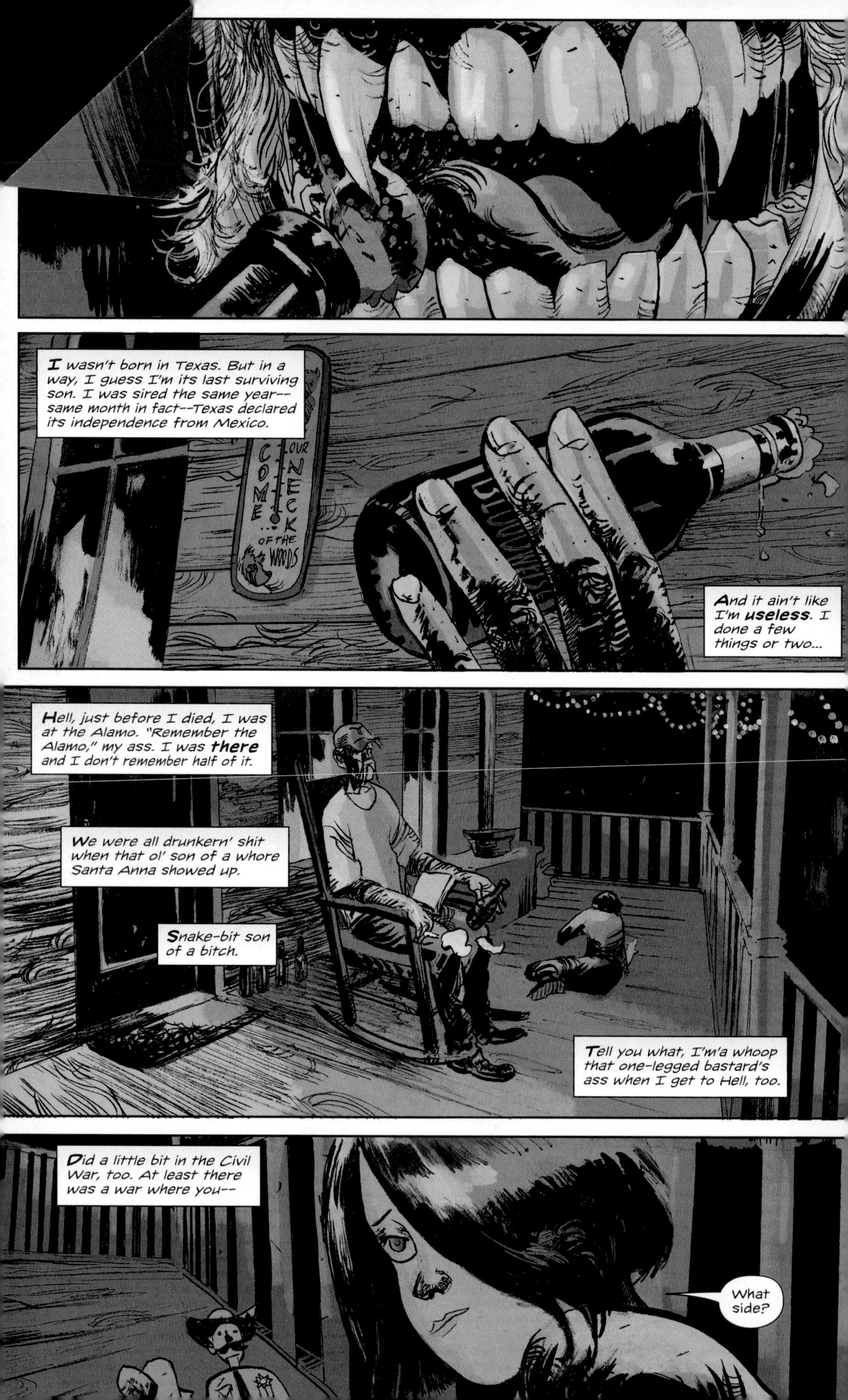

I wasn't born in Texas. But in a way, I guess I'm its last surviving son. I was sired the same year--same month in fact--Texas declared its independence from Mexico.
COME OUR NECK OF THE WOODS
And it ain't like I'm **useless**. I done a few things or two...
Hell, just before I died, I was at the Alamo. "Remember the Alamo," my ass. I was **there** and I don't remember half of it.
We were all drunkern' shit when that ol' son of a whore Santa Anna showed up.
Snake-bit son of a bitch.
Tell you what, I'm'a whoop that one-legged bastard's ass when I get to Hell, too.
Did a little bit in the Civil War, too. At least there was a war where you--
What side?

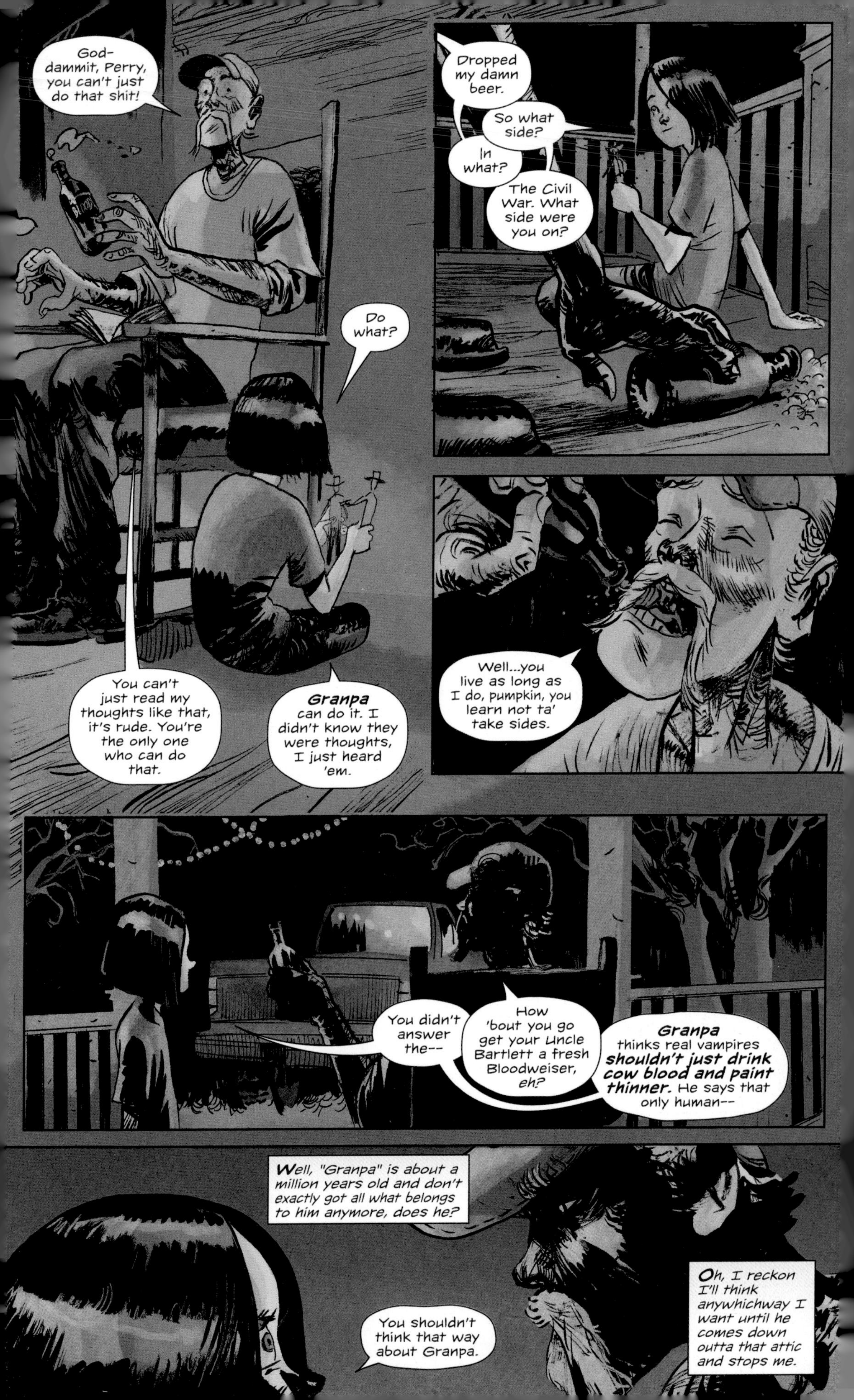
God-dammit, Perry, you can't just do that shit!
Do what?
You can't just read my thoughts like that, it's rude. You're the only one who can do that.
Granpa can do it. I didn't know they were thoughts, I just heard 'em.
Dropped my damn beer.
So what side?
In what?
The Civil War. What side were you on?
Well...you live as long as I do, pumpkin, you learn not ta' take sides.
You didn't answer the--
How 'bout you go get your Uncle Bartlett a fresh Bloodweiser, eh?
Granpa thinks real vampires *shouldn't just drink cow blood and paint thinner.* He says that only human--
Well, "Granpa" is about a million years old and don't exactly got all what belongs to him anymore, does he?
You shouldn't think that way about Granpa.
Oh, I reckon I'll think anywhichway I want until he comes down outta that attic and stops me.

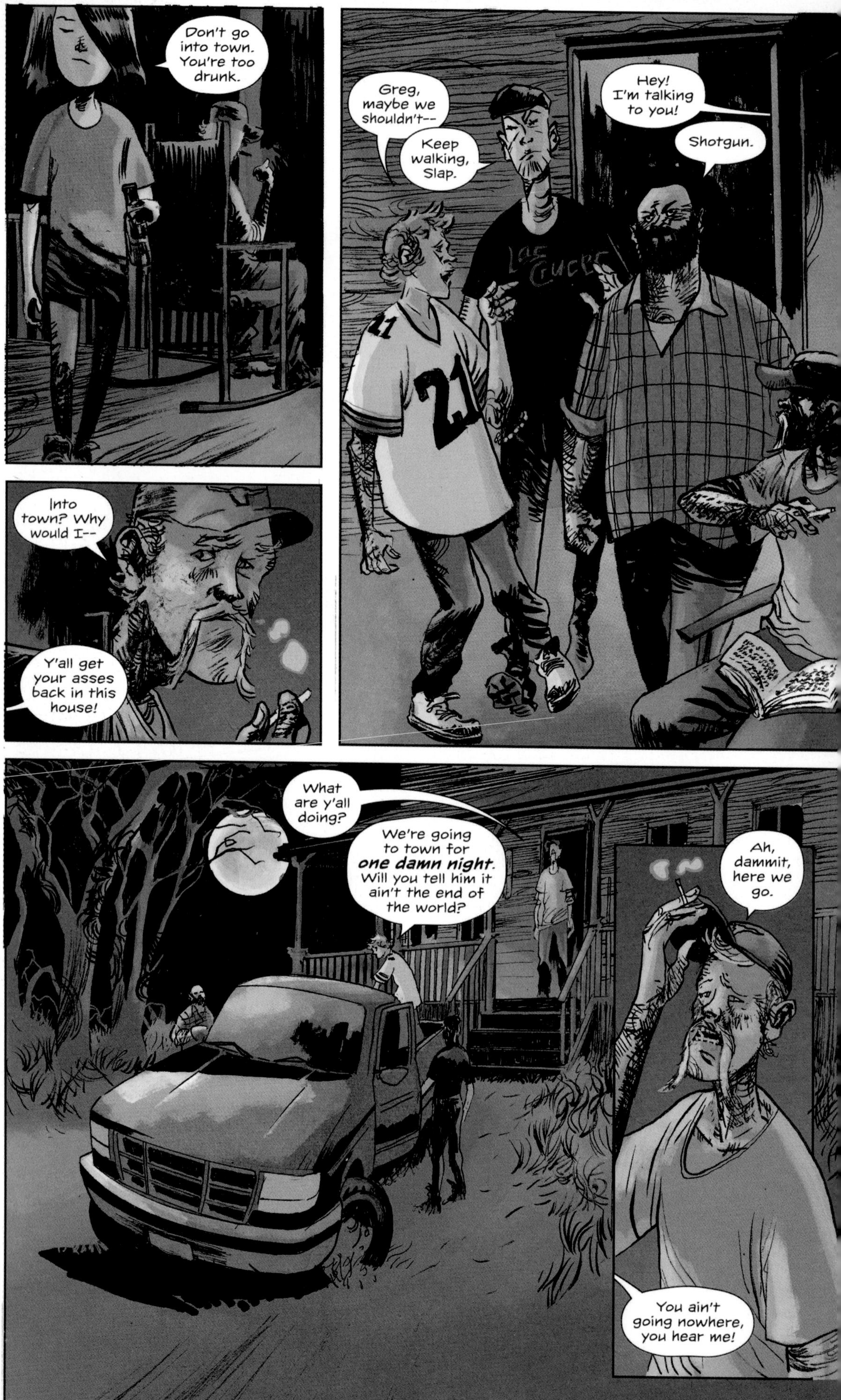

Don't go into town. You're too drunk.
Into town? Why would I--
Y'all get your asses back in this house!
Greg, maybe we shouldn't--
Keep walking, Slap.
Hey! I'm talking to you!
Shotgun.
What are y'all doing?
We're going to town for **one damn night**. Will you tell him it ain't the end of the world?
Ah, dammit, here we go.
You ain't going nowhere, you hear me!

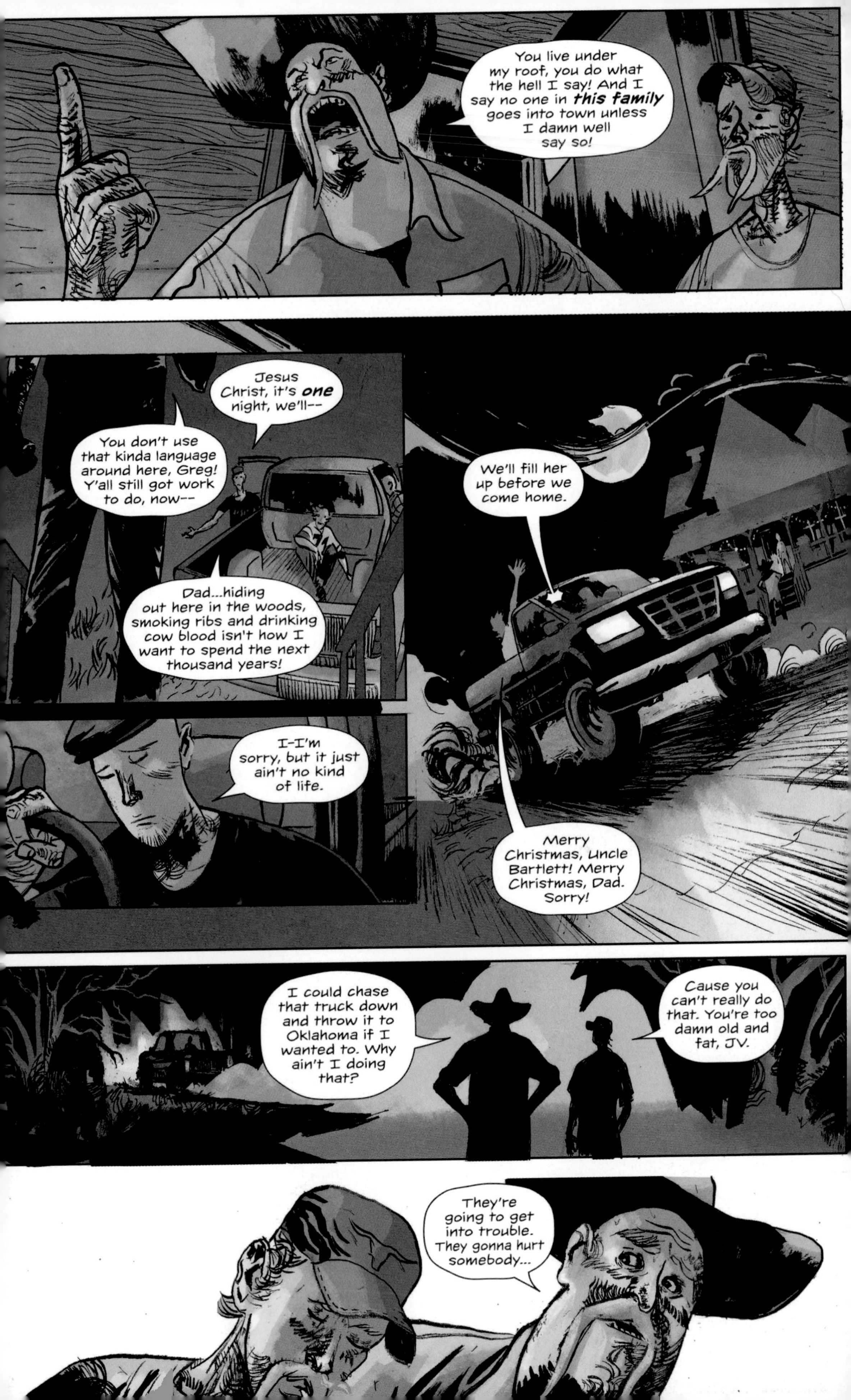
You live under my roof, you do what the hell I say! And I say no one in ***this family*** goes into town unless I damn well say so!
Jesus Christ, it's ***one*** night, we'll--
You don't use that kinda language around here, Greg! Y'all still got work to do, now--
Dad...hiding out here in the woods, smoking ribs and drinking cow blood isn't how I want to spend the next thousand years!
I-I'm sorry, but it just ain't no kind of life.
We'll fill her up before we come home.
Merry Christmas, Uncle Bartlett! Merry Christmas, Dad. Sorry!
I could chase that truck down and throw it to Oklahoma if I wanted to. Why ain't I doing that?
Cause you can't really do that. You're too damn old and fat, JV.
They're going to get into trouble. They gonna hurt somebody...

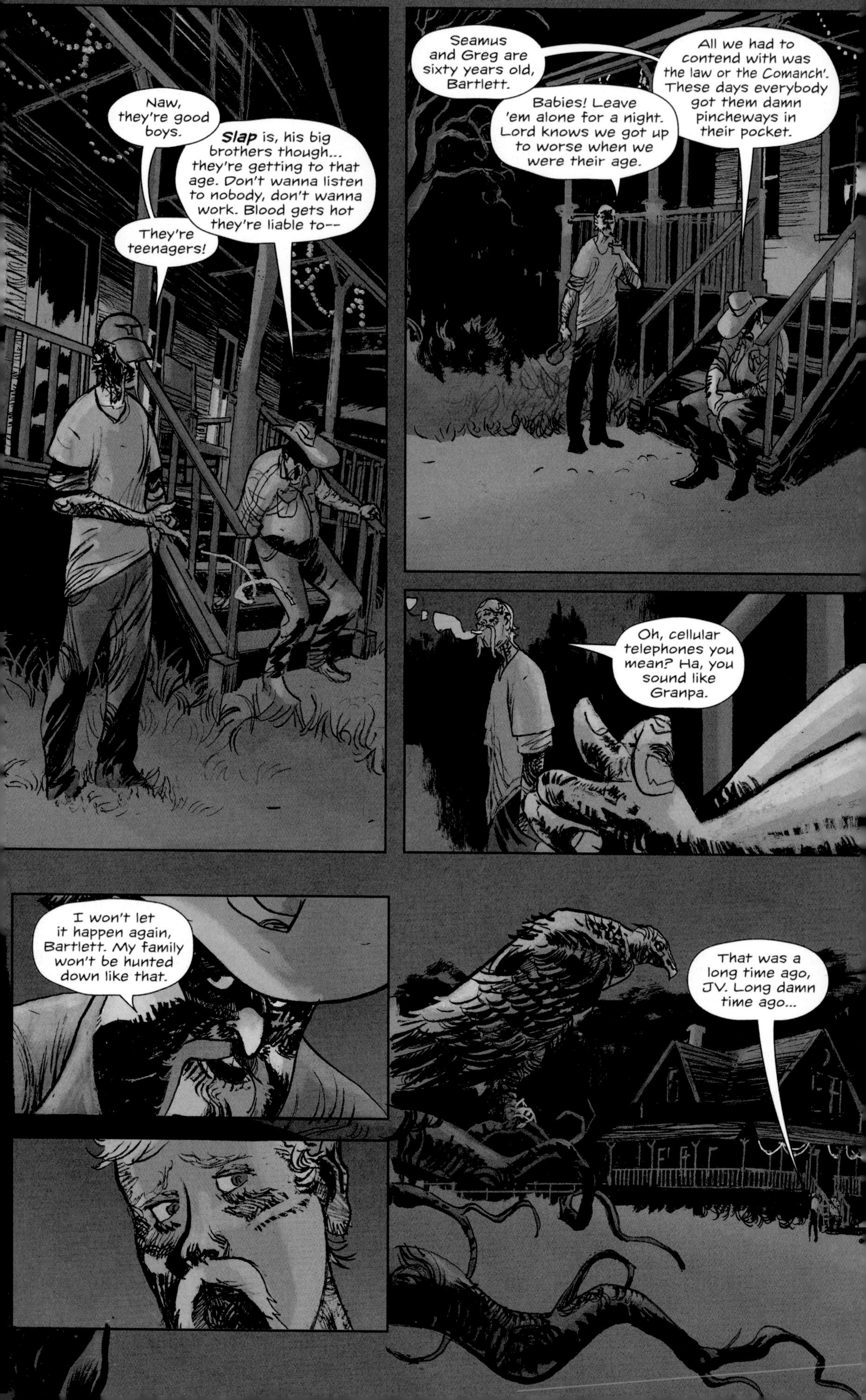
Naw, they're good boys.
Slap is, his big brothers though... they're getting to that age. Don't wanna listen to nobody, don't wanna work. Blood gets hot they're liable to--
They're teenagers!
Seamus and Greg are sixty years old, Bartlett.
Babies! Leave 'em alone for a night. Lord knows we got up to worse when we were their age.
All we had to contend with was the law or the Comanch'. These days everybody got them damn pincheways in their pocket.
Oh, cellular telephones you mean? Ha, you sound like Granpa.
I won't let it happen again, Bartlett. My family won't be hunted down like that.
That was a long time ago, JV. Long damn time ago...

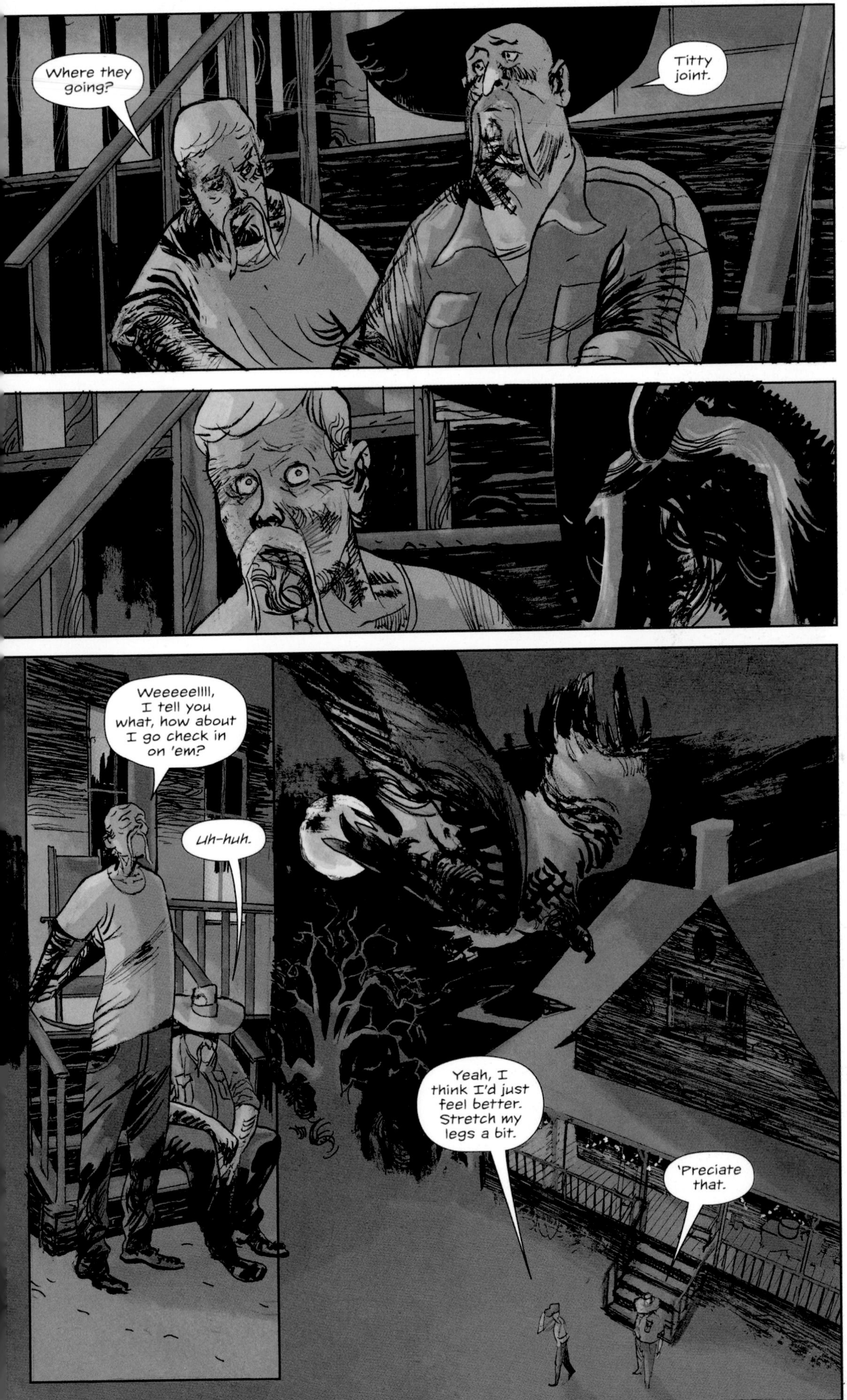
Where they going?
Titty joint.
Weeeeelll, I tell you what, how about I go check in on 'em?
Uh-huh.
Yeah, I think I'd just feel better. Stretch my legs a bit.
'Preciate that.

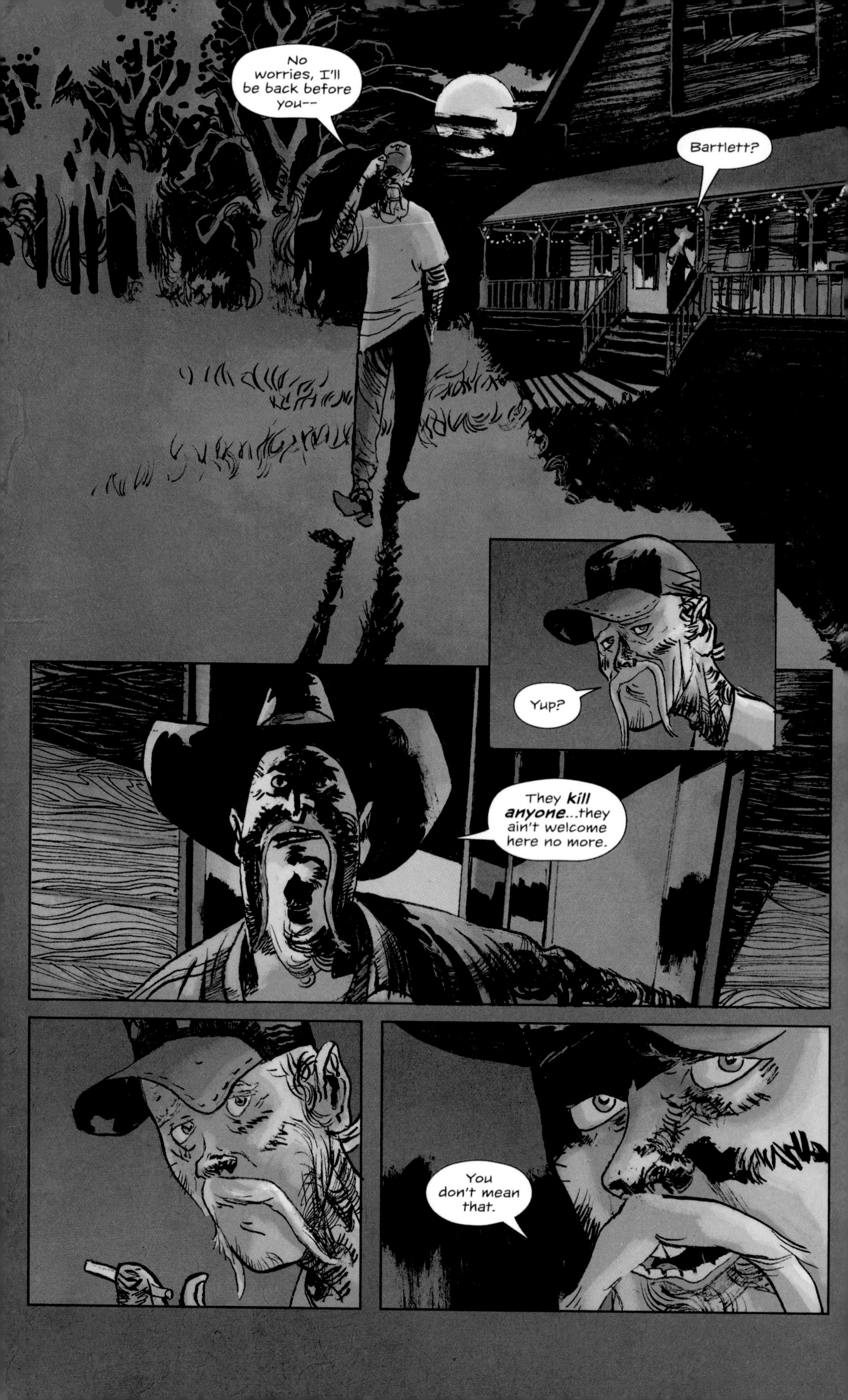
No worries, I'll be back before you--
Bartlett?
Yup?
They **kill** ***anyone***...they ain't welcome here no more.
You don't mean that.

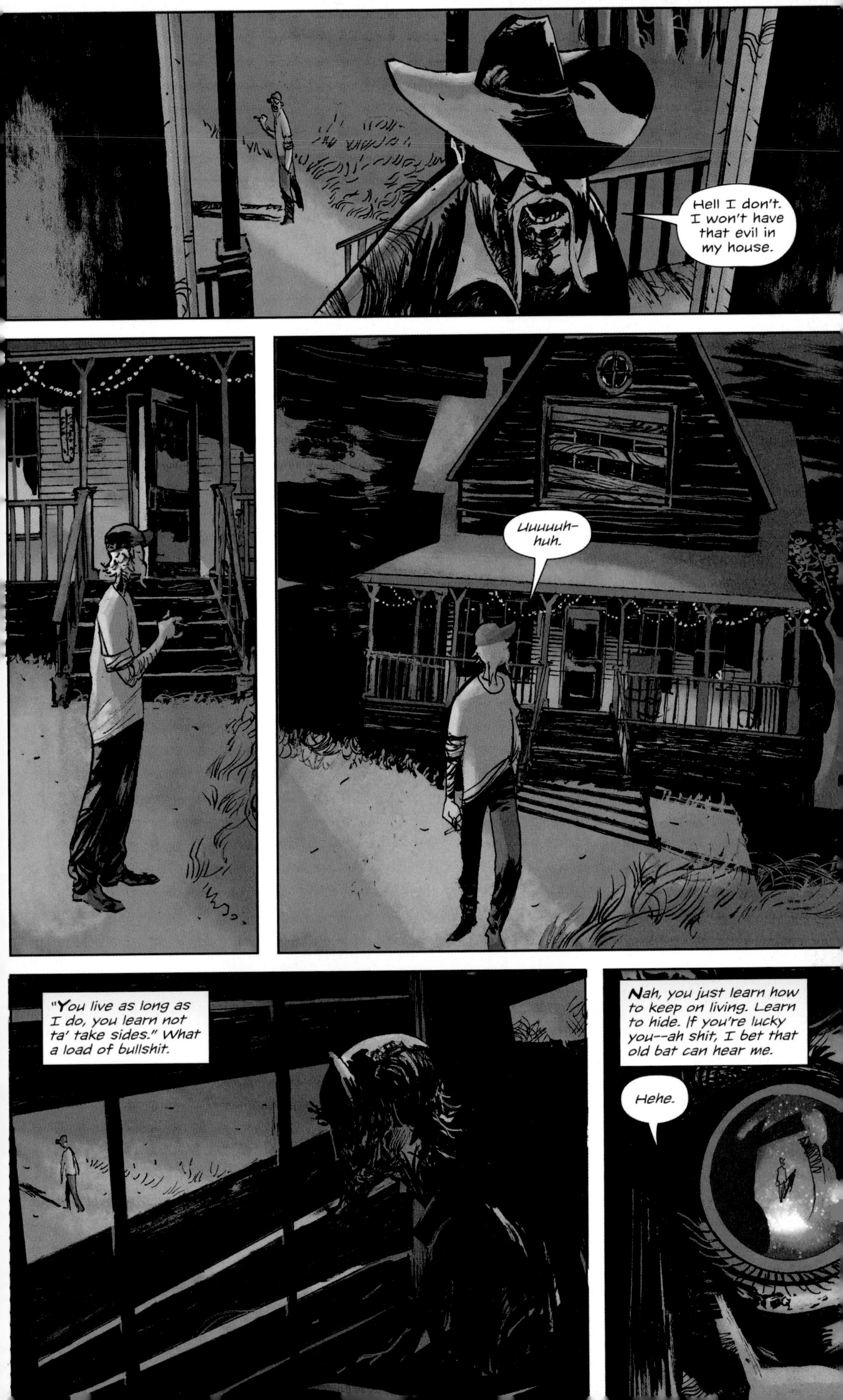

Hell I don't. I won't have that evil in my house.
Uuuuuh-huh.
"You live as long as I do, you learn not ta' take sides." What a load of bullshit.
Nah, you just learn how to keep on living. Learn to hide. If you're lucky you--ah shit, I bet that old bat can hear me.
Hehe.

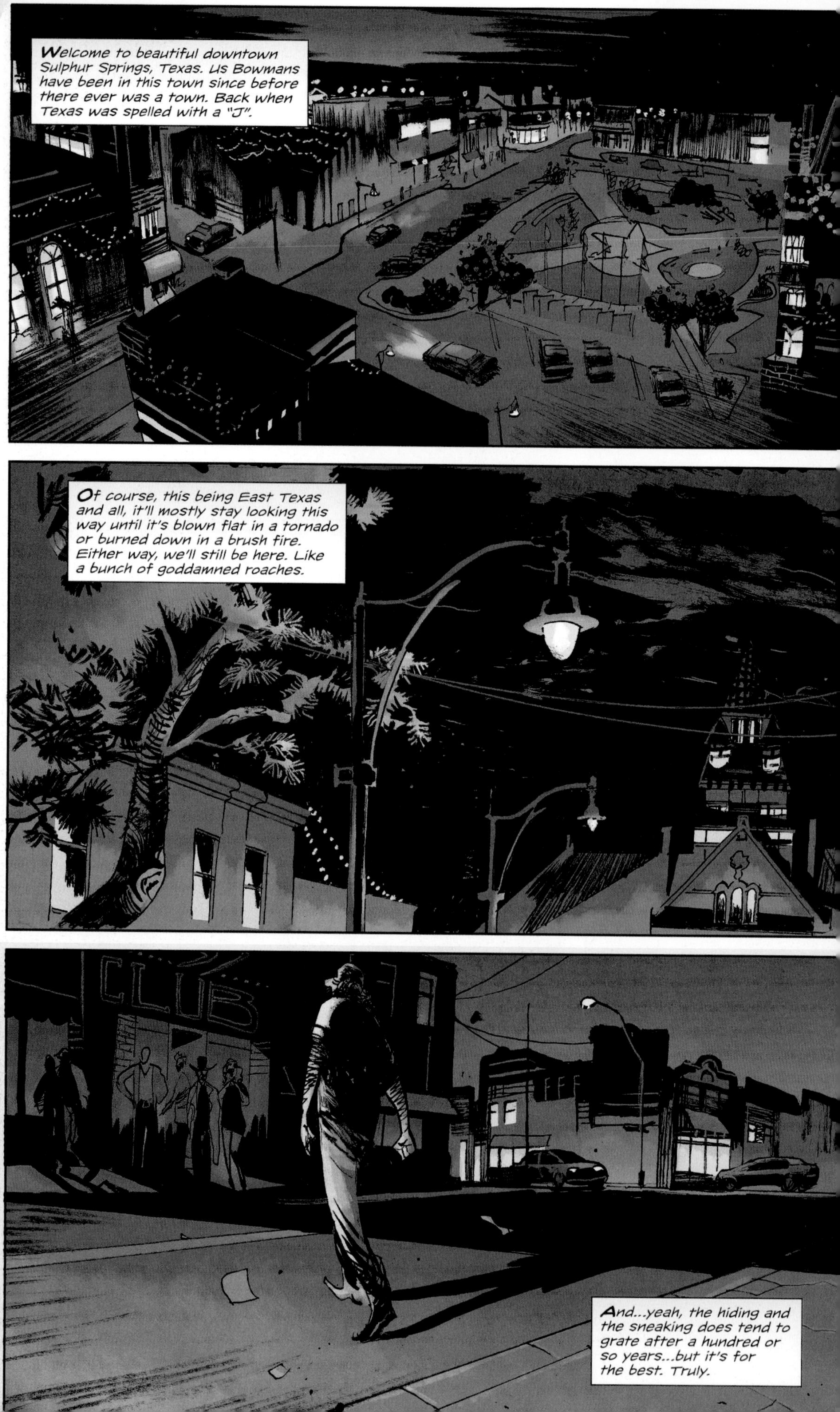
Welcome to beautiful downtown Sulphur Springs, Texas. Us Bowmans have been in this town since before there ever was a town. Back when Texas was spelled with a "J".
Of course, this being East Texas and all, it'll mostly stay looking this way until it's blown flat in a tornado or burned down in a brush fire. Either way, we'll still be here. Like a bunch of goddamned roaches.
CLUB
And...yeah, the hiding and the sneaking does tend to grate after a hundred or so years...but it's for the best. Truly.

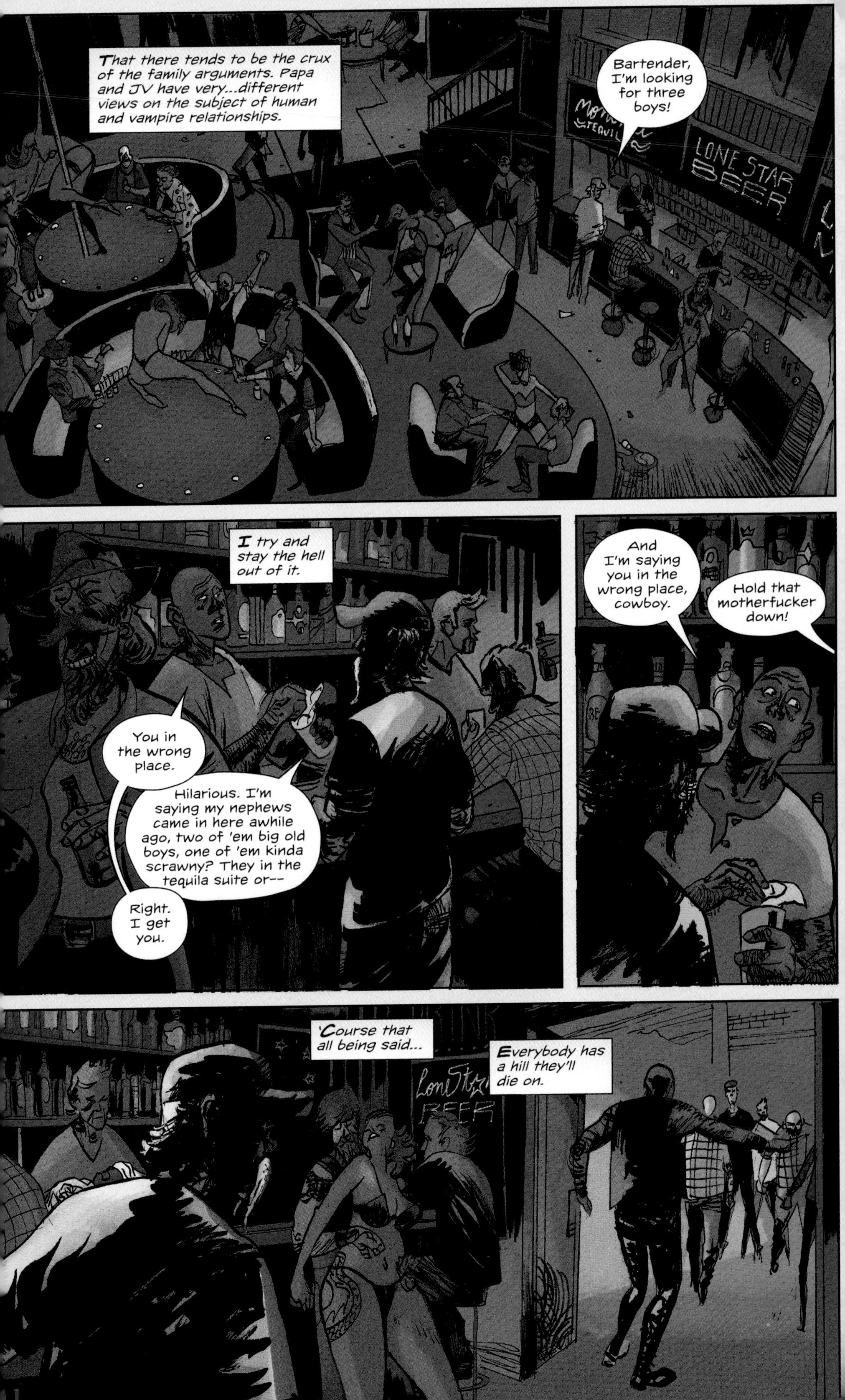
That there tends to be the crux of the family arguments. Papa and JV have very...different views on the subject of human and vampire relationships.
Bartender, I'm looking for three boys!
LONE STAR BEER
I try and stay the hell out of it.
You in the wrong place.
Hilarious. I'm saying my nephews came in here awhile ago, two of 'em big old boys, one of 'em kinda scrawny? They in the tequila suite or--
Right. I get you.
And I'm saying you in the wrong place, cowboy.
Hold that motherfucker down!
'Course that all being said...
Everybody has a hill they'll die on.

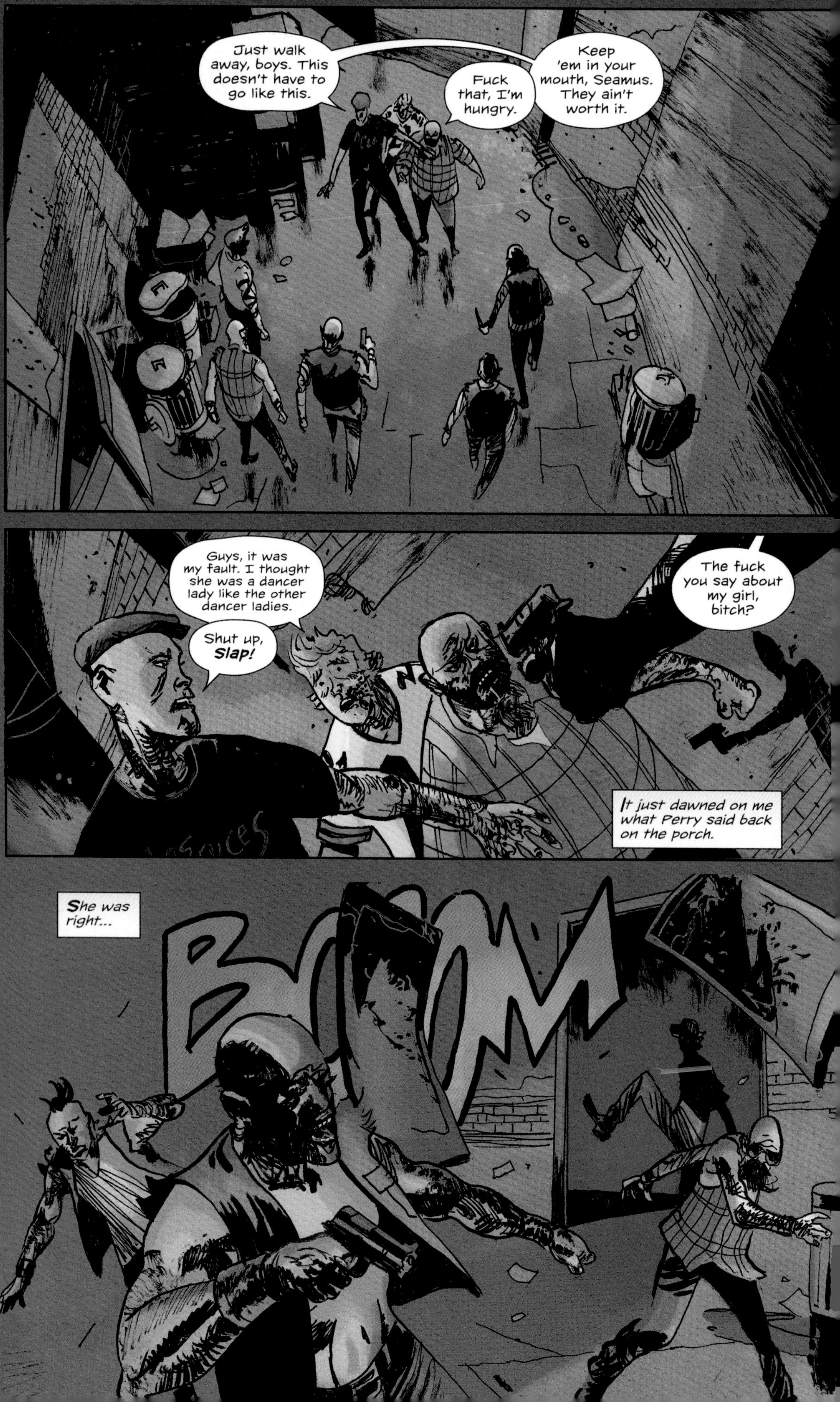
Just walk away, boys. This doesn't have to go like this.
Fuck that, I'm hungry.
Keep 'em in your mouth, Seamus. They ain't worth it.
Guys, it was my fault. I thought she was a dancer lady like the other dancer ladies.
Shut up, Slap!
The fuck you say about my girl, bitch?
It just dawned on me what Perry said back on the porch.
She was right...
BOOM

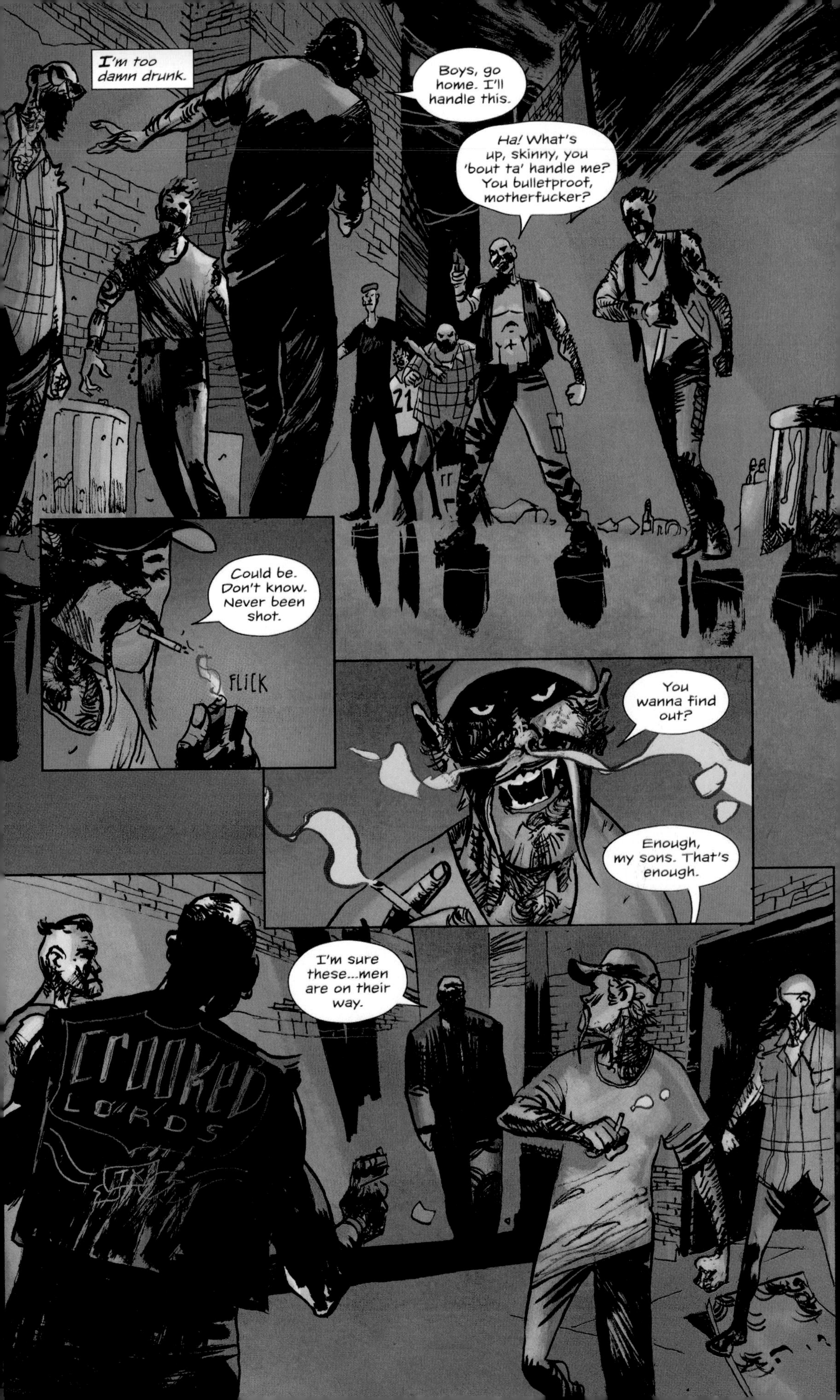

I'm too damn drunk.
Boys, go home. I'll handle this.
Ha! What's up, skinny, you 'bout ta' handle me? You bulletproof, motherfucker?
Could be. Don't know. Never been shot.
FLICK
You wanna find out?
Enough, my sons. That's enough.
I'm sure these...men are on their way.
CROOKED LORDS

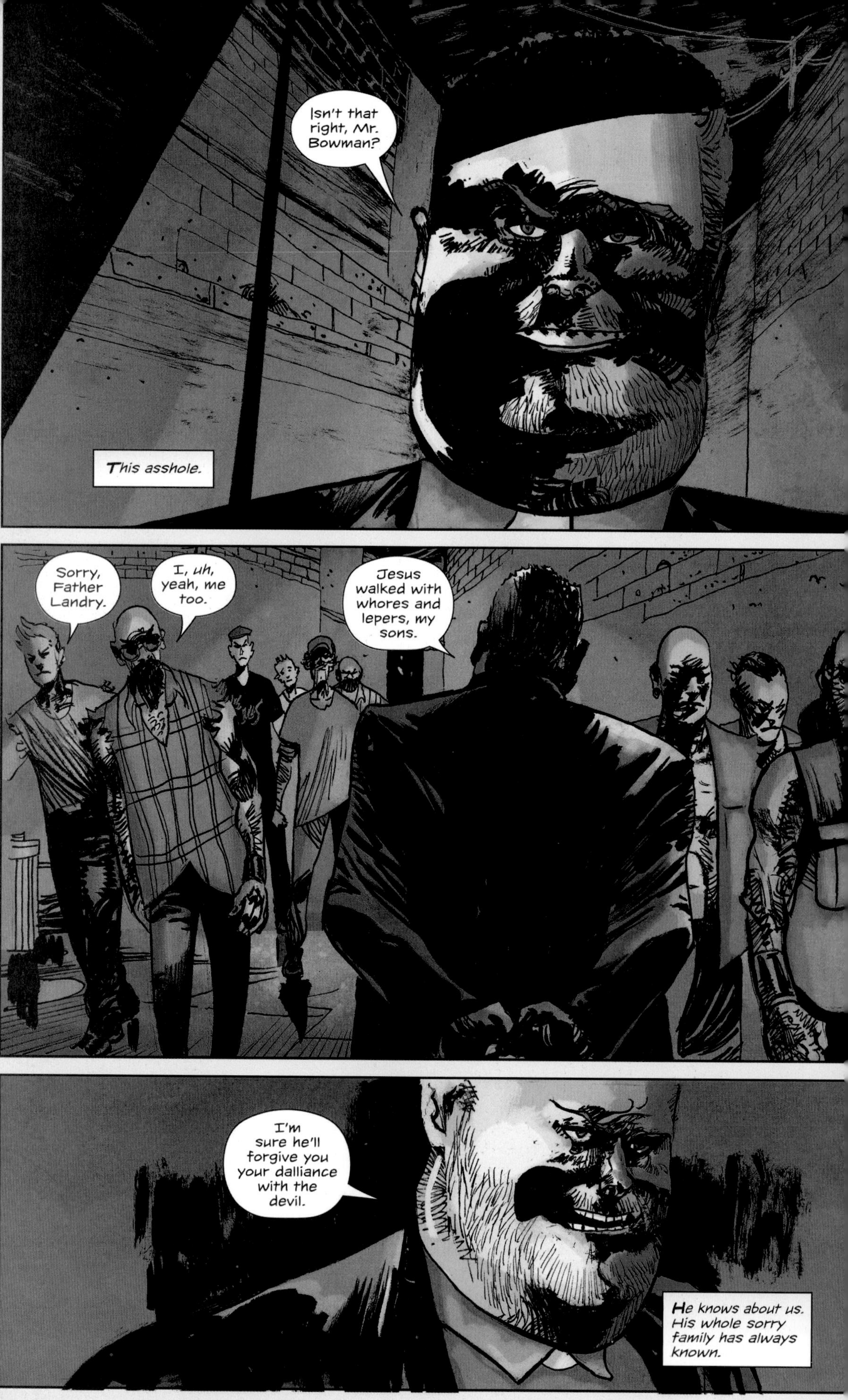
Isn't that right, Mr. Bowman?
This asshole.
Sorry, Father Landry.
I, uh, yeah, me too.
Jesus walked with whores and lepers, my sons.
I'm sure he'll forgive you your dalliance with the devil.
He knows about us. His whole sorry family has always known.

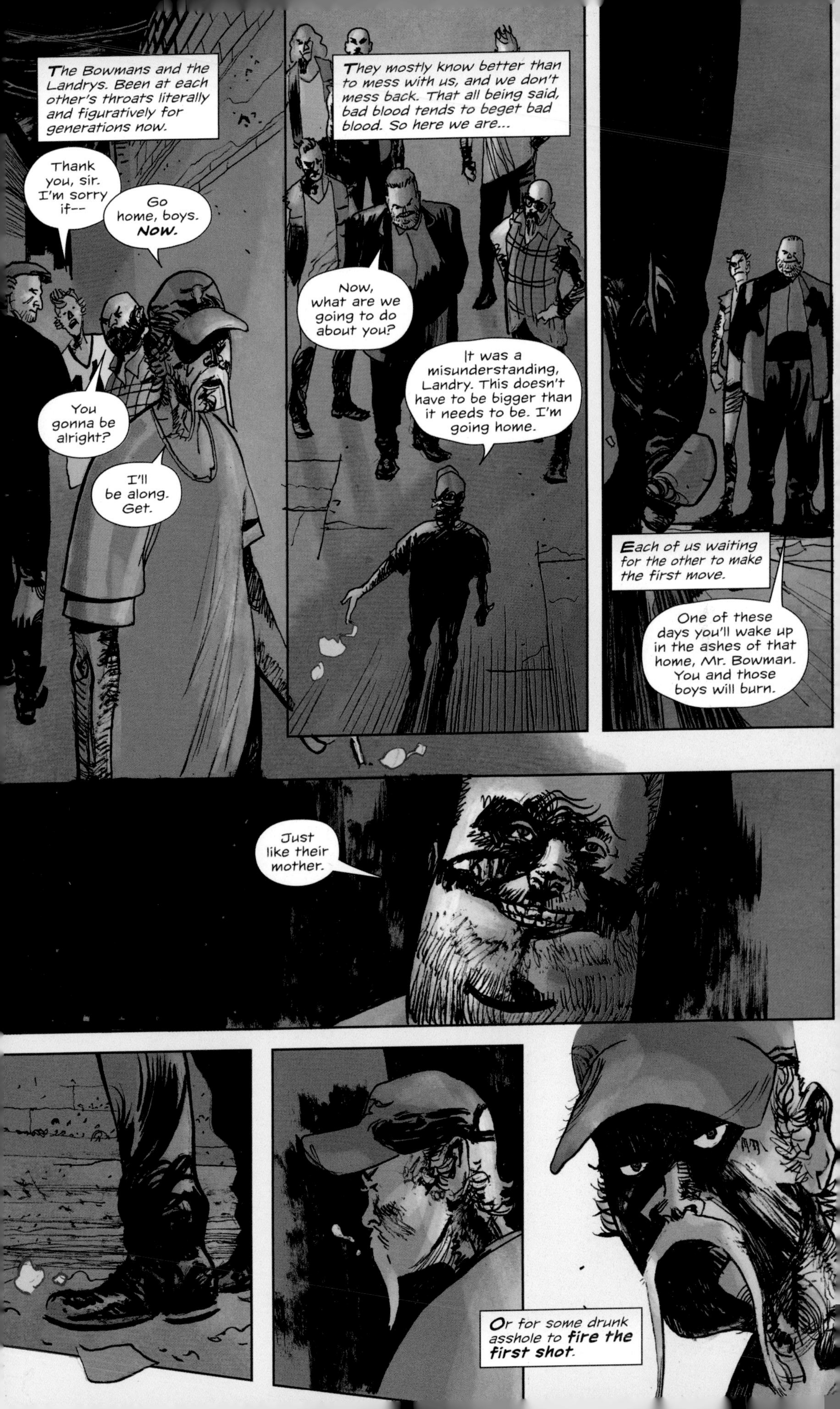

The Bowmans and the Landrys. Been at each other's throats literally and figuratively for generations now.
Thank you, sir. I'm sorry if--
Go home, boys. NOW.
You gonna be alright?
I'll be along. Get.
They mostly know better than to mess with us, and we don't mess back. That all being said, bad blood tends to beget bad blood. So here we are...
Now, what are we going to do about you?
It was a misunderstanding, Landry. This doesn't have to be bigger than it needs to be. I'm going home.
Each of us waiting for the other to make the first move.
One of these days you'll wake up in the ashes of that home, Mr. Bowman. You and those boys will burn.
Just like their mother.
Or for some drunk asshole to fire the first shot.

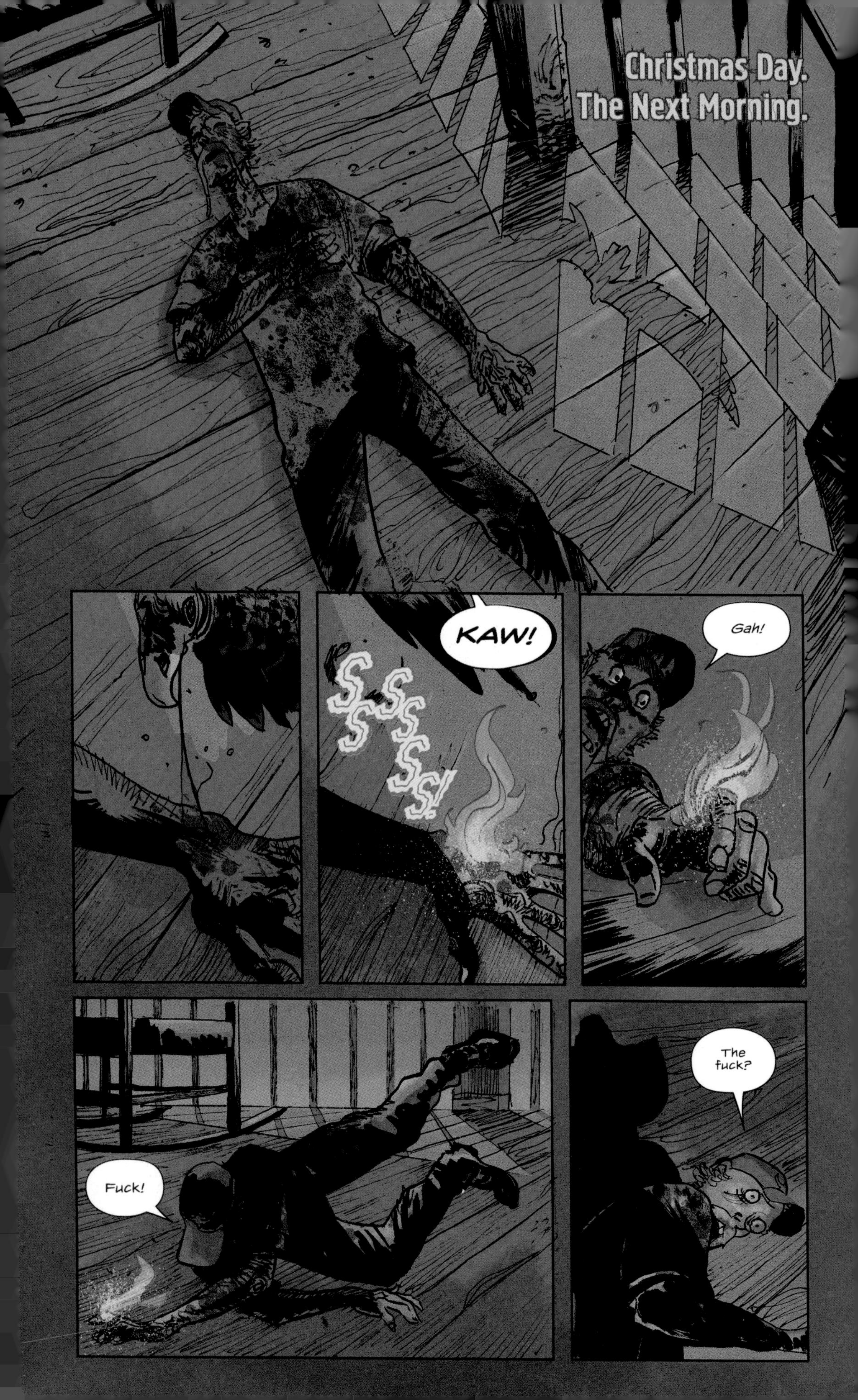
Christmas Day.
The Next Morning.
KAW!
SSSSSS!
Gah!
Fuck!
The fuck?

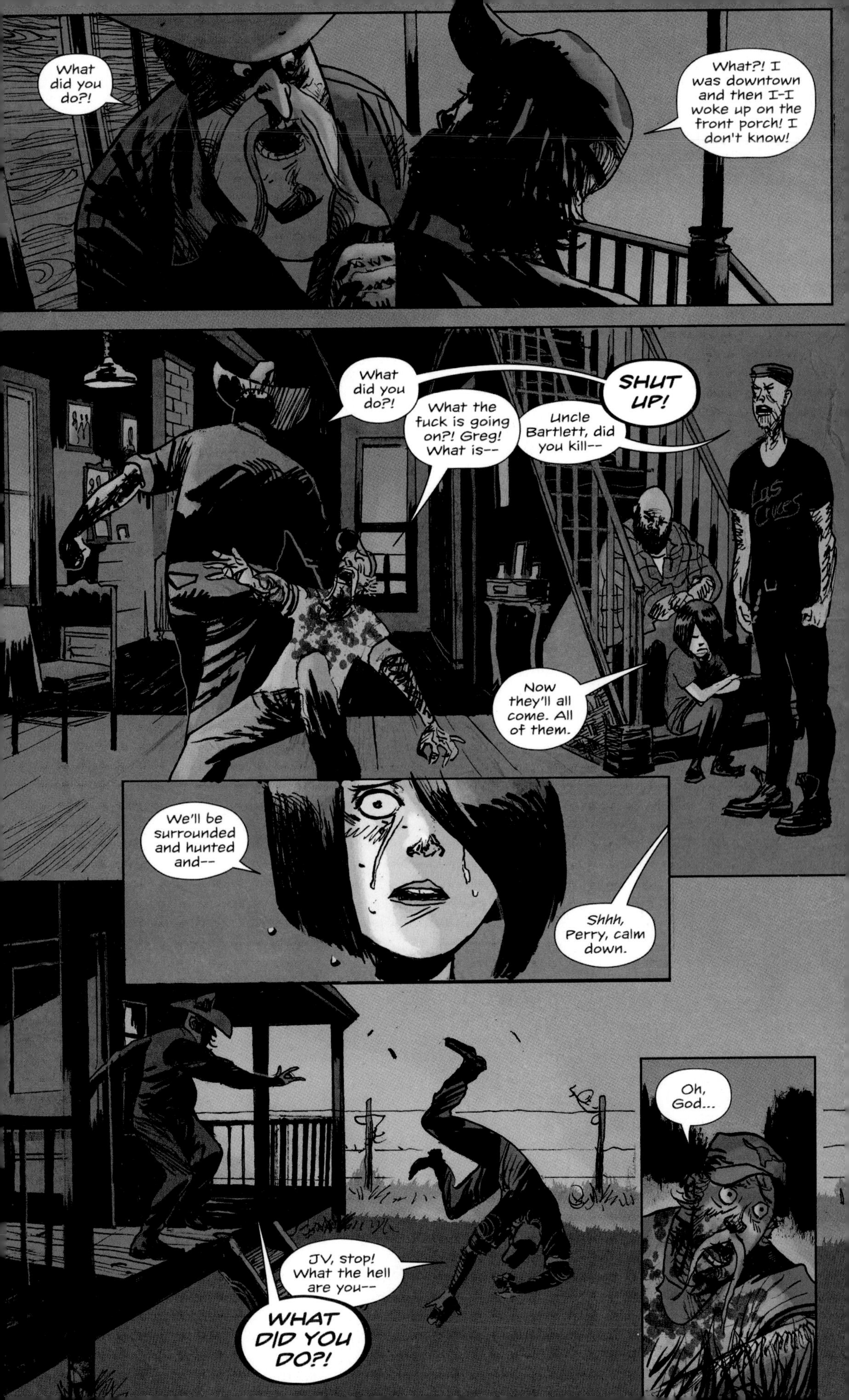
What did you do?!
What?! I was downtown and then I-I woke up on the front porch! I don't know!
What did you do?!
SHUT UP!
What the fuck is going on?! Greg! What is--
Uncle Bartlett, did you kill--
Now they'll all come. All of them.
We'll be surrounded and hunted and--
Shhh, Perry, calm down.
JV, stop! What the hell are you--
WHAT DID YOU DO?!
Oh, God...

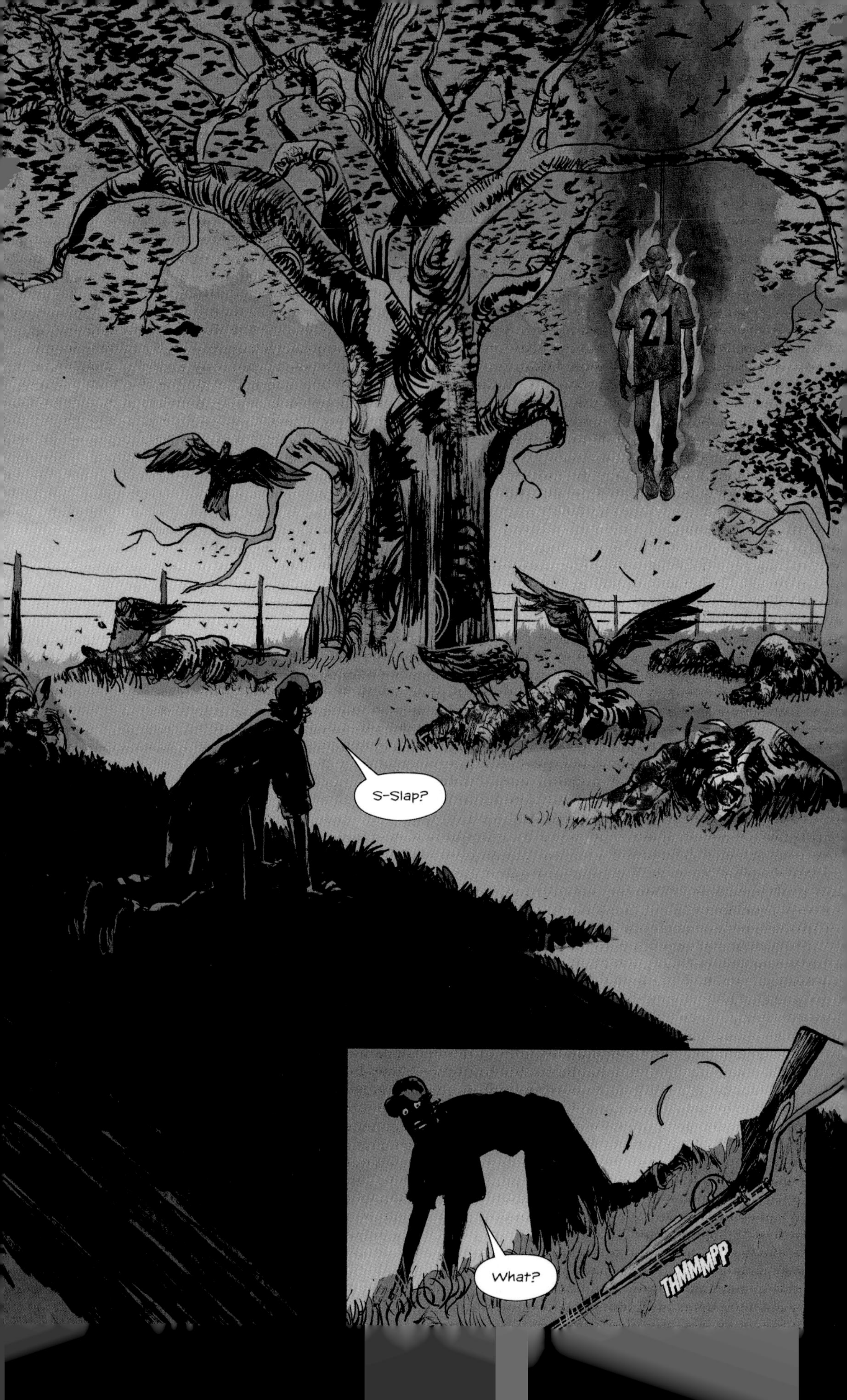
S-Slap?
What?
THMMMPP

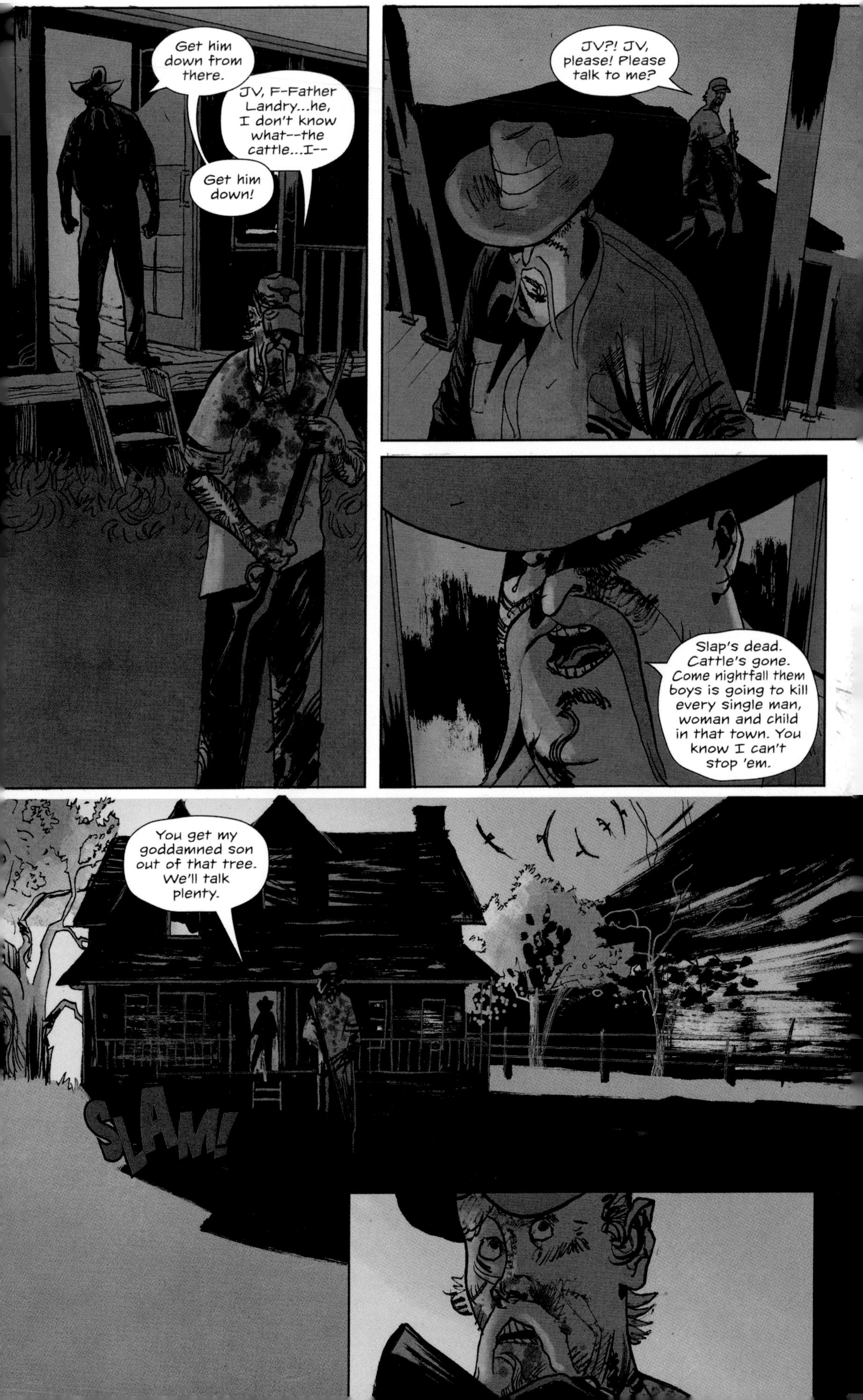
Get him down from there.
JV, F-Father Landry...he, I don't know what--the cattle...I--
Get him down!
JV?! JV, please! Please talk to me?
Slap's dead. Cattle's gone. Come nightfall them boys is going to kill every single man, woman and child in that town. You know I can't stop 'em.
You get my goddamned son out of that tree. We'll talk plenty.
SLAM!

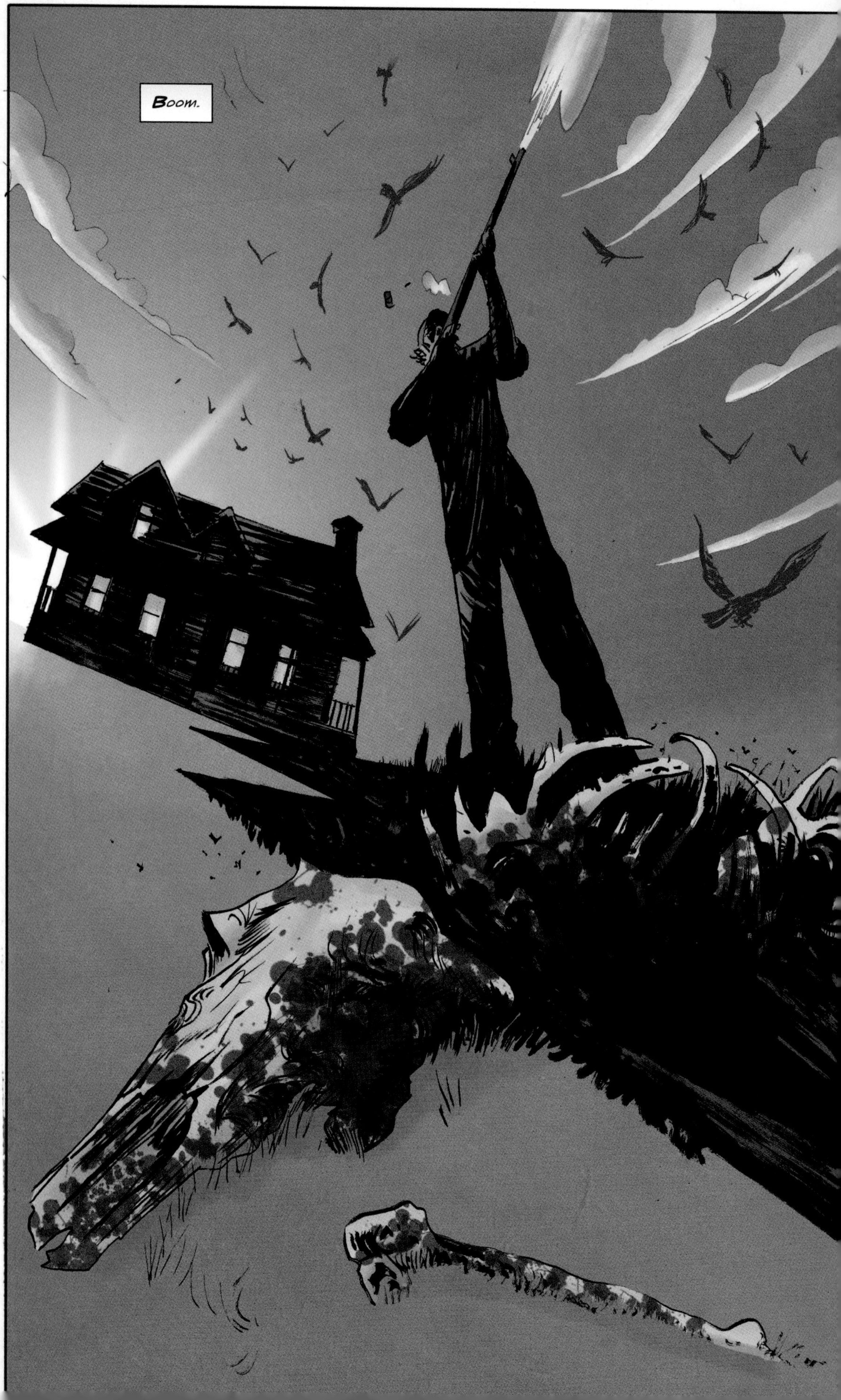
Boom.

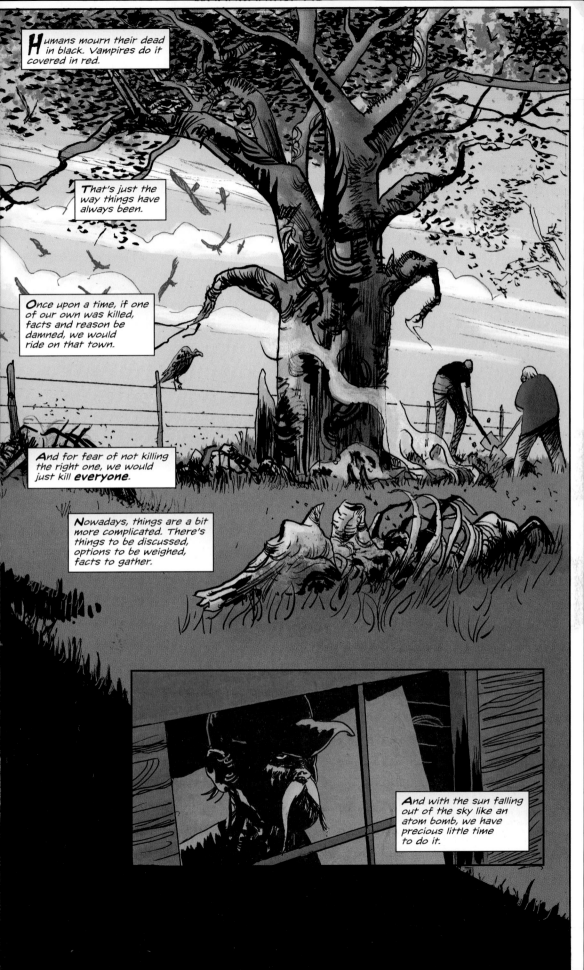

Humans mourn their dead in black. Vampires do it covered in red.

That's just the way things have always been.

Once upon a time, if one of our own was killed, facts and reason be damned, we would ride on that town.

And for fear of not killing the right one, we would just kill **everyone**.

Nowadays, things are a bit more complicated. There's things to be discussed, options to be weighed, facts to gather.

And with the sun falling out of the sky like an atom bomb, we have precious little time to do it.

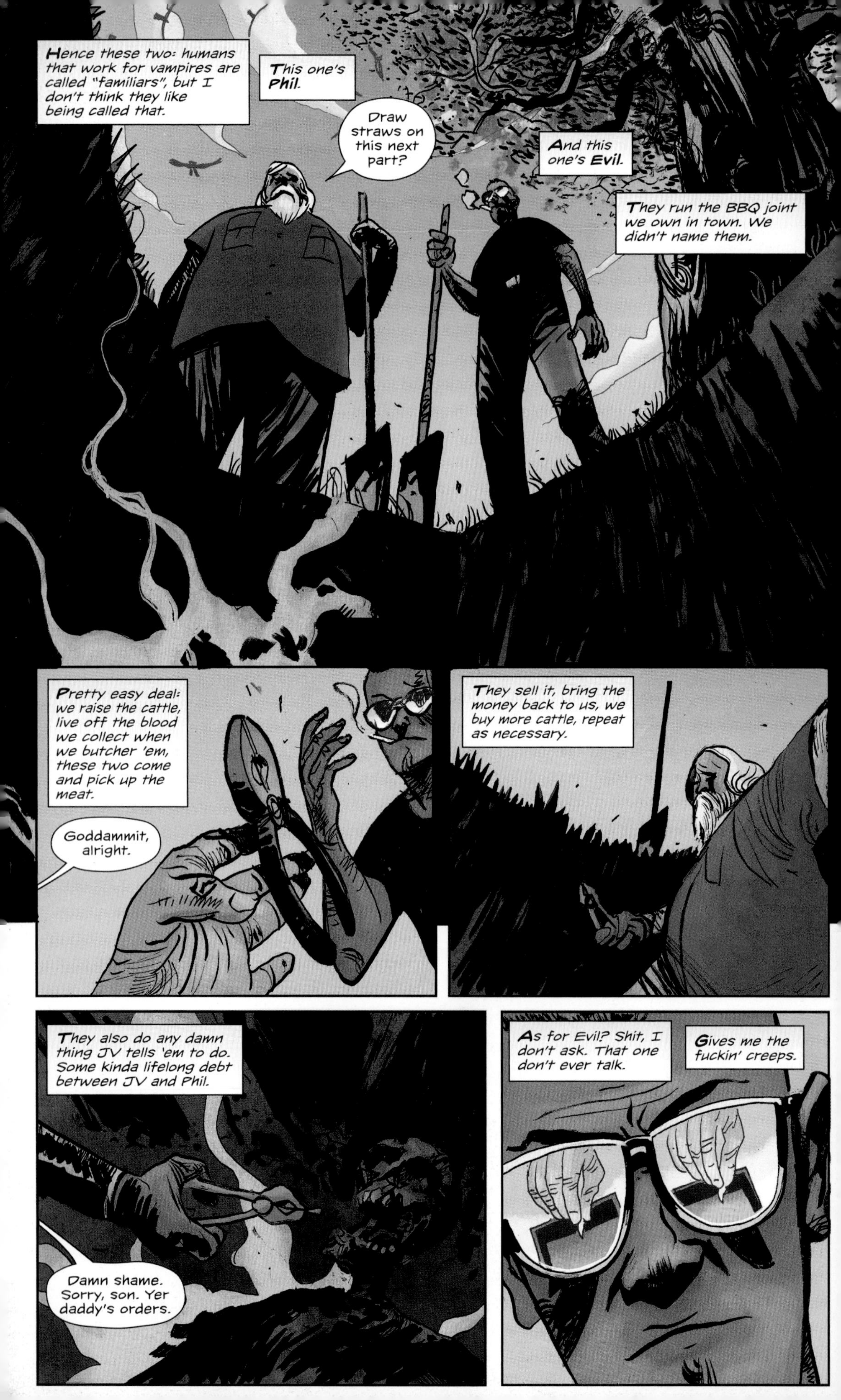
Hence these two: humans that work for vampires are called "familiars", but I don't think they like being called that.
This one's Phil.
Draw straws on this next part?
And this one's Evil.
They run the BBQ joint we own in town. We didn't name them.
Pretty easy deal: we raise the cattle, live off the blood we collect when we butcher 'em, these two come and pick up the meat.
Goddammit, alright.
They sell it, bring the money back to us, we buy more cattle, repeat as necessary.
They also do any damn thing JV tells 'em to do. Some kinda lifelong debt between JV and Phil.
Damn shame. Sorry, son. Yer daddy's orders.
As for Evil? Shit, I don't ask. That one don't ever talk.
Gives me the fuckin' creeps.

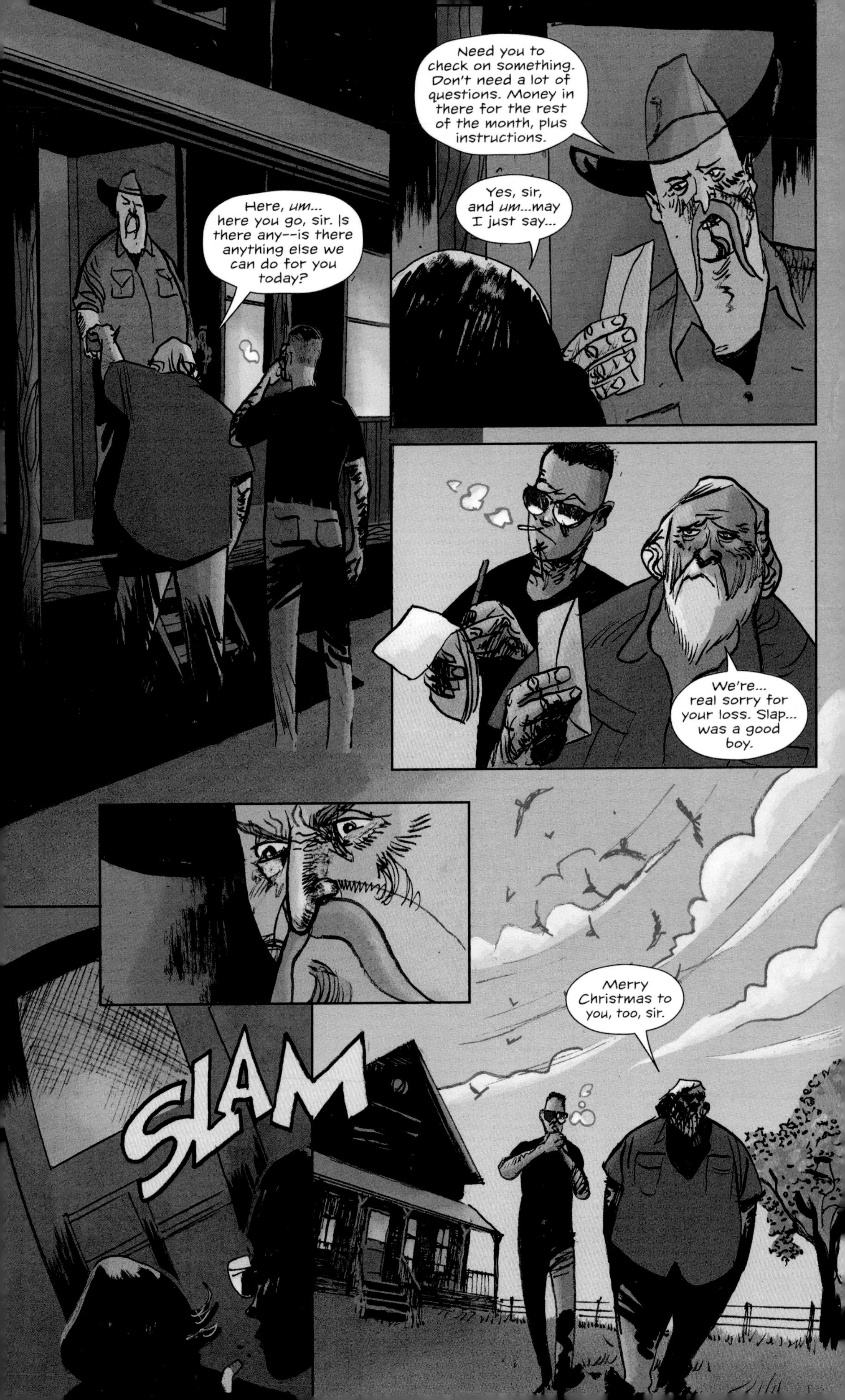
Here, *um*... here you go, sir. Is there any--is there anything else we can do for you today?
Need you to check on something. Don't need a lot of questions. Money in there for the rest of the month, plus instructions.
Yes, sir, and *um*...may I just say...
We're... real sorry for your loss. Slap... was a good boy.
SLAM
Merry Christmas to you, too, sir.

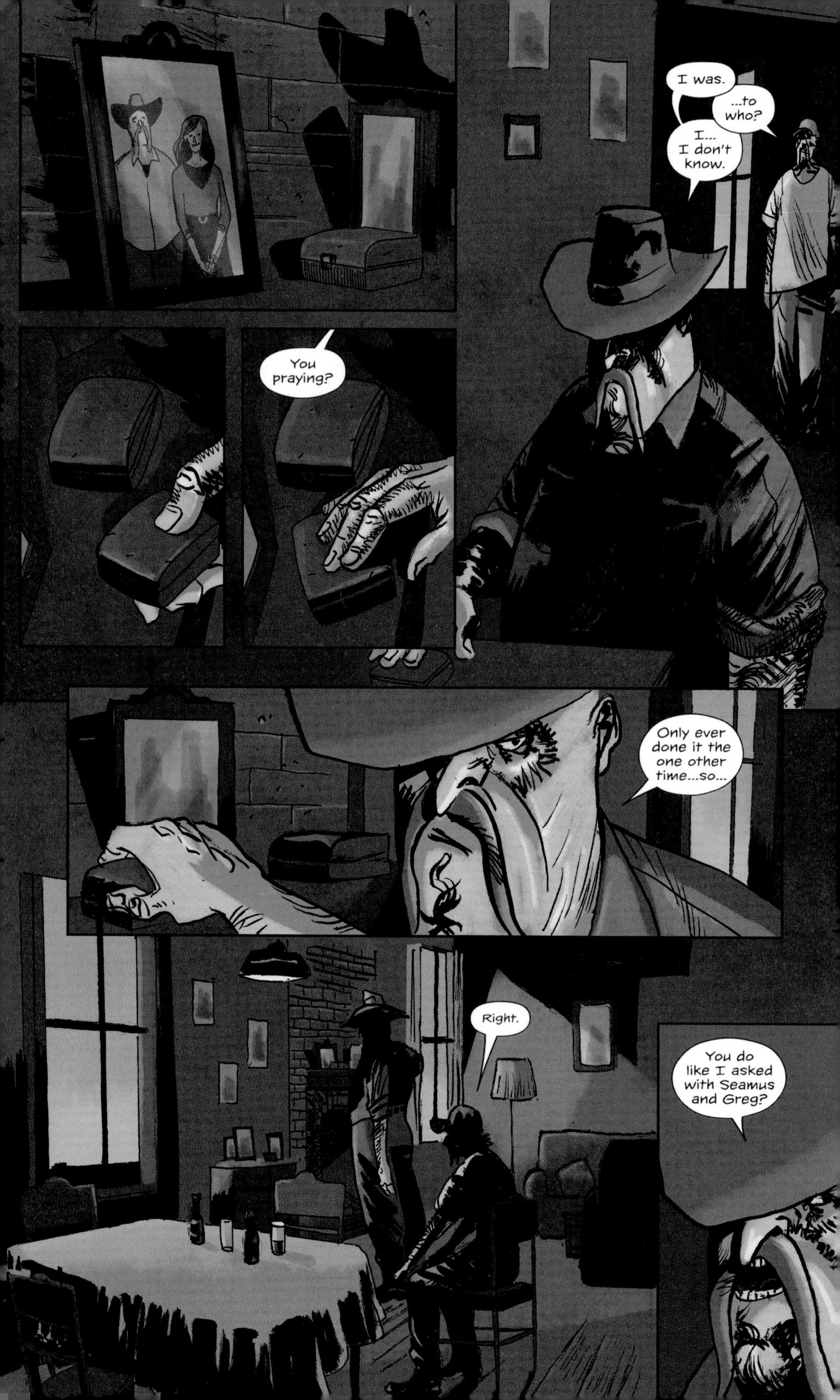
I was.
...to who?
I... I don't know.
You praying?
Only ever done it the one other time...so...
Right.
You do like I asked with Seamus and Greg?

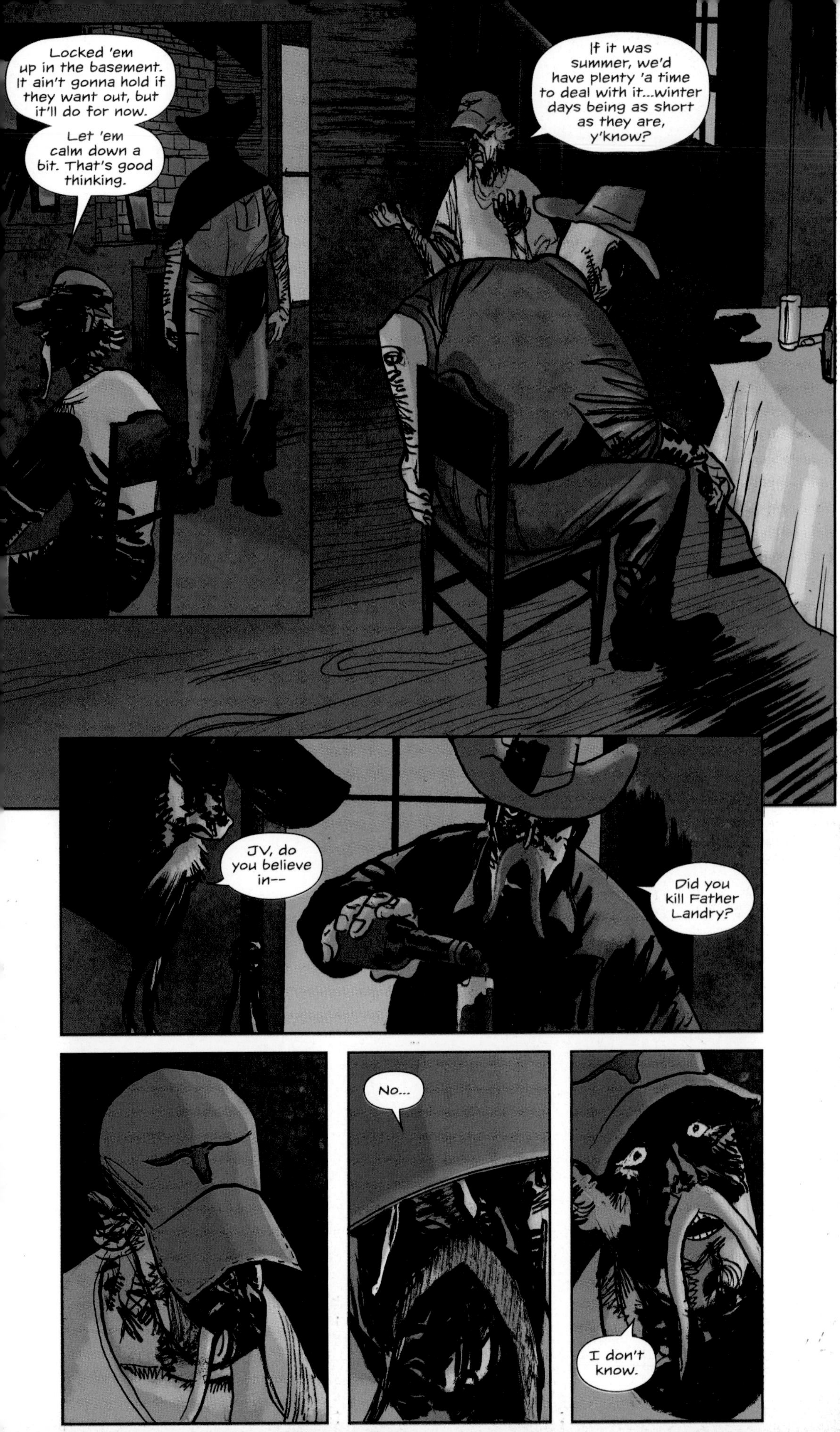
Locked 'em up in the basement. It ain't gonna hold if they want out, but it'll do for now.
Let 'em calm down a bit. That's good thinking.
If it was summer, we'd have plenty 'a time to deal with it...winter days being as short as they are, y'know?
JV, do you believe in--
Did you kill Father Landry?
No...
I don't know.

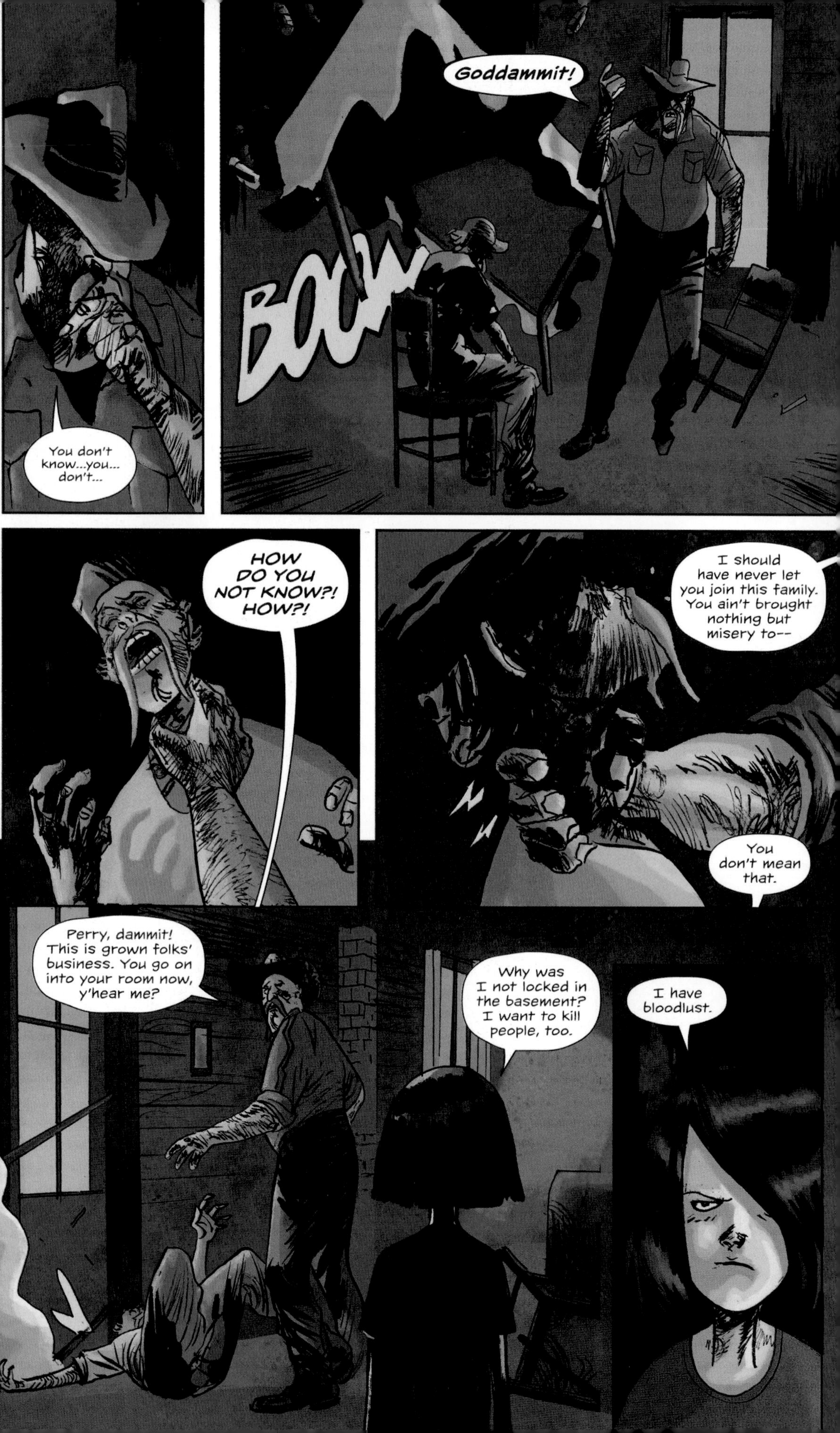

You don't know...you... don't...
Goddammit!
BOOM
HOW DO YOU NOT KNOW?! HOW?!
I should have never let you join this family. You ain't brought nothing but misery to--
You don't mean that.
Perry, dammit! This is grown folks' business. You go on into your room now, y'hear me?
Why was I not locked in the basement? I want to kill people, too.
I have bloodlust.

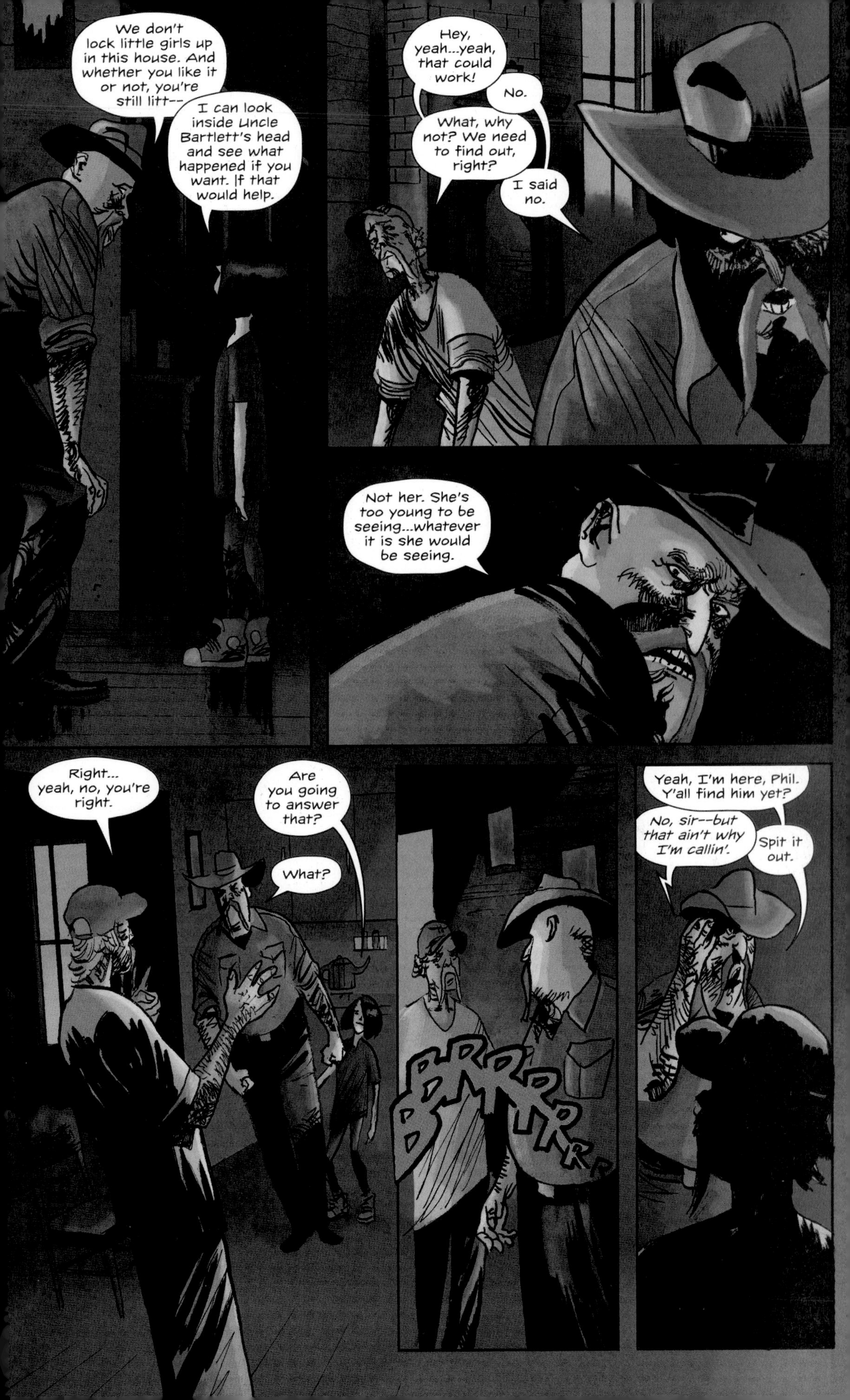
We don't lock little girls up in this house. And whether you like it or not, you're still litt--
I can look inside Uncle Bartlett's head and see what happened if you want. If that would help.
Hey, yeah...yeah, that could work!
No.
What, why not? We need to find out, right?
I said no.
Not her. She's too young to be seeing...whatever it is she would be seeing.
Right... yeah, no, you're right.
Are you going to answer that?
What?
BBRRRRRRRR
Yeah, I'm here, Phil. Y'all find him yet?
No, sir--but that ain't why I'm callin'.
Spit it out.

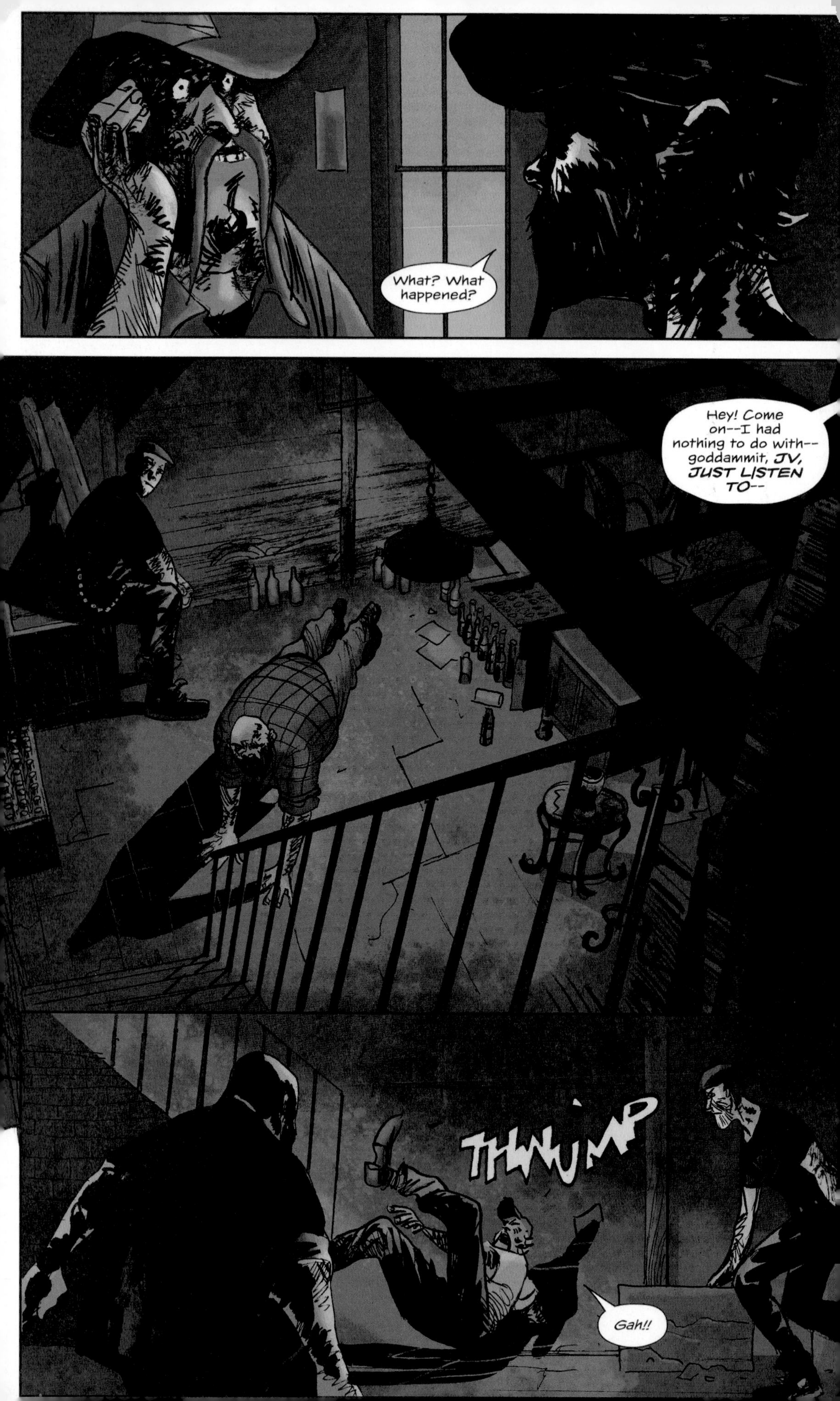
What? What happened?
Hey! Come on--I had nothing to do with--goddammit, JV, JUST LISTEN TO--
THWUMP
Gah!!

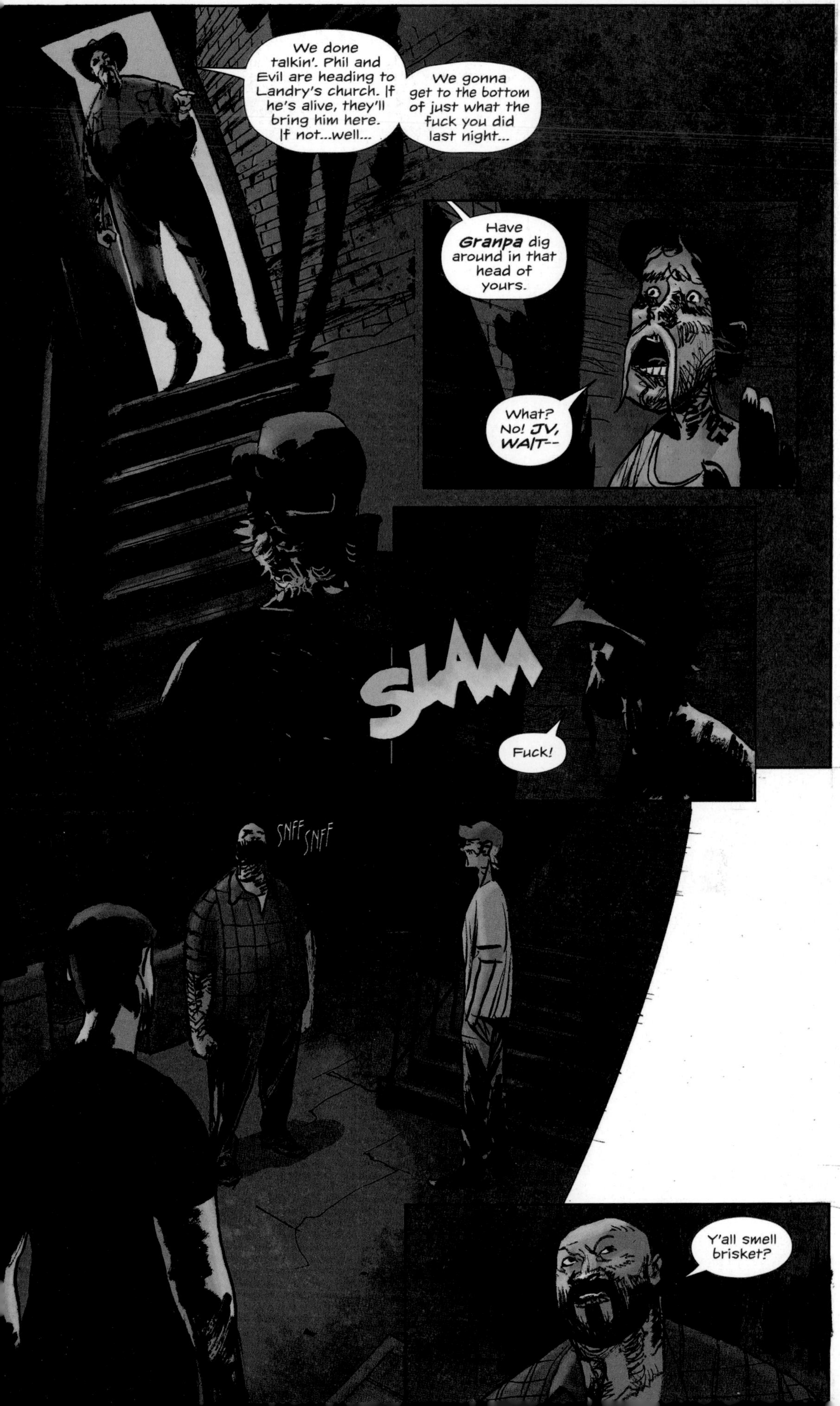
We done talkin'. Phil and Evil are heading to Landry's church. If he's alive, they'll bring him here. If not...well...
We gonna get to the bottom of just what the fuck you did last night...
Have Granpa dig around in that head of yours.
What? No! JV, WAIT--
SLAM
Fuck!
SNFF SNFF
Y'all smell brisket?

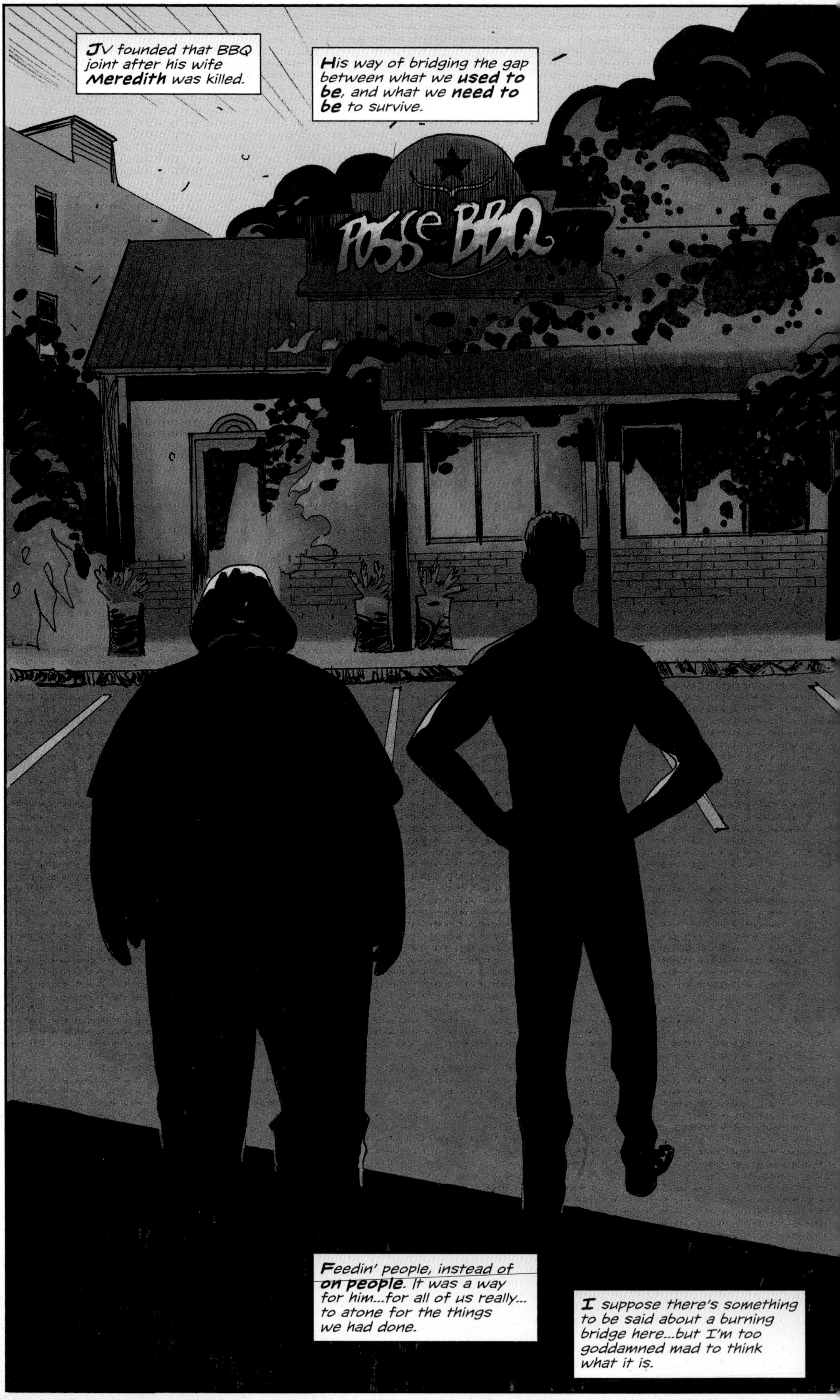
JV founded that BBQ joint after his wife Meredith was killed.
His way of bridging the gap between what we used to be, and what we need to be to survive.
POSSE BBQ
Feedin' people, instead of on people. It was a way for him...for all of us really... to atone for the things we had done.
I suppose there's something to be said about a burning bridge here...but I'm too goddamned mad to think what it is.

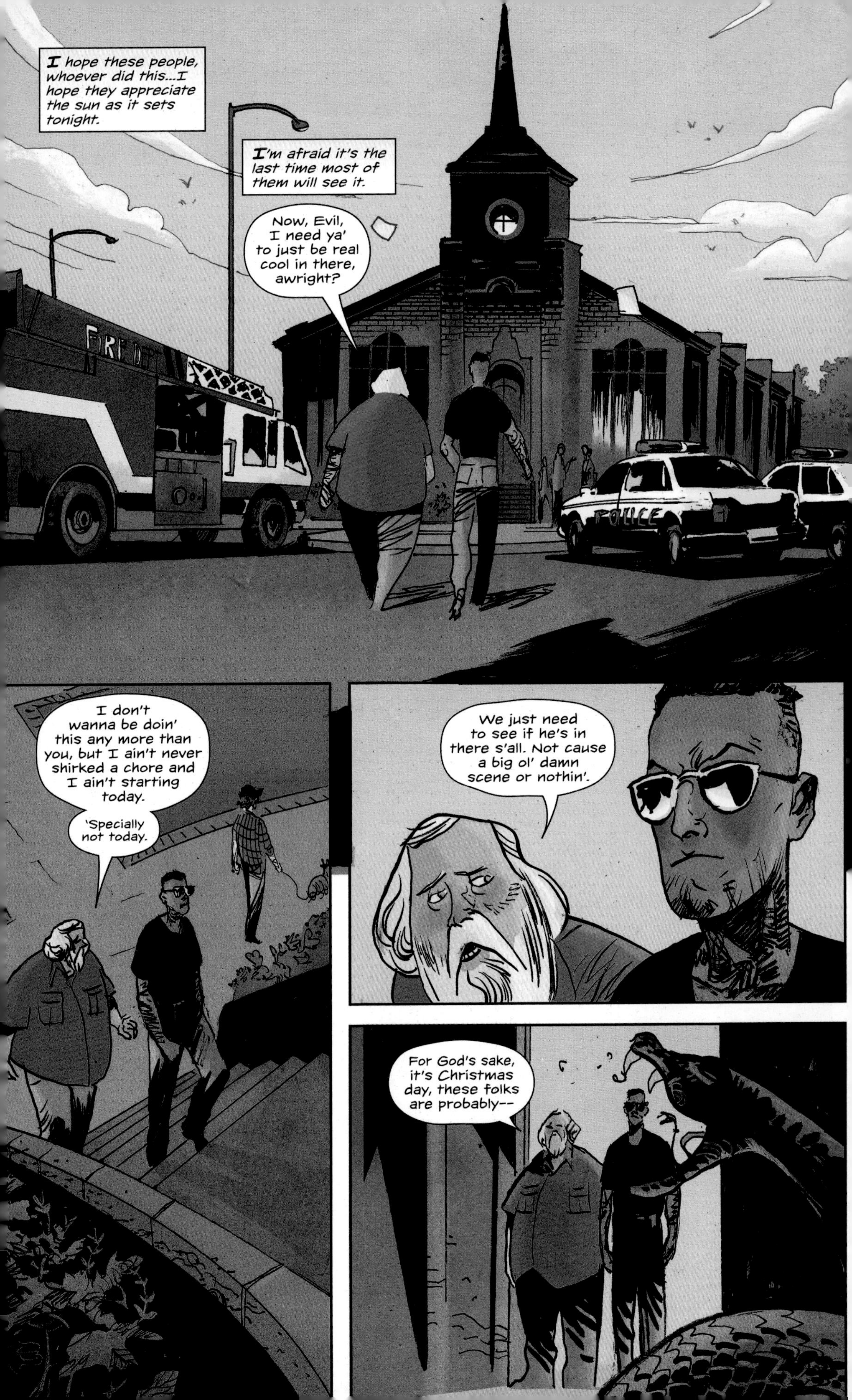
I hope these people, whoever did this...I hope they appreciate the sun as it sets tonight.
I'm afraid it's the last time most of them will see it.
Now, Evil, I need ya' to just be real cool in there, awright?
FIRE DEPT
POLICE
I don't wanna be doin' this any more than you, but I ain't never shirked a chore and I ain't starting today.
'Specially not today.
We just need to see if he's in there s'all. Not cause a big ol' damn scene or nothin'.
For God's sake, it's Christmas day, these folks are probably--

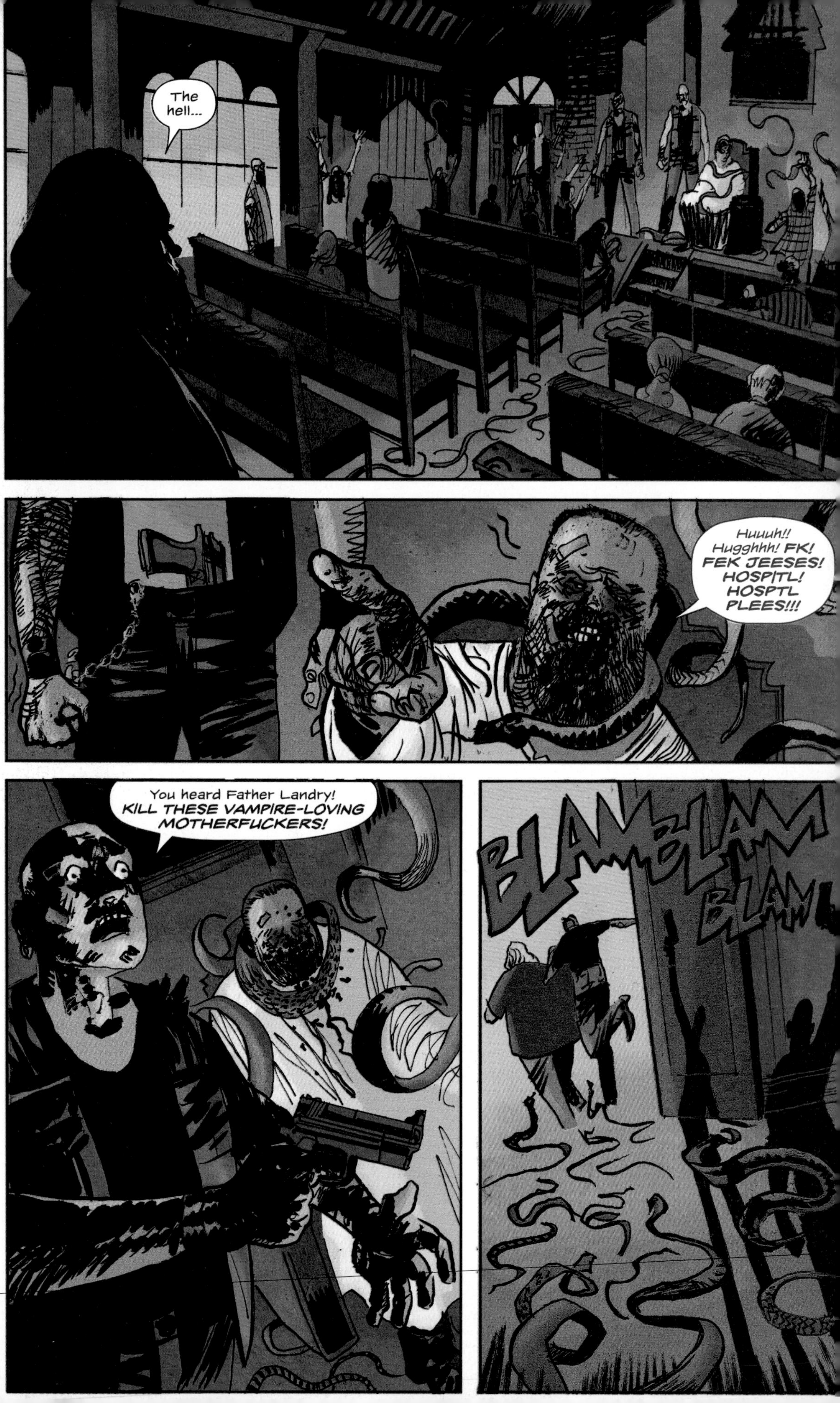

The hell...
Huuuh!! Hugghhh! FK! FEK JEESES! HOSPITL! HOSPTL PLEES!!!
You heard Father Landry! KILL THESE VAMPIRE-LOVING MOTHERFUCKERS!
BLAM BLAM BLAM

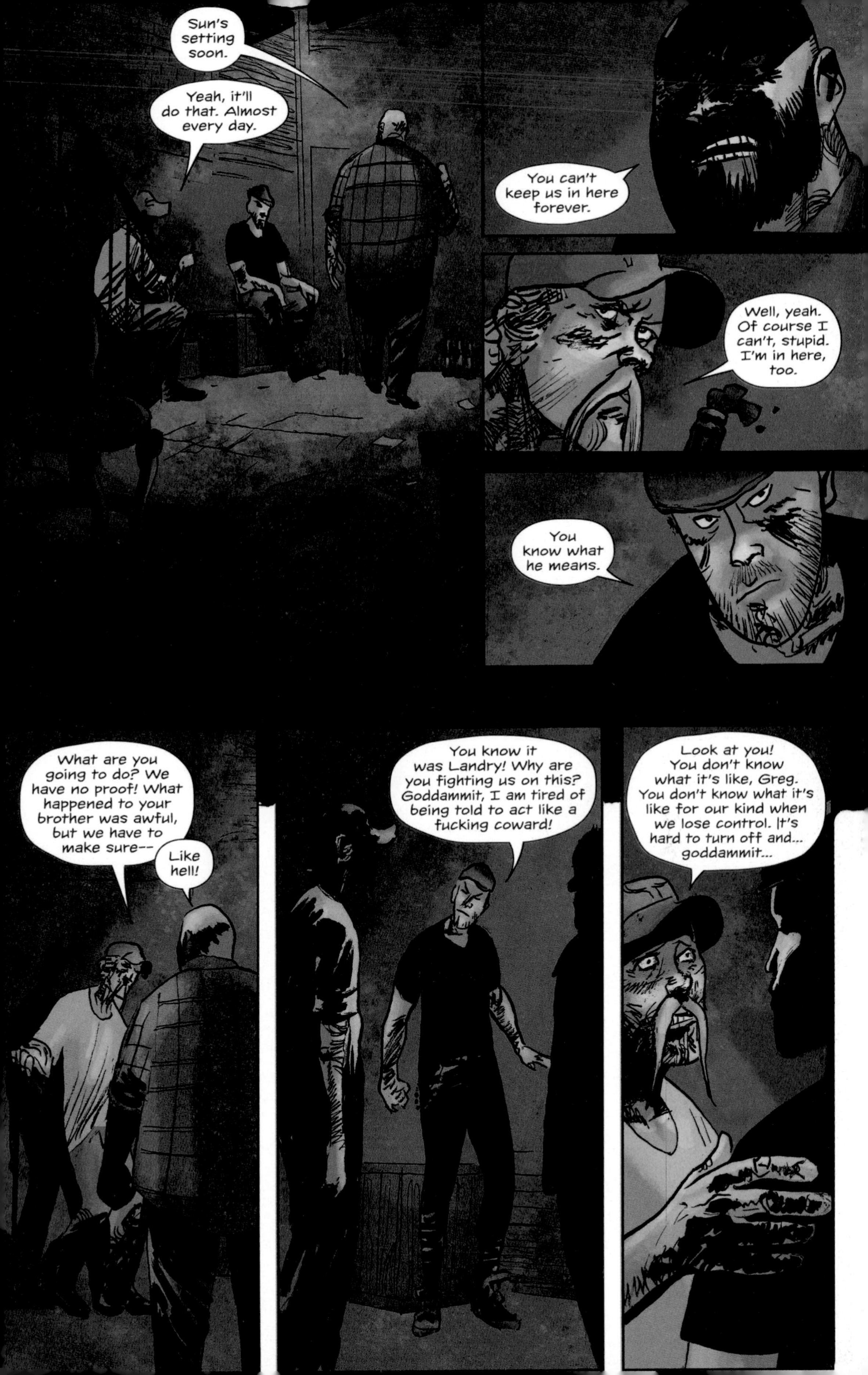
Sun's setting soon.
Yeah, it'll do that. Almost every day.
You can't keep us in here forever.
Well, yeah. Of course I can't, stupid. I'm in here, too.
You know what he means.
What are you going to do? We have no proof! What happened to your brother was awful, but we have to make sure--
Like hell!
You know it was Landry! Why are you fighting us on this? Goddammit, I am tired of being told to act like a fucking coward!
Look at you! You don't know what it's like, Greg. You don't know what it's like for our kind when we lose control. It's hard to turn off and... goddammit...

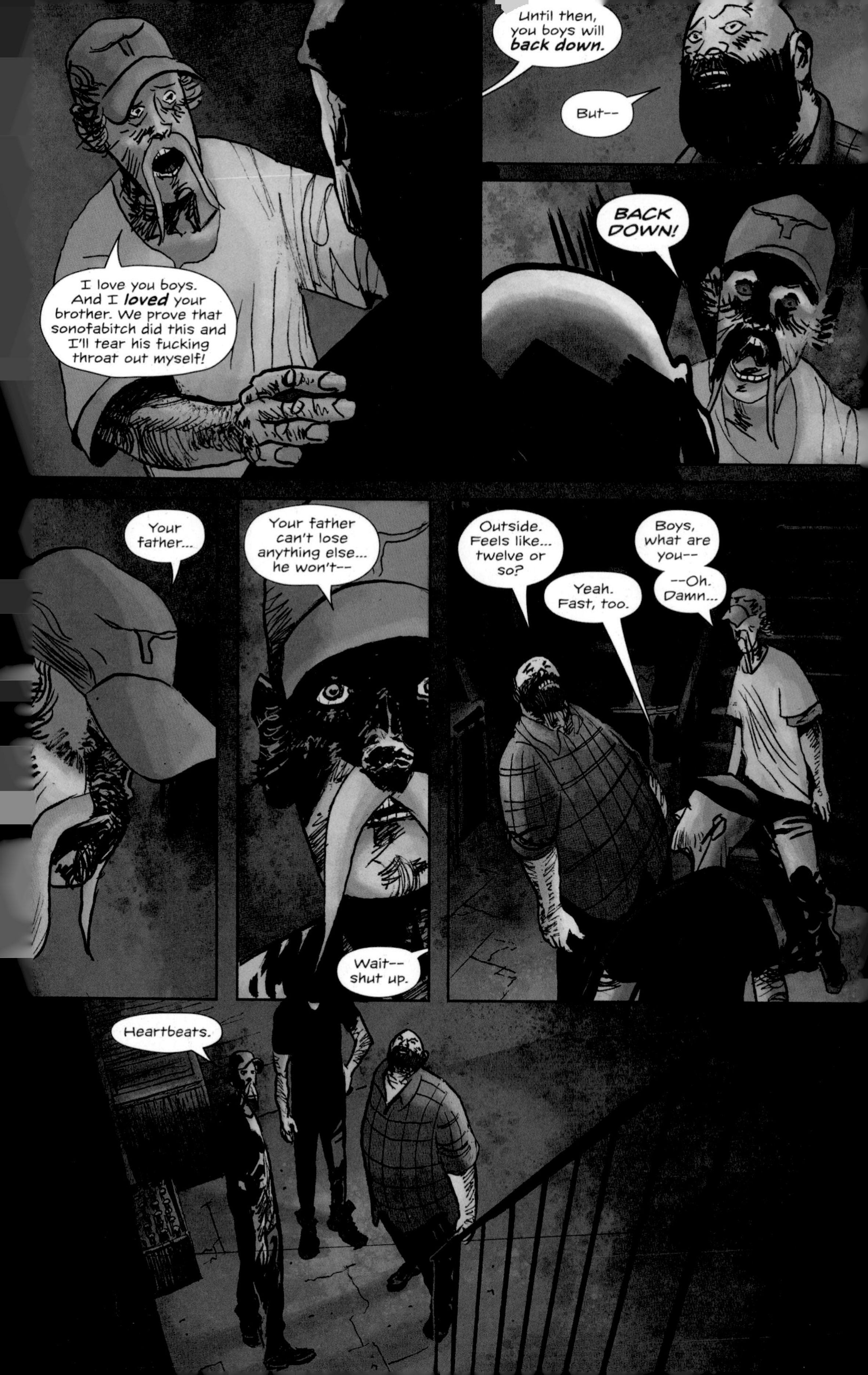
I love you boys. And I *loved* your brother. We prove that sonofabitch did this and I'll tear his fucking throat out myself!
Until then, you boys will **back down.**
But--
BACK DOWN!
Your father...
Your father can't lose anything else... he won't--
Wait-- shut up.
Outside. Feels like... twelve or so?
Yeah. Fast, too.
Boys, what are you--
--Oh. Damn...
Heartbeats.

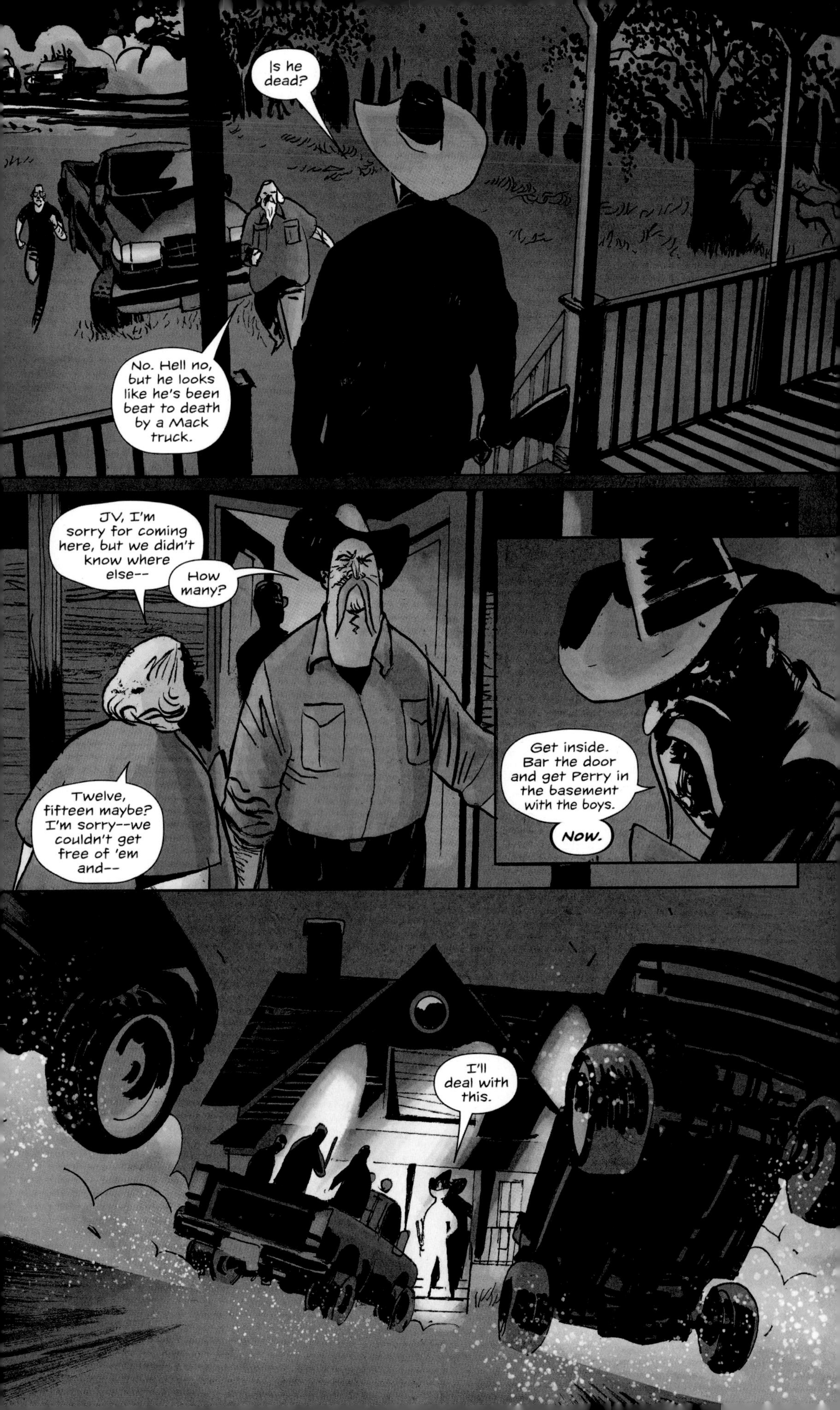
Is he dead?
No. Hell no, but he looks like he's been beat to death by a Mack truck.
JV, I'm sorry for coming here, but we didn't know where else--
How many?
Twelve, fifteen maybe? I'm sorry--we couldn't get free of 'em and--
Get inside. Bar the door and get Perry in the basement with the boys.
NOW.
I'll deal with this.

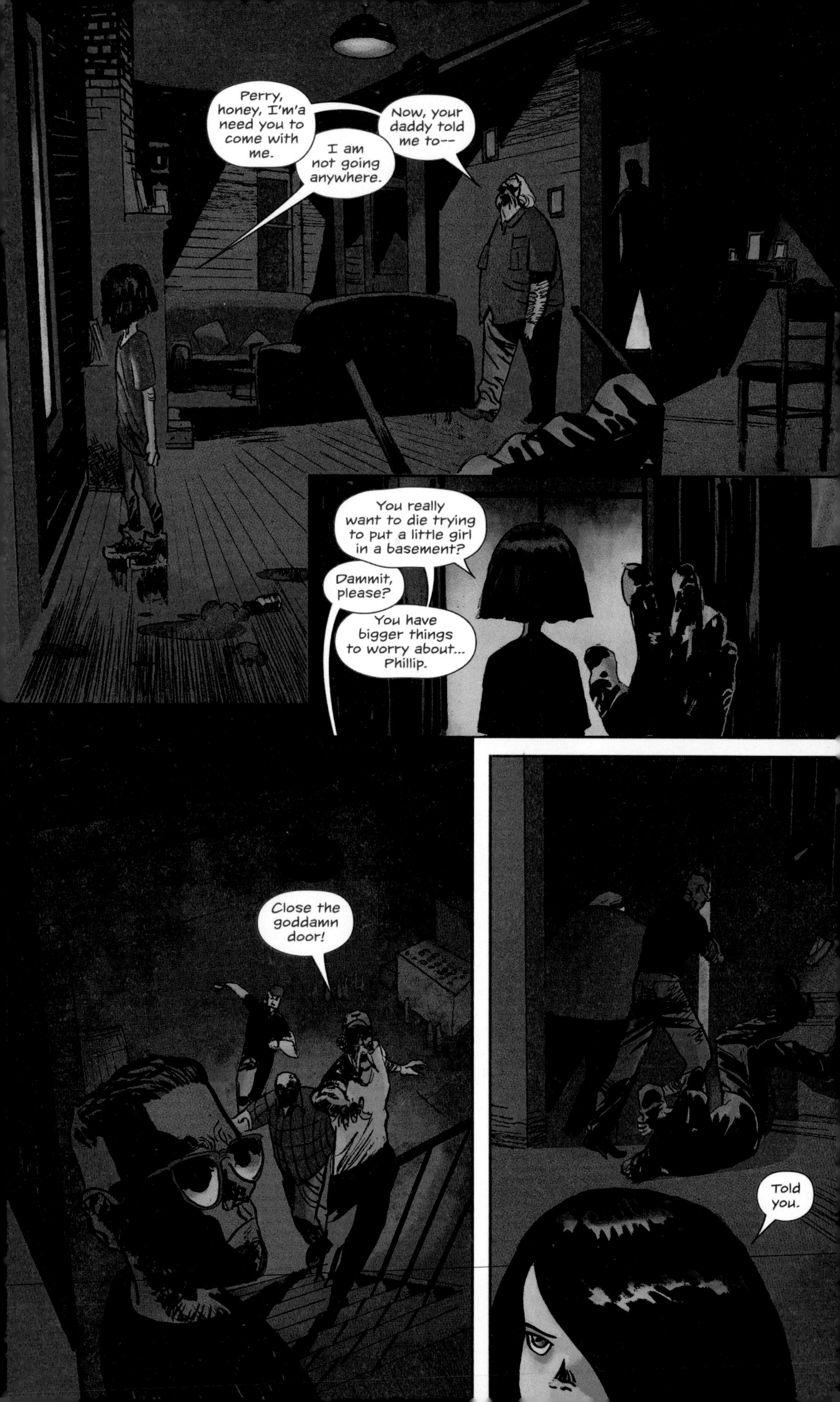
Perry, honey, I'm'a need you to come with me.
Now, your daddy told me to--
I am not going anywhere.
You really want to die trying to put a little girl in a basement?
Dammit, please?
You have bigger things to worry about... Phillip.
Close the goddamn door!
Told you.

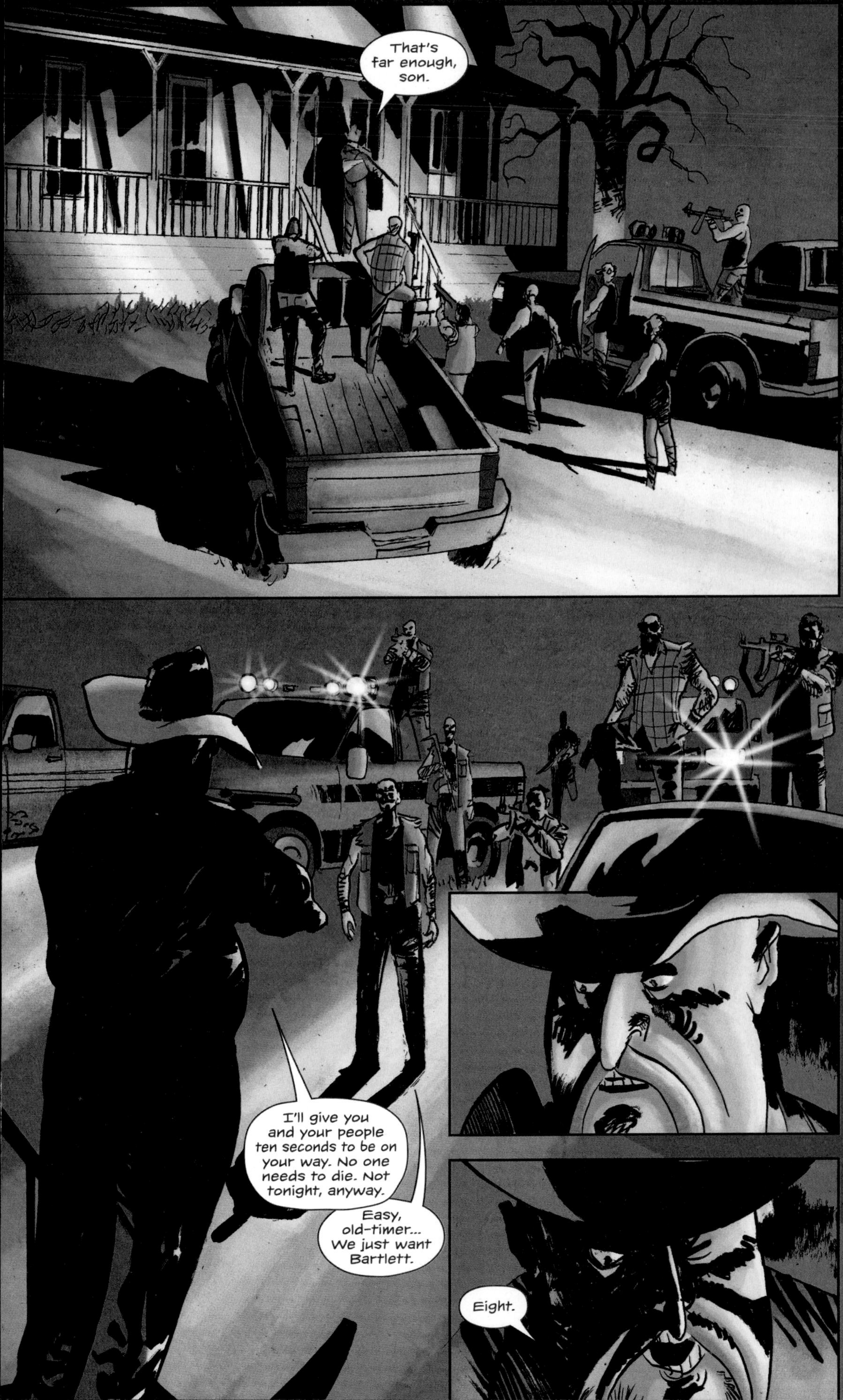
That's far enough, son.
I'll give you and your people ten seconds to be on your way. No one needs to die. Not tonight, anyway.
Easy, old-timer... We just want Bartlett.
Eight.

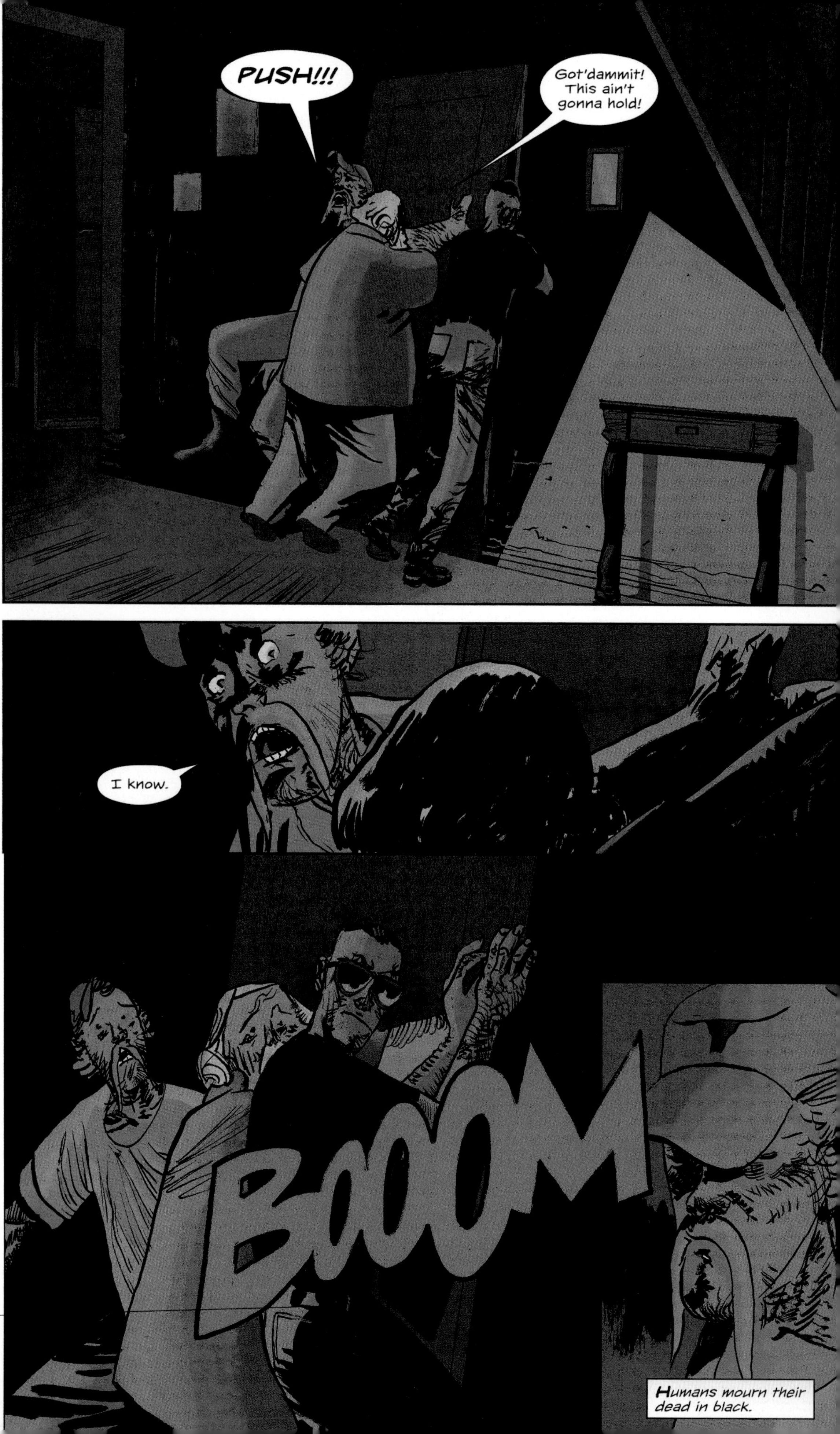
PUSH!!!
Got'dammit! This ain't gonna hold!
I know.
BOOOM
Humans mourn their dead in black.

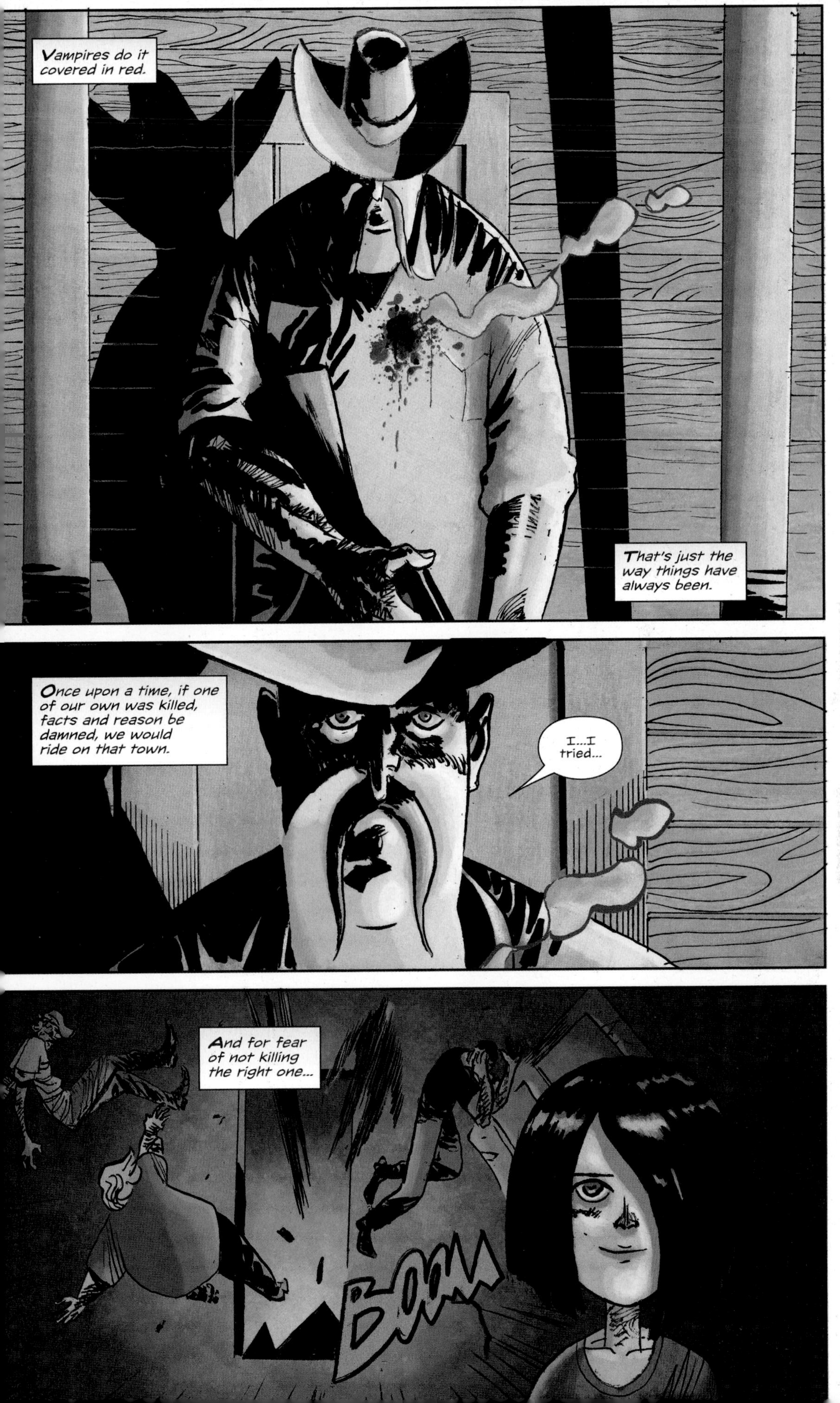

Vampires do it covered in red.
That's just the way things have always been.
Once upon a time, if one of our own was killed, facts and reason be damned, we would ride on that town.
I...I tried...
And for fear of not killing the right one...
BOOM

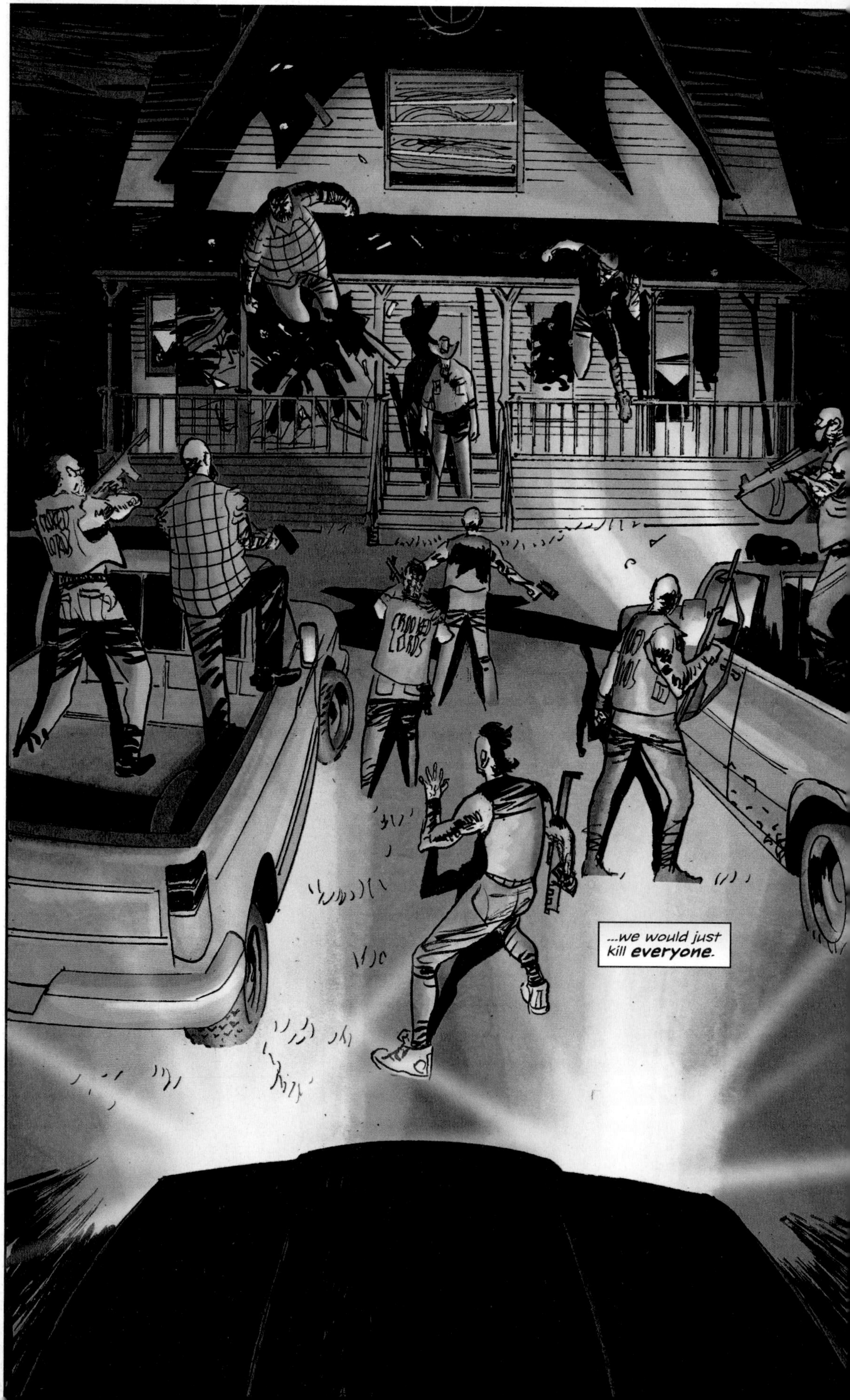
...we would just kill everyone.

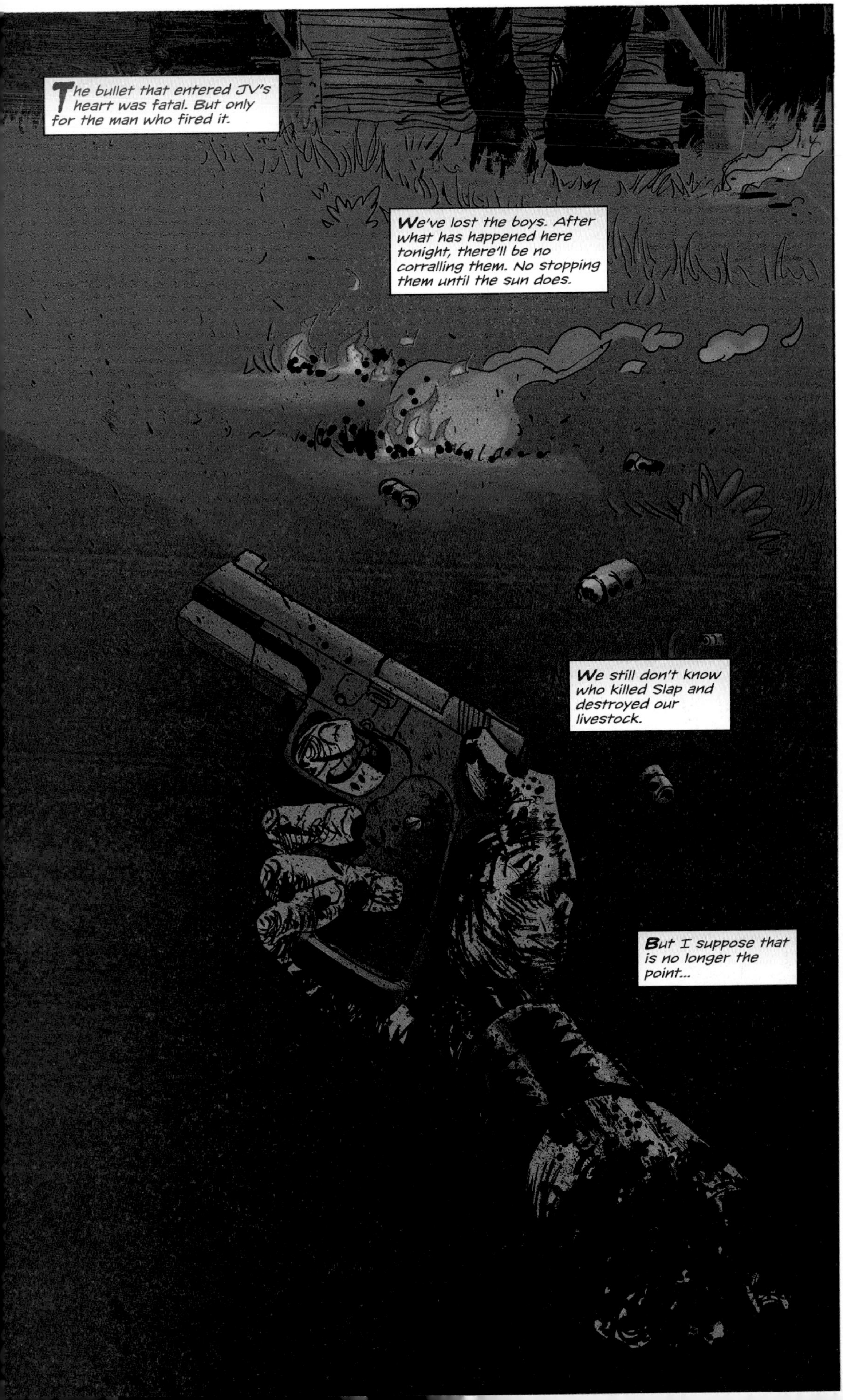
The bullet that entered JV's heart was fatal. But only for the man who fired it.
We've lost the boys. After what has happened here tonight, there'll be no corralling them. No stopping them until the sun does.
We still don't know who killed Slap and destroyed our livestock.
But I suppose that is no longer the point...

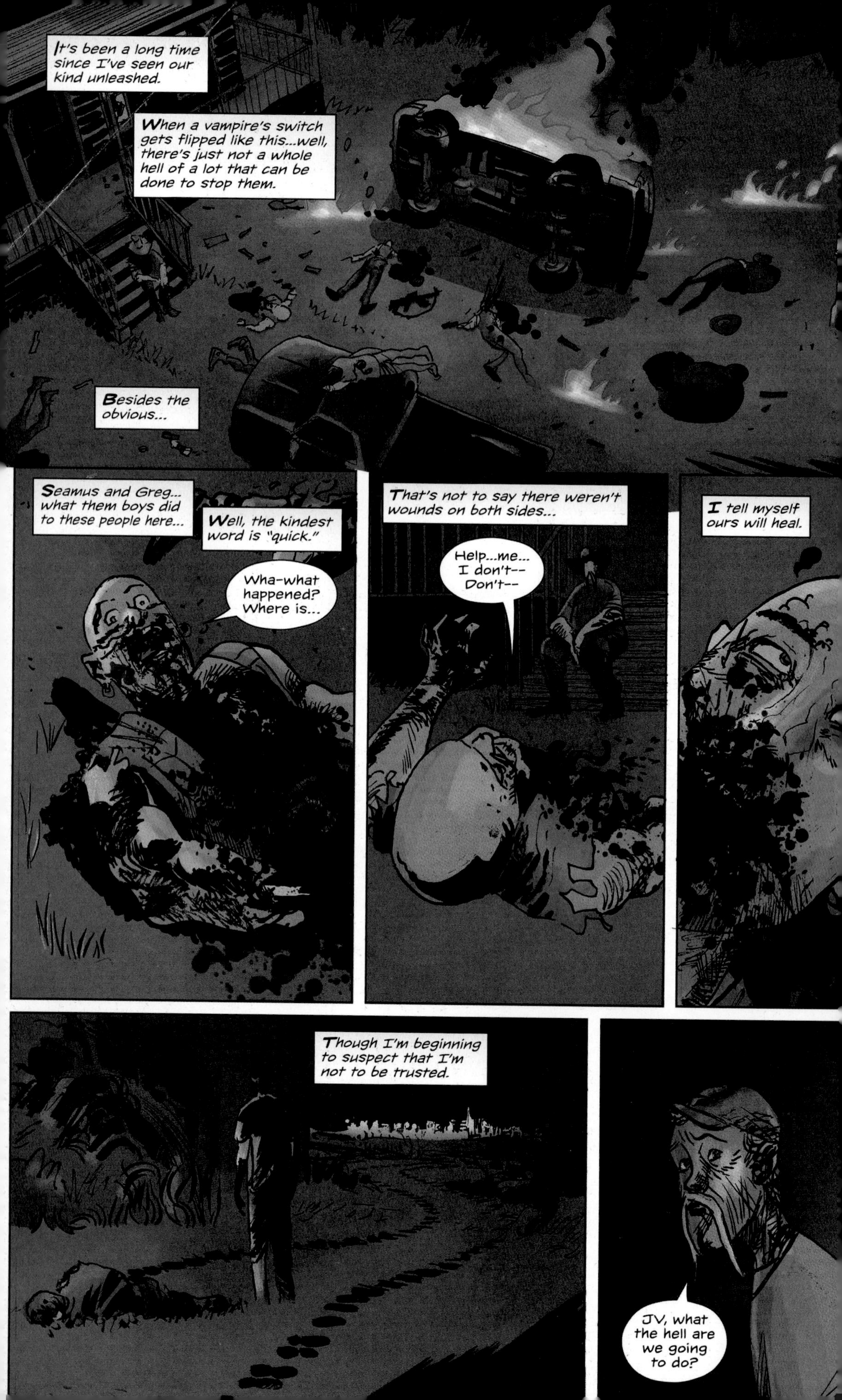
It's been a long time since I've seen our kind unleashed.
When a vampire's switch gets flipped like this...well, there's just not a whole hell of a lot that can be done to stop them.
Besides the obvious...
Seamus and Greg... what them boys did to these people here...
Well, the kindest word is "quick."
Wha-what happened? Where is...
That's not to say there weren't wounds on both sides...
Help...me... I don't-- Don't--
I tell myself ours will heal.
Though I'm beginning to suspect that I'm not to be trusted.
JV, what the hell are we going to do?

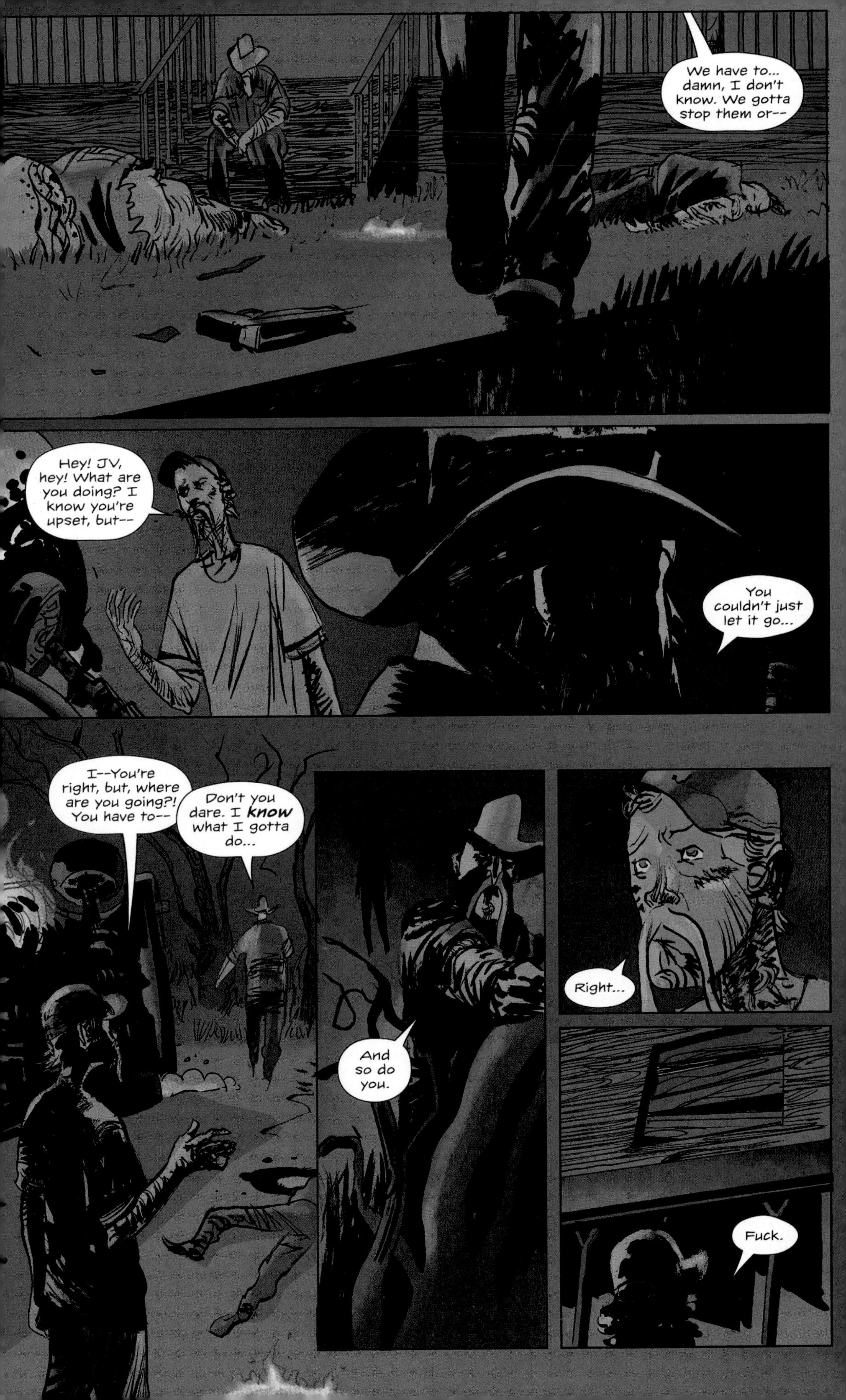
We have to... damn, I don't know. We gotta stop them or--
Hey! JV, hey! What are you doing? I know you're upset, but--
You couldn't just let it go...
I--You're right, but, where are you going?! You have to--
Don't you dare. I **know** what I gotta do...
And so do you.
Right...
Fuck.

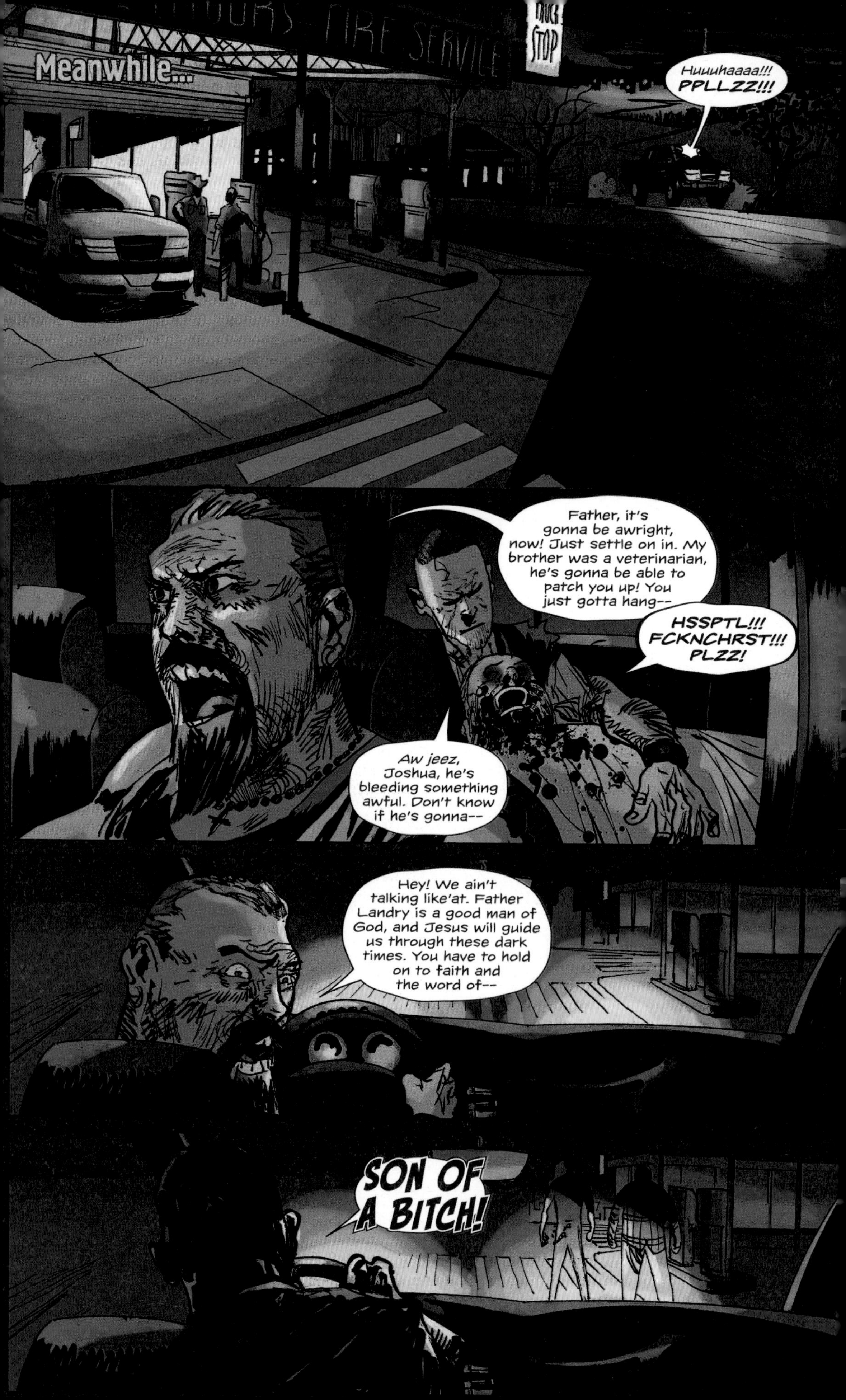
Meanwhile...
Huuuhaaaa!!! PPLLZZ!!!
Father, it's gonna be awright, now! Just settle on in. My brother was a veterinarian, he's gonna be able to patch you up! You just gotta hang--
HSSPTL!!! FCKNCHRST!!! PLZZ!
Aw jeez, Joshua, he's bleeding something awful. Don't know if he's gonna--
Hey! We ain't talking like'at. Father Landry is a good man of God, and Jesus will guide us through these dark times. You have to hold on to faith and the word of--
SON OF A BITCH!

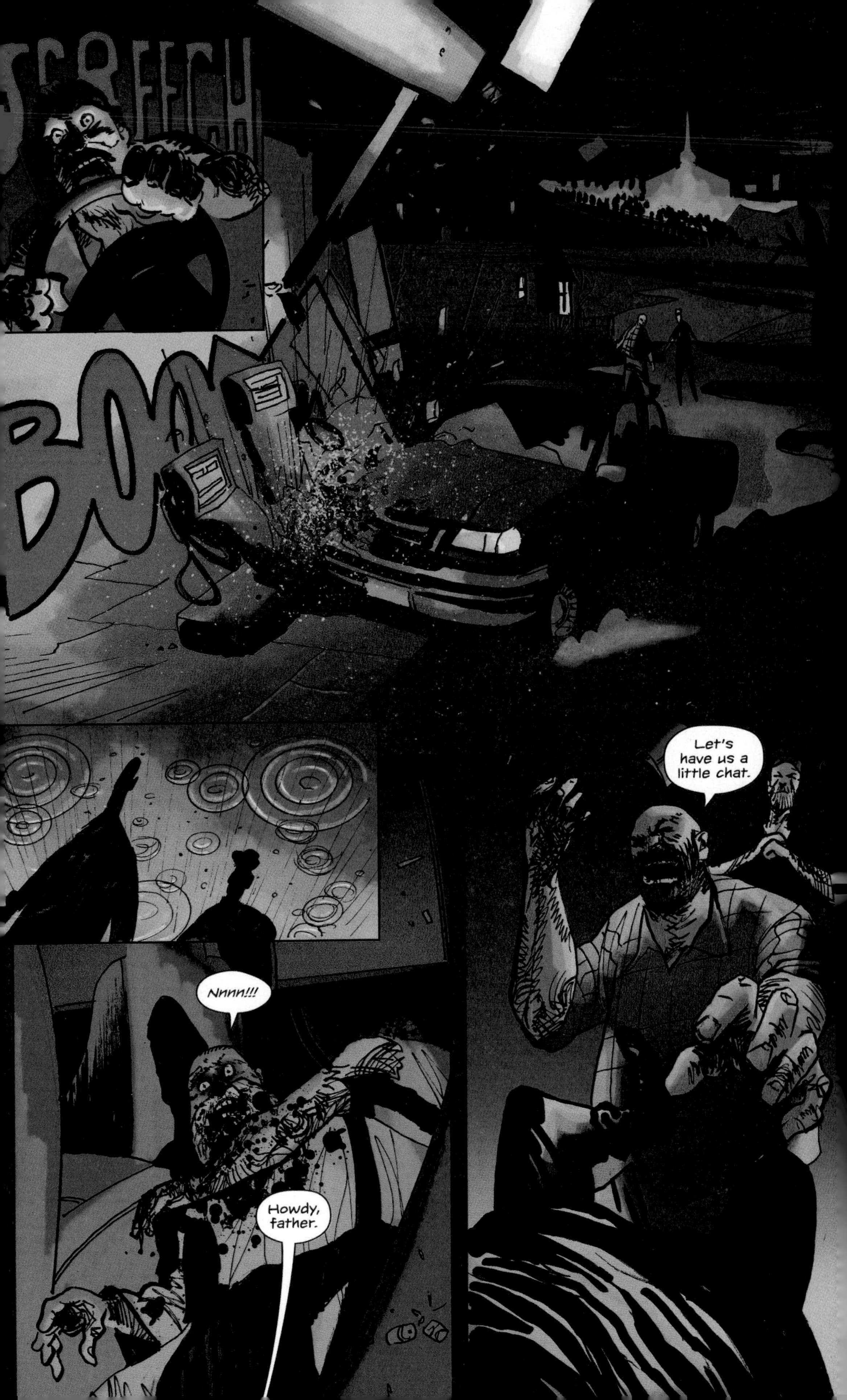
SCREECH
BOOM
Let's have us a little chat.
Nnnn!!!
Howdy, father.

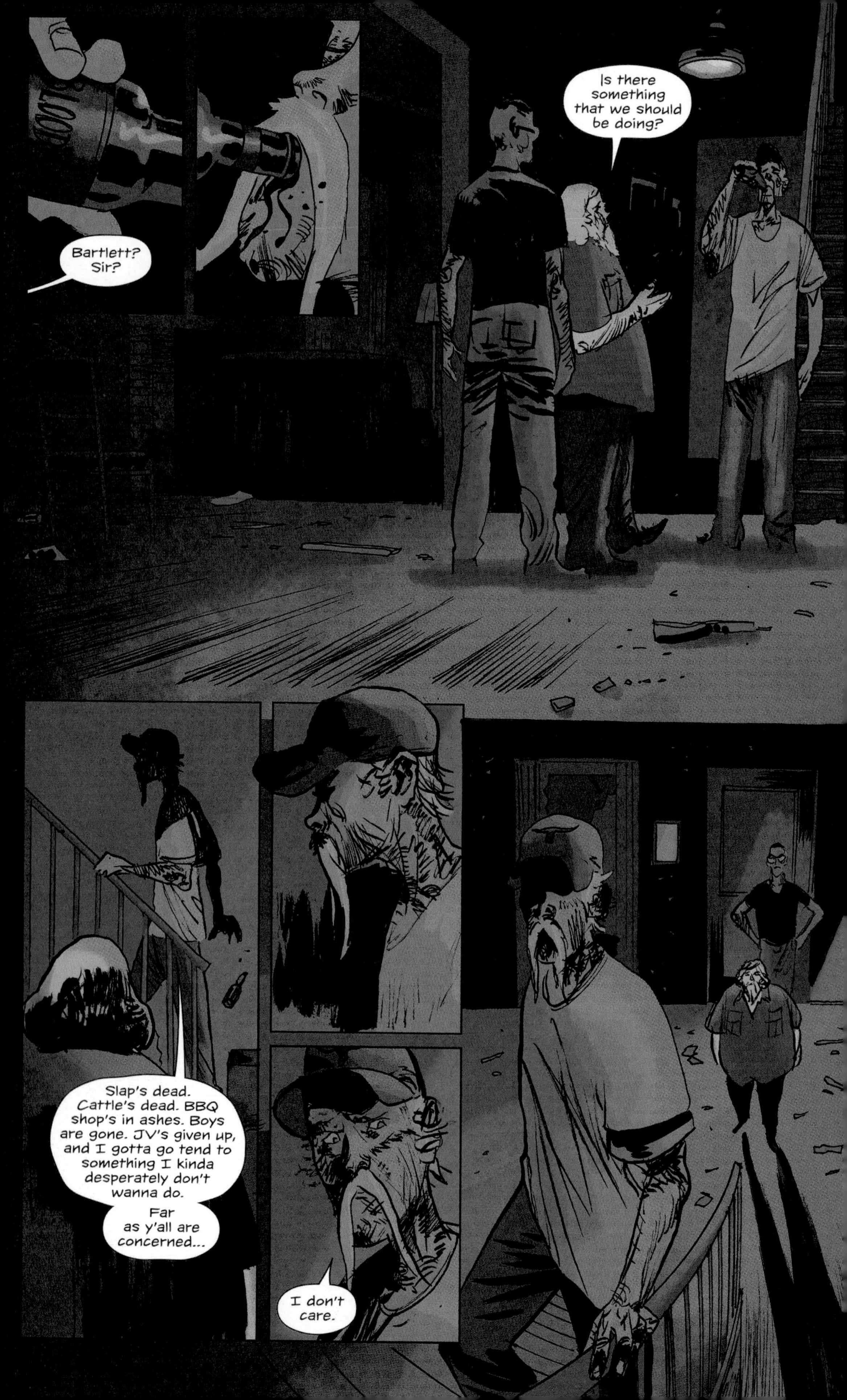
Bartlett? Sir?
Is there something that we should be doing?
Slap's dead. Cattle's dead. BBQ shop's in ashes. Boys are gone. JV's given up, and I gotta go tend to something I kinda desperately don't wanna do.
Far as y'all are concerned...
I don't care.

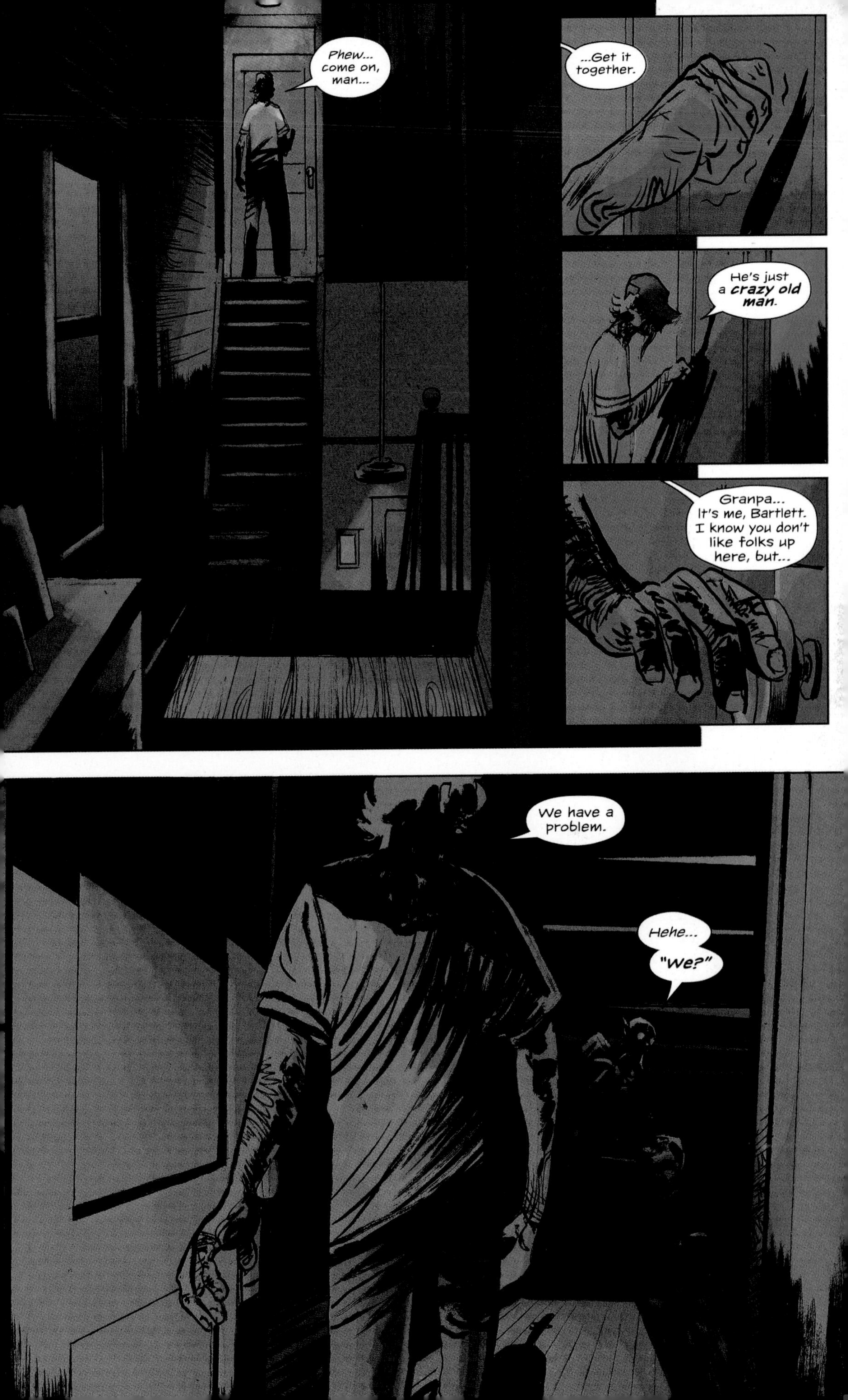
Phew... come on, man...
...Get it together.
He's just a crazy old man.
Granpa... It's me, Bartlett. I know you don't like folks up here, but...
We have a problem.
Hehe...
"We?"

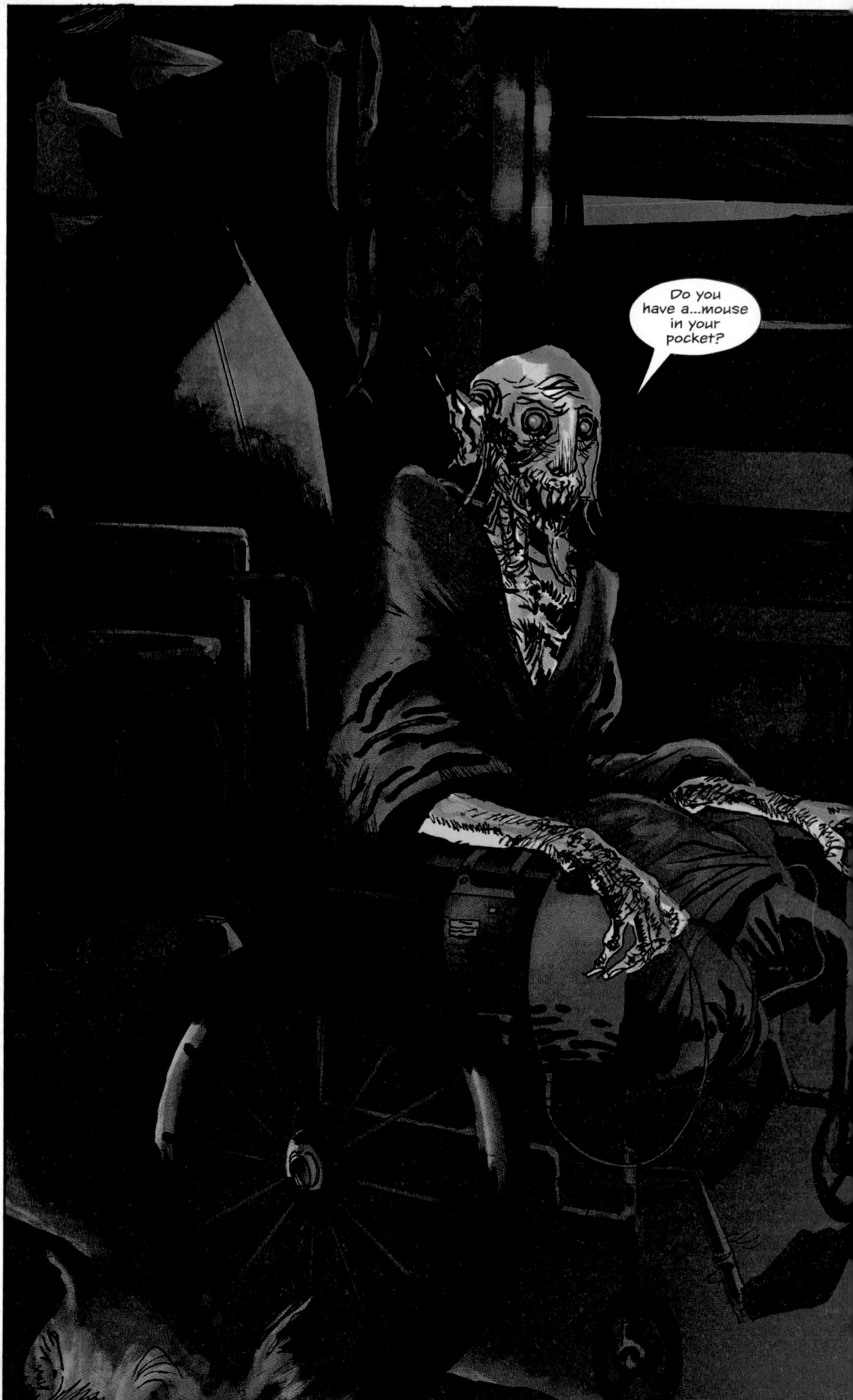
Do you have a...mouse in your pocket?

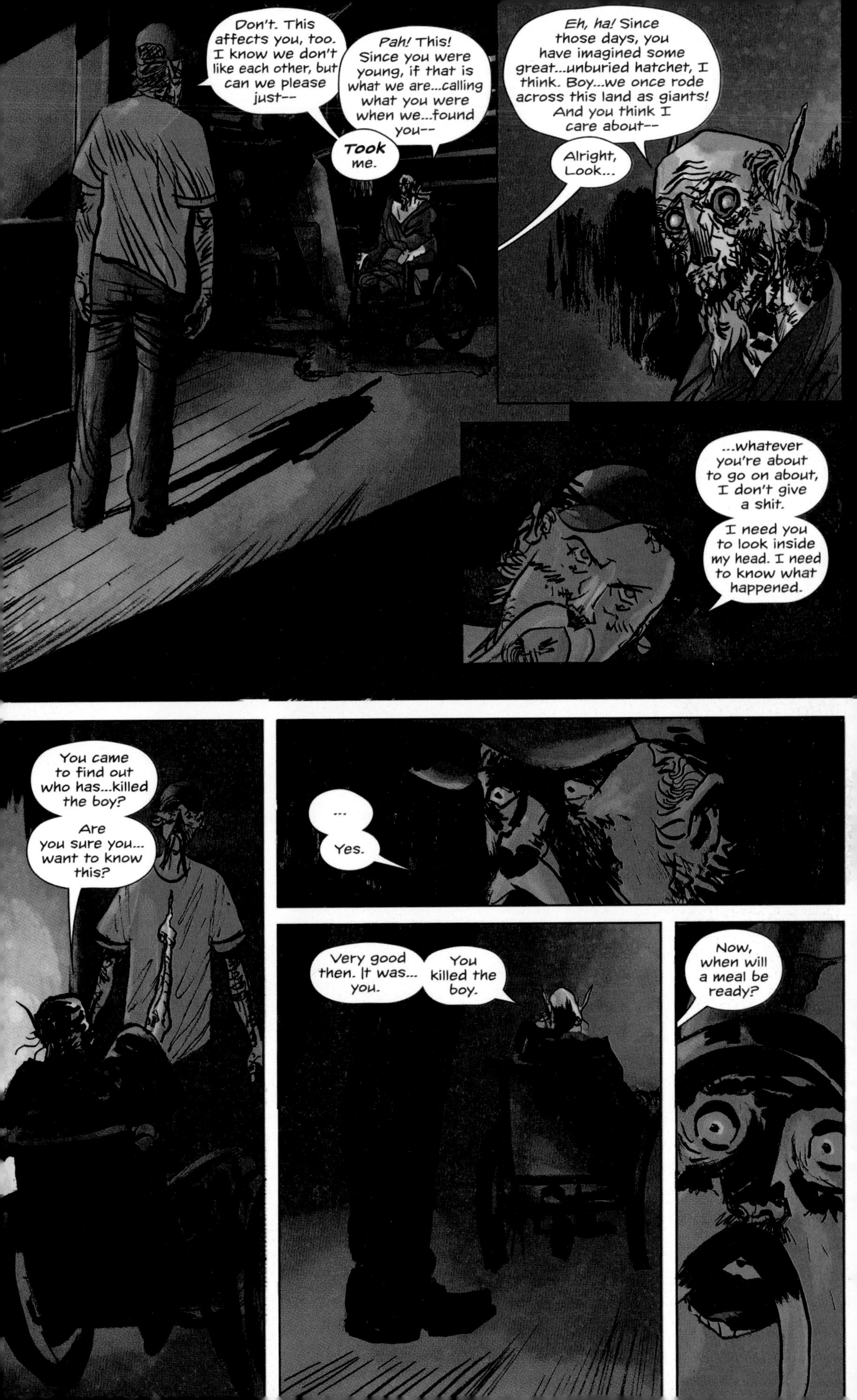

Don't. This affects you, too. I know we don't like each other, but can we please just--
Pah! This! Since you were young, if that is what we are...calling what you were when we...found you--
Took me.
Eh, ha! Since those days, you have imagined some great...unburied hatchet, I think. Boy...we once rode across this land as giants! And you think I care about--
Alright, Look...
...whatever you're about to go on about, I don't give a shit.
I need you to look inside my head. I need to know what happened.
You came to find out who has...killed the boy?
Are you sure you... want to know this?
...
Yes.
Very good then. It was... you.
You killed the boy.
Now, when will a meal be ready?

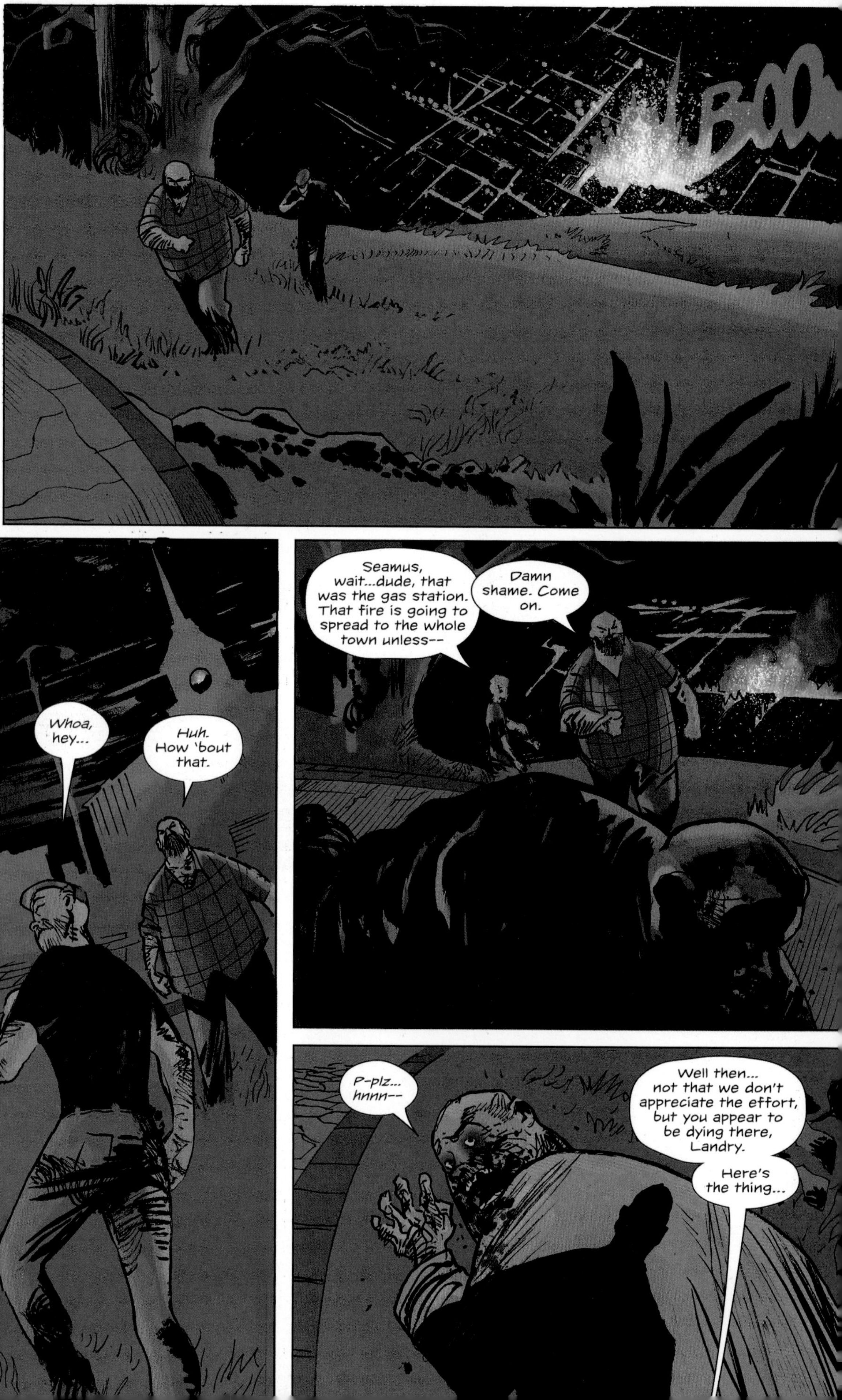
BOO
Whoa, hey...
Huh. How 'bout that.
Seamus, wait...dude, that was the gas station. That fire is going to spread to the whole town unless--
Damn shame. Come on.
P-plz... hnnn--
Well then... not that we don't appreciate the effort, but you appear to be dying there, Landry.
Here's the thing...

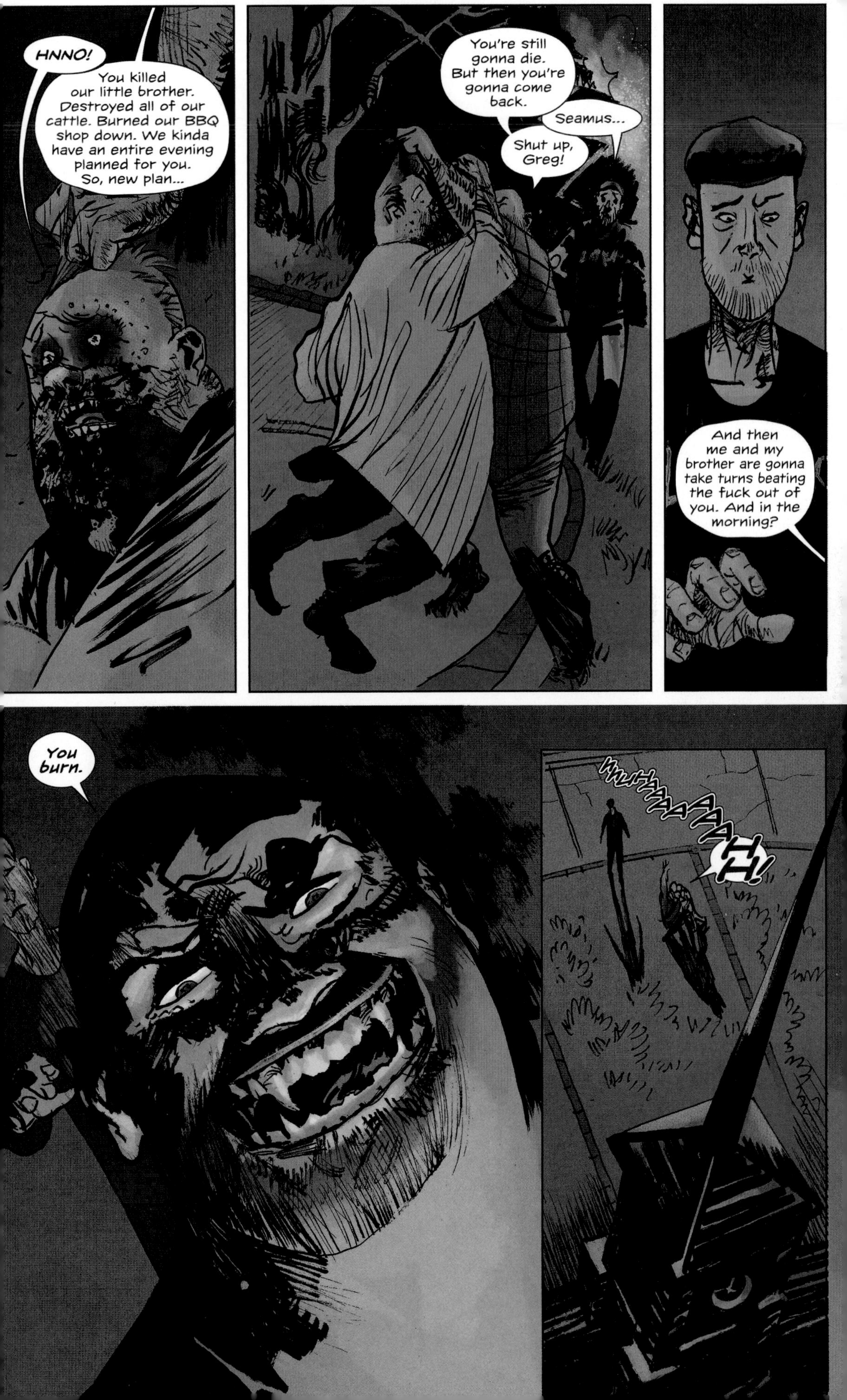
HNNO!
You killed our little brother. Destroyed all of our cattle. Burned our BBQ shop down. We kinda have an entire evening planned for you. So, new plan...
You're still gonna die. But then you're gonna come back.
Seamus...
Shut up, Greg!
And then me and my brother are gonna take turns beating the fuck out of you. And in the morning?
You burn.
WUHHAAAAAAHH!

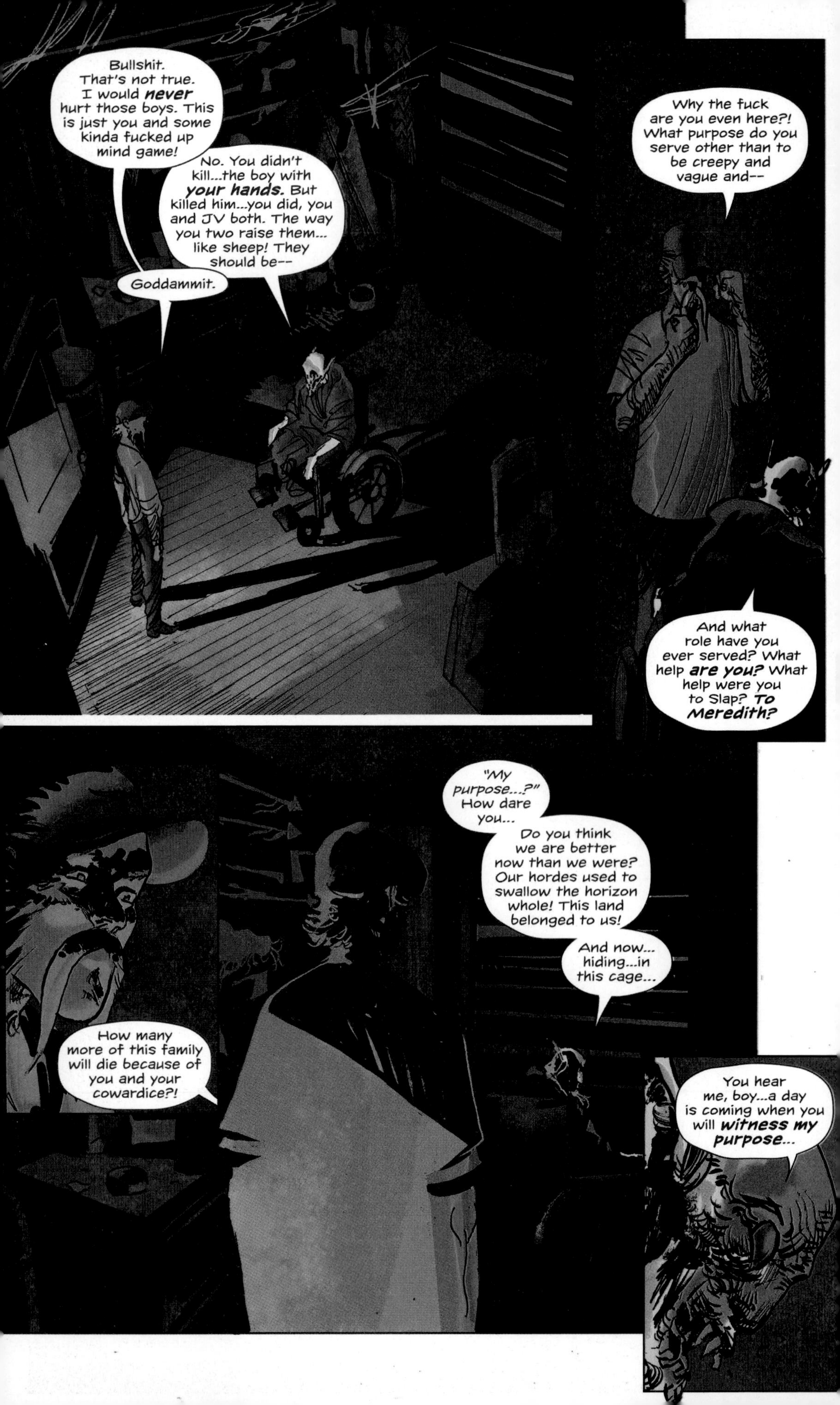
Bullshit. That's not true. I would never hurt those boys. This is just you and some kinda fucked up mind game!
No. You didn't kill...the boy with your hands. But killed him...you did, you and JV both. The way you two raise them... like sheep! They should be--
Goddammit.
Why the fuck are you even here?! What purpose do you serve other than to be creepy and vague and--
And what role have you ever served? What help are you? What help were you to Slap? To Meredith?
"My purpose...?" How dare you...
Do you think we are better now than we were? Our hordes used to swallow the horizon whole! This land belonged to us!
And now... hiding...in this cage...
How many more of this family will die because of you and your cowardice?!
You hear me, boy...a day is coming when you will witness my purpose...

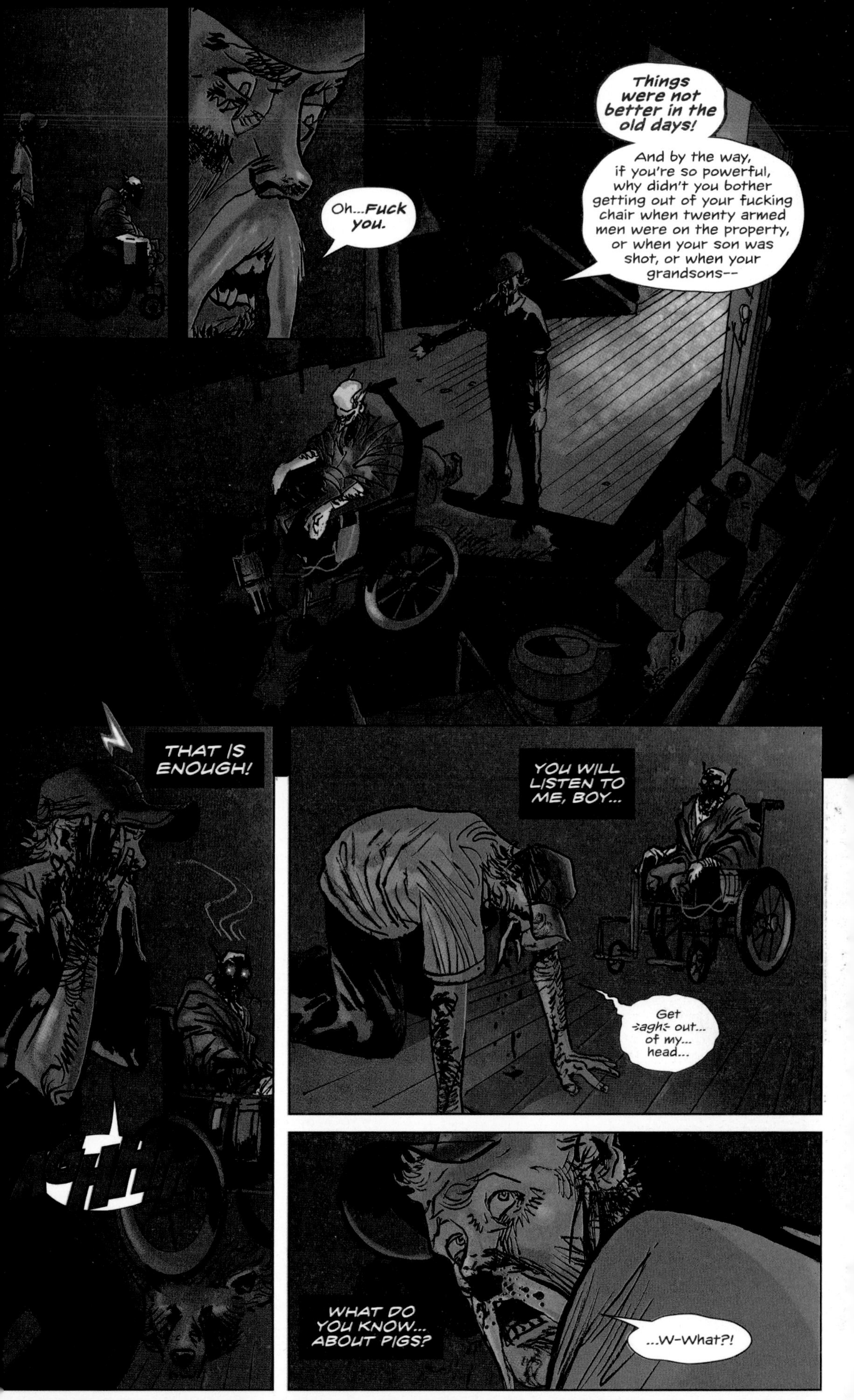

Oh...Fuck you.
Things were not better in the old days!
And by the way, if you're so powerful, why didn't you bother getting out of your fucking chair when twenty armed men were on the property, or when your son was shot, or when your grandsons--
THAT IS ENOUGH!
YOU WILL LISTEN TO ME, BOY...
Get -agh- out... of my... head...
WHAT DO YOU KNOW... ABOUT PIGS?
...W-What?!

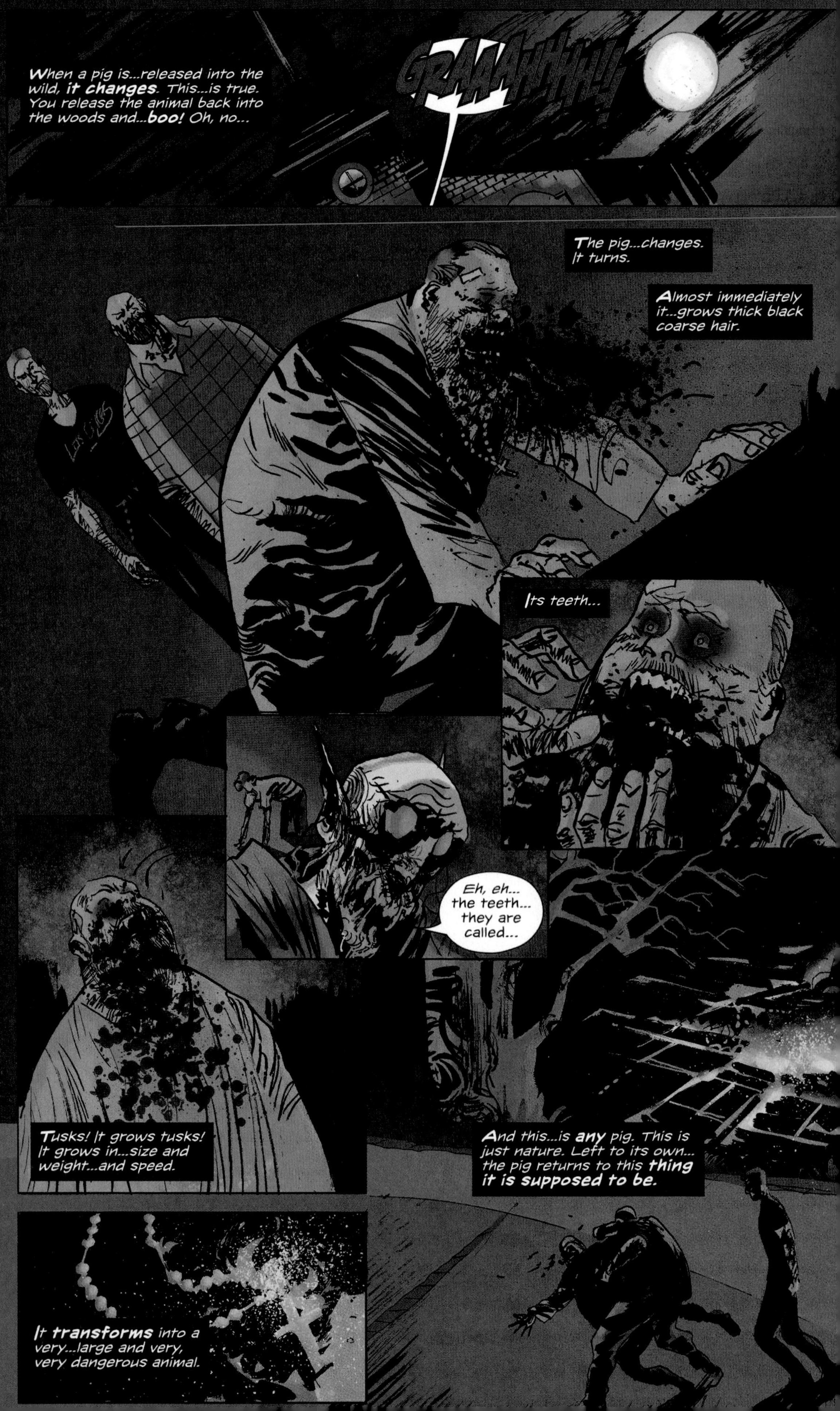
When a pig is...released into the wild, it changes. This...is true. You release the animal back into the woods and...boo! Oh, no...
GRAAAHHH!!
The pig...changes. It turns.
Almost immediately it...grows thick black coarse hair.
Its teeth...
Eh, eh... the teeth... they are called...
Tusks! It grows tusks! It grows in...size and weight...and speed.
And this...is any pig. This is just nature. Left to its own... the pig returns to this thing it is supposed to be.
It transforms into a very...large and very, very dangerous animal.

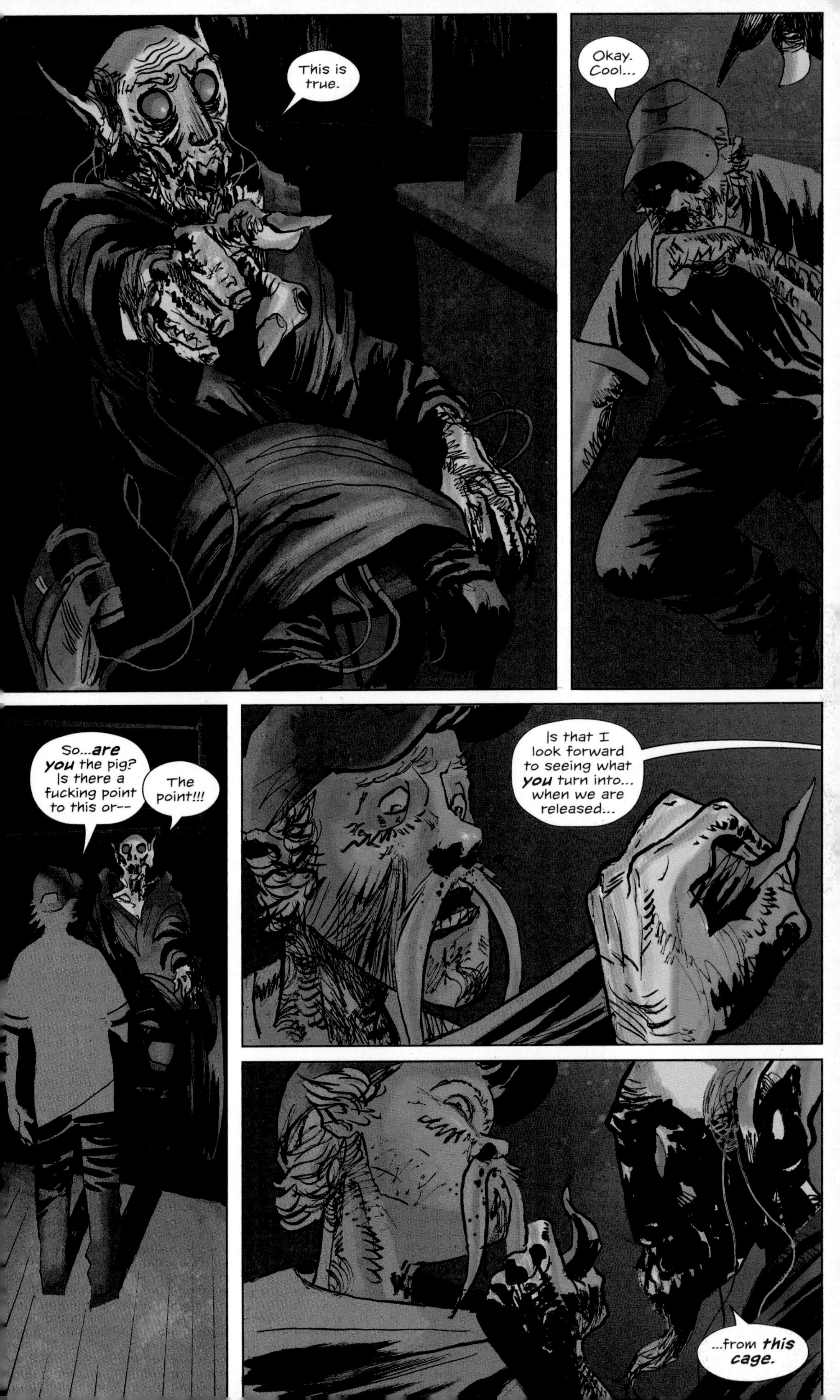
This is true.
Okay. Cool...
So...**are you** the pig? Is there a fucking point to this or--
The point!!!
Is that I look forward to seeing what **you** turn into... when we are released...
...from **this cage.**

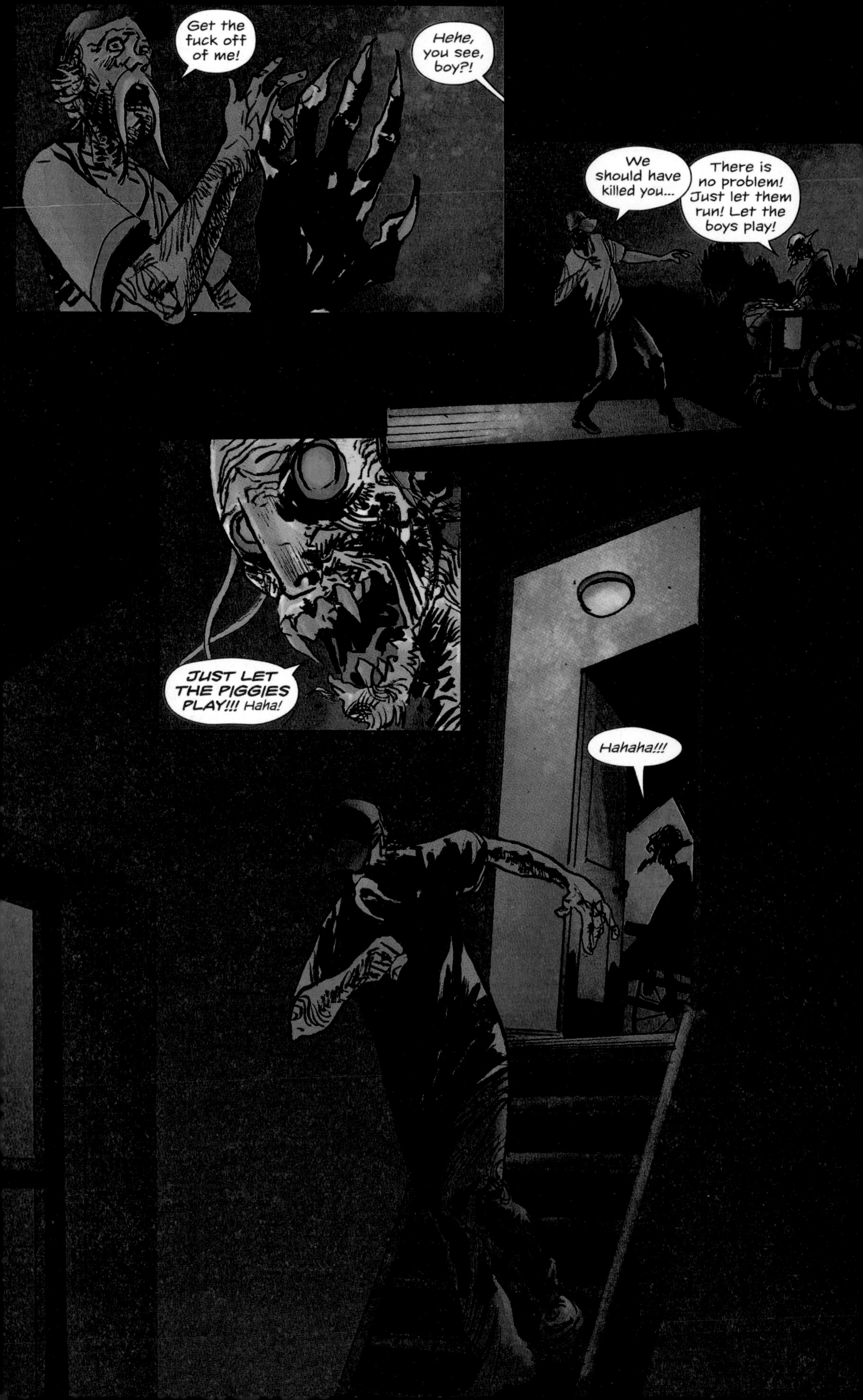

Get the fuck off of me!
Hehe, you see, boy?!
We should have killed you...
There is no problem! Just let them run! Let the boys play!
JUST LET THE PIGGIES PLAY!!! Haha!
Hahaha!!!

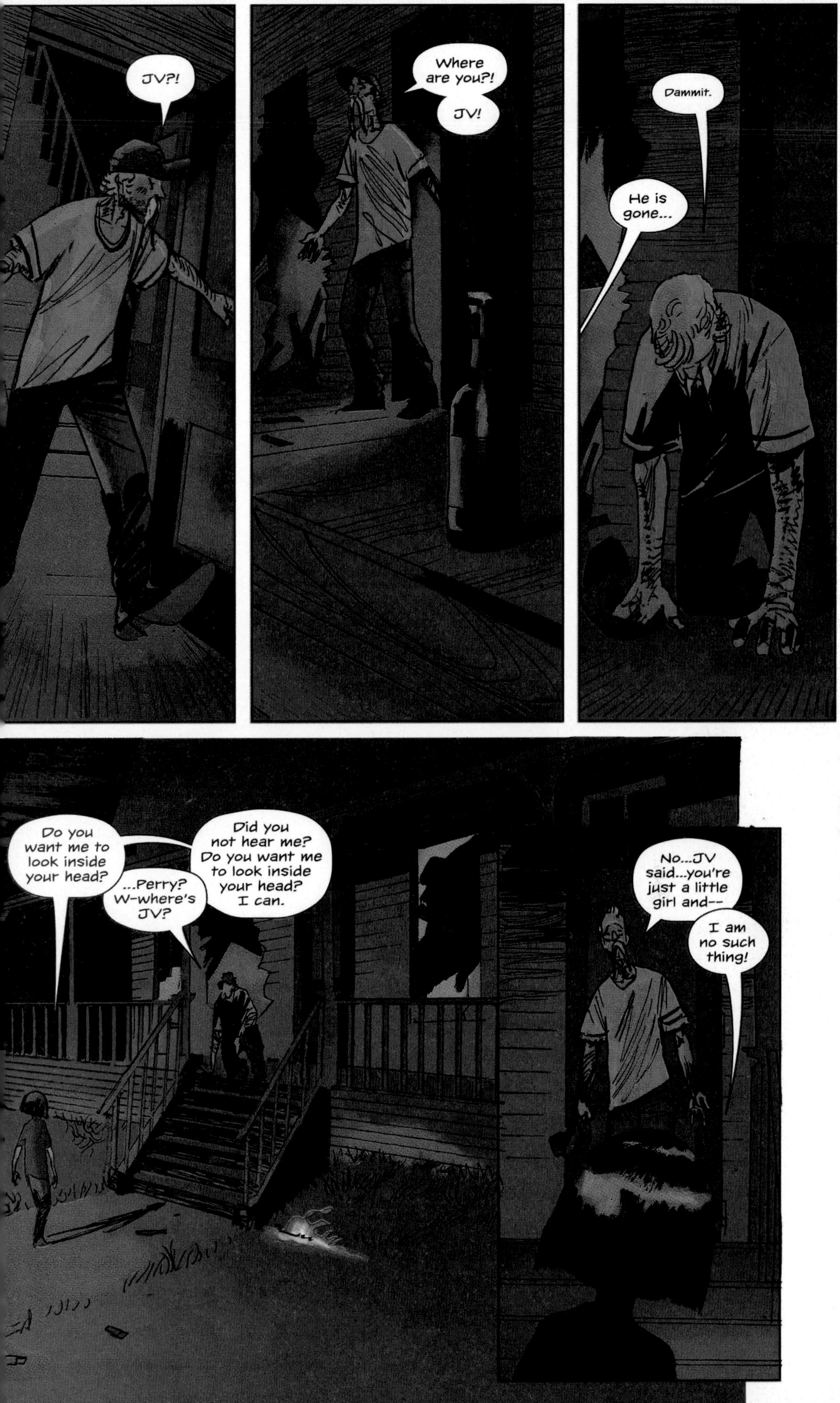
JV?!
Where are you?!
JV!
Dammit.
He is gone...
Do you want me to look inside your head?
...Perry? W-where's JV?
Did you not hear me? Do you want me to look inside your head? I can.
No...JV said...you're just a little girl and--
I am no such thing!

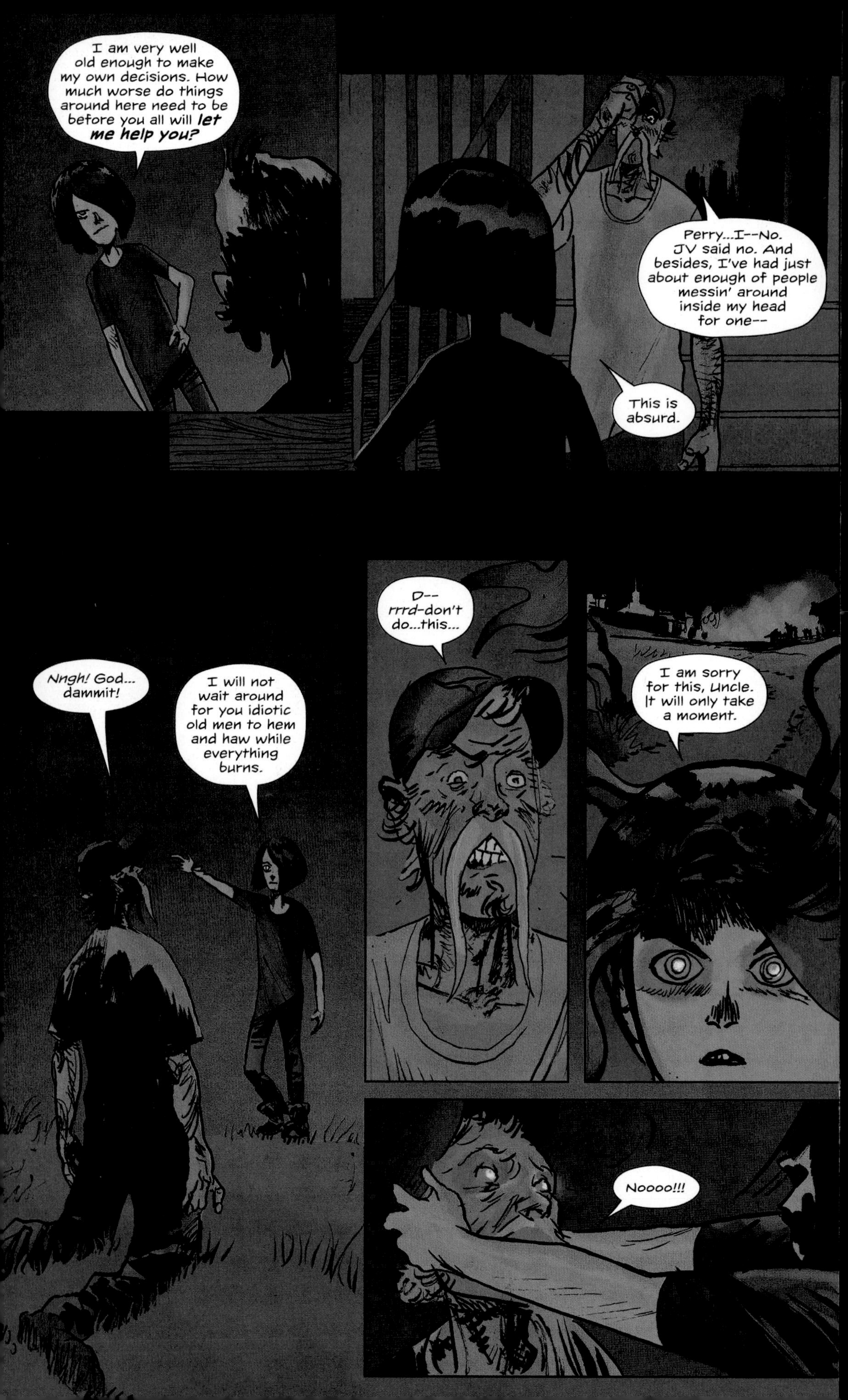

I am very well old enough to make my own decisions. How much worse do things around here need to be before you all will ***let me help you?***
Perry...I--No. JV said no. And besides, I've had just about enough of people messin' around inside my head for one--
This is absurd.
Nngh! God... dammit!
I will not wait around for you idiotic old men to hem and haw while everything burns.
D-- rrrd-don't do...this...
I am sorry for this, Uncle. It will only take a moment.
Noooo!!!

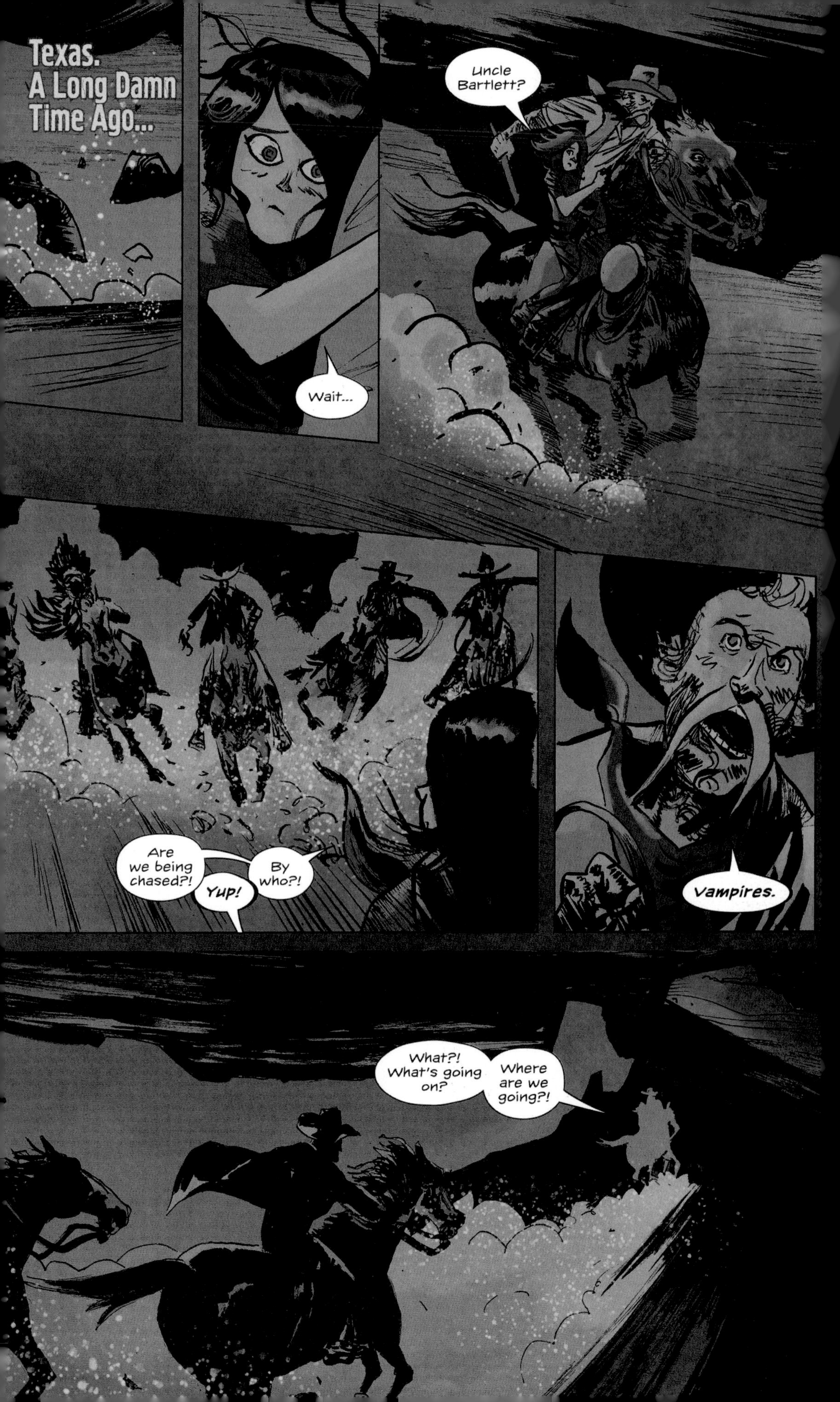
Texas.
A Long Damn
Time Ago...
Wait...
Uncle
Bartlett?
Are
we being
chased?!
Yup!
By
who?!
Vampires.
What?!
What's going
on?
Where
are we
going?!

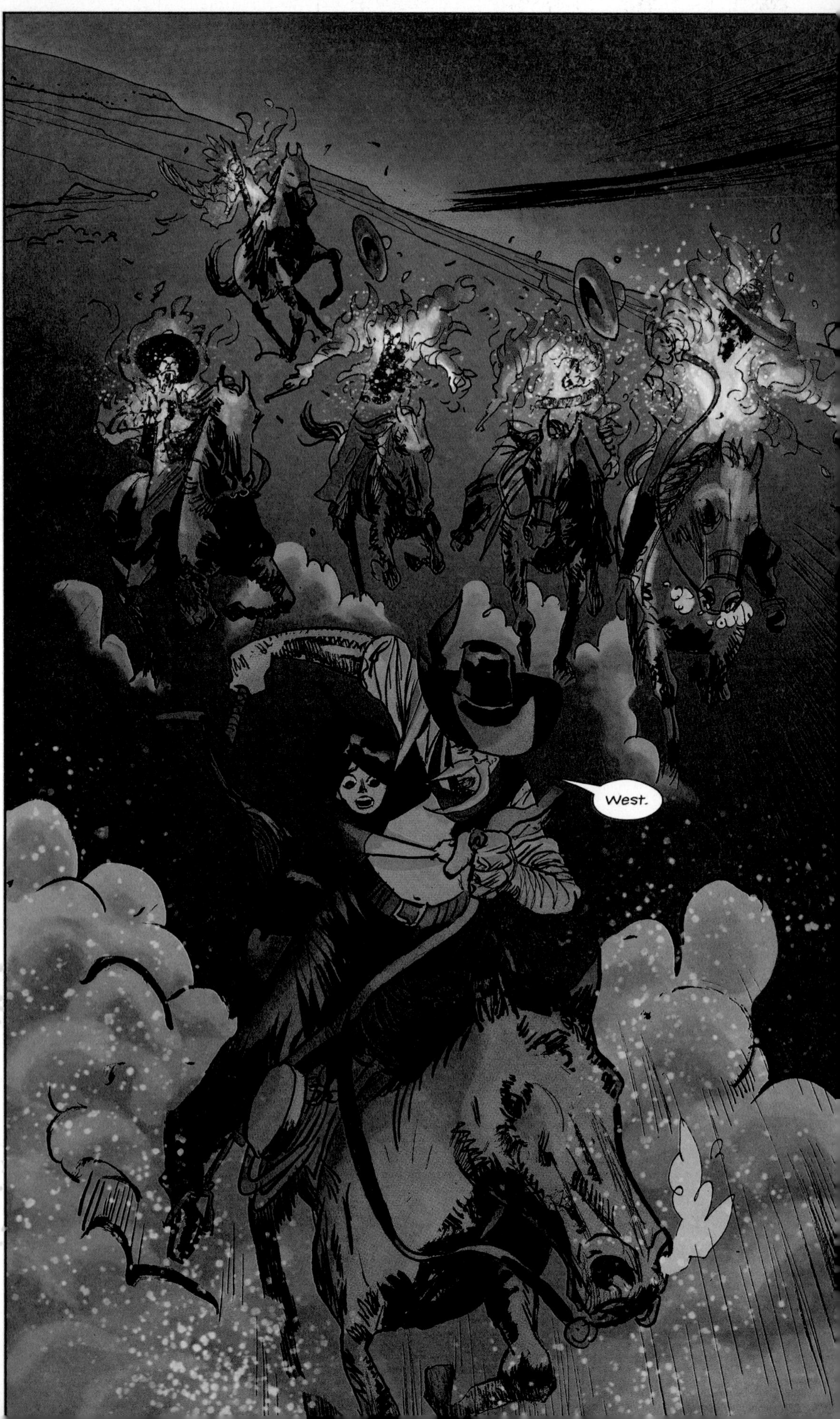
West.

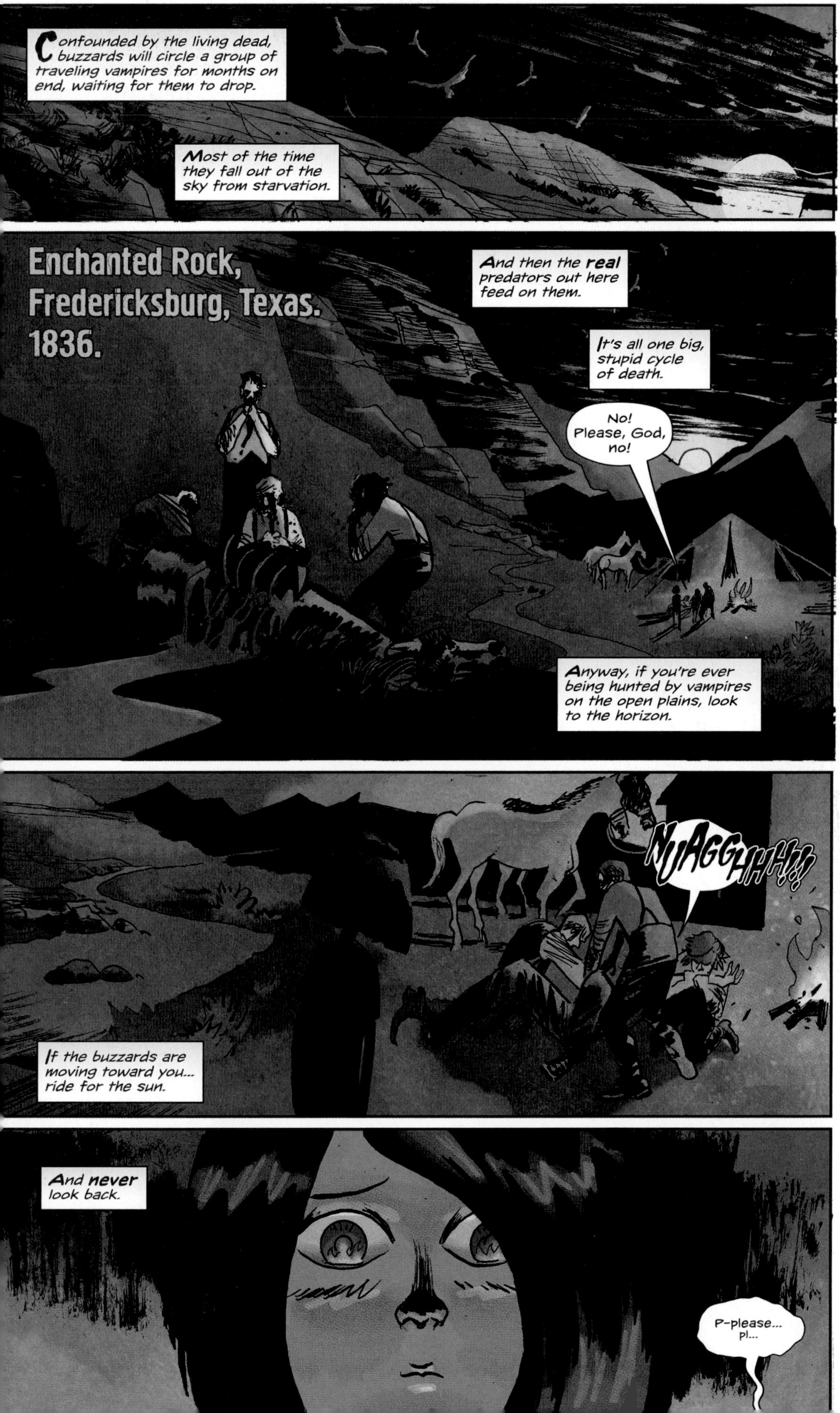
Confounded by the living dead, buzzards will circle a group of traveling vampires for months on end, waiting for them to drop.
Most of the time they fall out of the sky from starvation.
Enchanted Rock, Fredericksburg, Texas. 1836.
And then the real predators out here feed on them.
It's all one big, stupid cycle of death.
No! Please, God, no!
Anyway, if you're ever being hunted by vampires on the open plains, look to the horizon.
NUAGGHHH!!
If the buzzards are moving toward you... ride for the sun.
And never look back.
P-please... pl...

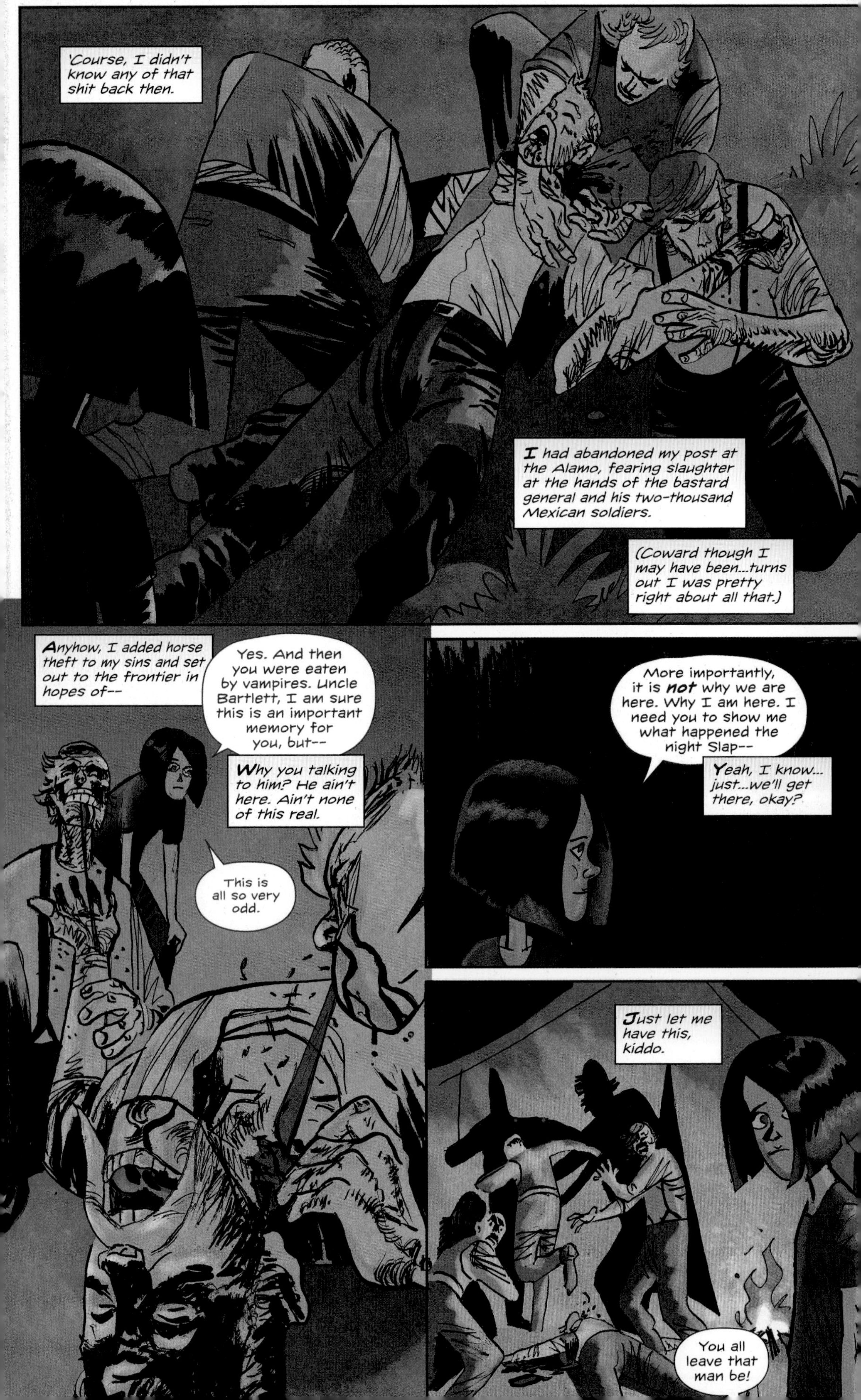
'Course, I didn't know any of that shit back then.
I had abandoned my post at the Alamo, fearing slaughter at the hands of the bastard general and his two-thousand Mexican soldiers.
(Coward though I may have been...turns out I was pretty right about all that.)
Anyhow, I added horse theft to my sins and set out to the frontier in hopes of--
Yes. And then you were eaten by vampires. Uncle Bartlett, I am sure this is an important memory for you, but--
Why you talking to him? He ain't here. Ain't none of this real.
This is all so very odd.
More importantly, it is not why we are here. Why I am here. I need you to show me what happened the night Slap--
Yeah, I know... just...we'll get there, okay?
Just let me have this, kiddo.
You all leave that man be!

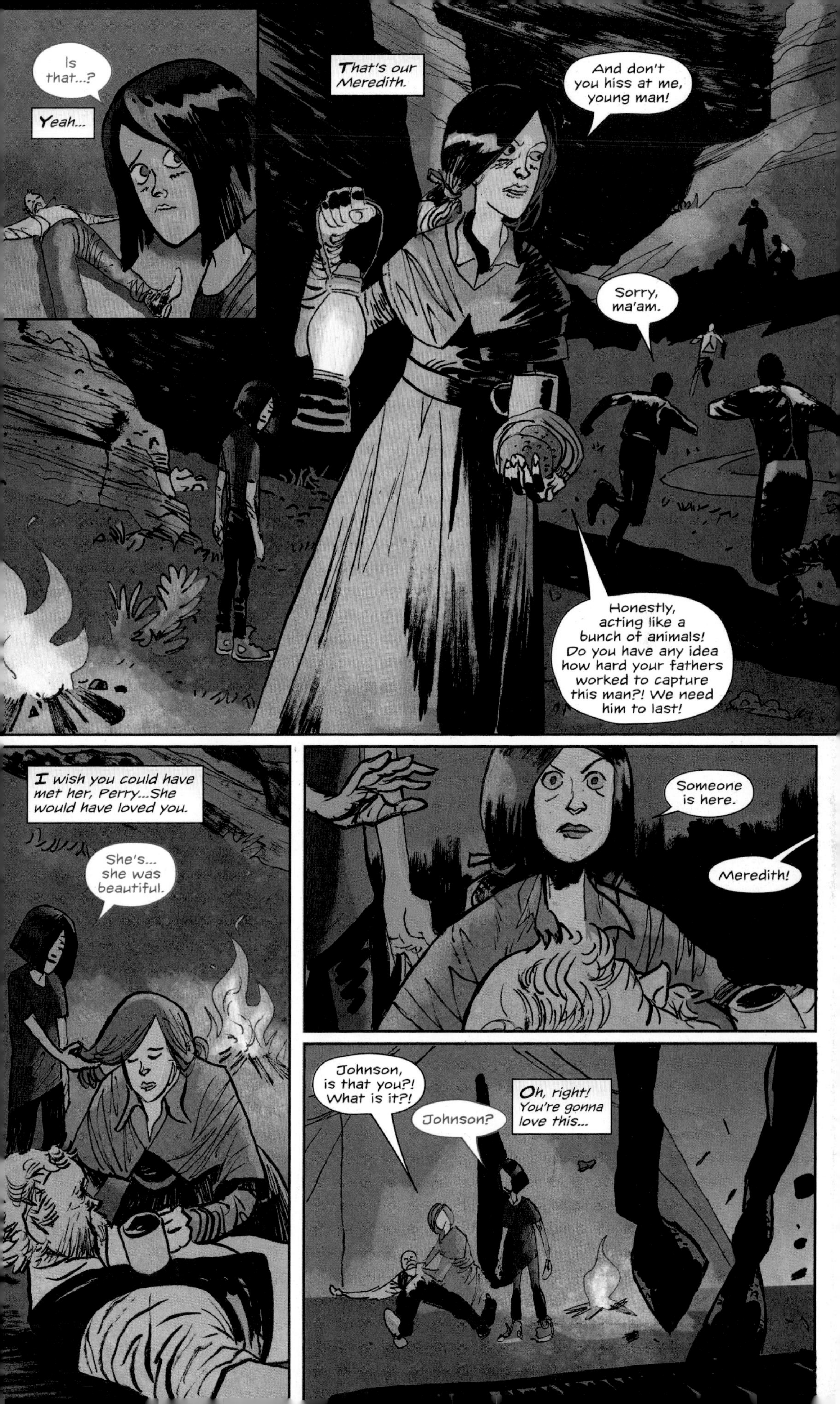

Is that...?
Yeah...
That's our Meredith.
And don't you hiss at me, young man!
Sorry, ma'am.
Honestly, acting like a bunch of animals! Do you have any idea how hard your fathers worked to capture this man?! We need him to last!
I wish you could have met her, Perry...She would have loved you.
She's... she was beautiful.
Someone is here.
Meredith!
Johnson, is that you?! What is it?!
Johnson?
Oh, right! You're gonna love this...

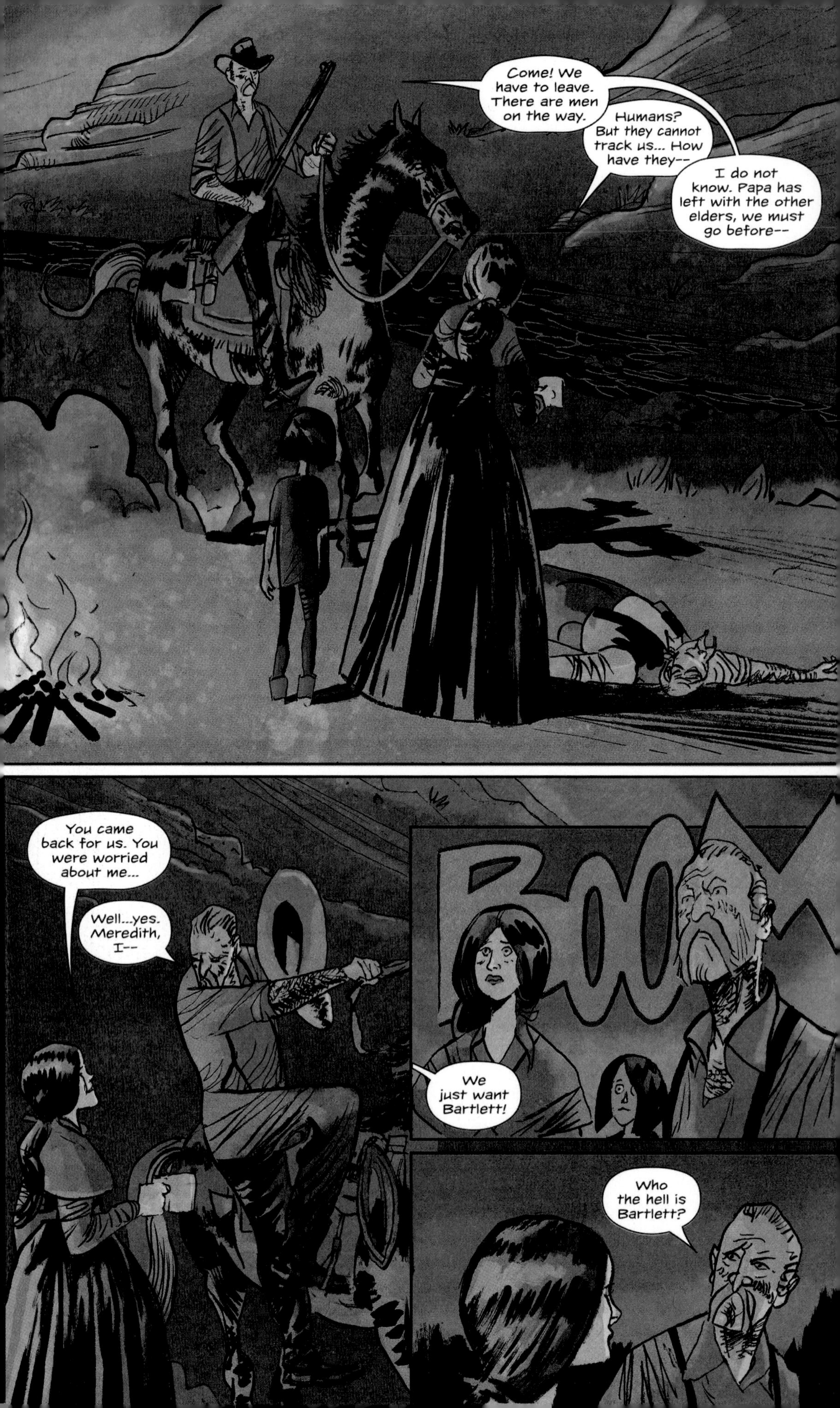
Come! We have to leave. There are men on the way.
Humans? But they cannot track us... How have they--
I do not know. Papa has left with the other elders, we must go before--
You came back for us. You were worried about me...
Well...yes. Meredith, I--
BOOM
We just want Bartlett!
Who the hell is Bartlett?

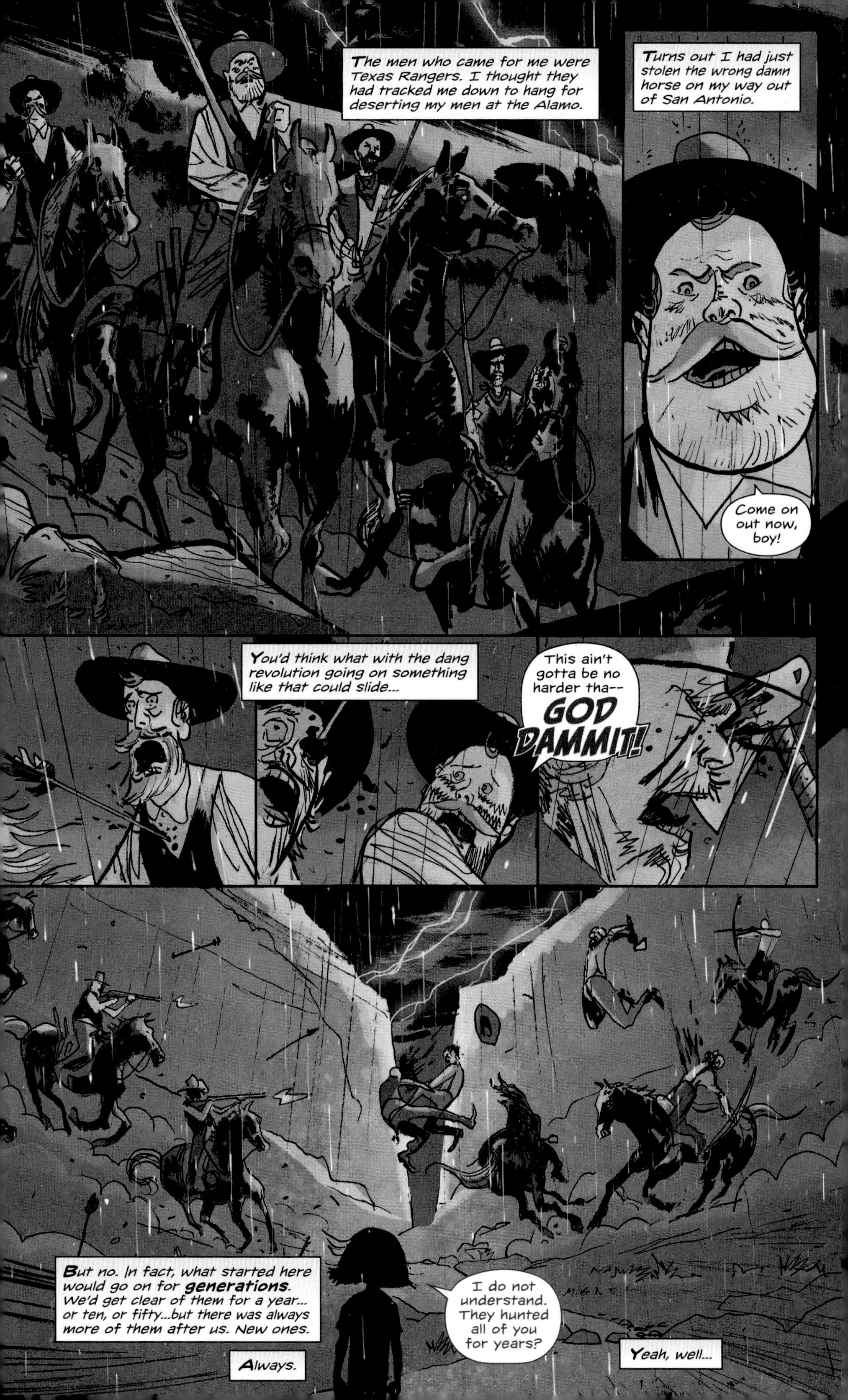
The men who came for me were Texas Rangers. I thought they had tracked me down to hang for deserting my men at the Alamo.
Turns out I had just stolen the wrong damn horse on my way out of San Antonio.
Come on out now, boy!
You'd think what with the dang revolution going on something like that could slide...
This ain't gotta be no harder tha-- GOD DAMMIT!
But no. In fact, what started here would go on for generations. We'd get clear of them for a year... or ten, or fifty...but there was always more of them after us. New ones.
Always.
I do not understand. They hunted all of you for years?
Yeah, well...

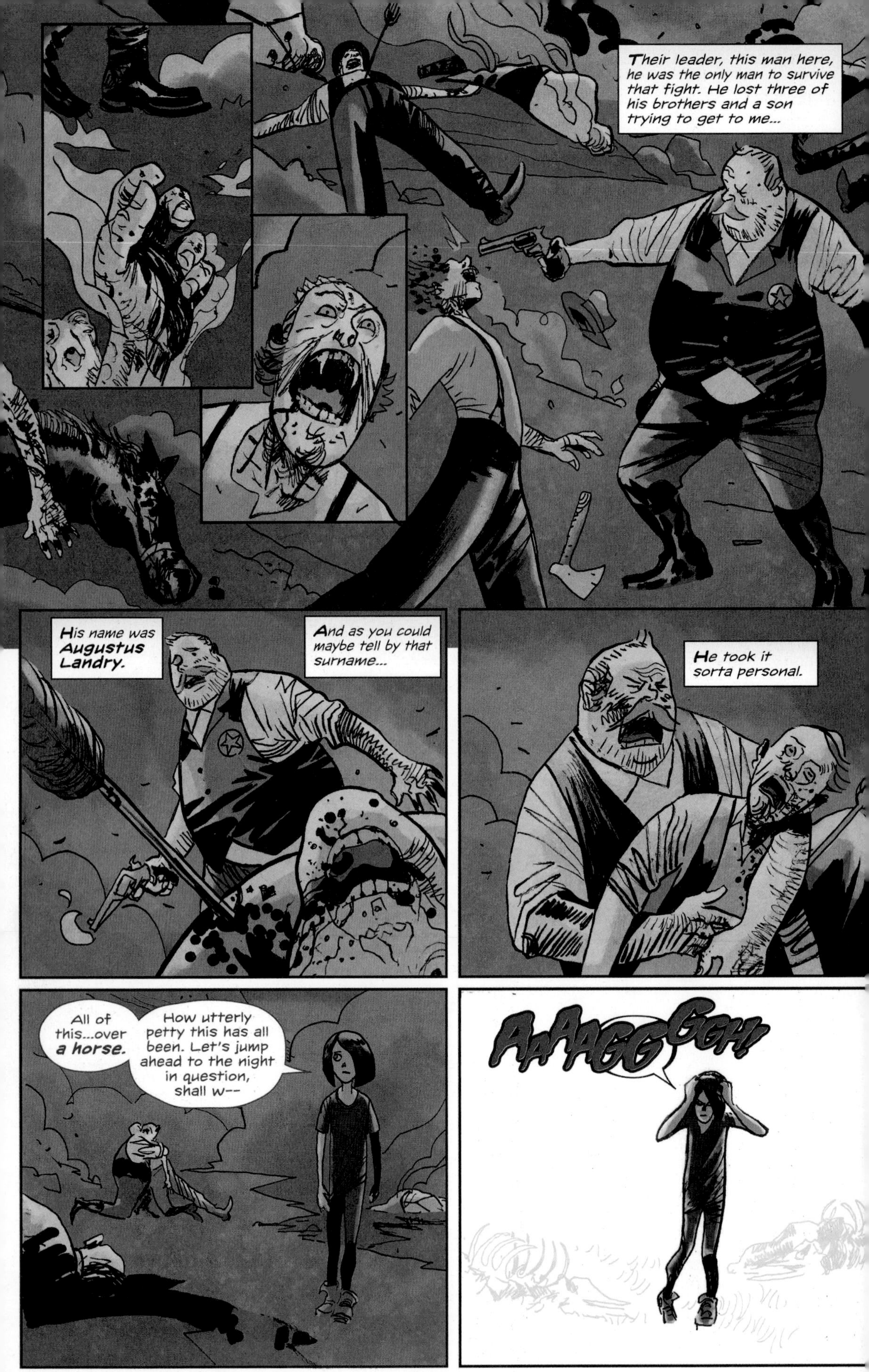
Their leader, this man here, he was the only man to survive that fight. He lost three of his brothers and a son trying to get to me...
His name was Augustus Landry.
And as you could maybe tell by that surname...
He took it sorta personal.
All of this...over a horse.
How utterly petty this has all been. Let's jump ahead to the night in question, shall w--
AAAAGGGGH!

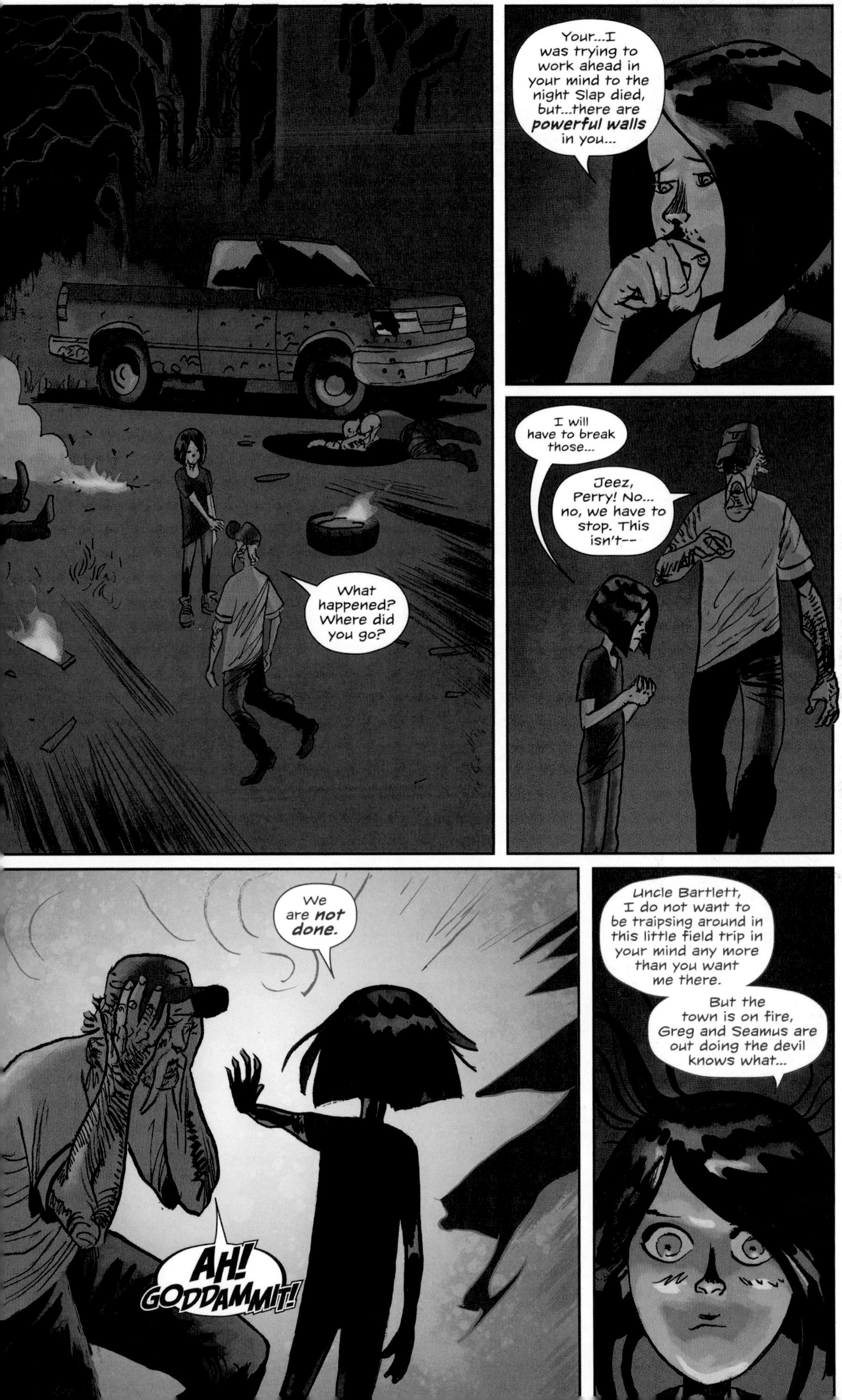
What happened? Where did you go?
Your...I was trying to work ahead in your mind to the night Slap died, but...there are powerful walls in you...
I will have to break those...
Jeez, Perry! No... no, we have to stop. This isn't--
We are not done.
AH! GODDAMMIT!
Uncle Bartlett, I do not want to be traipsing around in this little field trip in your mind any more than you want me there.
But the town is on fire, Greg and Seamus are out doing the devil knows what...

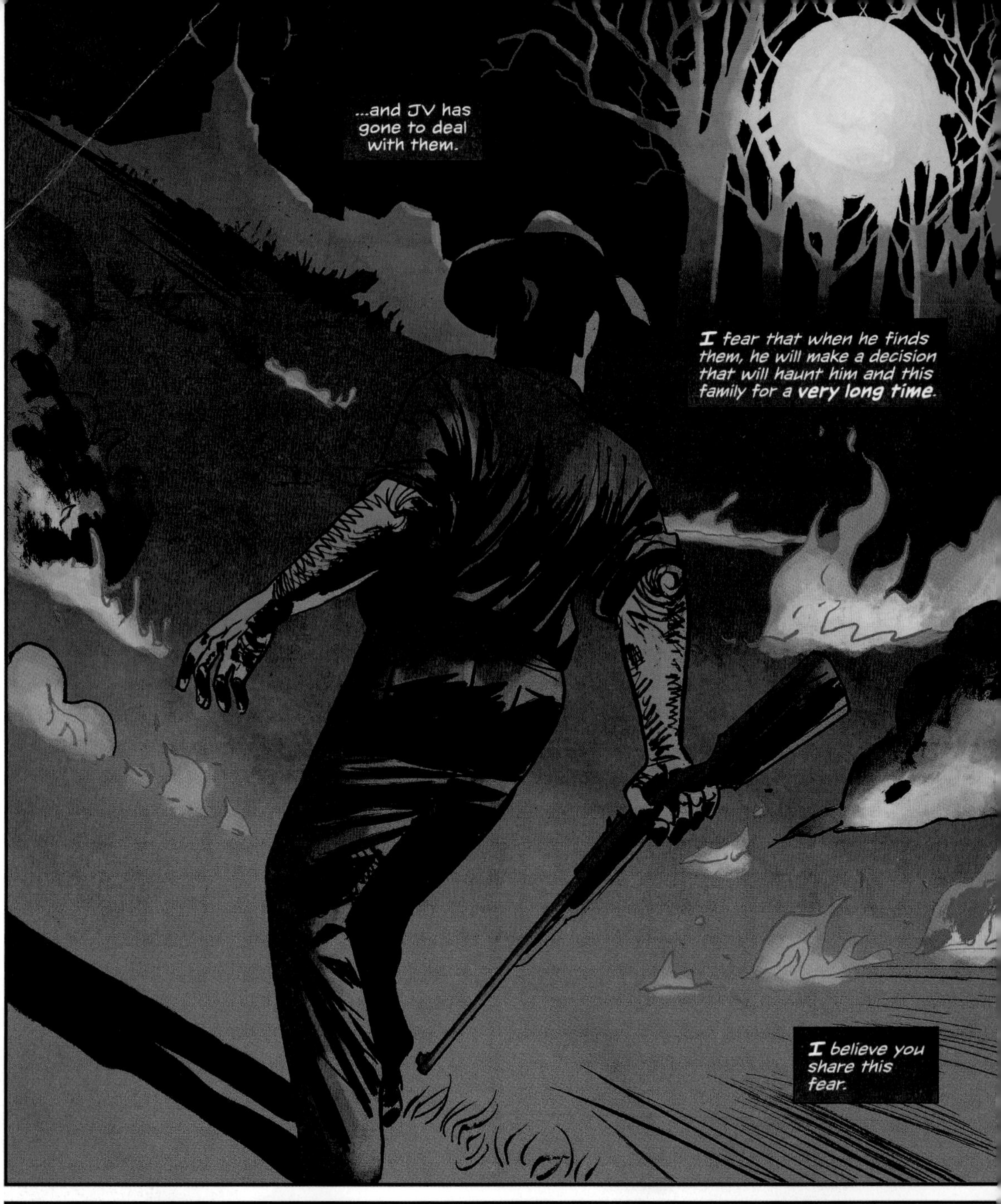
...and JV has gone to deal with them.
I fear that when he finds them, he will make a decision that will haunt him and this family for a **very long time**.
I believe you share this fear.

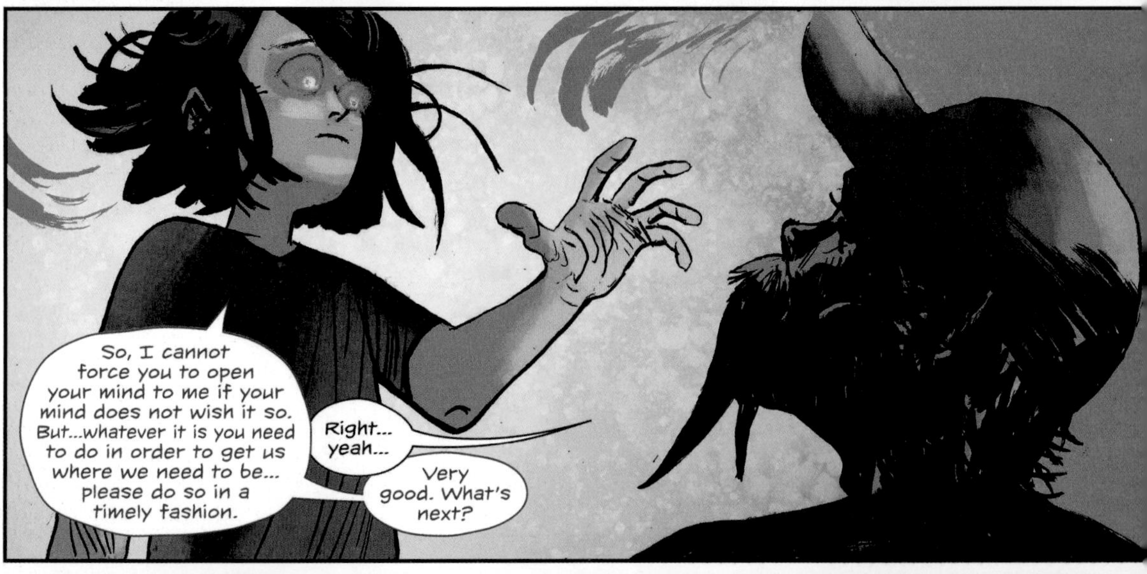
So, I cannot force you to open your mind to me if your mind does not wish it so. But...whatever it is you need to do in order to get us where we need to be... please do so in a timely fashion.
Right... yeah...
Very good. What's next?

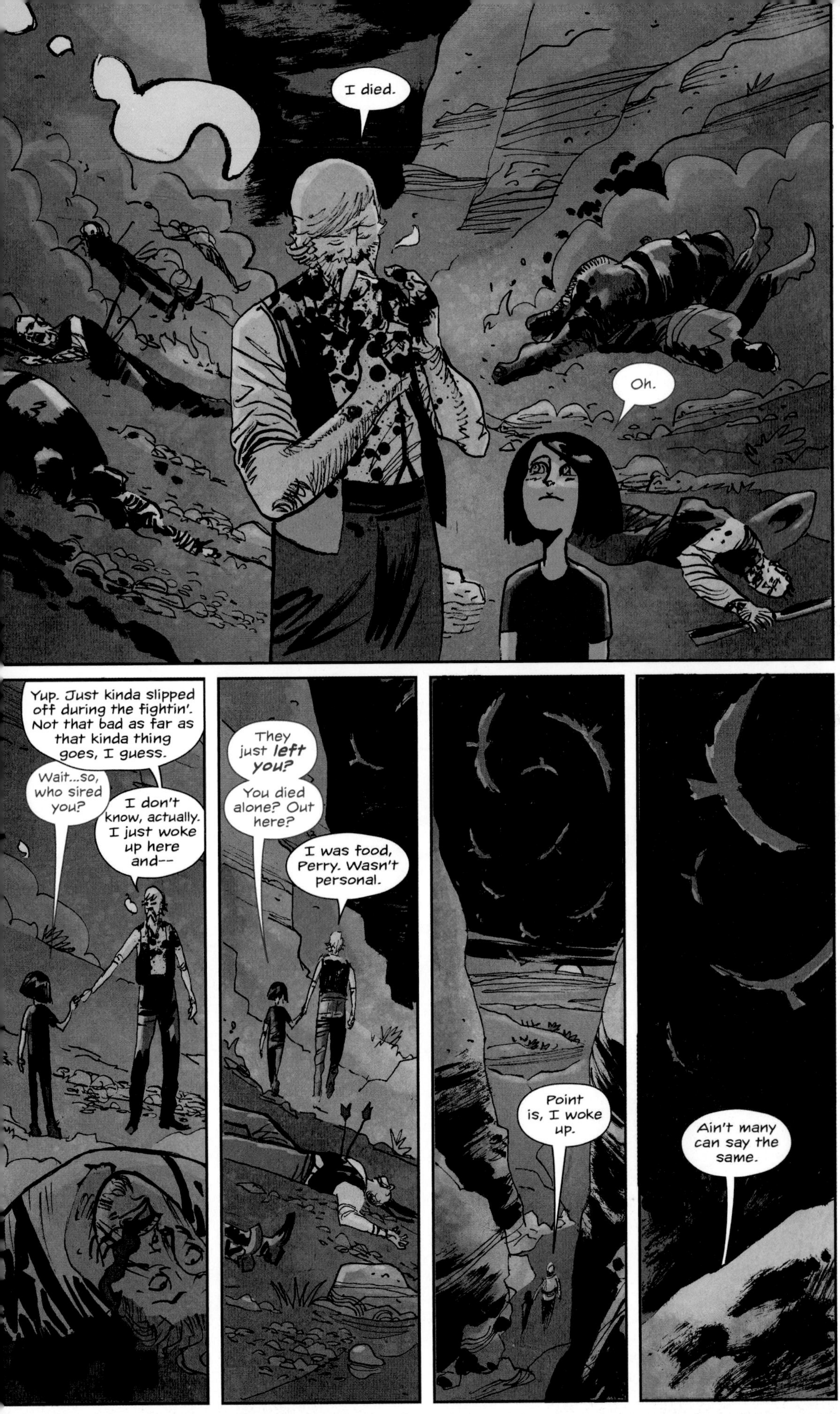
I died.
Oh.
Yup. Just kinda slipped off during the fightin'. Not that bad as far as that kinda thing goes, I guess.
Wait...so, who sired you?
I don't know, actually. I just woke up here and--
They just *left you?*
You died alone? Out here?
I was food, Perry. Wasn't personal.
Point is, I woke up.
Ain't many can say the same.

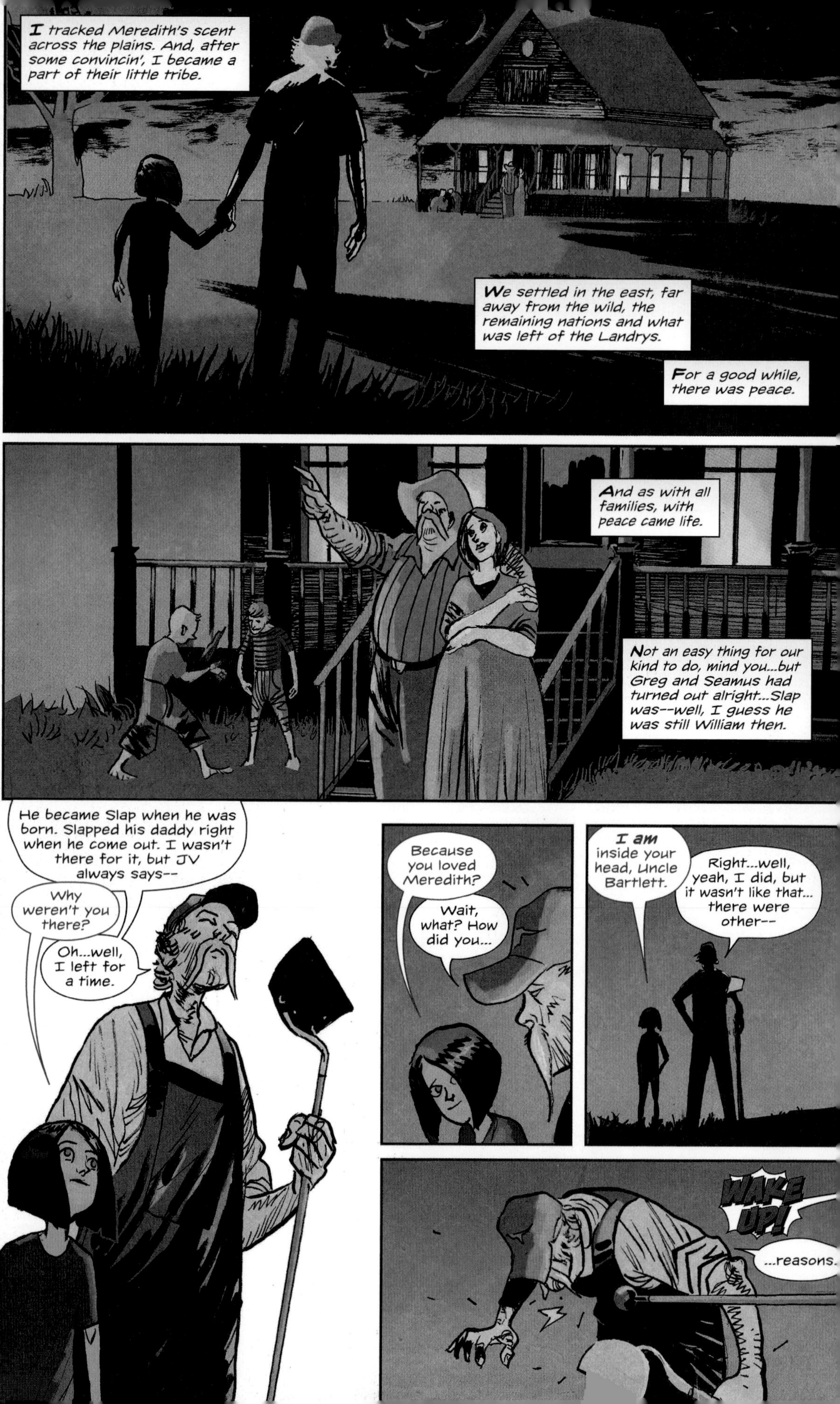
I tracked Meredith's scent across the plains. And, after some convincin', I became a part of their little tribe.
We settled in the east, far away from the wild, the remaining nations and what was left of the Landrys.
For a good while, there was peace.
And as with all families, with peace came life.
Not an easy thing for our kind to do, mind you...but Greg and Seamus had turned out alright...Slap was--well, I guess he was still William then.
He became Slap when he was born. Slapped his daddy right when he come out. I wasn't there for it, but JV always says--
Why weren't you there?
Oh...well, I left for a time.
Because you loved Meredith?
Wait, what? How did you...
I am inside your head, Uncle Bartlett.
Right...well, yeah, I did, but it wasn't like that... there were other--
WAKE UP!
...reasons.

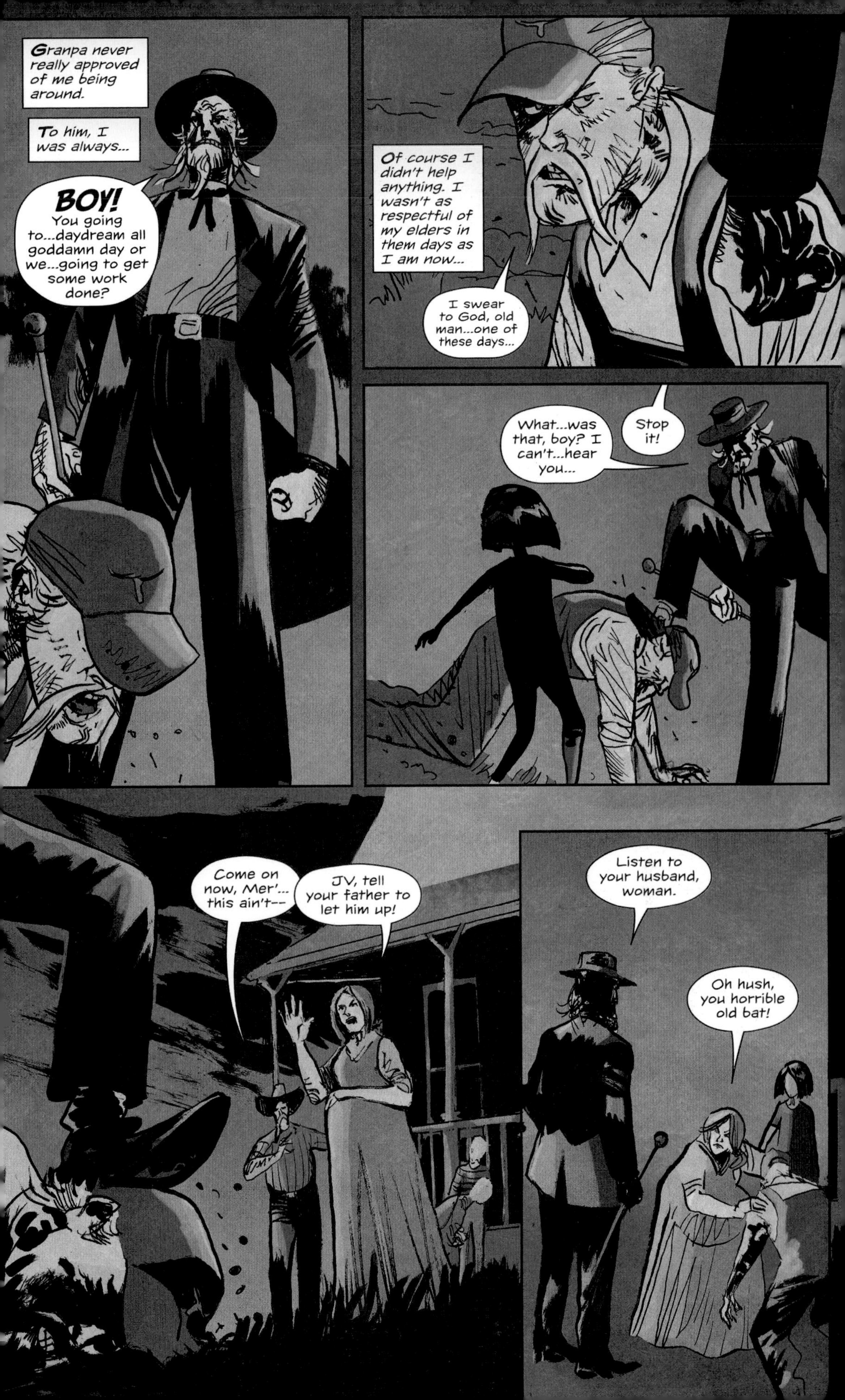

Granpa never really approved of me being around.
To him, I was always...
BOY! You going to...daydream all goddamn day or we...going to get some work done?
Of course I didn't help anything. I wasn't as respectful of my elders in them days as I am now...
I swear to God, old man...one of these days...
Stop it!
What...was that, boy? I can't...hear you...
Come on now, Mer'... this ain't--
JV, tell your father to let him up!
Listen to your husband, woman.
Oh hush, you horrible old bat!

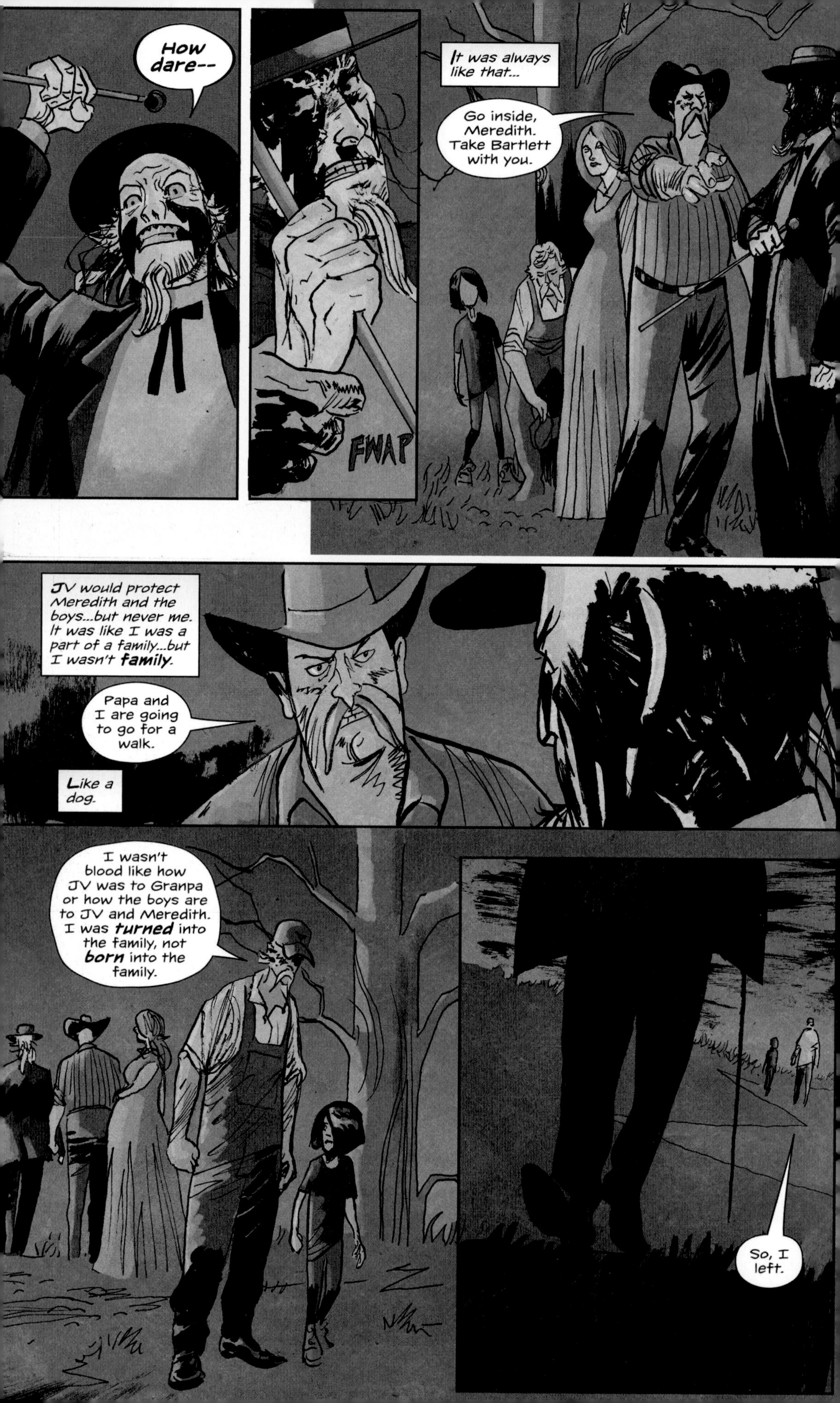

How dare--
FWAP
It was always like that...
Go inside, Meredith. Take Bartlett with you.
JV would protect Meredith and the boys...but never me. It was like I was a part of a family...but I wasn't **family**.
Papa and I are going to go for a walk.
Like a dog.
I wasn't blood like how JV was to Granpa or how the boys are to JV and Meredith. I was **turned** into the family, not **born** into the family.
So, I left.

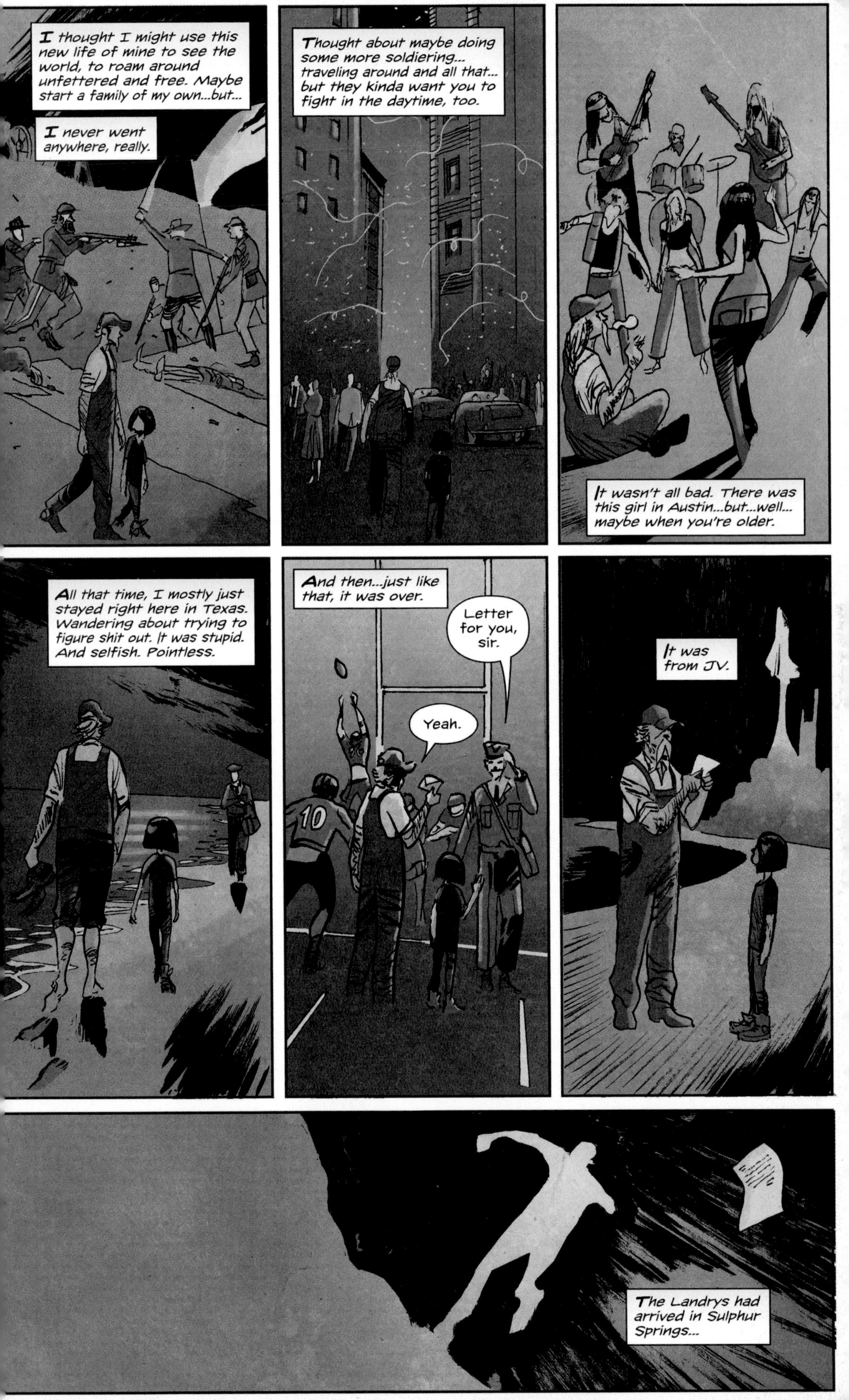
I thought I might use this new life of mine to see the world, to roam around unfettered and free. Maybe start a family of my own...but...
I never went anywhere, really.
Thought about maybe doing some more soldiering... traveling around and all that... but they kinda want you to fight in the daytime, too.
It wasn't all bad. There was this girl in Austin...but...well... maybe when you're older.
All that time, I mostly just stayed right here in Texas. Wandering about trying to figure shit out. It was stupid. And selfish. Pointless.
And then...just like that, it was over.
Letter for you, sir.
Yeah.
10
It was from JV.
The Landrys had arrived in Sulphur Springs...

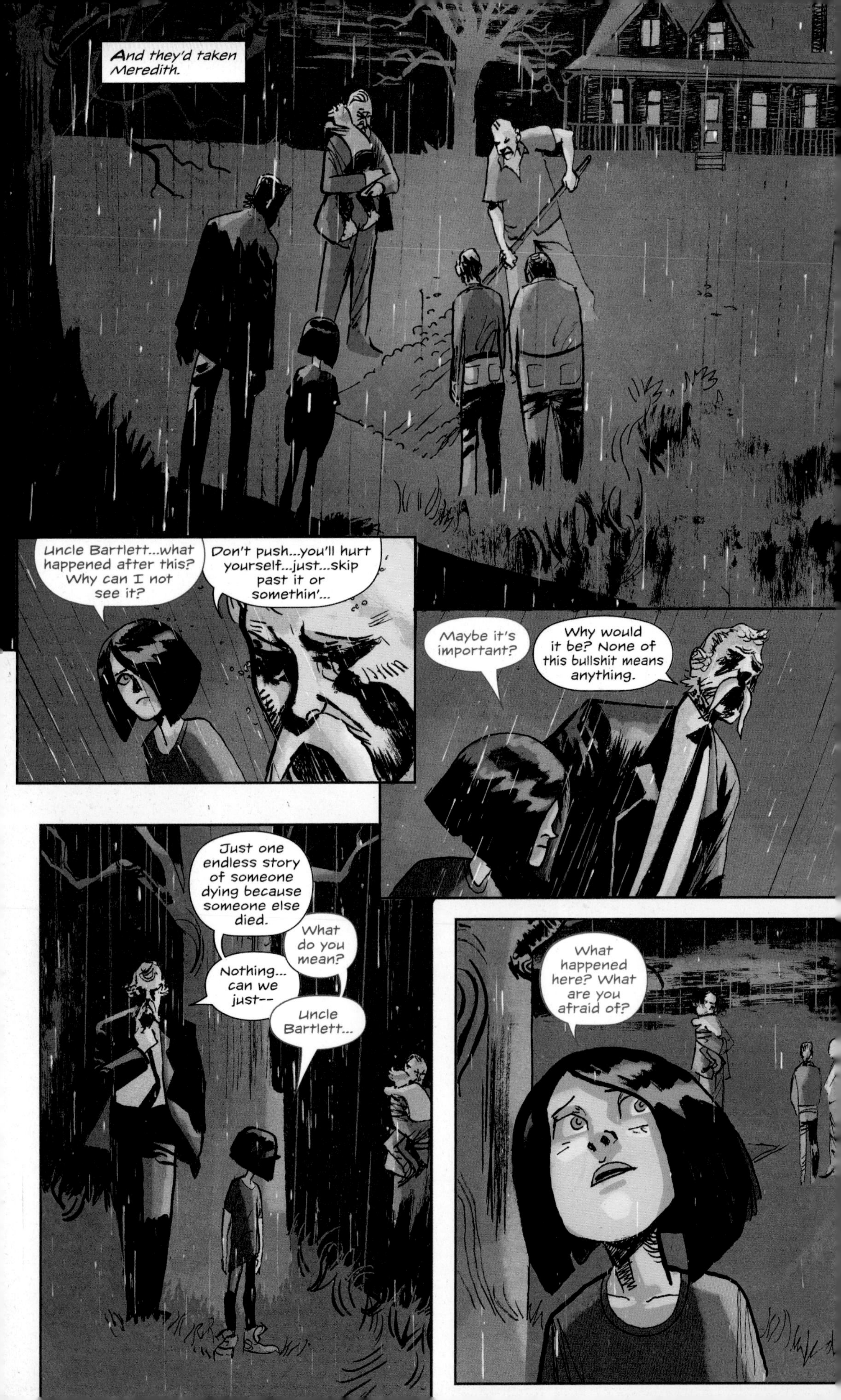
And they'd taken Meredith.
Uncle Bartlett...what happened after this? Why can I not see it?
Don't push...you'll hurt yourself...just...skip past it or somethin'...
Maybe it's important?
Why would it be? None of this bullshit means anything.
Just one endless story of someone dying because someone else died.
What do you mean?
Nothing... can we just--
Uncle Bartlett...
What happened here? What are you afraid of?

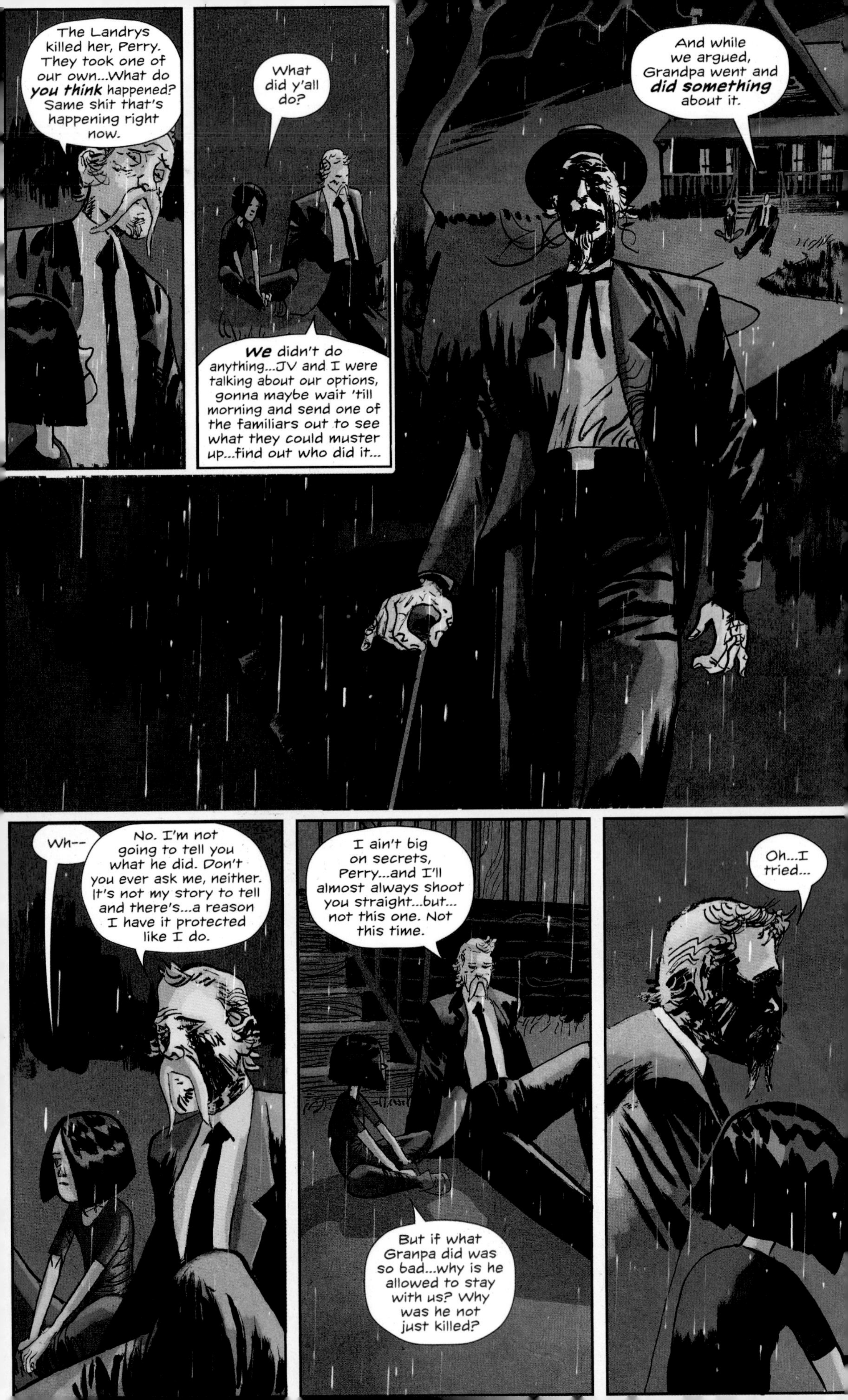
The Landrys killed her, Perry. They took one of our own...What do *you think* happened? Same shit that's happening right now.
What did y'all do?
We didn't do anything...JV and I were talking about our options, gonna maybe wait 'till morning and send one of the familiars out to see what they could muster up...find out who did it...
And while we argued, Grandpa went and *did something* about it.
Wh--
No. I'm not going to tell you what he did. Don't you ever ask me, neither. It's not my story to tell and there's...a reason I have it protected like I do.
I ain't big on secrets, Perry...and I'll almost always shoot you straight...but... not this one. Not this time.
But if what Granpa did was so bad...why is he allowed to stay with us? Why was he not just killed?
Oh...I tried...

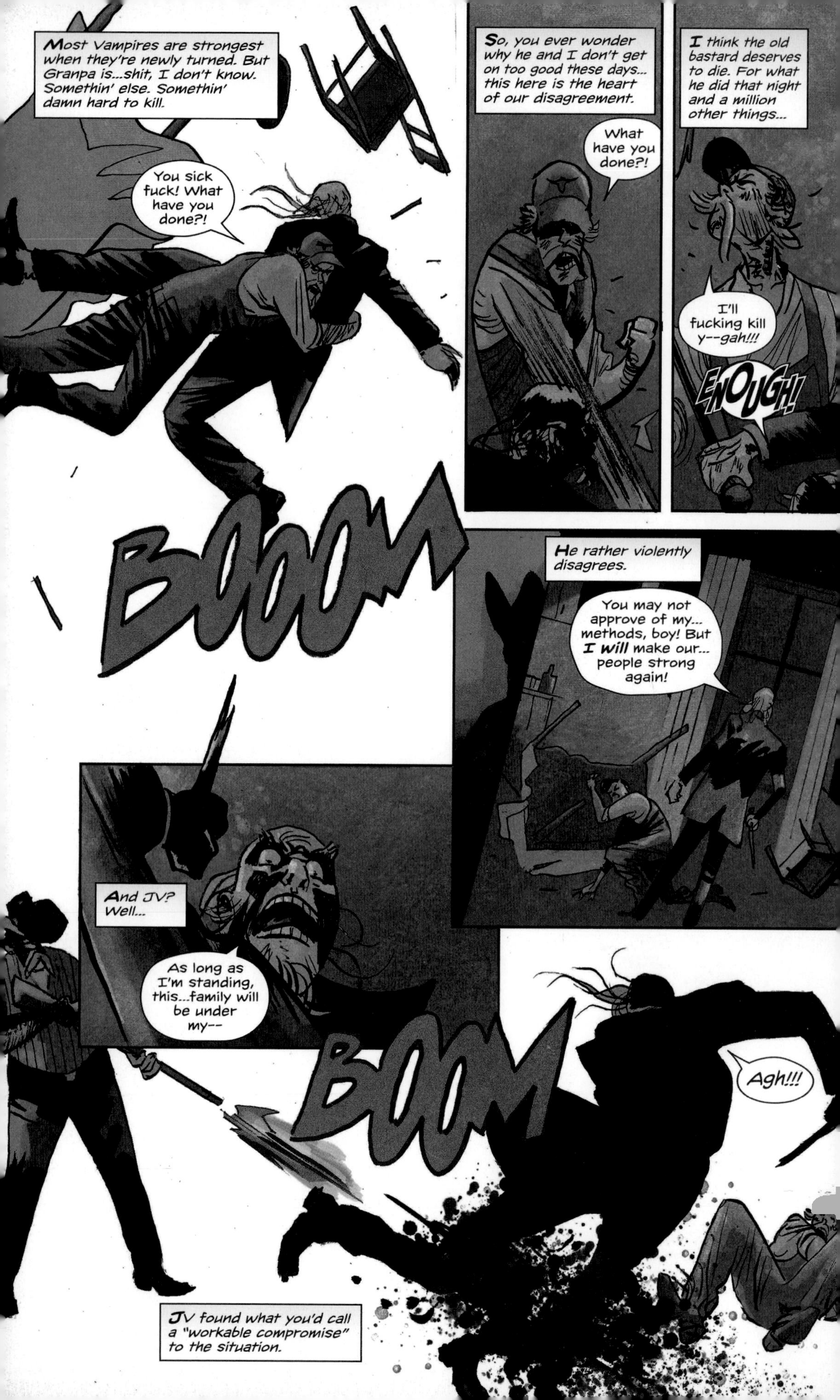
Most Vampires are strongest when they're newly turned. But Granpa is...shit, I don't know. Somethin' else. Somethin' damn hard to kill.
You sick fuck! What have you done?!
BOOOM
So, you ever wonder why he and I don't get on too good these days... this here is the heart of our disagreement.
What have you done?!
I think the old bastard deserves to die. For what he did that night and a million other things...
I'll fucking kill y--gah!!!
ENOUGH!
He rather violently disagrees.
You may not approve of my... methods, boy! But I will make our... people strong again!
And JV? Well...
As long as I'm standing, this...family will be under my--
BOOM
Agh!!!
JV found what you'd call a "workable compromise" to the situation.

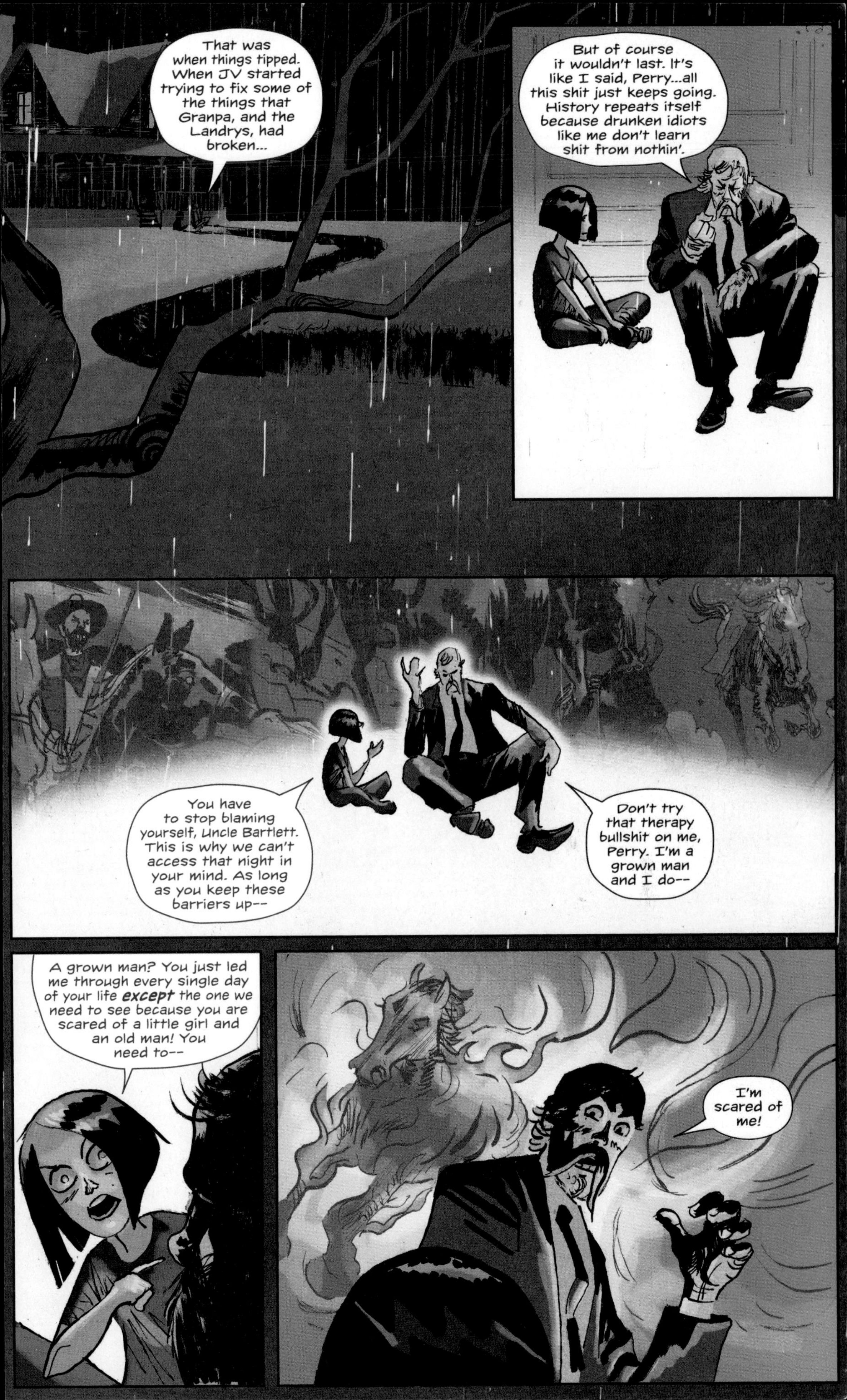
That was when things tipped. When JV started trying to fix some of the things that Granpa, and the Landrys, had broken...
But of course it wouldn't last. It's like I said, Perry...all this shit just keeps going. History repeats itself because drunken idiots like me don't learn shit from nothin'.
You have to stop blaming yourself, Uncle Bartlett. This is why we can't access that night in your mind. As long as you keep these barriers up--
Don't try that therapy bullshit on me, Perry. I'm a grown man and I do--
A grown man? You just led me through every single day of your life *except* the one we need to see because you are scared of a little girl and an old man! You need to--
I'm scared of me!

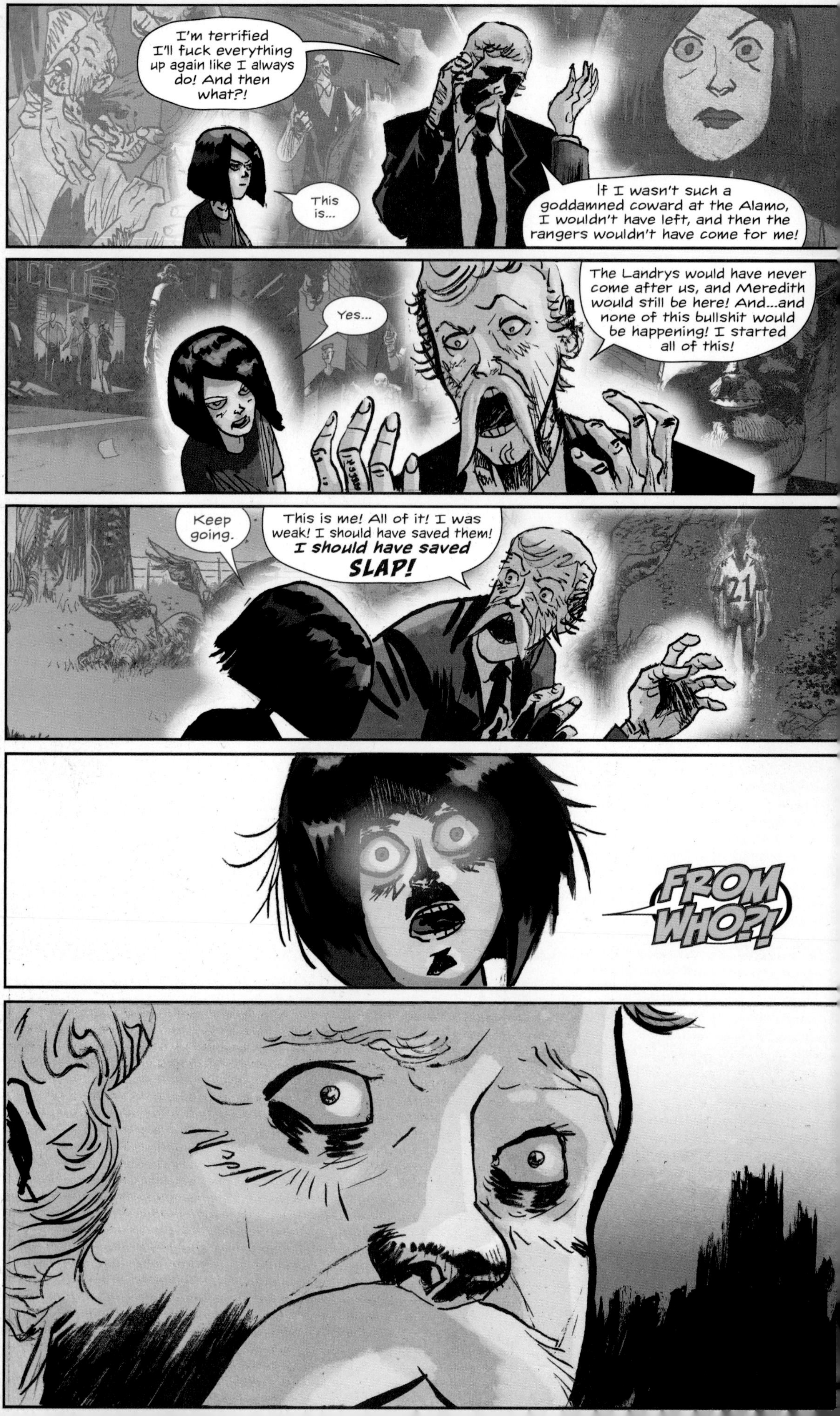
I'm terrified I'll fuck everything up again like I always do! And then what?!
This is...
If I wasn't such a goddamned coward at the Alamo, I wouldn't have left, and then the rangers wouldn't have come for me!
Yes...
The Landrys would have never come after us, and Meredith would still be here! And...and none of this bullshit would be happening! I started all of this!
Keep going.
This is me! All of it! I was weak! I should have saved them! I should have saved
SLAP!
FROM WHO?!

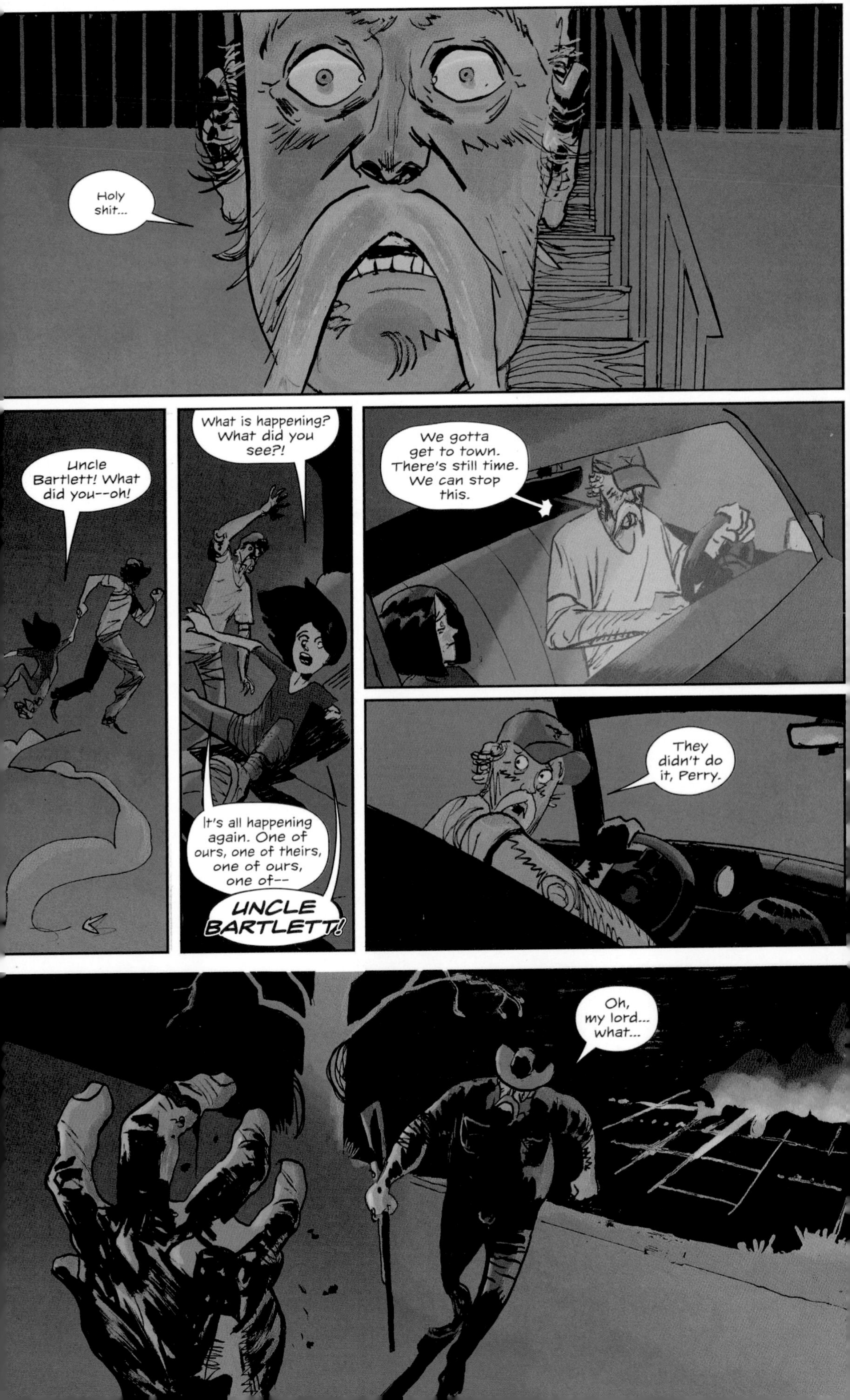

Holy shit...
Uncle Bartlett! What did you--oh!
What is happening? What did you see?!
It's all happening again. One of ours, one of theirs, one of ours, one of--
UNCLE BARTLETT!
We gotta get to town. There's still time. We can stop this.
They didn't do it, Perry.
Oh, my lord... what...

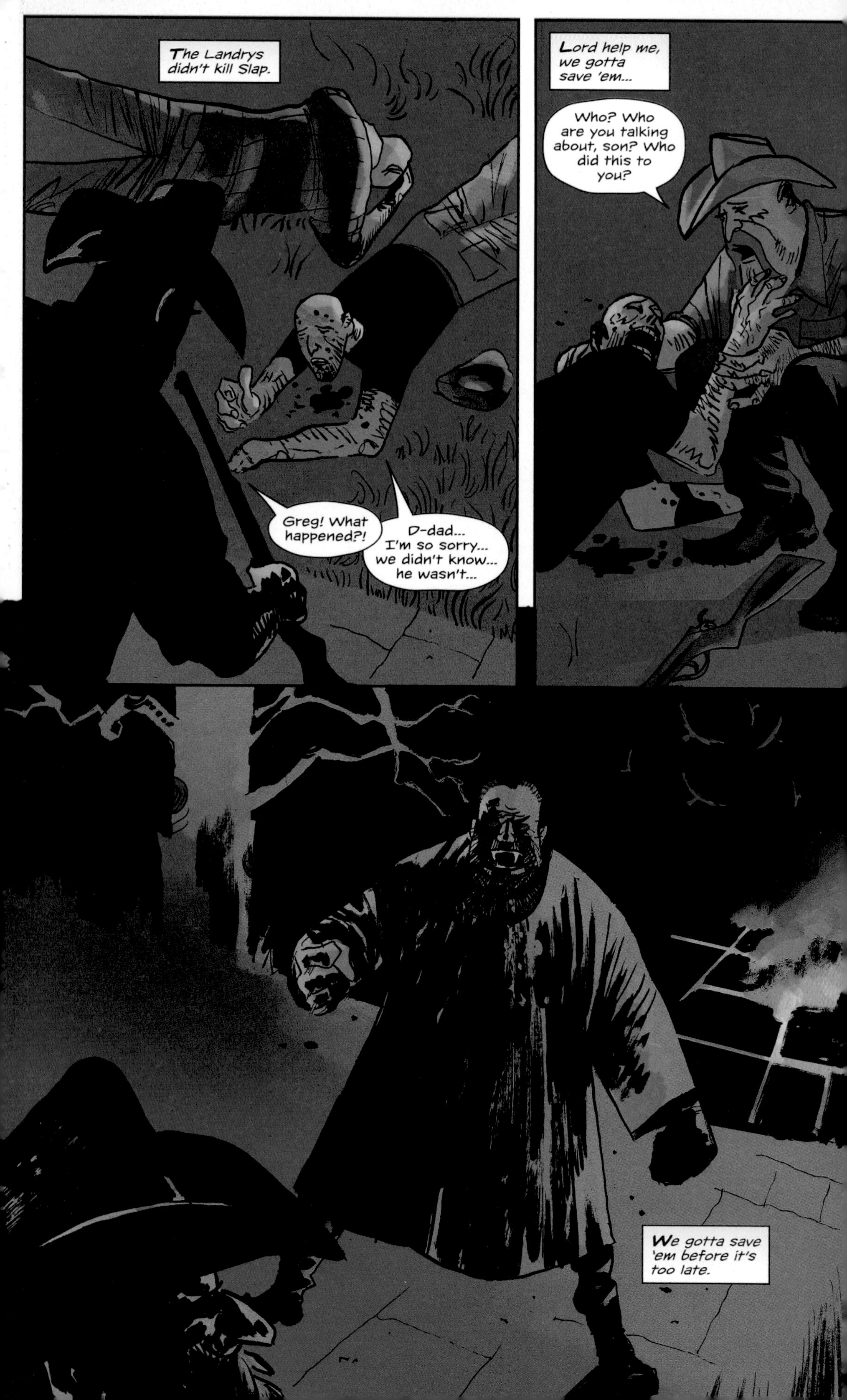
The Landrys didn't kill Slap.
Greg! What happened?!
D-dad... I'm so sorry... we didn't know... he wasn't...
Lord help me, we gotta save 'em...
Who? Who are you talking about, son? Who did this to you?
We gotta save 'em before it's too late.

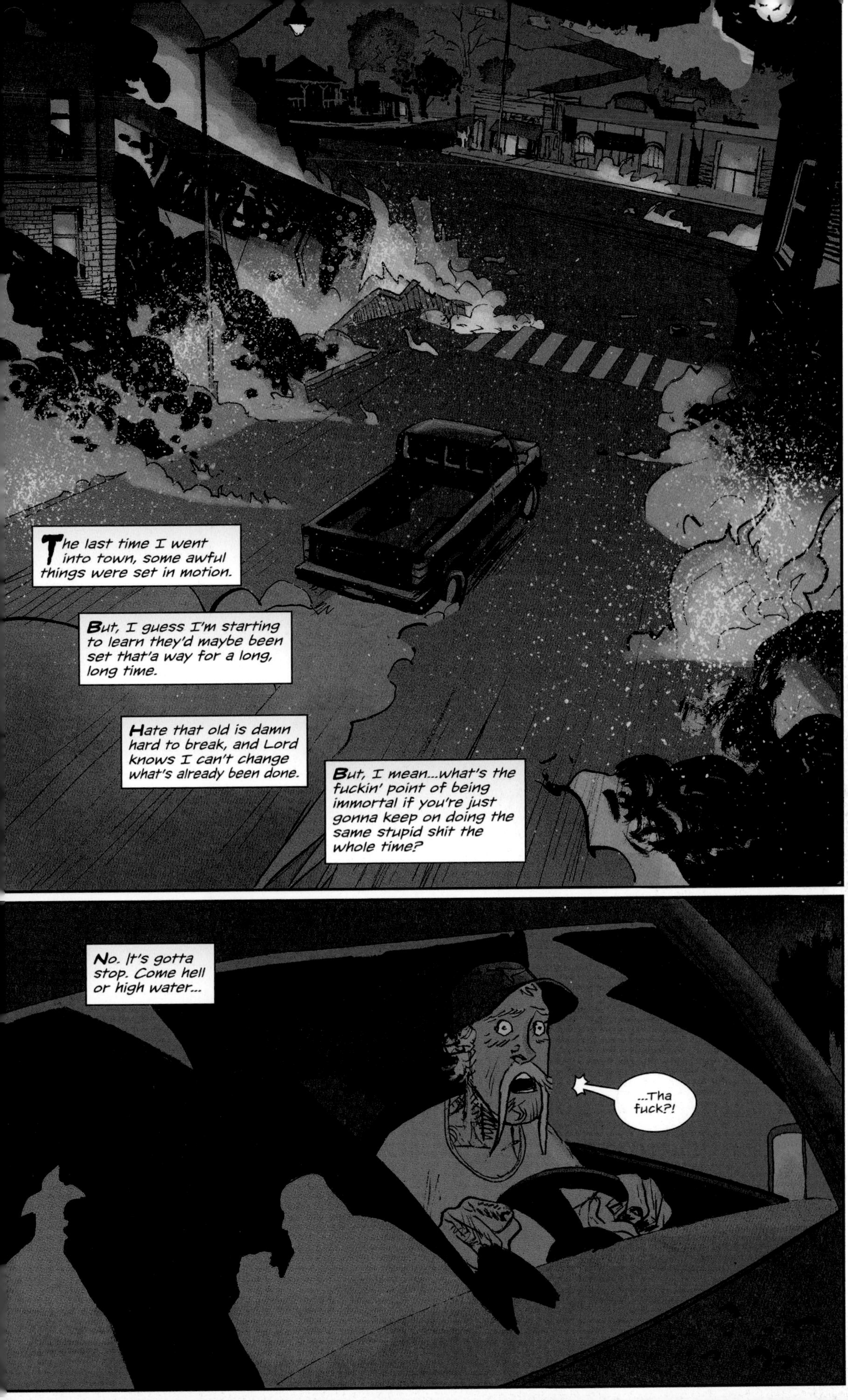
The last time I went into town, some awful things were set in motion.
But, I guess I'm starting to learn they'd maybe been set that'a way for a long, long time.
Hate that old is damn hard to break, and Lord knows I can't change what's already been done.
But, I mean...what's the fuckin' point of being immortal if you're just gonna keep on doing the same stupid shit the whole time?
No. It's gotta stop. Come hell or high water...
...Tha fuck?!

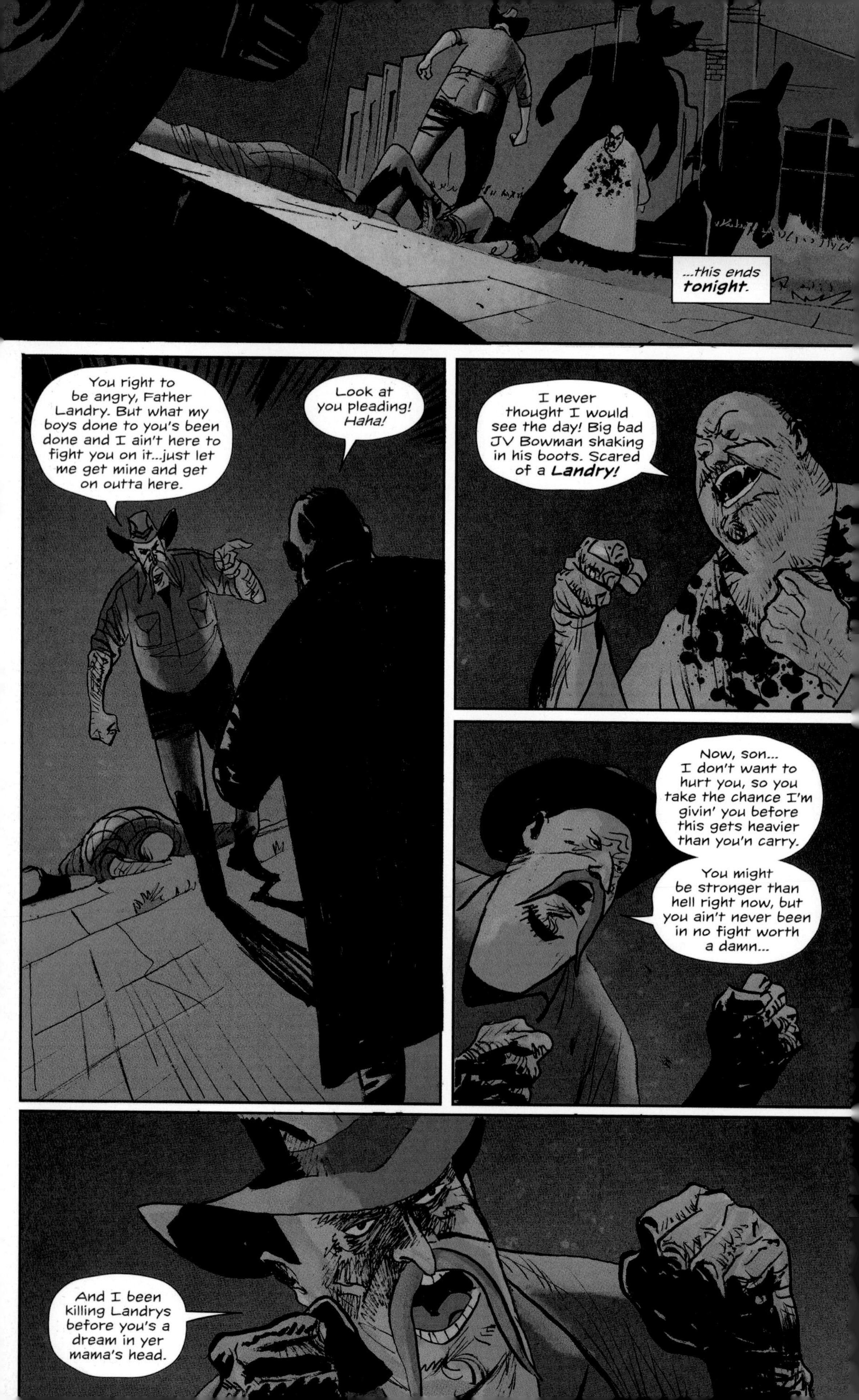
...this ends tonight.
You right to be angry, Father Landry. But what my boys done to you's been done and I ain't here to fight you on it...just let me get mine and get on outta here.
Look at you pleading! Haha!
I never thought I would see the day! Big bad JV Bowman shaking in his boots. Scared of a Landry!
Now, son... I don't want to hurt you, so you take the chance I'm givin' you before this gets heavier than you'n carry.
You might be stronger than hell right now, but you ain't never been in no fight worth a damn...
And I been killing Landrys before you's a dream in yer mama's head.

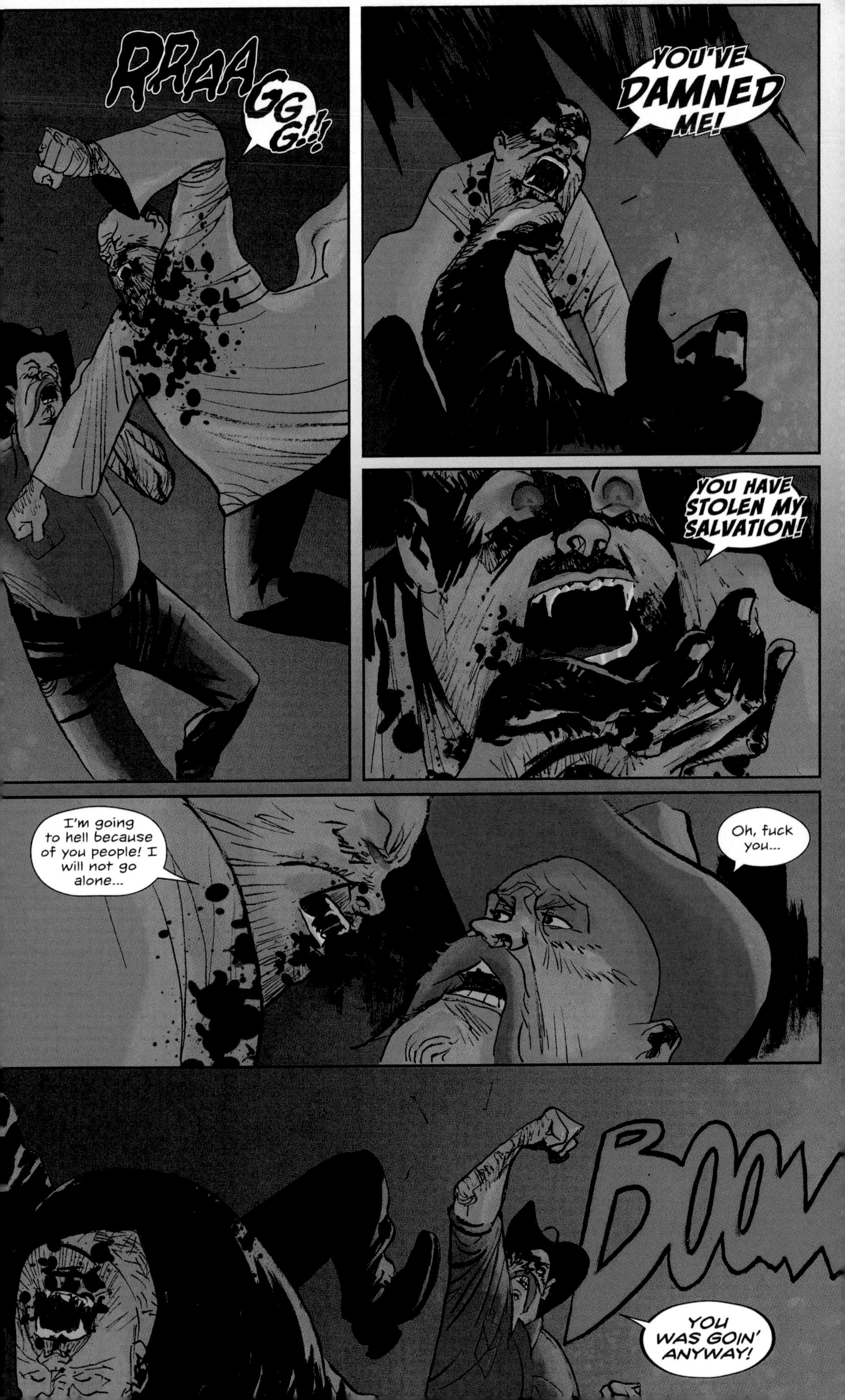
RRAAGGG!!!
YOU'VE DAMNED ME!
YOU HAVE STOLEN MY SALVATION!
I'm going to hell because of you people! I will not go alone...
Oh, fuck you...
BOOM
YOU WAS GOIN' ANYWAY!

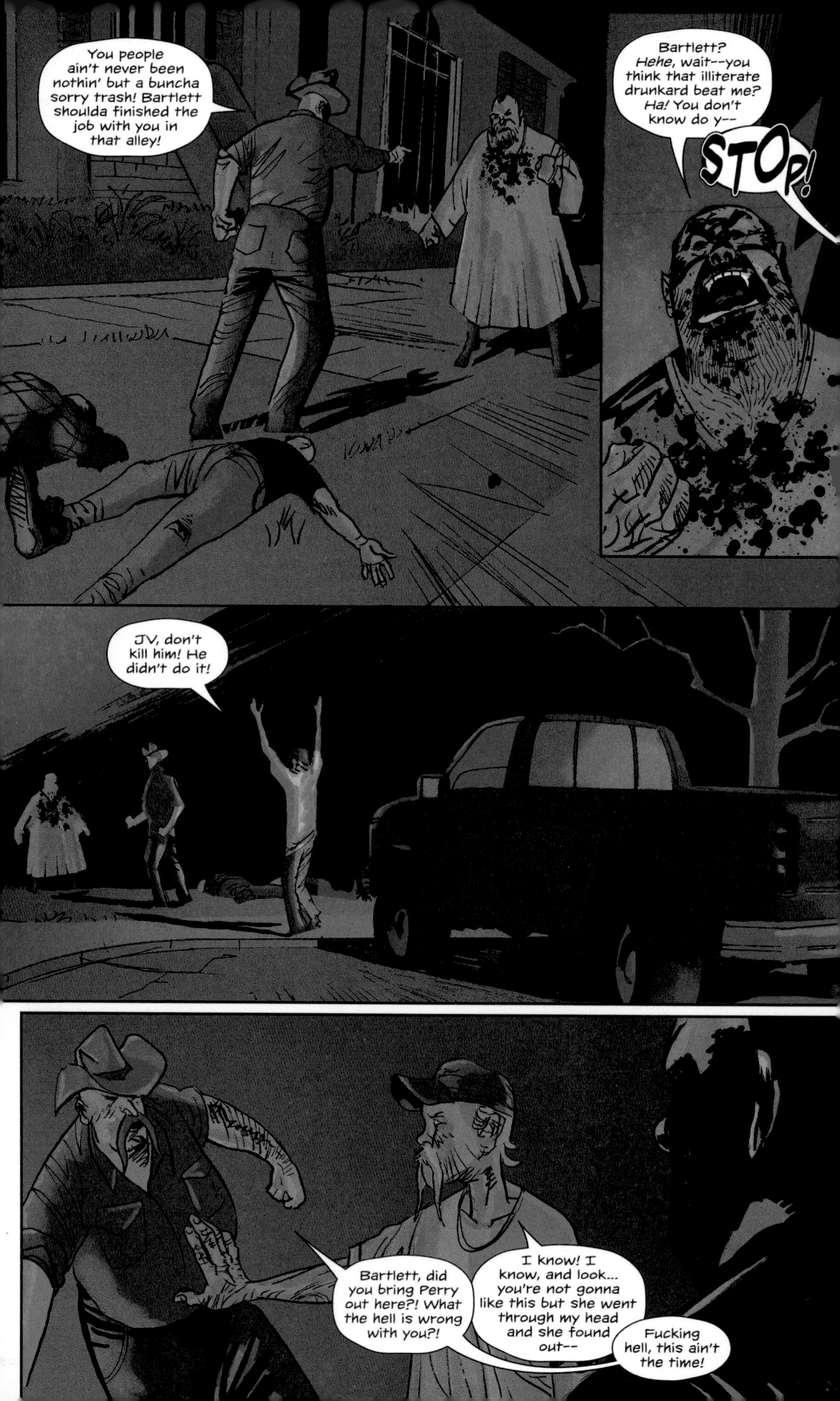
You people ain't never been nothin' but a buncha sorry trash! Bartlett shoulda finished the job with you in that alley!
Bartlett? *Hehe,* wait--you think that illiterate drunkard beat me? *Ha!* You don't know do y--
STOP!
JV, don't kill him! He didn't do it!
Bartlett, did you bring Perry out here?! What the hell is wrong with you?!
I know! I know, and look... you're not gonna like this but she went through my head and she found out--
Fucking hell, this ain't the time!

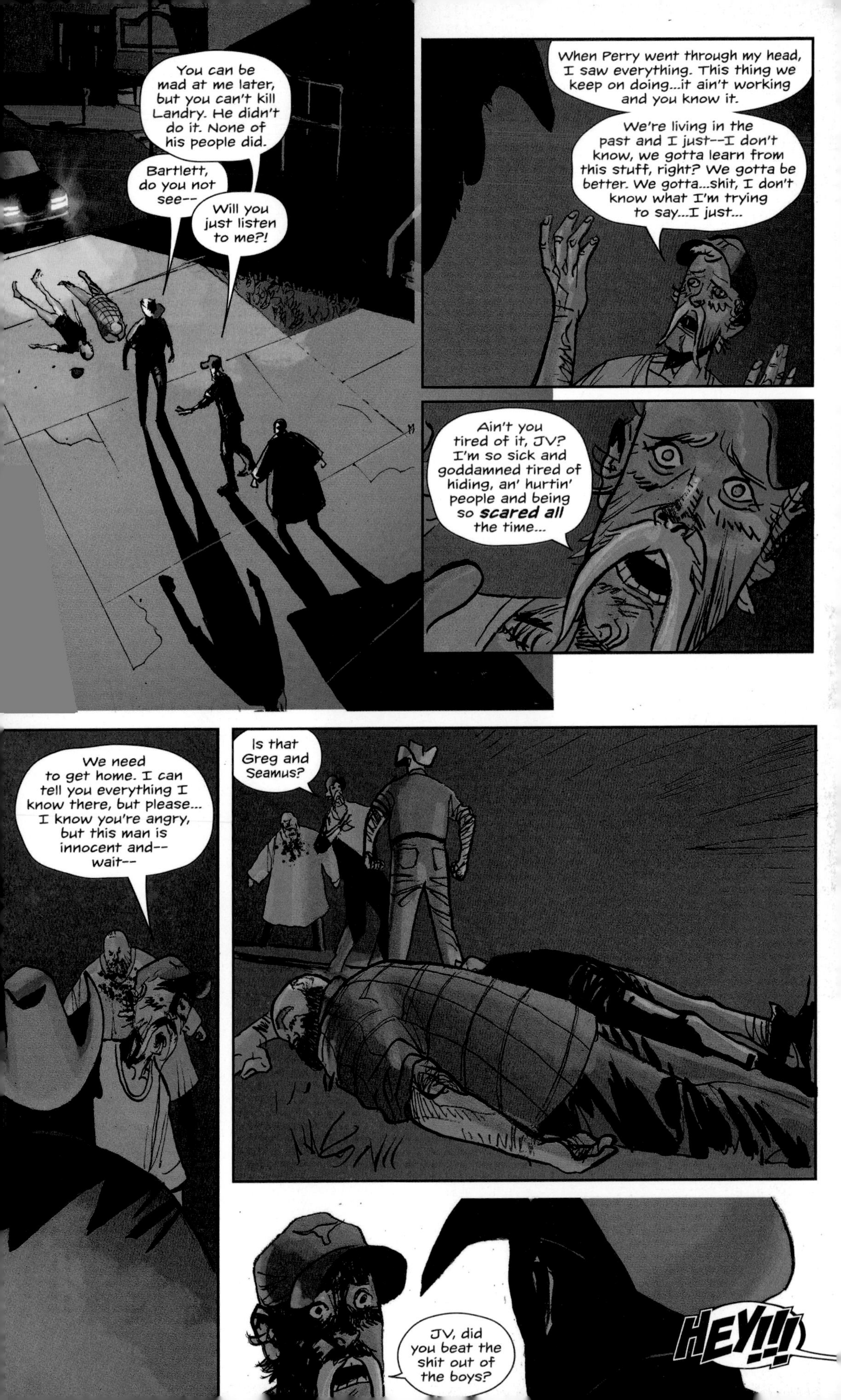
You can be mad at me later, but you can't kill Landry. He didn't do it. None of his people did.
Bartlett, do you not see--
Will you just listen to me?!
When Perry went through my head, I saw everything. This thing we keep on doing...it ain't working and you know it.
We're living in the past and I just--I don't know, we gotta learn from this stuff, right? We gotta be better. We gotta...shit, I don't know what I'm trying to say...I just...
Ain't you tired of it, JV? I'm so sick and goddamned tired of hiding, an' hurtin' people and being so scared all the time...
We need to get home. I can tell you everything I know there, but please... I know you're angry, but this man is innocent and-- wait--
Is that Greg and Seamus?
HEY!!!
JV, did you beat the shit out of the boys?

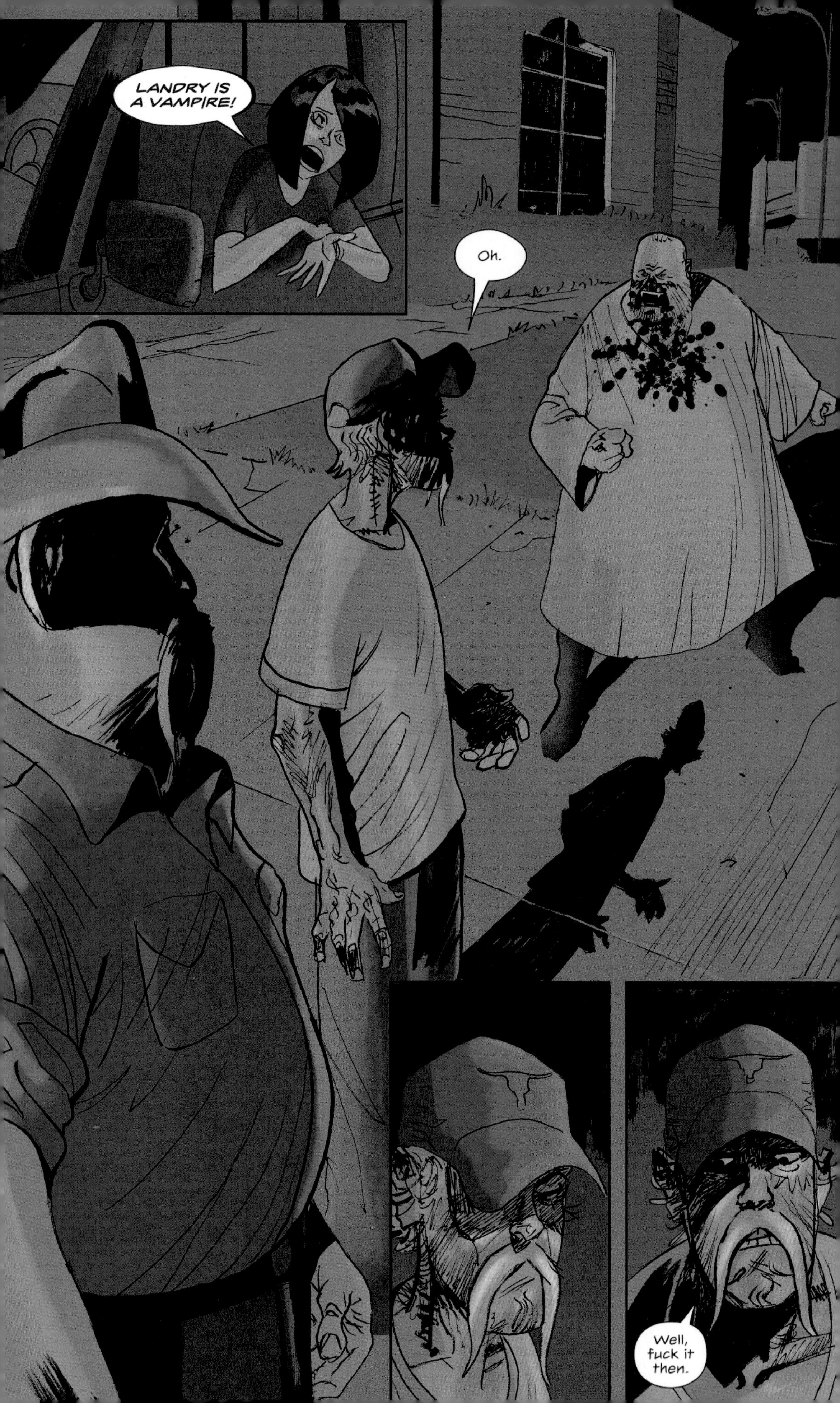
LANDRY IS
A VAMPIRE!
Oh.
Well,
fuck it
then.

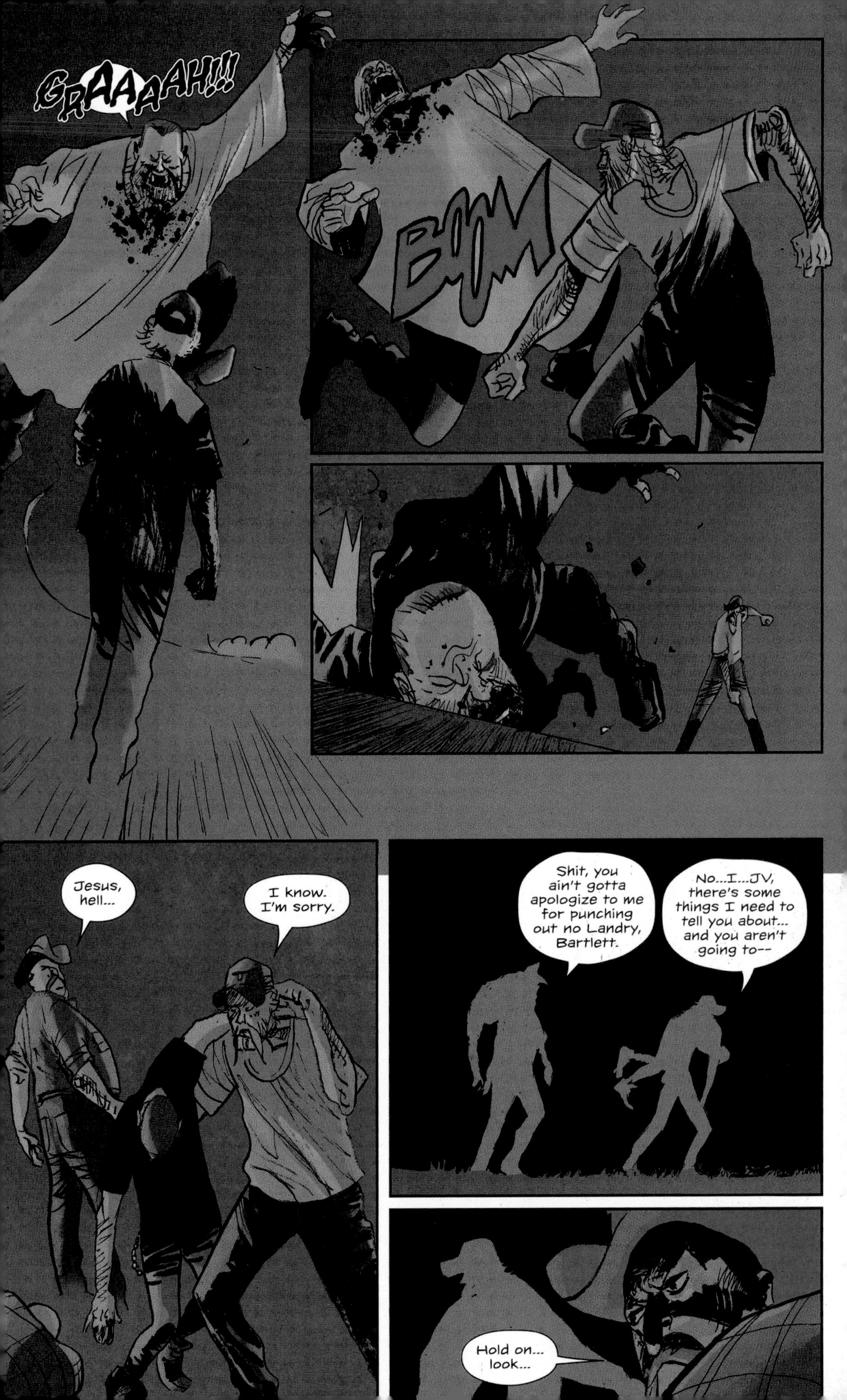
GRAAAAH!!!
BOOM
Jesus, hell...
I know. I'm sorry.
Shit, you ain't gotta apologize to me for punching out no Landry, Bartlett.
No...I...JV, there's some things I need to tell you about... and you aren't going to--
Hold on... look...

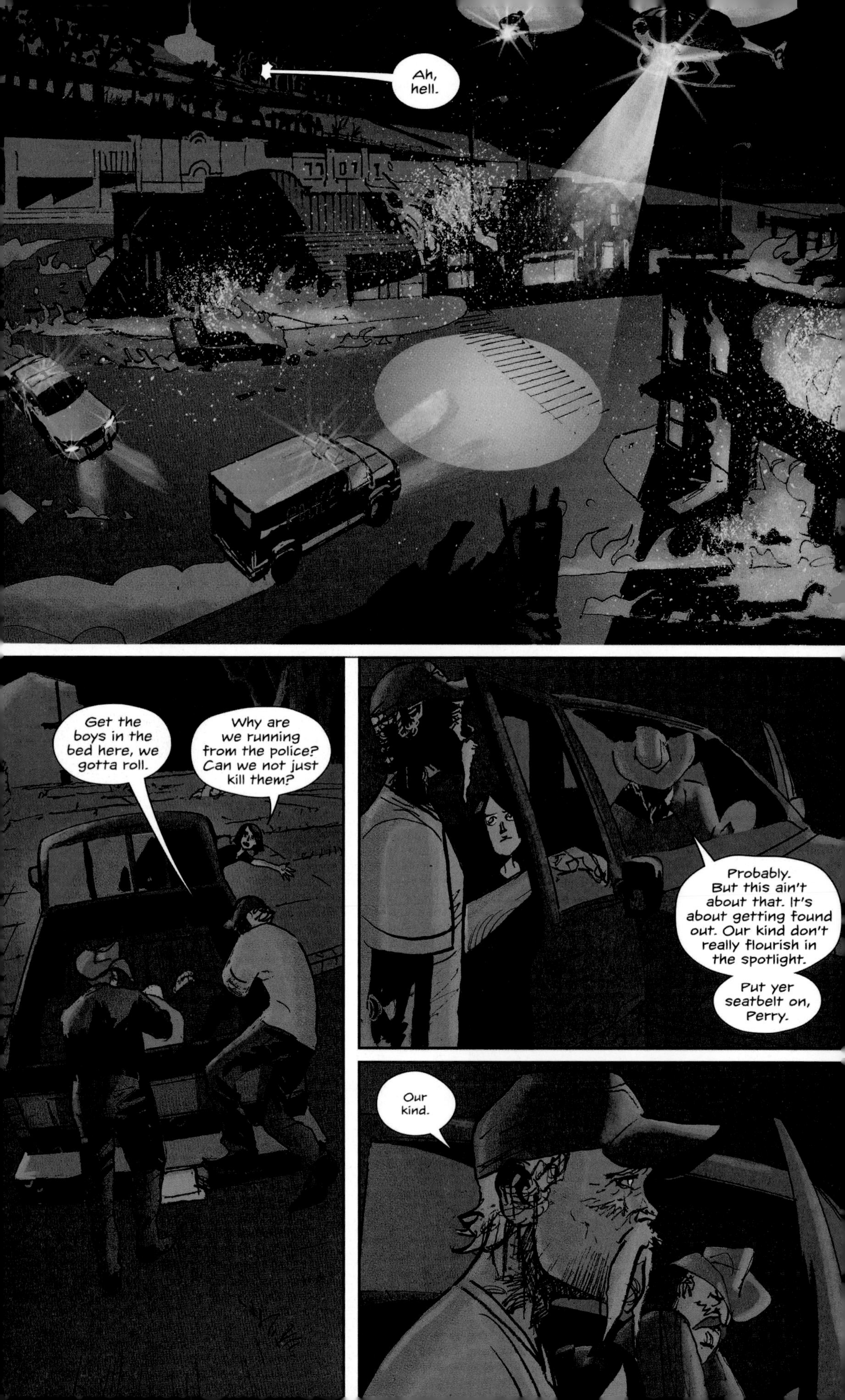
Ah, hell.
Get the boys in the bed here, we gotta roll.
Why are we running from the police? Can we not just kill them?
Probably. But this ain't about that. It's about getting found out. Our kind don't really flourish in the spotlight.
Put yer seatbelt on, Perry.
Our kind.

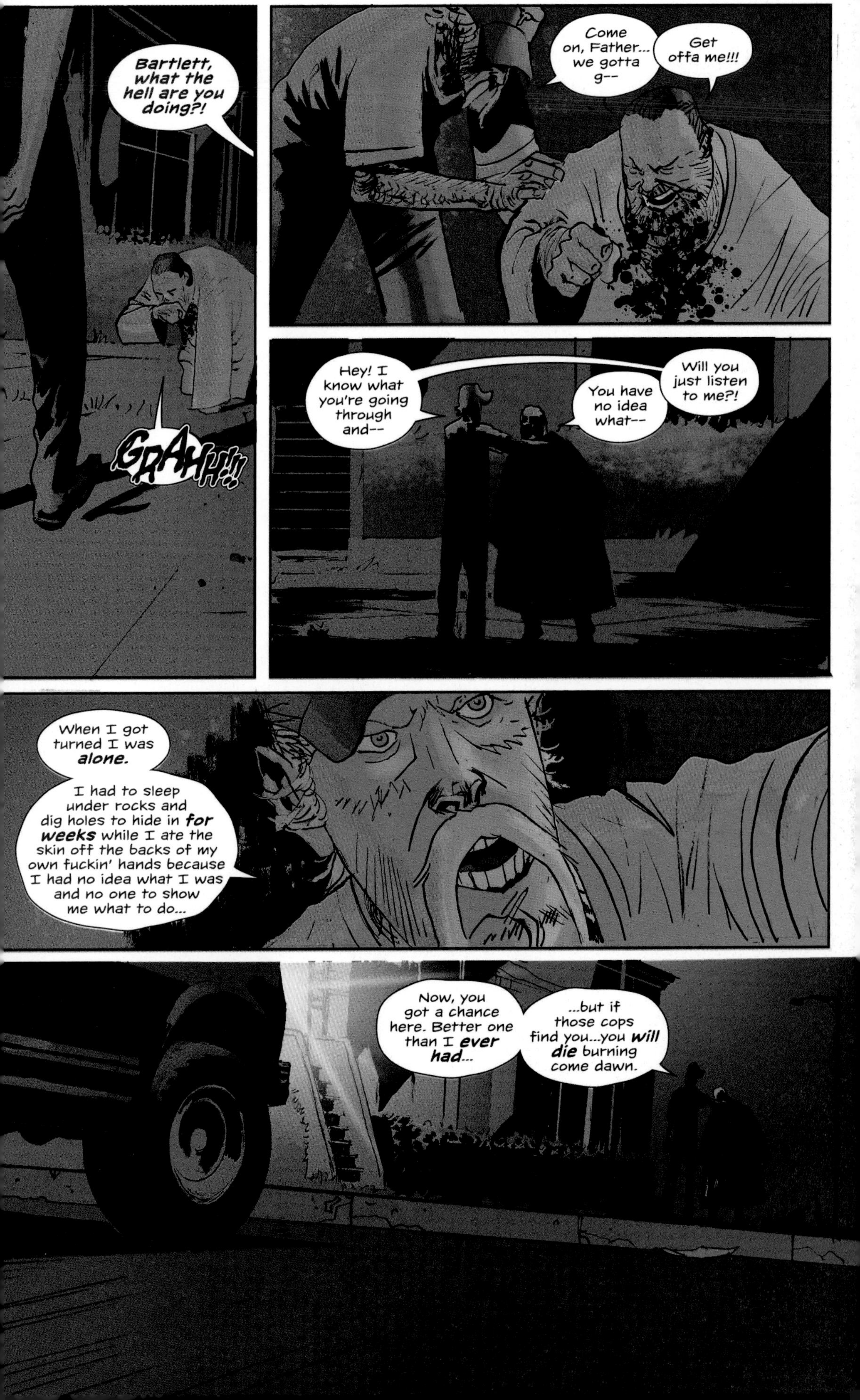
Bartlett, what the hell are you doing?!
GRAHH!!
Come on, Father... we gotta g--
Get offa me!!!
Hey! I know what you're going through and--
You have no idea what--
Will you just listen to me?!
When I got turned I was **alone.**
I had to sleep under rocks and dig holes to hide in **for weeks** while I ate the skin off the backs of my own fuckin' hands because I had no idea what I was and no one to show me what to do...
Now, you got a chance here. Better one than I **ever had...**
...but if those cops find you...you **will die** burning come dawn.

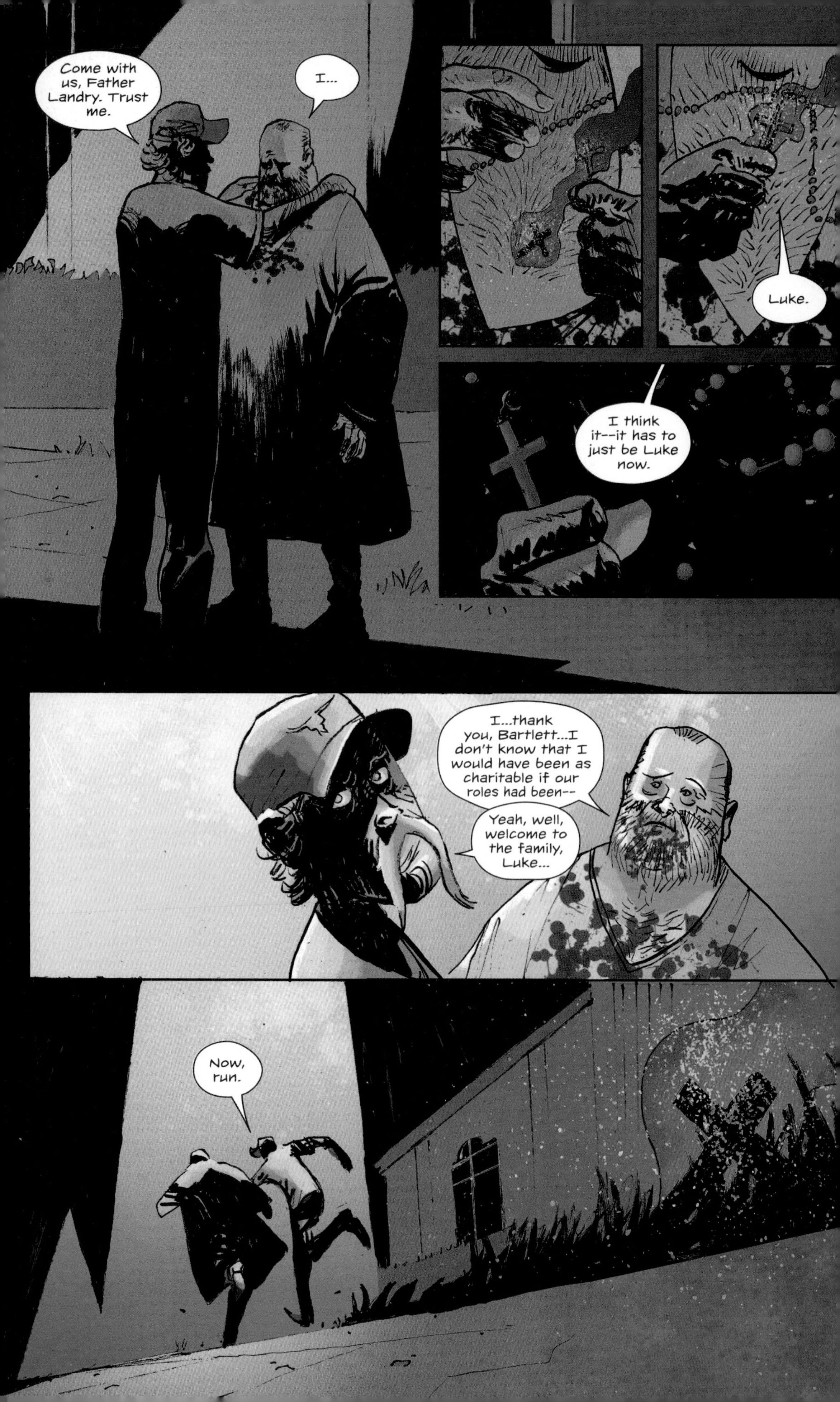
Come with us, Father Landry. Trust me.
I...
Luke.
I think it--it has to just be Luke now.
I...thank you, Bartlett...I don't know that I would have been as charitable if our roles had been--
Yeah, well, welcome to the family, Luke...
Now, run.

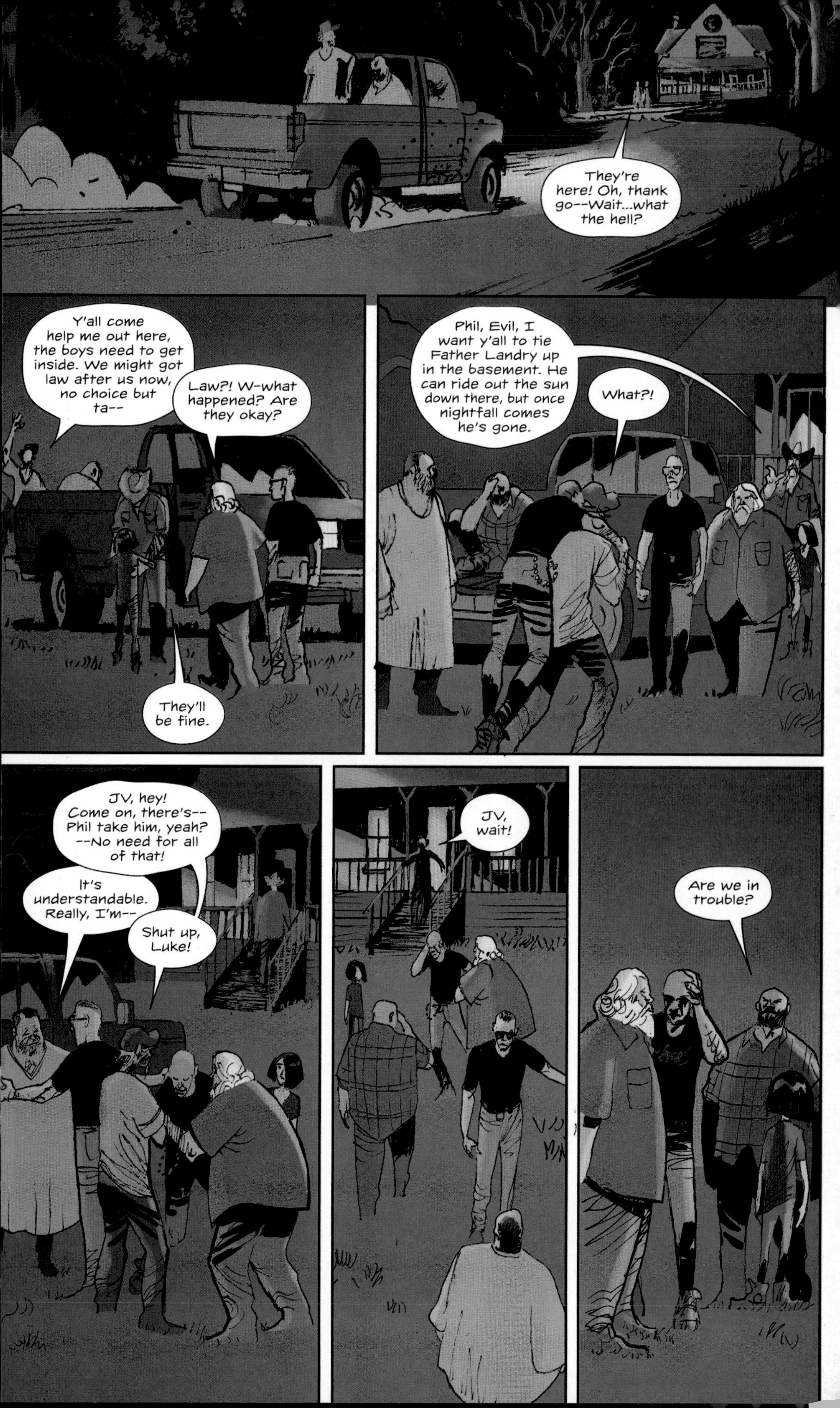
They're here! Oh, thank go--Wait...what the hell?
Y'all come help me out here, the boys need to get inside. We might got law after us now, no choice but ta--
Law?! W-what happened? Are they okay?
They'll be fine.
Phil, Evil, I want y'all to tie Father Landry up in the basement. He can ride out the sun down there, but once nightfall comes he's gone.
What?!
JV, hey! Come on, there's-- Phil take him, yeah? --No need for all of that!
It's understandable. Really, I'm--
Shut up, Luke!
JV, wait!
Are we in trouble?

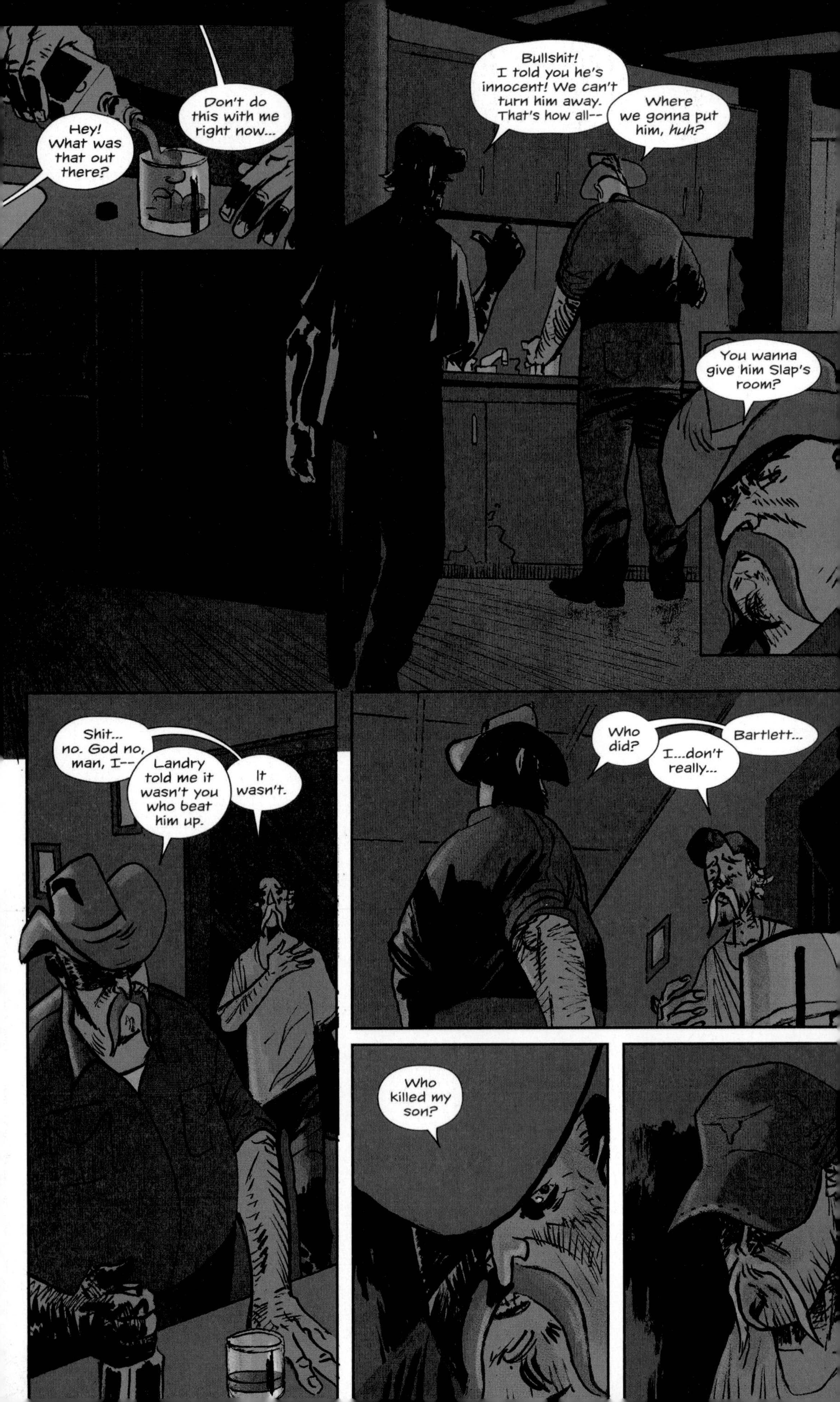
Hey! What was that out there?
Don't do this with me right now...
Bullshit! I told you he's innocent! We can't turn him away. That's how all--
Where we gonna put him, *huh?*
You wanna give him Slap's room?
Shit... no. God no, man, I--
Landry told me it wasn't you who beat him up.
It wasn't.
Who did?
Bartlett...
I...don't really...
Who killed my son?

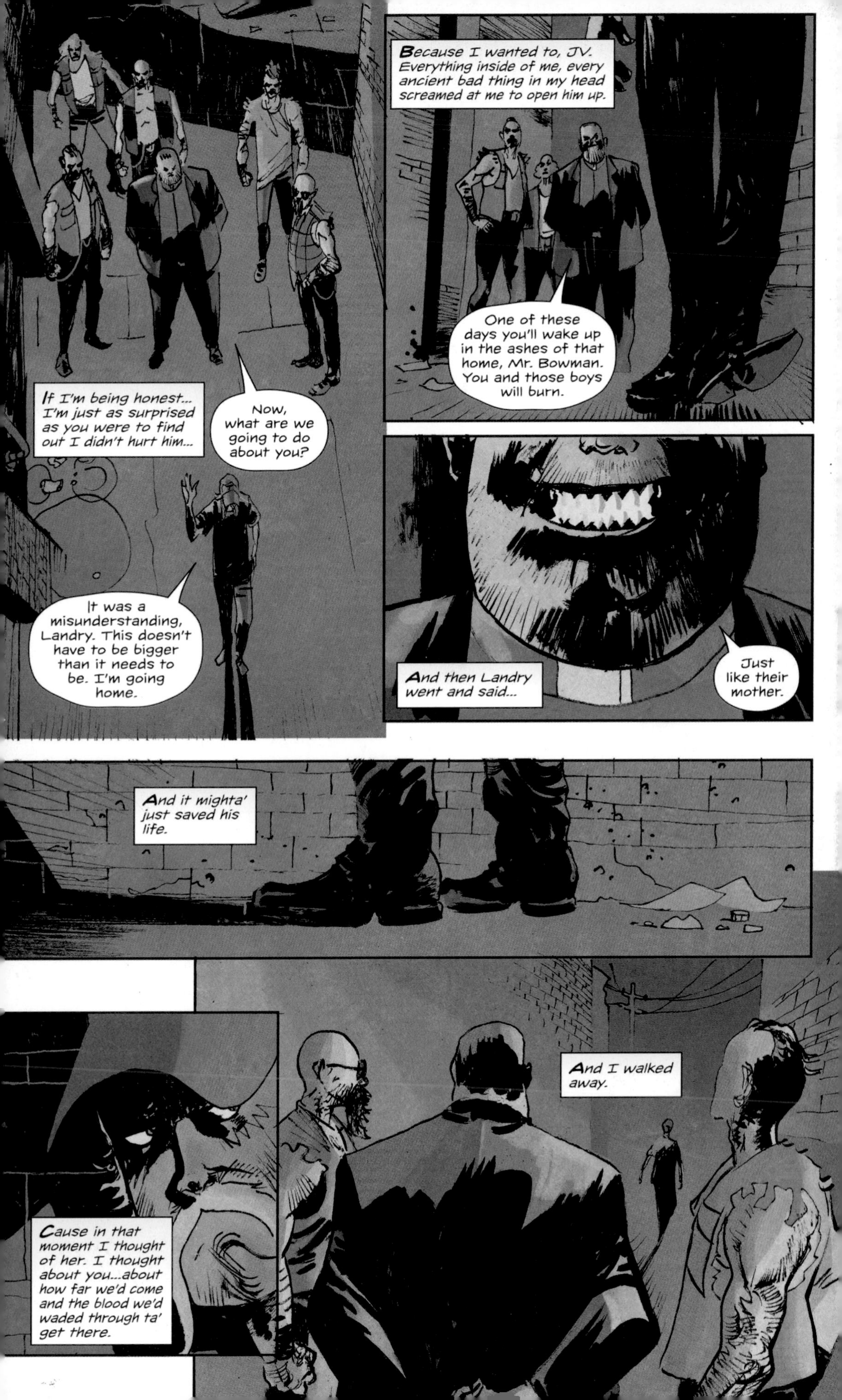
If I'm being honest... I'm just as surprised as you were to find out I didn't hurt him...
Now, what are we going to do about you?
It was a misunderstanding, Landry. This doesn't have to be bigger than it needs to be. I'm going home.
Because I wanted to, JV. Everything inside of me, every ancient bad thing in my head screamed at me to open him up.
One of these days you'll wake up in the ashes of that home, Mr. Bowman. You and those boys will burn.
And then Landry went and said...
Just like their mother.
And it mighta' just saved his life.
Cause in that moment I thought of her. I thought about you...about how far we'd come and the blood we'd waded through ta' get there.
And I walked away.

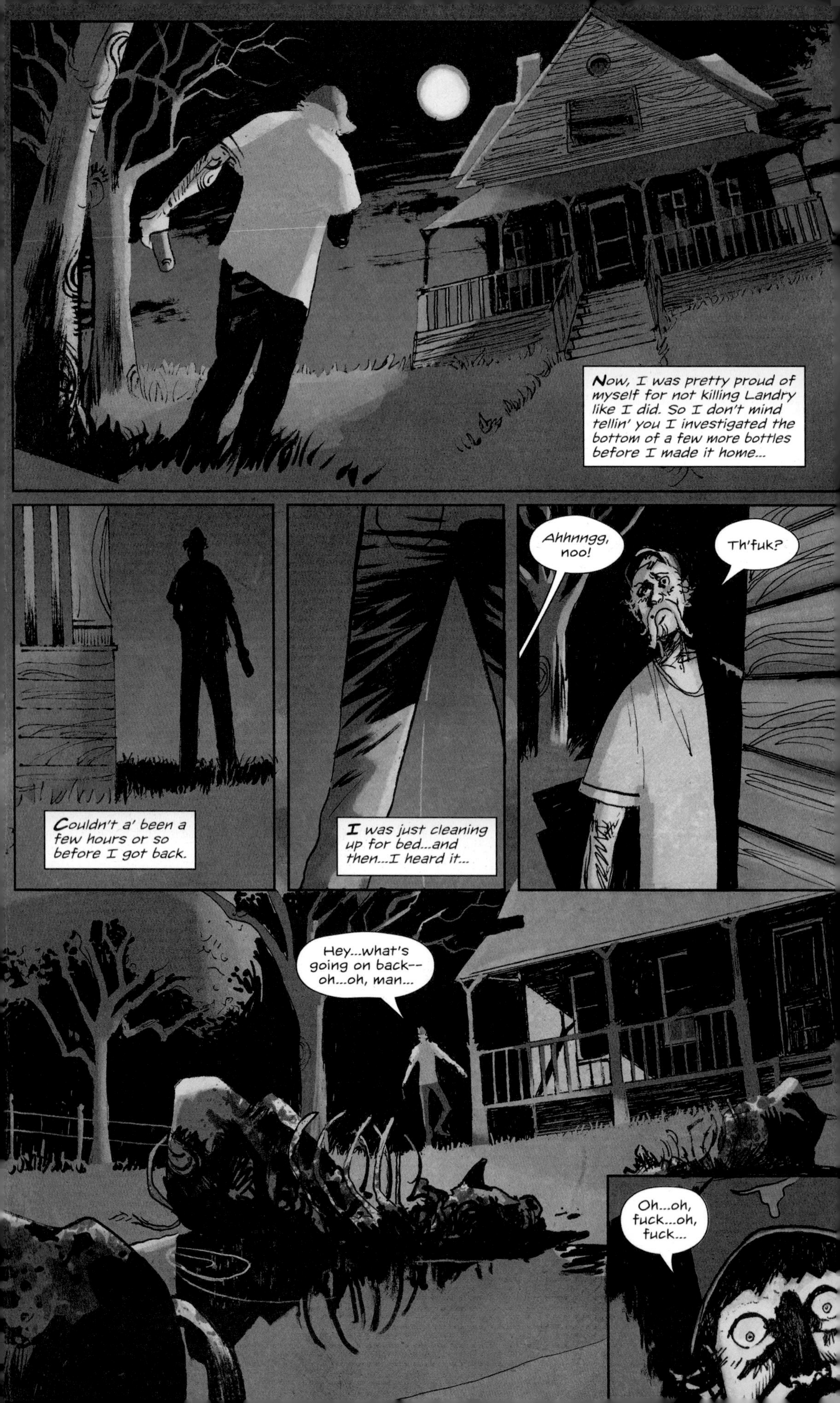
Now, I was pretty proud of myself for not killing Landry like I did. So I don't mind tellin' you I investigated the bottom of a few more bottles before I made it home...
Couldn't a' been a few hours or so before I got back.
I was just cleaning up for bed...and then...I heard it...
Ahhnngg, noo!
Th'fuk?
Hey...what's going on back-- oh...oh, man...
Oh...oh, fuck...oh, fuck...

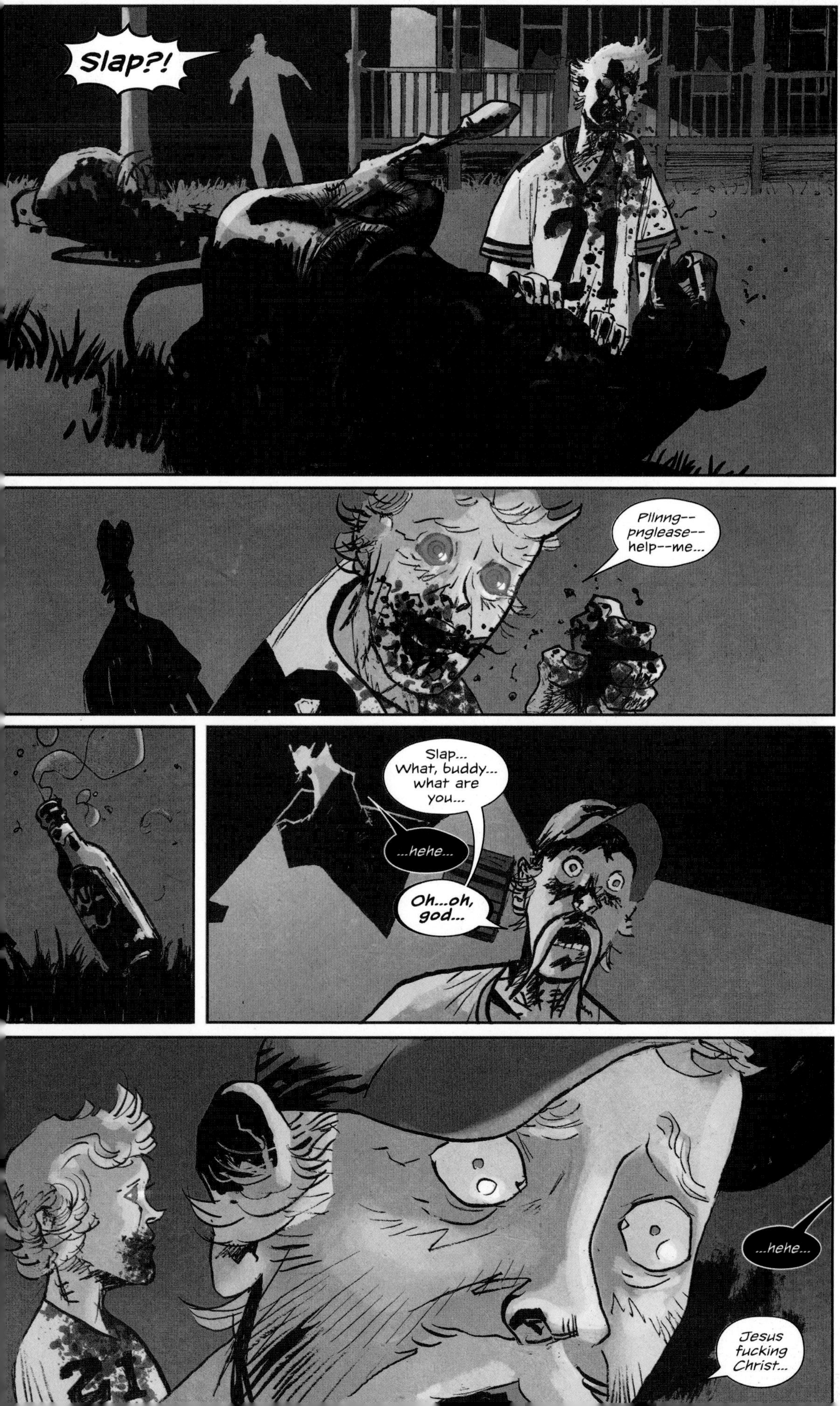
Slap?!
Pllnng--
pnglease--
help--me...
Slap...
What, buddy...
what are
you...
...hehe...
Oh...oh,
god...
...hehe...
Jesus
fucking
Christ...

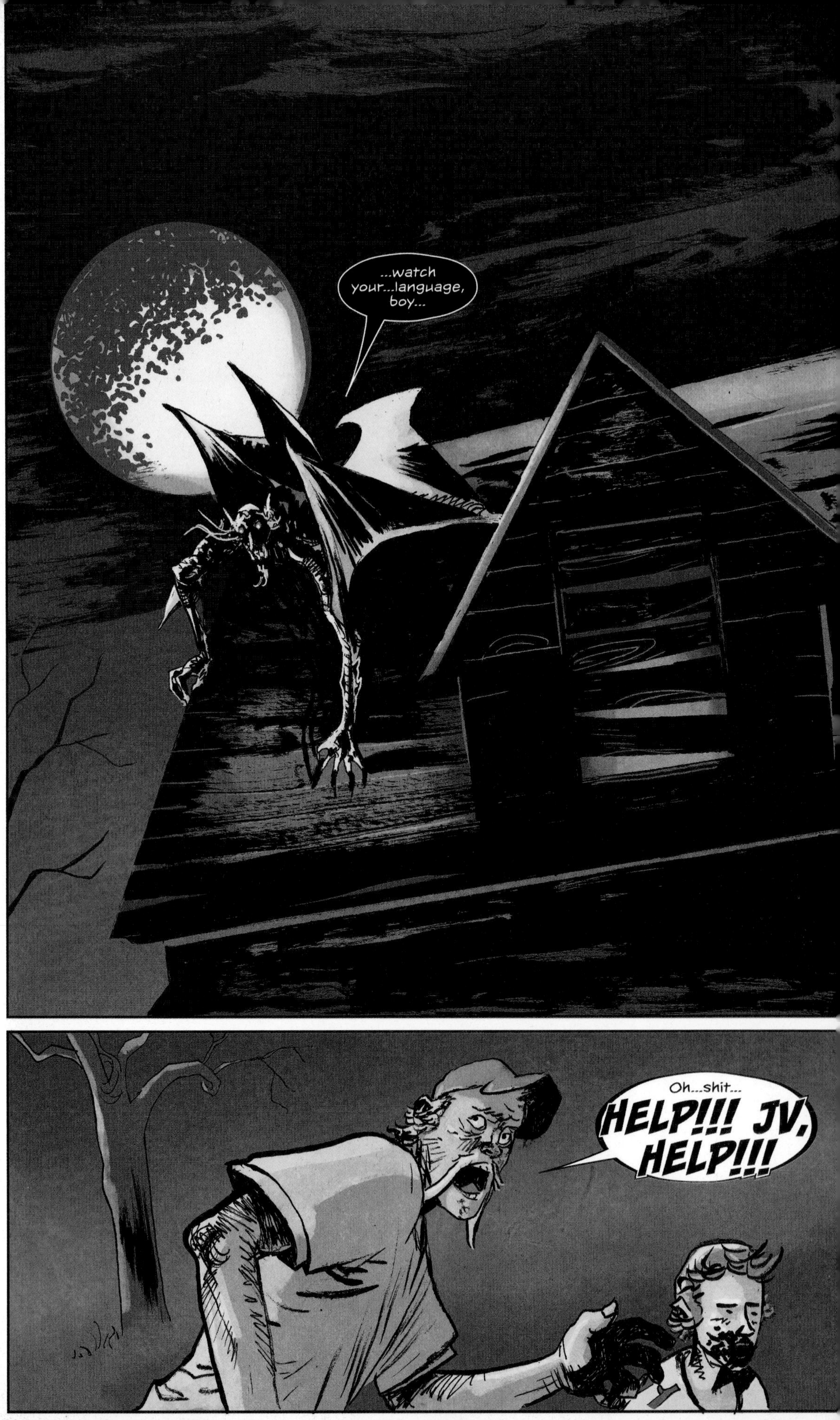
...watch your...language, boy...
Oh...shit...
HELP!!! JV, HELP!!!

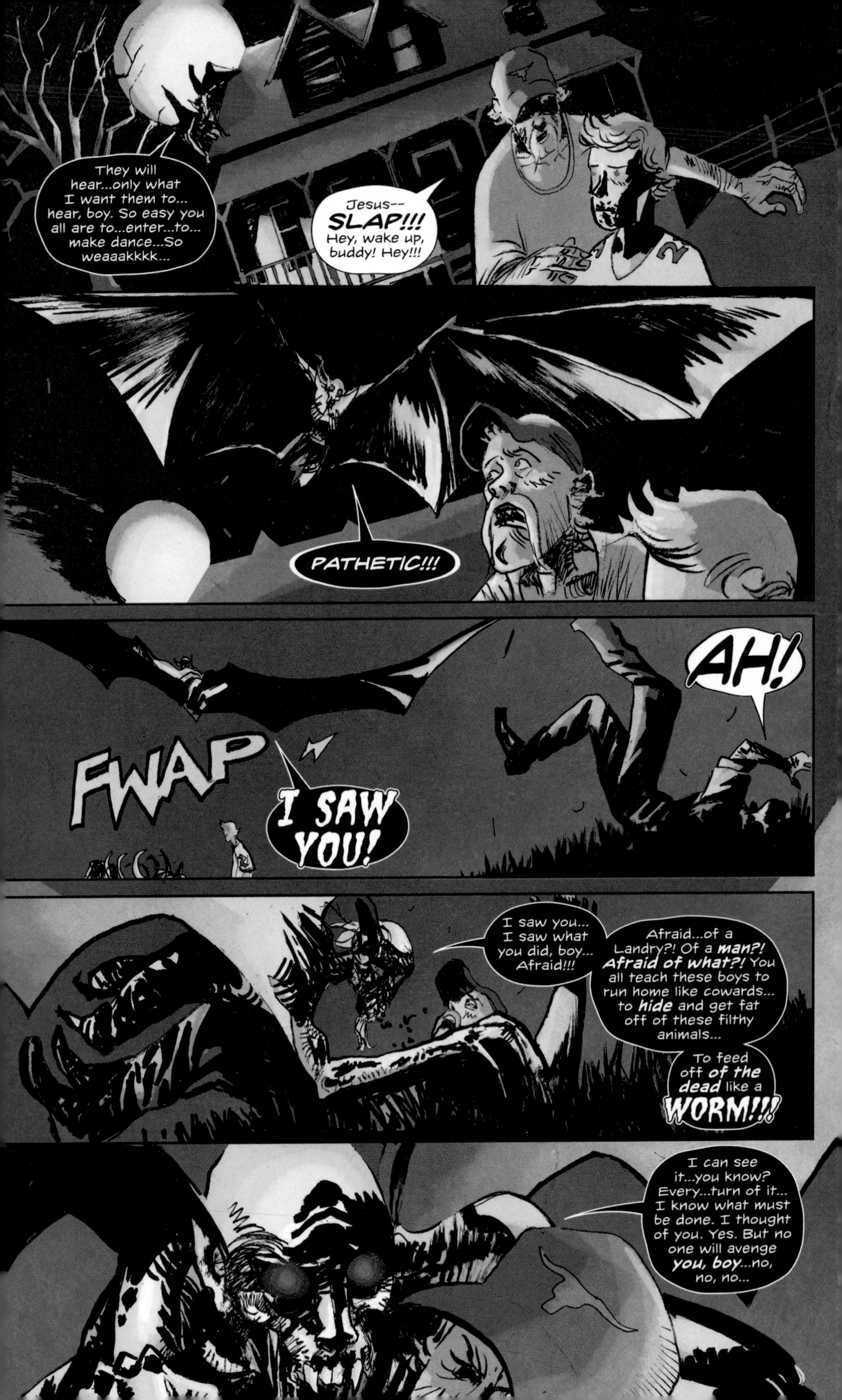
They will hear...only what I want them to... hear, boy. So easy you all are to...enter...to... make dance...So weaaakkkk...
Jesus-- SLAP!!! Hey, wake up, buddy! Hey!!!
PATHETIC!!!
AH!
FWAP
I SAW YOU!
I saw you... I saw what you did, boy... Afraid!!!
Afraid...of a Landry?! Of a man?! Afraid of what?! You all teach these boys to run home like cowards... to hide and get fat off of these filthy animals...
To feed off of the dead like a WORM!!!
I can see it...you know? Every...turn of it... I know what must be done. I thought of you. Yes. But no one will avenge you, boy...no, no, no...

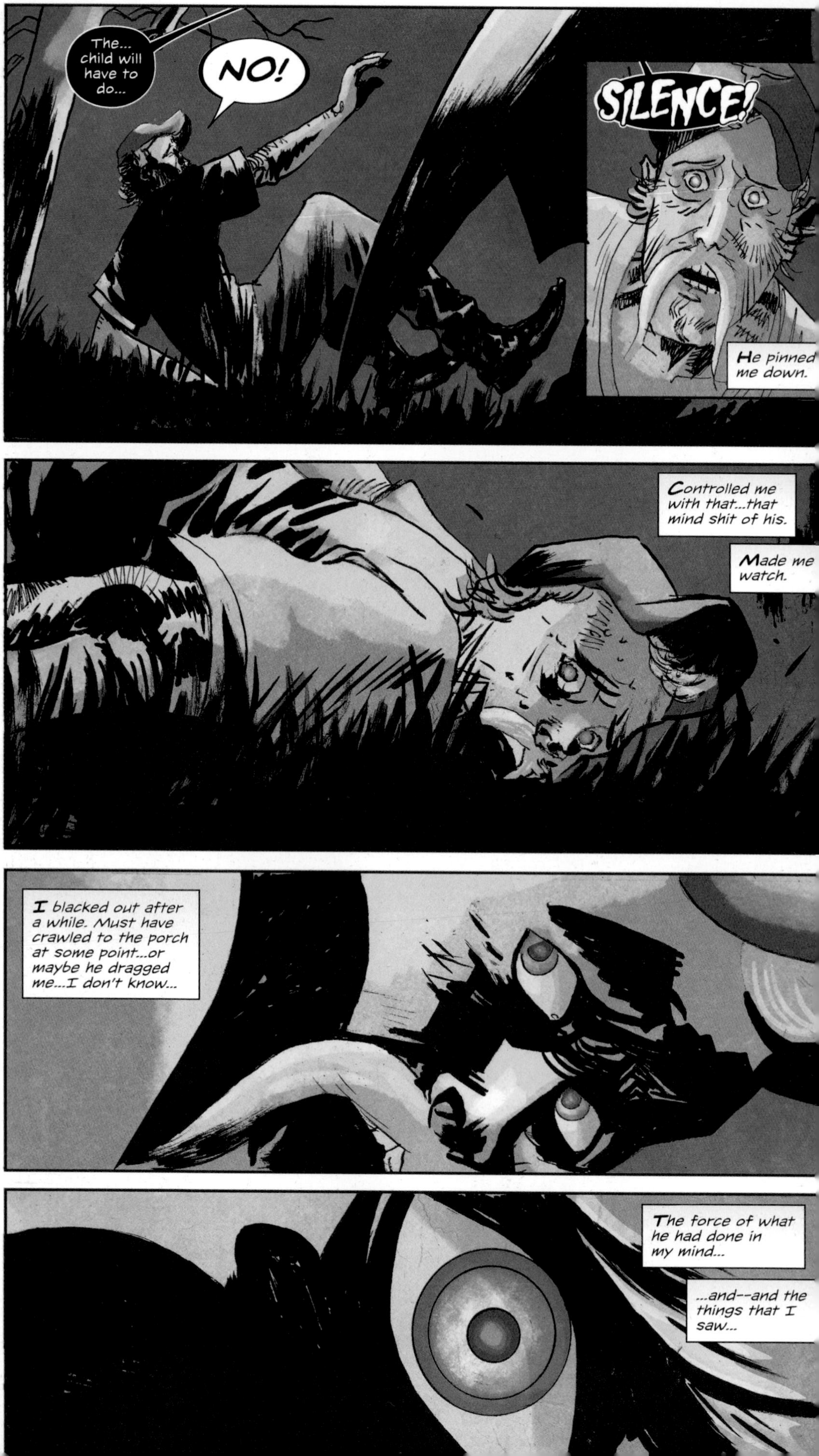

The... child will have to do...
NO!
SILENCE!
He pinned me down.
Controlled me with that...that mind shit of his.
Made me watch.
I blacked out after a while. Must have crawled to the porch at some point...or maybe he dragged me...I don't know...
The force of what he had done in my mind...
...and--and the things that I saw...

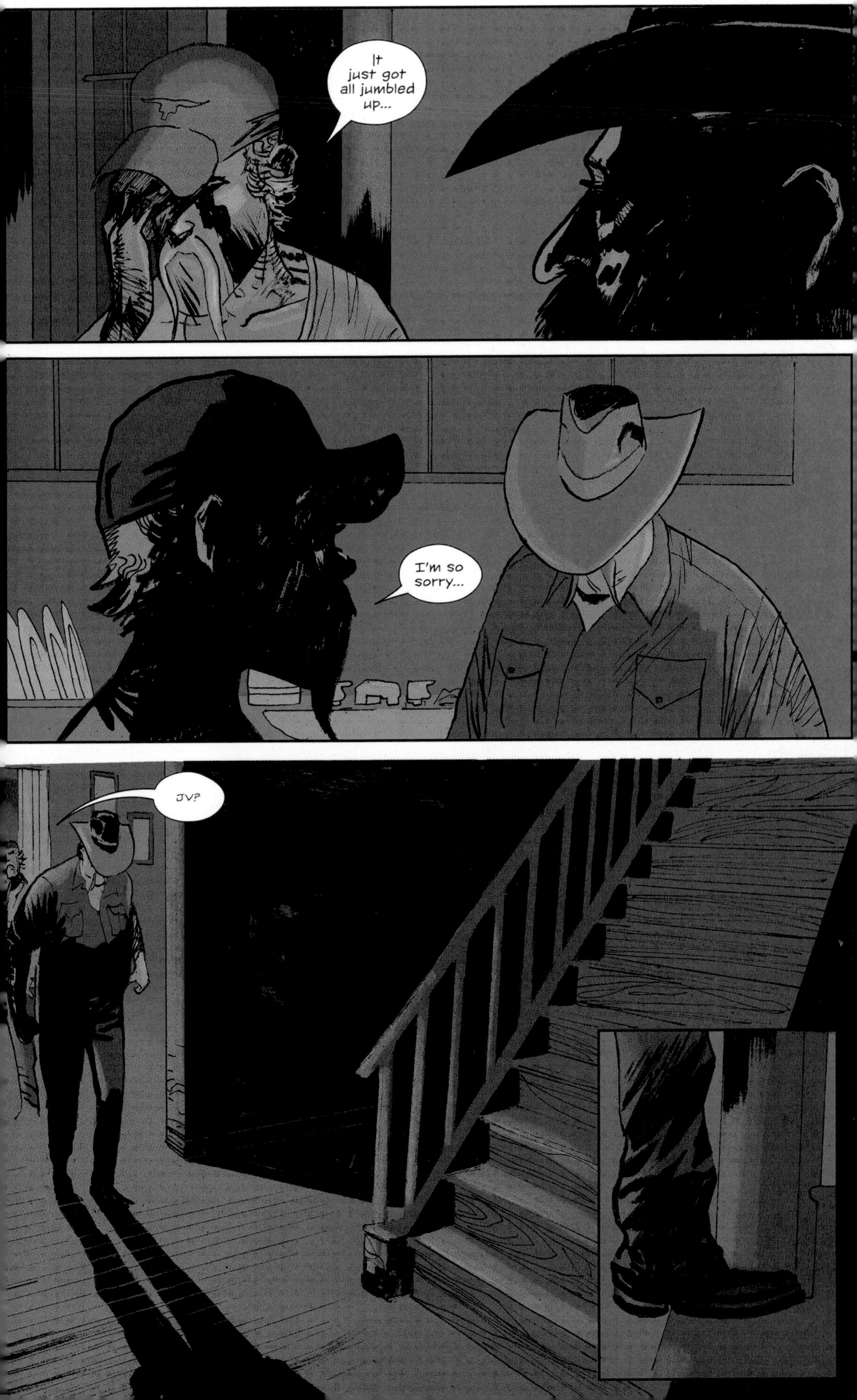
It just got all jumbled up...
I'm so sorry...
JV?

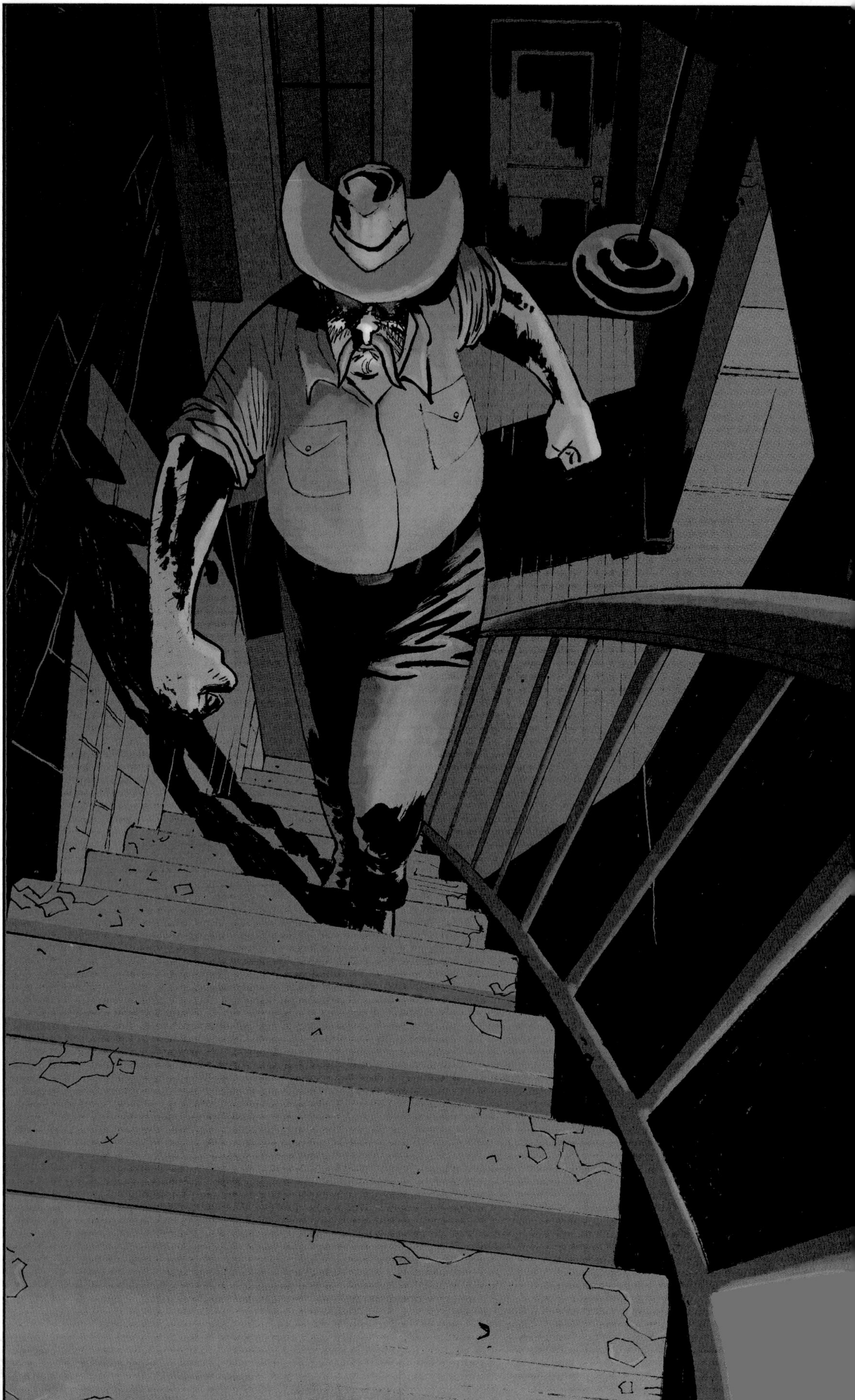

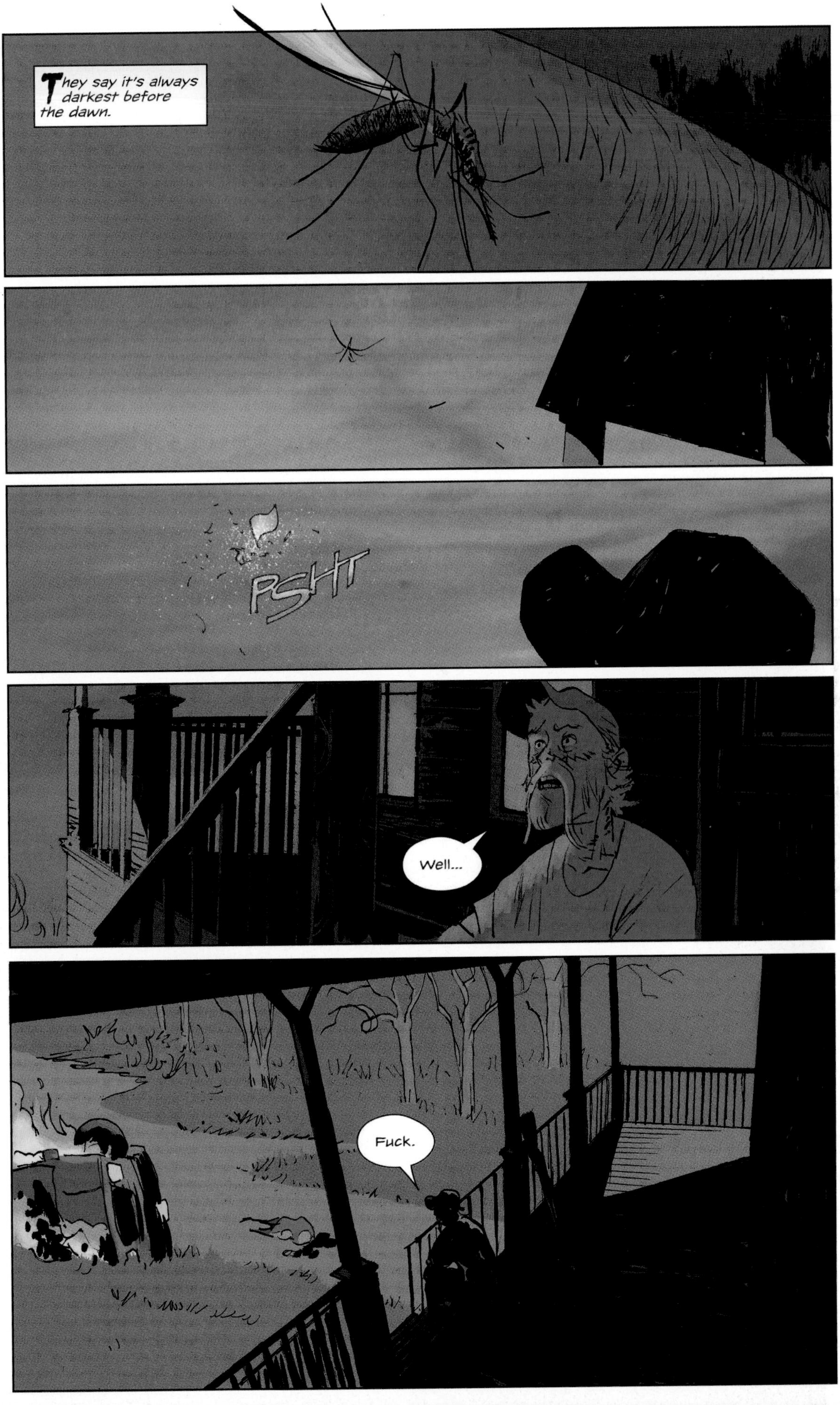
They say it's always darkest before the dawn.
PSHT
Well...
Fuck.

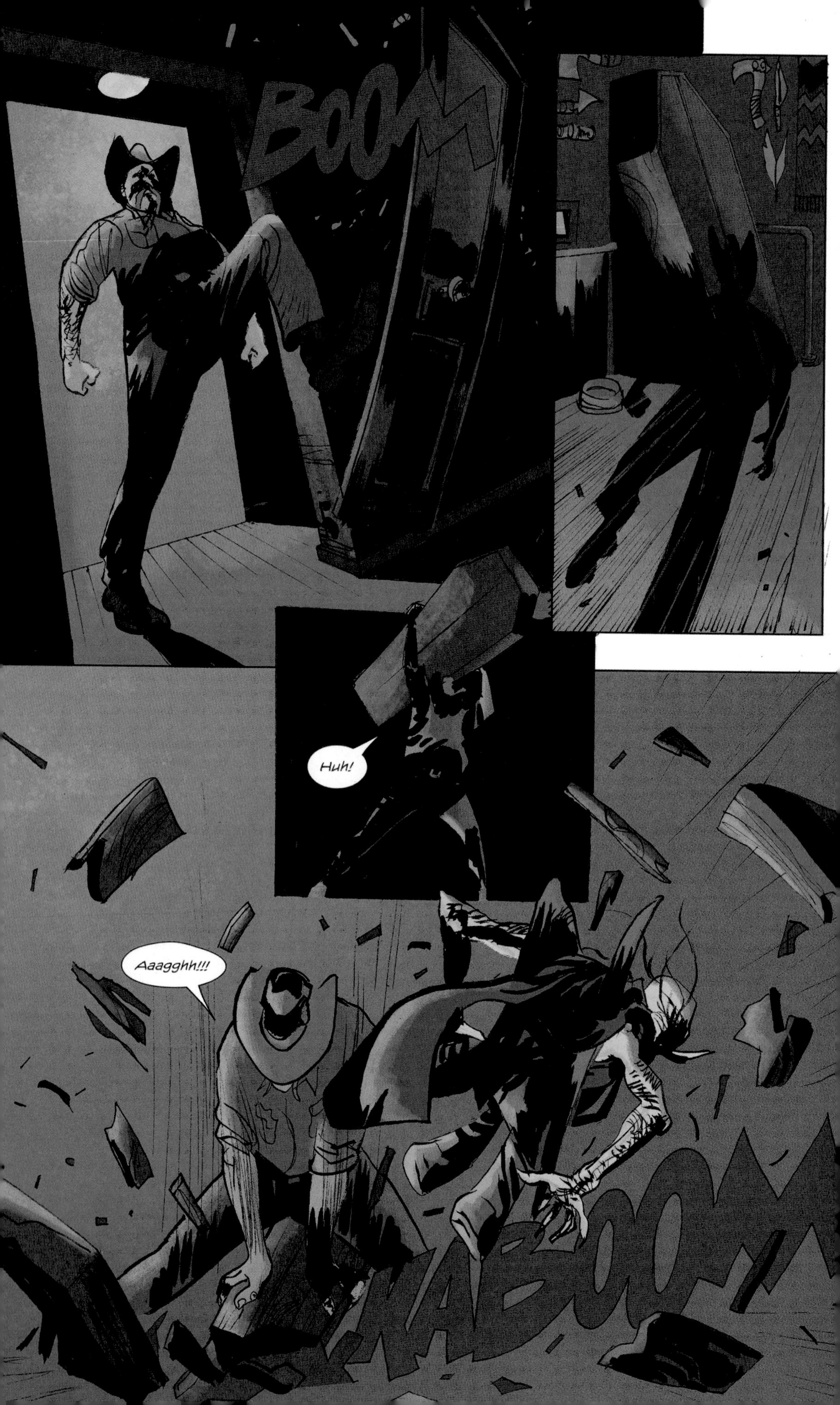

BOOM
Huh!
Aaagghh!!!
KABOOM

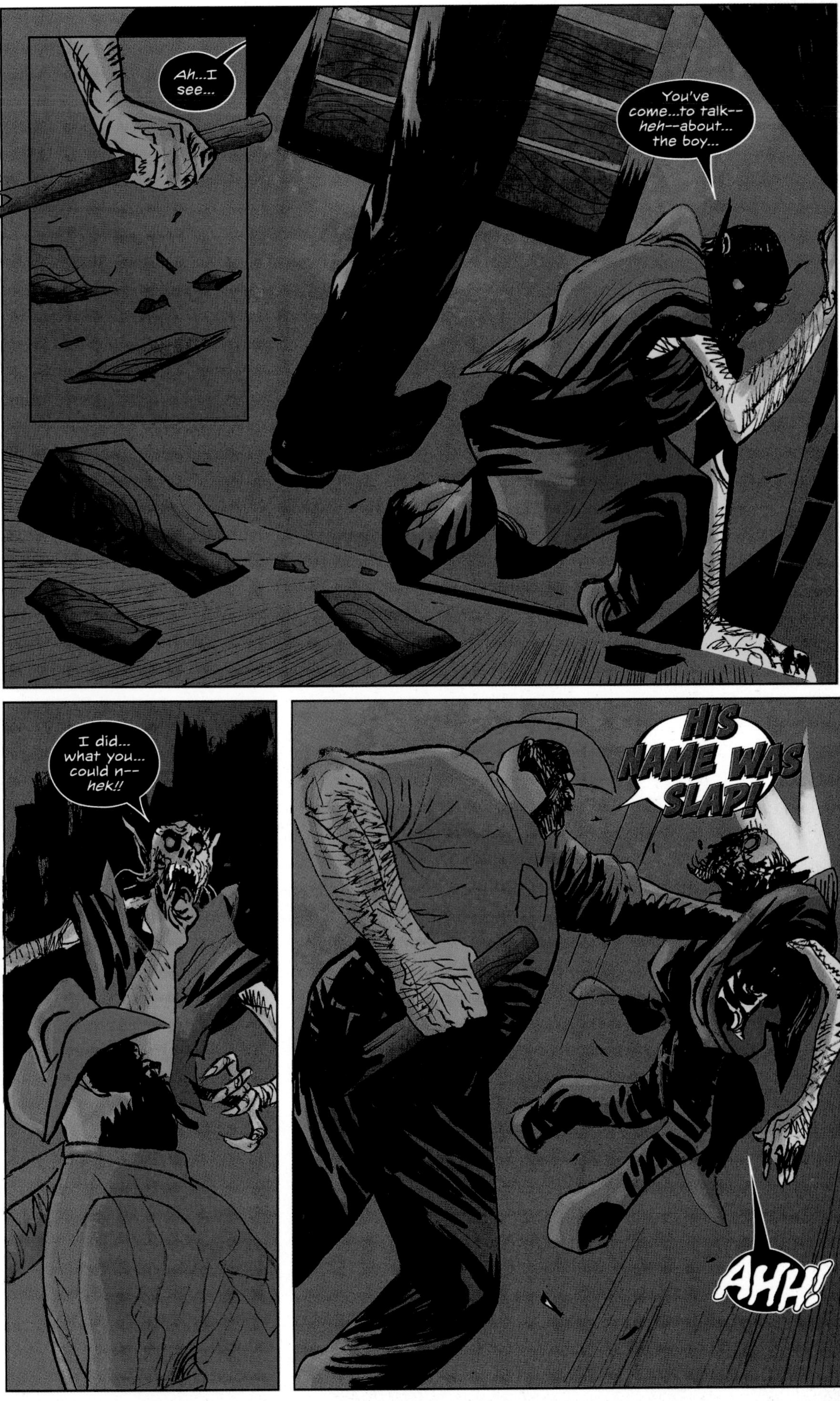
Ah...I see...
You've come...to talk--heh--about... the boy...
I did... what you... could n--hek!!
HIS NAME WAS SLAP!
AHH!

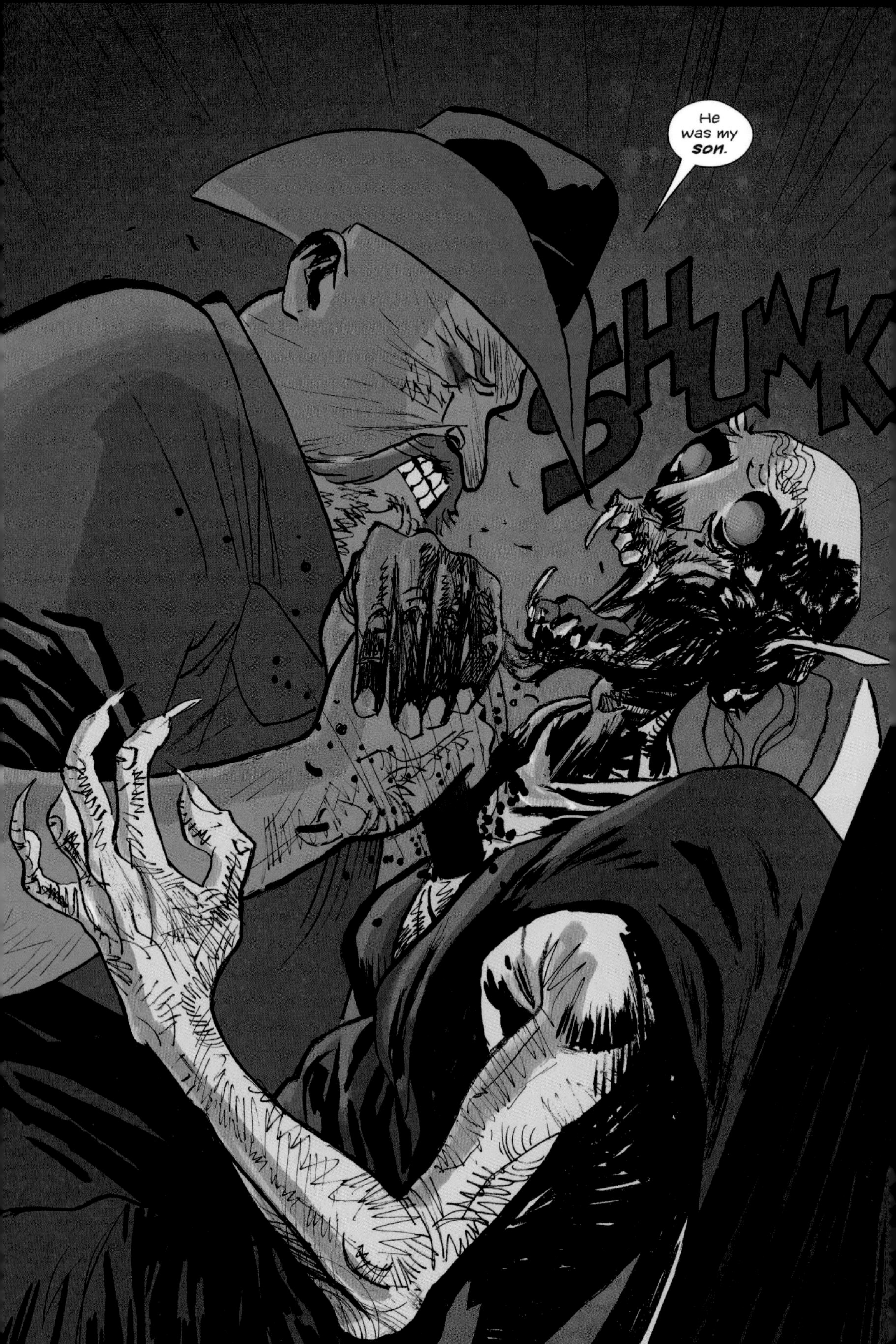
He was my son.
SHUNK!

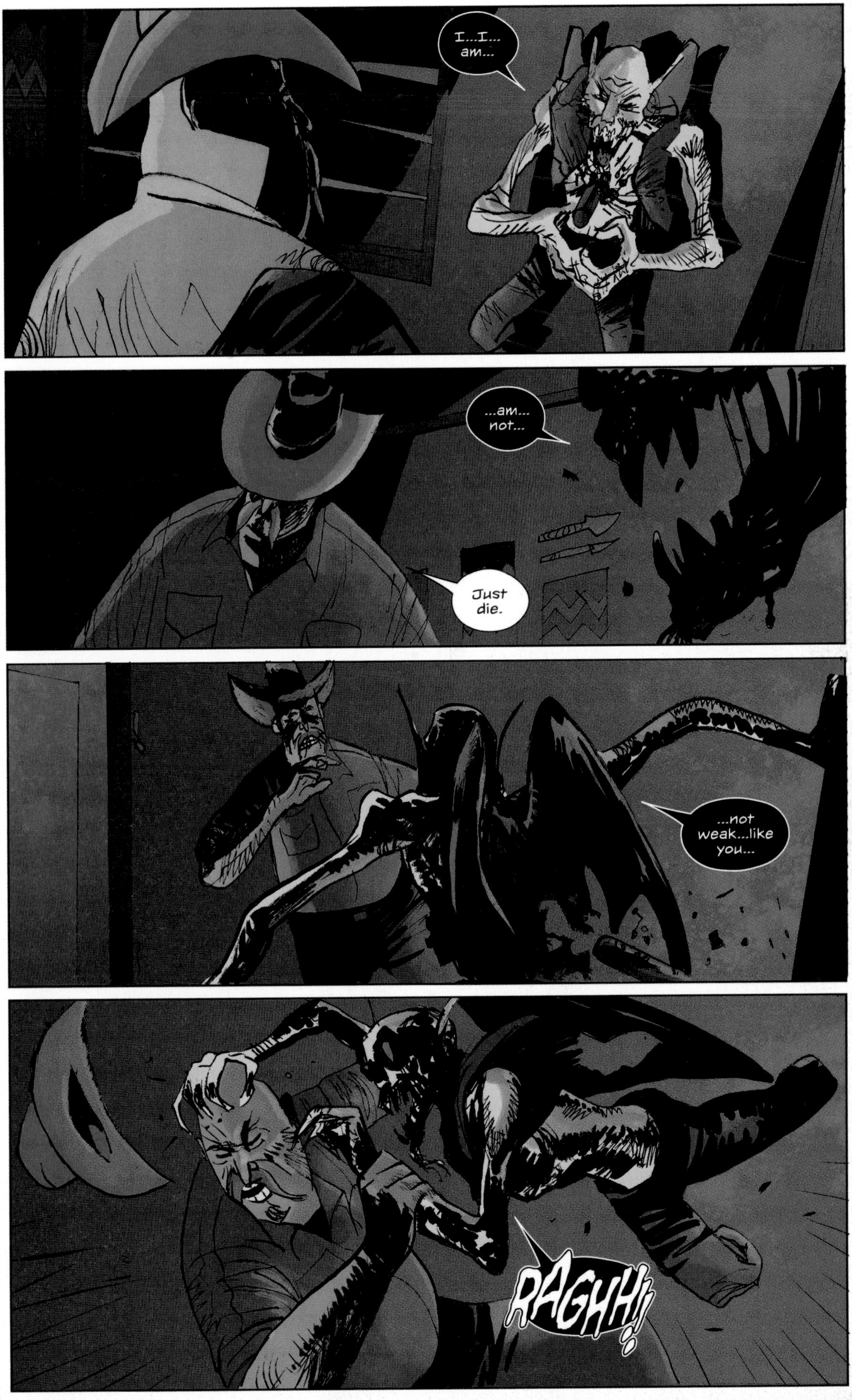
I...I... am...
...am... not...
Just die.
...not weak...like you...
RAGHH!!

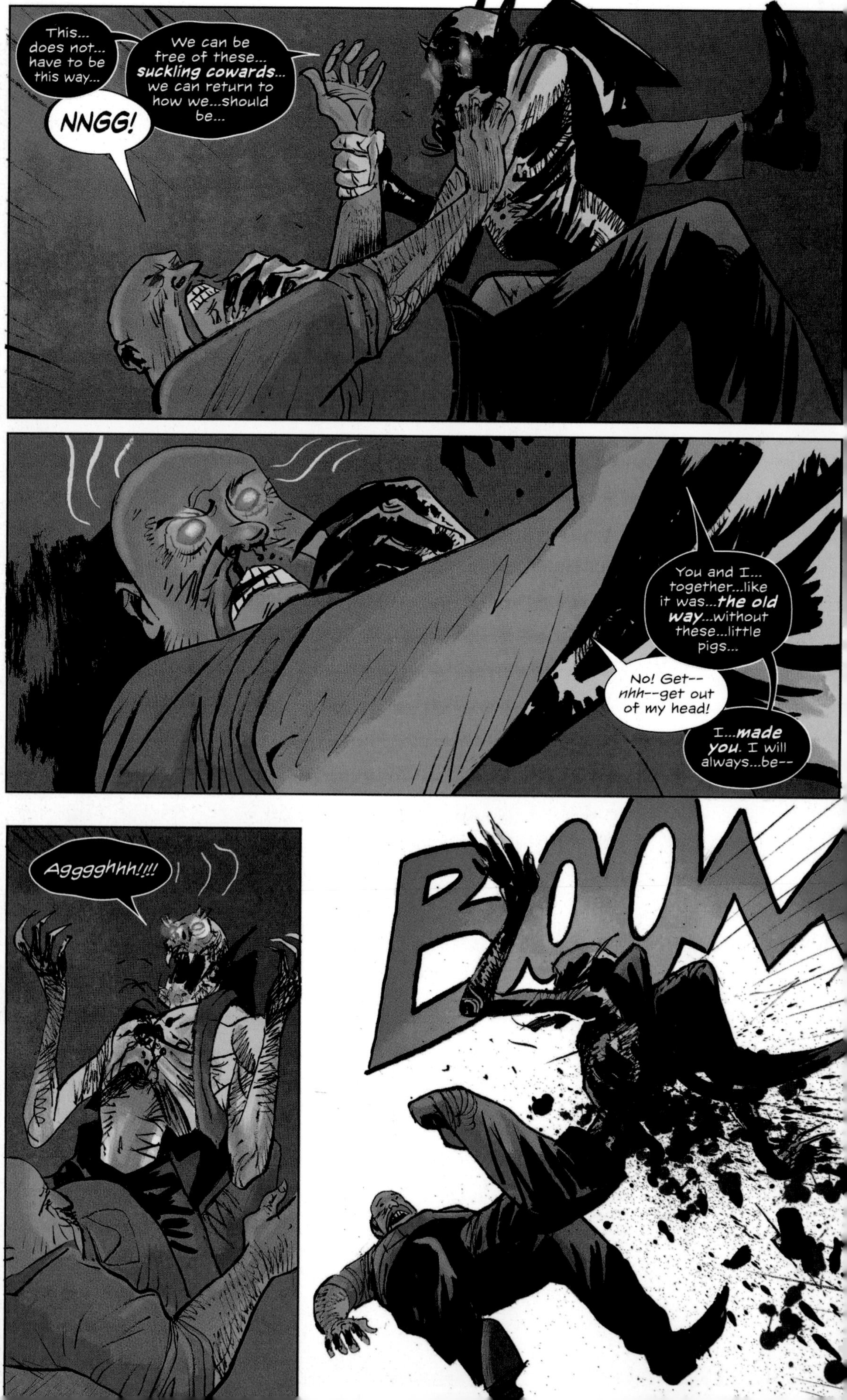

This... does not... have to be this way...
We can be free of these... **suckling cowards**... we can return to how we...should be...
NNGG!
You and I... together...like it was...***the old way***...without these...little pigs...
No! Get-- nhh--get out of my head!
I...***made you***. I will always...be--
Agggghhh!!!!
BOOM

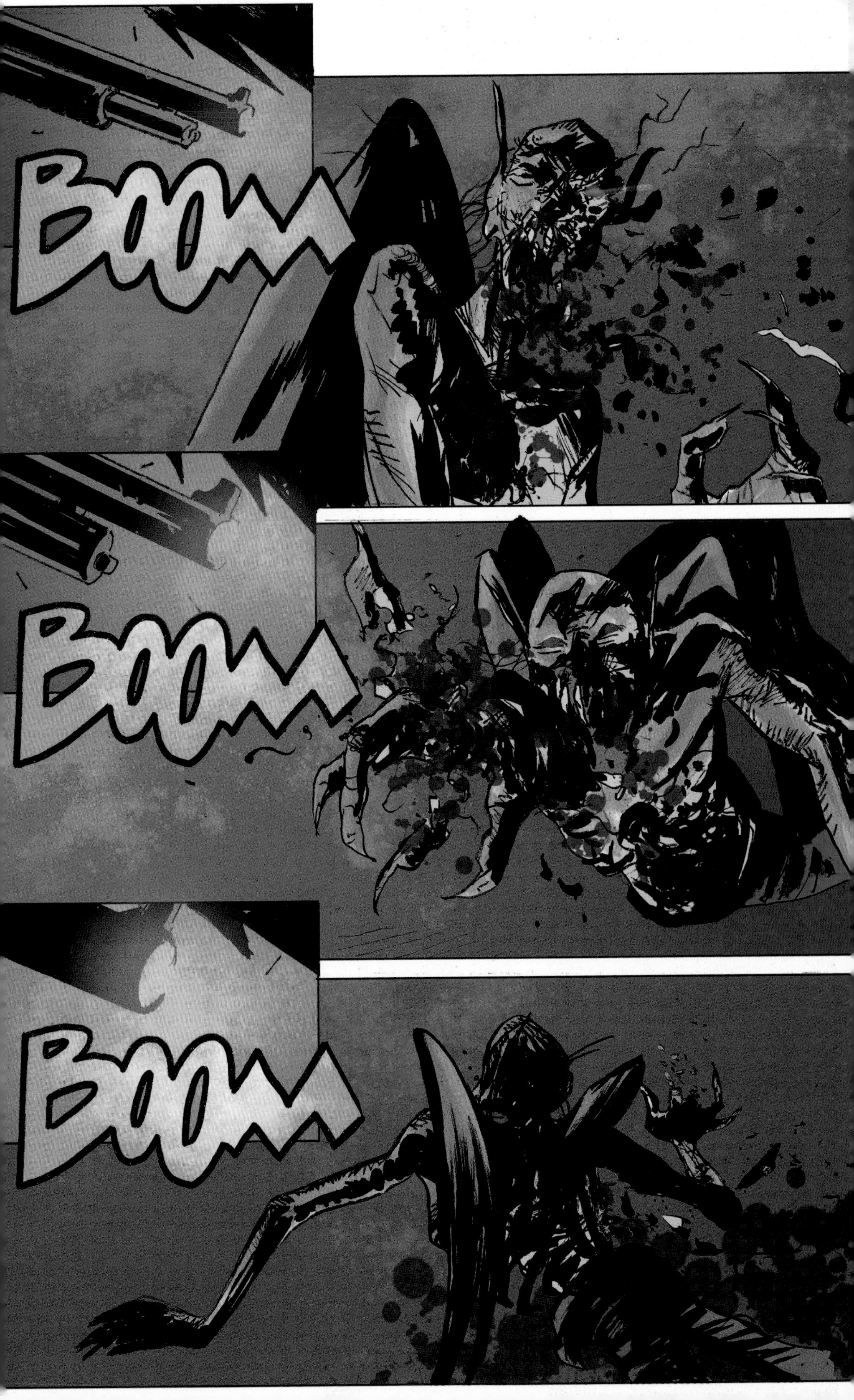
BOOM
BOOM
BOOM

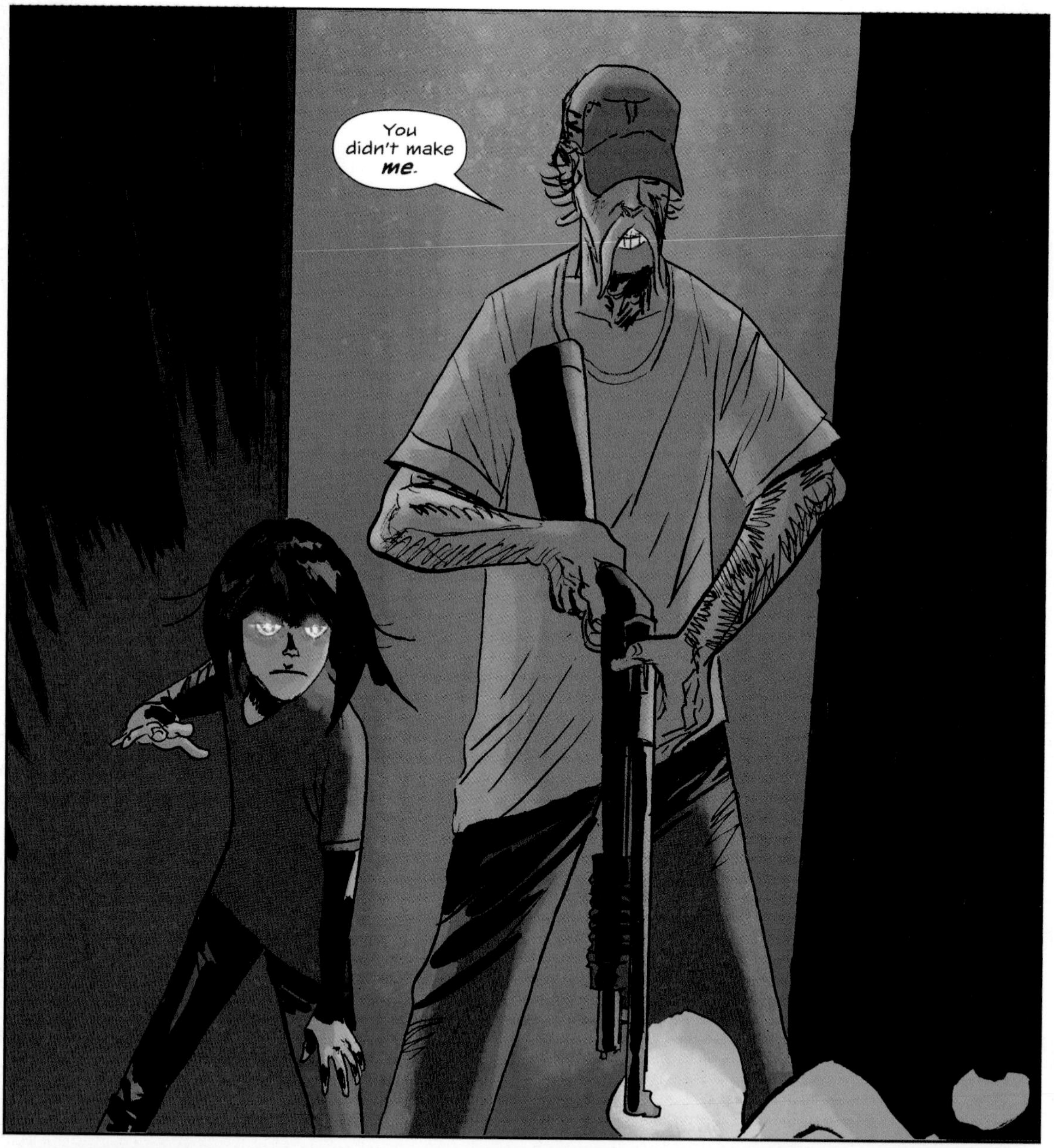
You didn't make **me**.

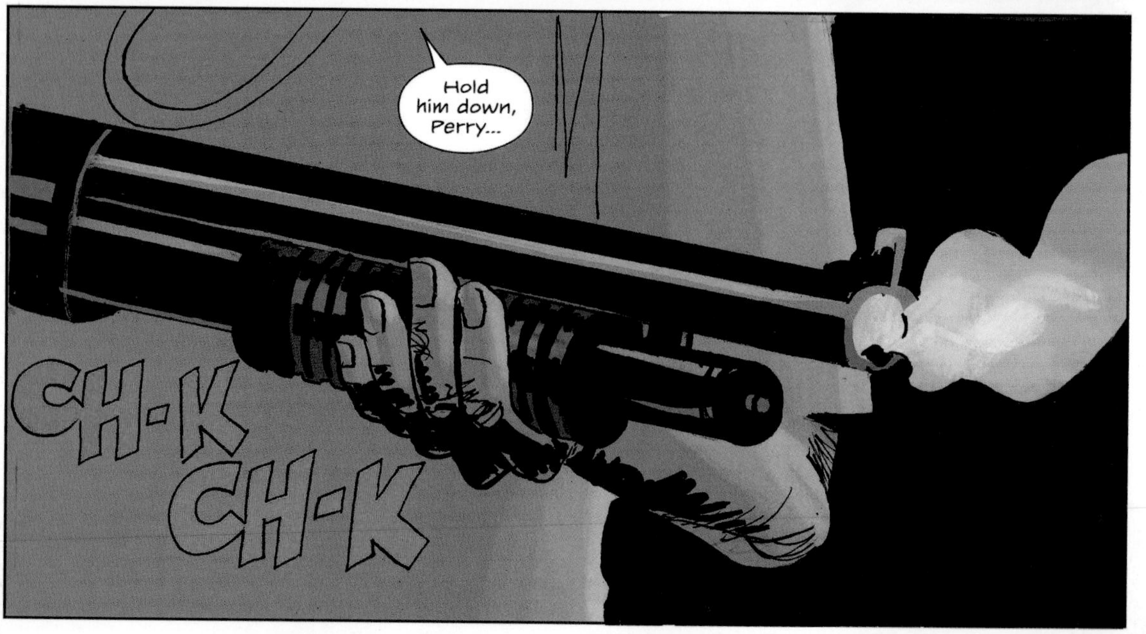
Hold him down, Perry...
CH-K
CH-K

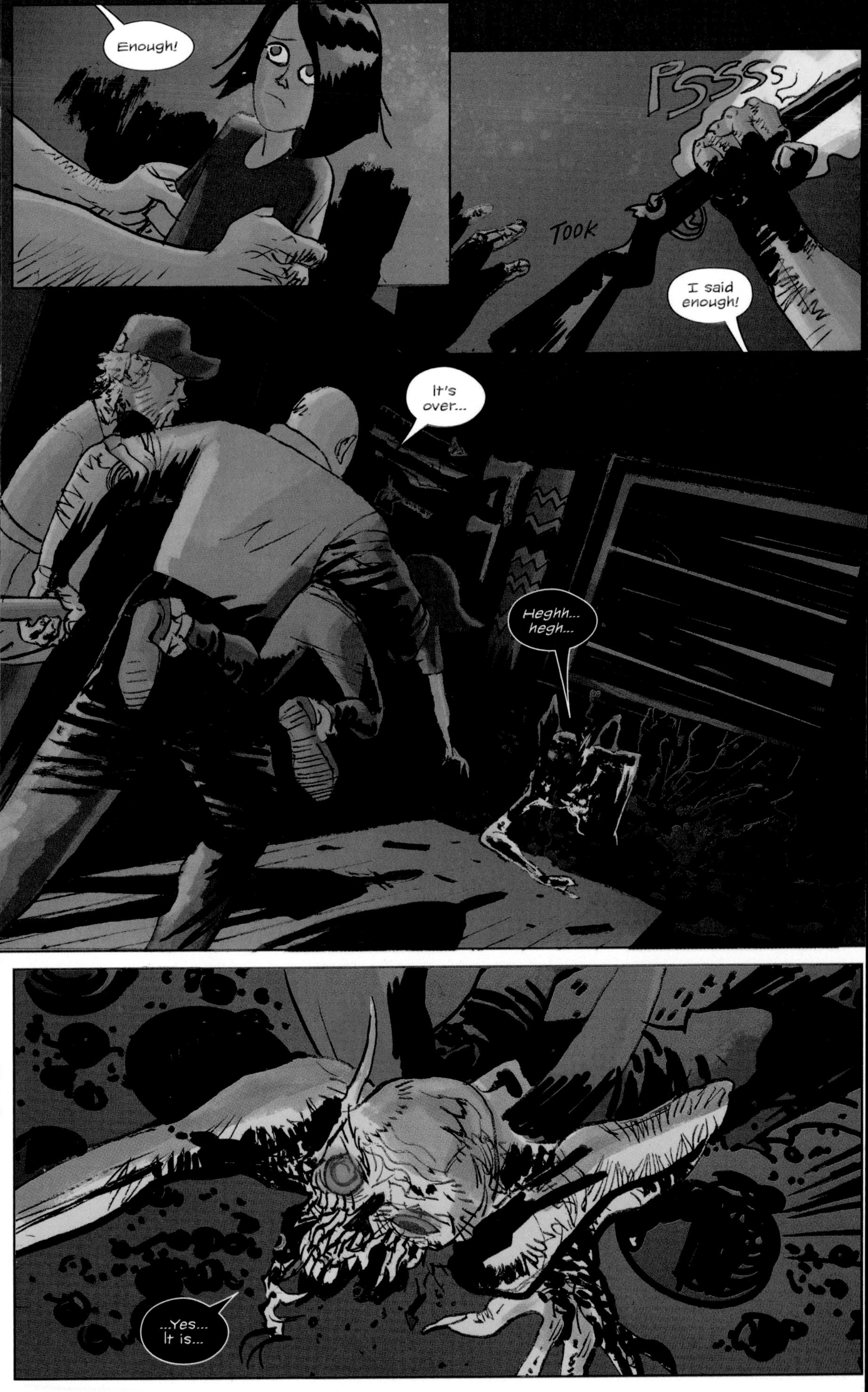
Enough!
PSSSSS
TOOK
I said enough!
It's over...
Heghh... hegh...
...Yes... It is...

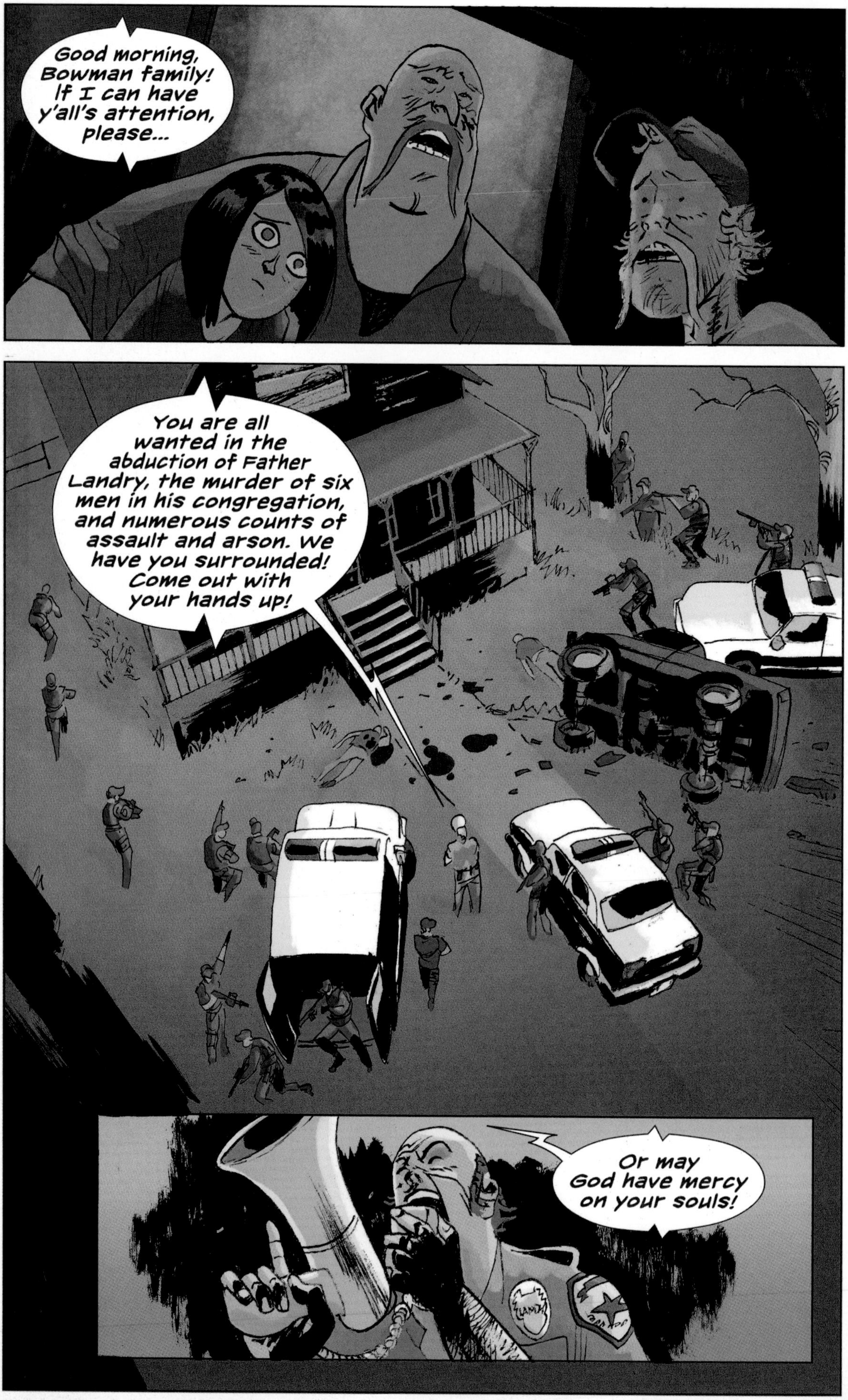
Good morning, Bowman family! If I can have y'all's attention, please...
You are all wanted in the abduction of Father Landry, the murder of six men in his congregation, and numerous counts of assault and arson. We have you surrounded! Come out with your hands up!
Or may God have mercy on your souls!

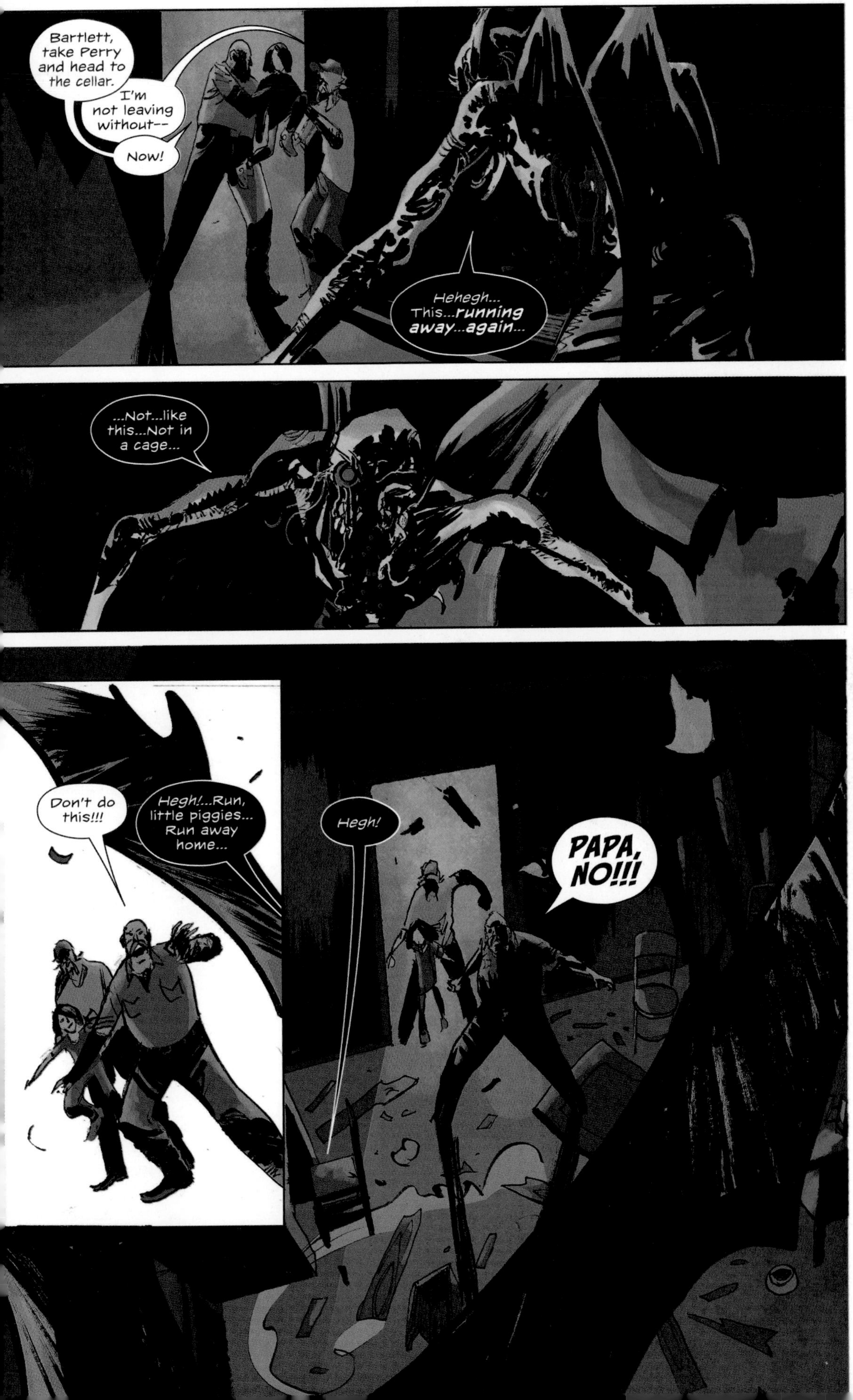
Bartlett, take Perry and head to the cellar.
I'm not leaving without--
Now!
Hehegh... This...running away...again...
...Not...like this...Not in a cage...
Don't do this!!!
Hegh!...Run, little piggies... Run away home...
Hegh!
PAPA, NO!!!

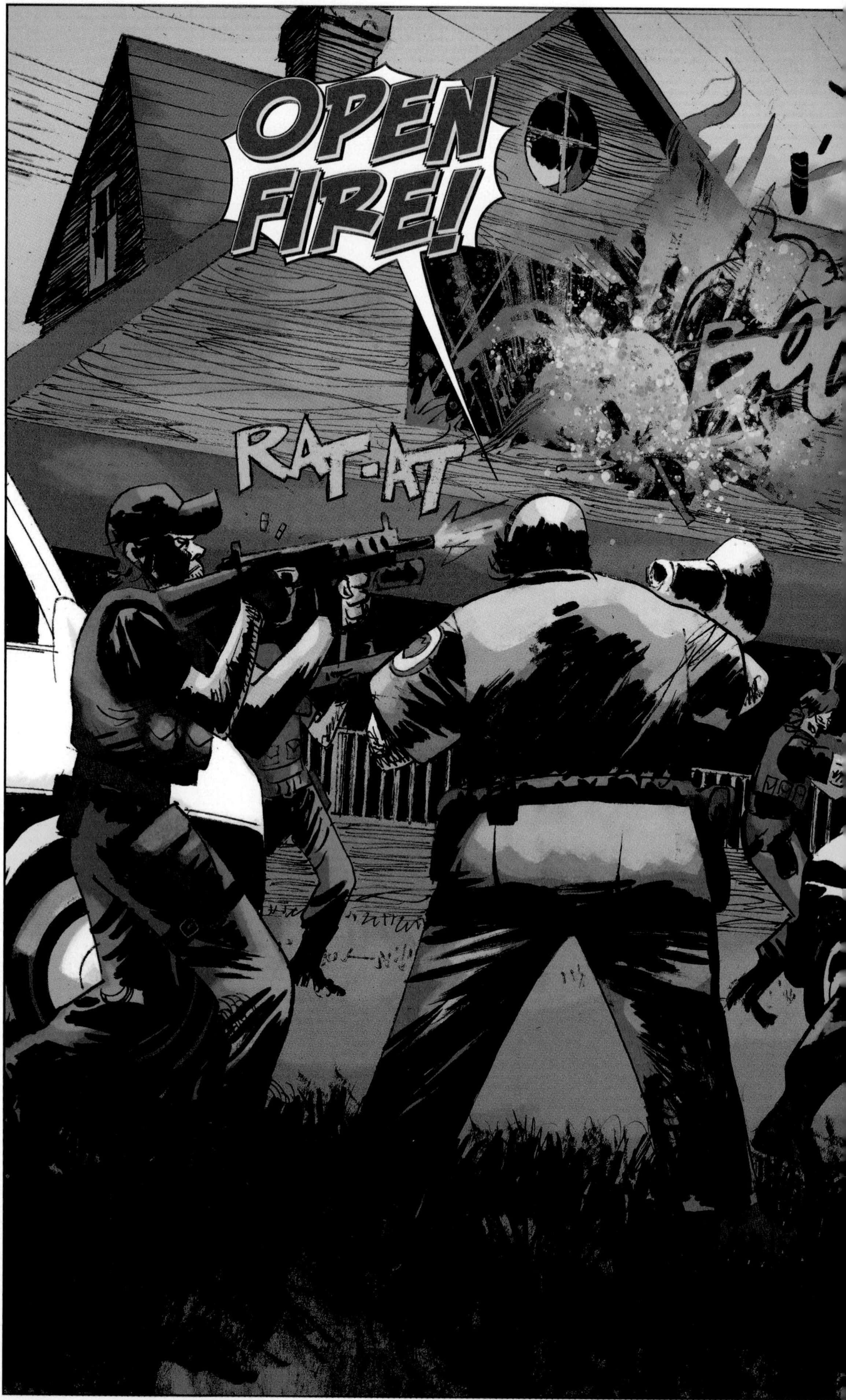
OPEN FIRE!
RAT-AT

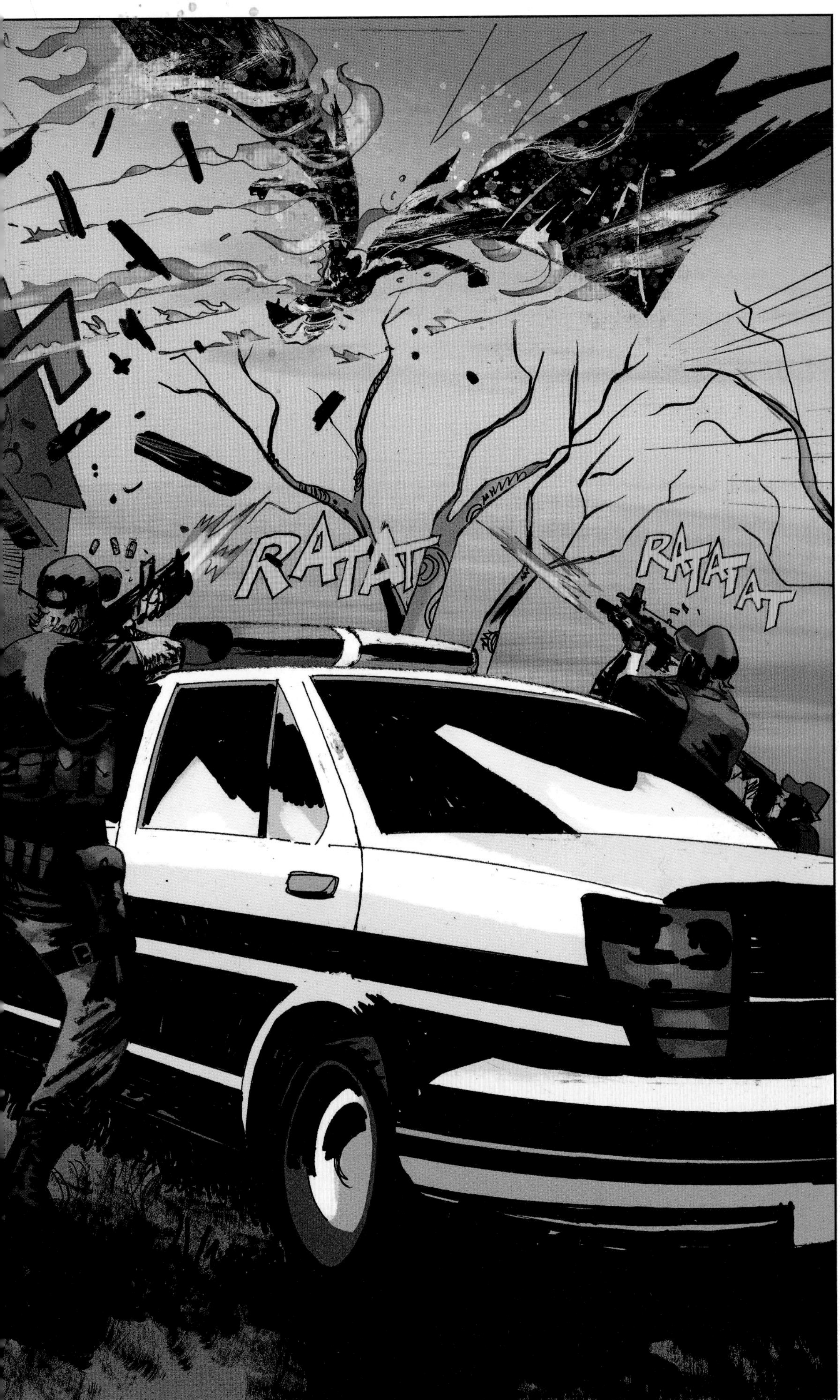
RATAT
RATATAT

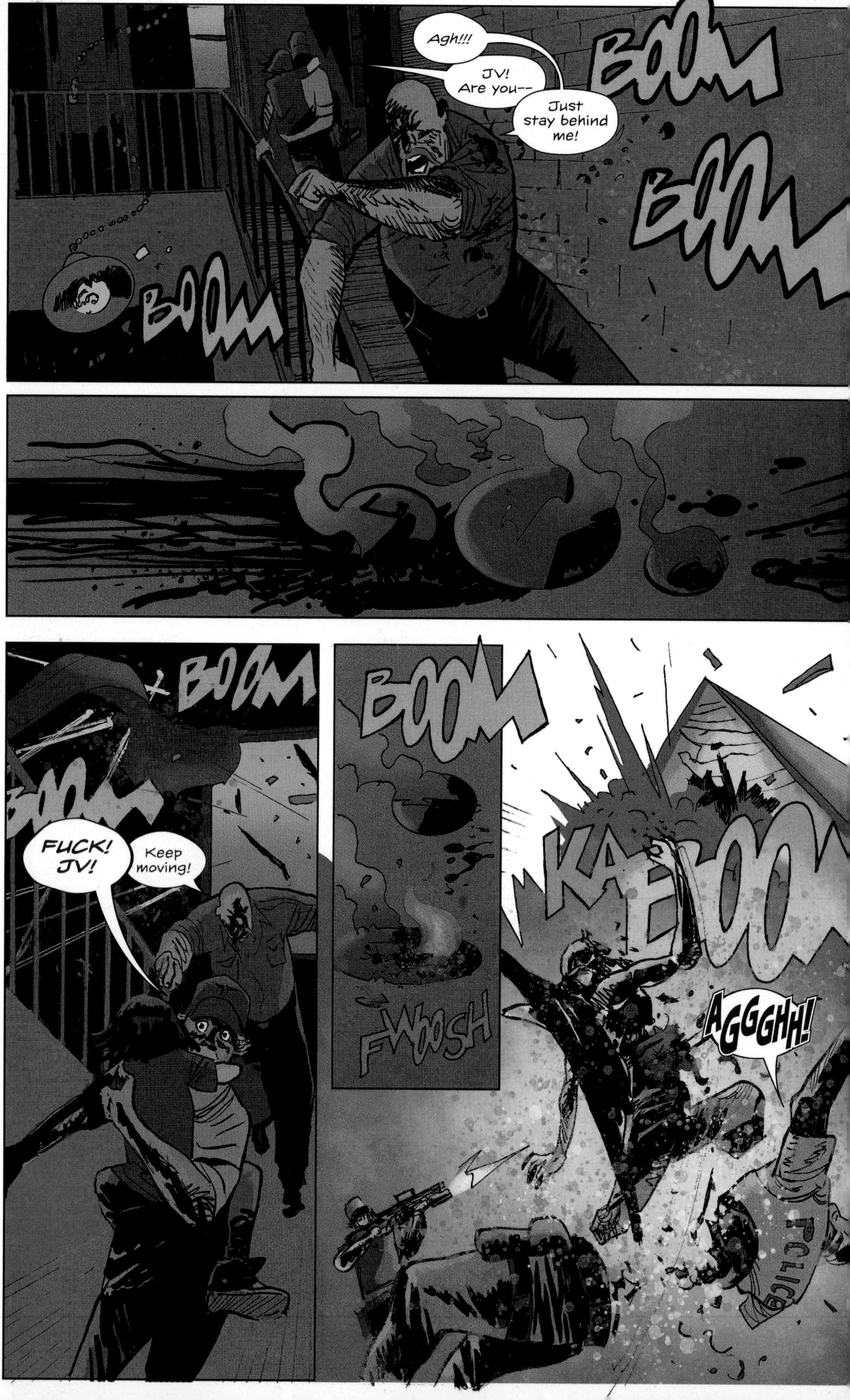
Agh!!!
JV! Are you--
Just stay behind me!
BOOM
BOOM
BOOM
BOOM
BOOM
FUCK! JV!
Keep moving!
BOOM
FWOOSH
KABOOM
AGGGHH!
POLICE

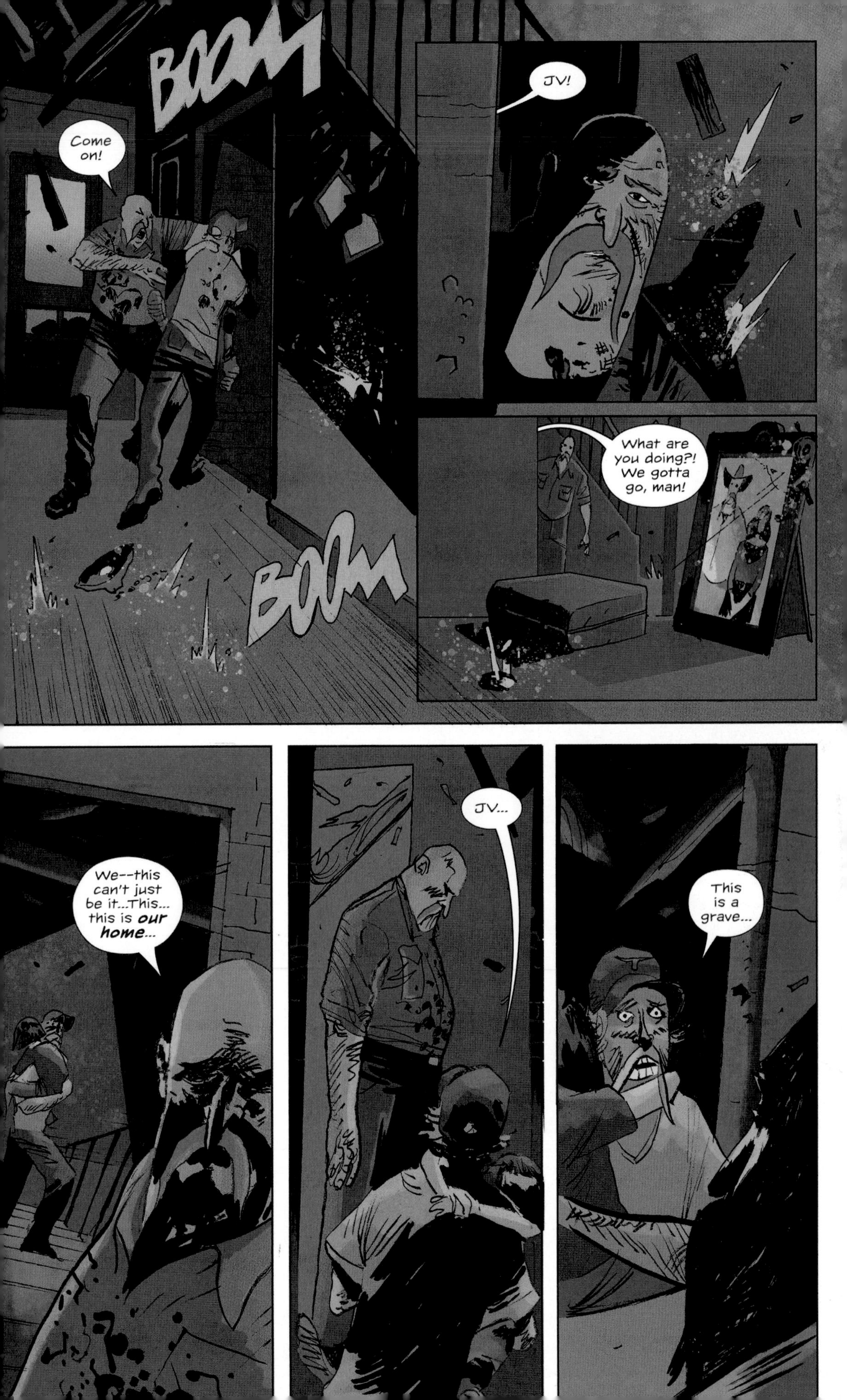
BOOM
Come on!
JV!
What are you doing?! We gotta go, man!
BOOM
We--this can't just be it...This... this is **our home**...
JV...
This is a grave...

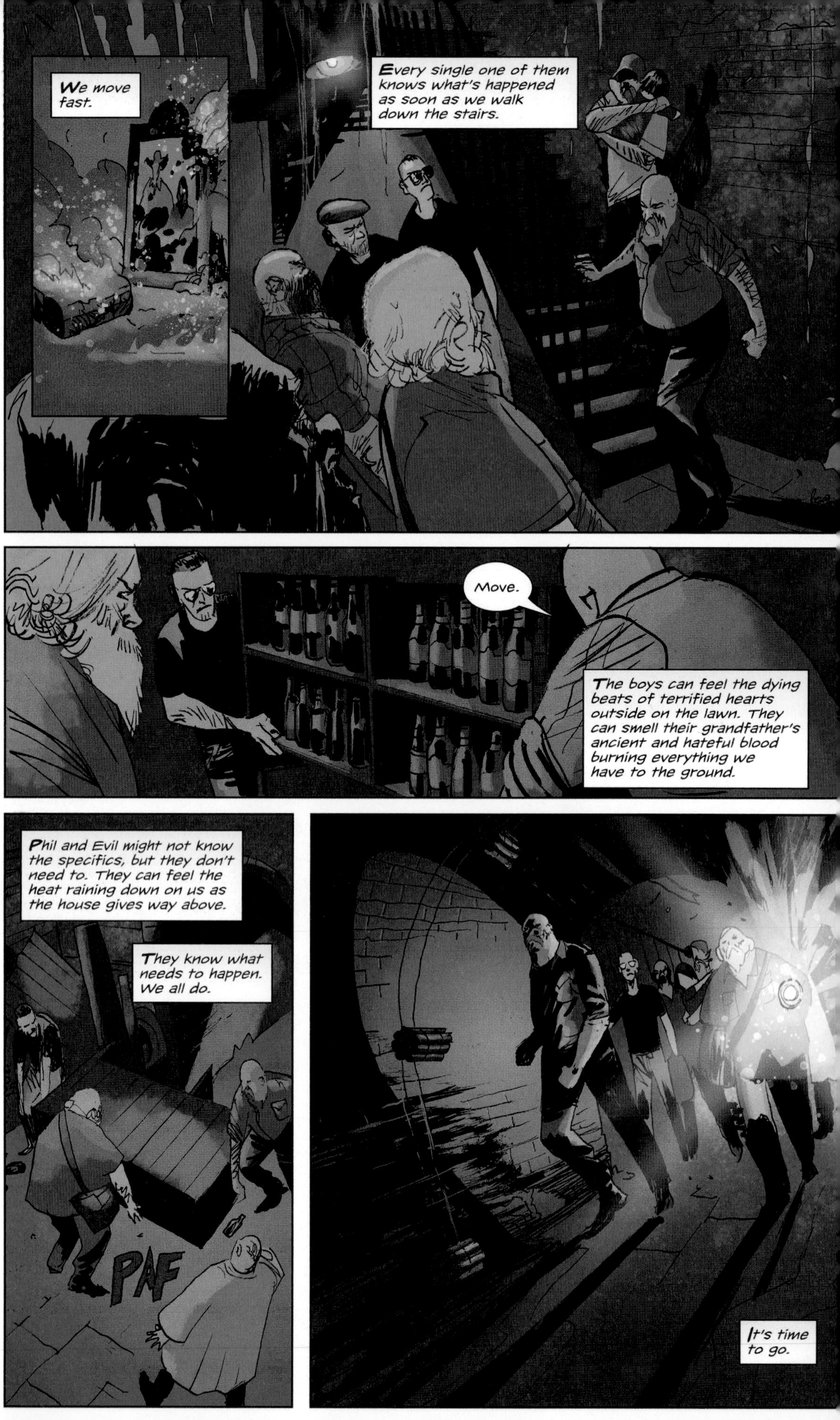
We move fast.
Every single one of them knows what's happened as soon as we walk down the stairs.
Move.
The boys can feel the dying beats of terrified hearts outside on the lawn. They can smell their grandfather's ancient and hateful blood burning everything we have to the ground.
Phil and Evil might not know the specifics, but they don't need to. They can feel the heat raining down on us as the house gives way above.
They know what needs to happen. We all do.
PAF
It's time to go.

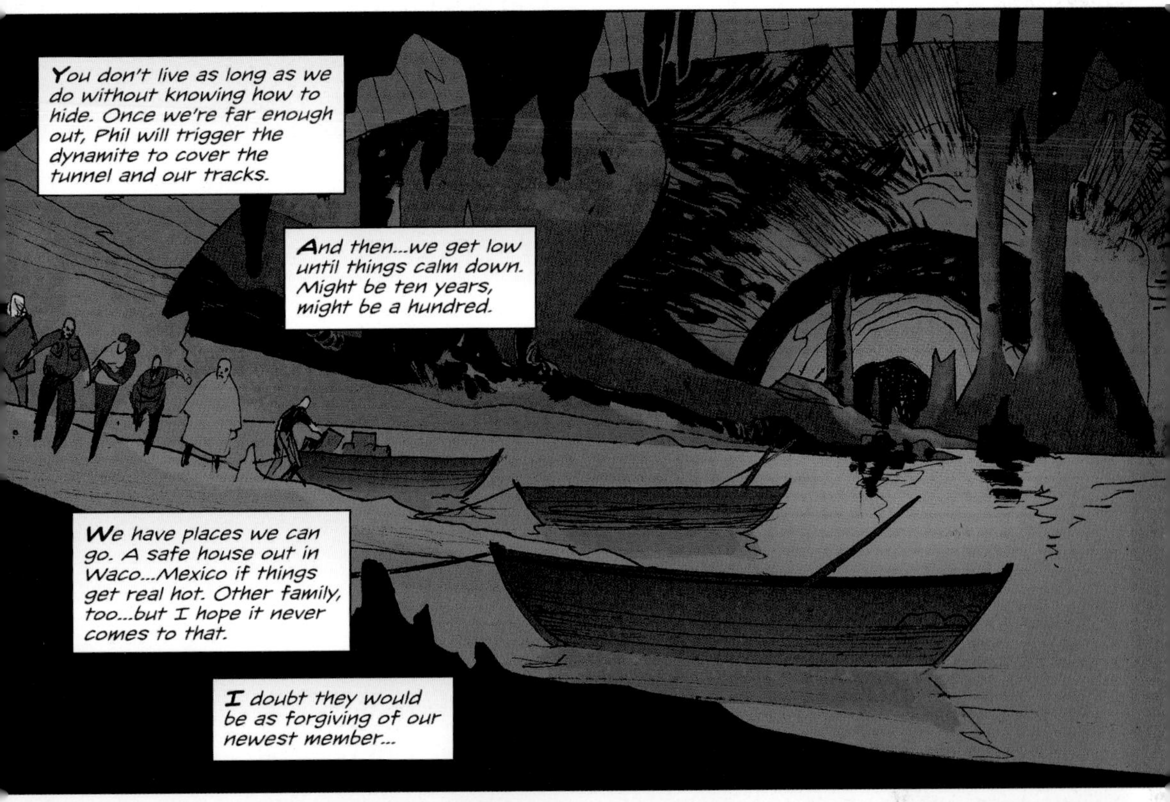
You don't live as long as we do without knowing how to hide. Once we're far enough out, Phil will trigger the dynamite to cover the tunnel and our tracks.
And then...we get low until things calm down. Might be ten years, might be a hundred.
We have places we can go. A safe house out in Waco...Mexico if things get real hot. Other family, too...but I hope it never comes to that.
I doubt they would be as forgiving of our newest member...
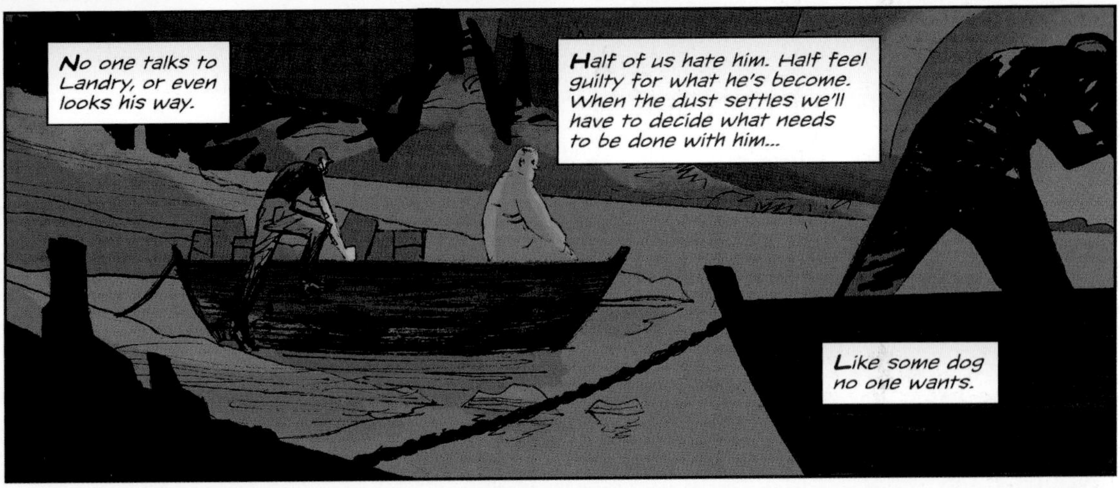
No one talks to Landry, or even looks his way.
Half of us hate him. Half feel guilty for what he's become. When the dust settles we'll have to decide what needs to be done with him...
Like some dog no one wants.
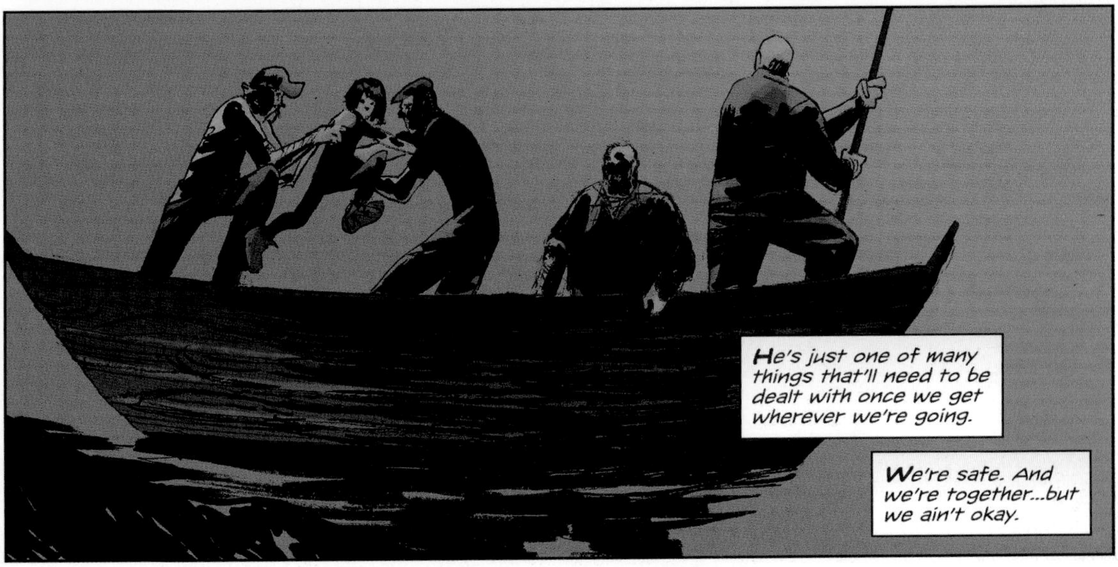
He's just one of many things that'll need to be dealt with once we get wherever we're going.
We're safe. And we're together...but we ain't okay.

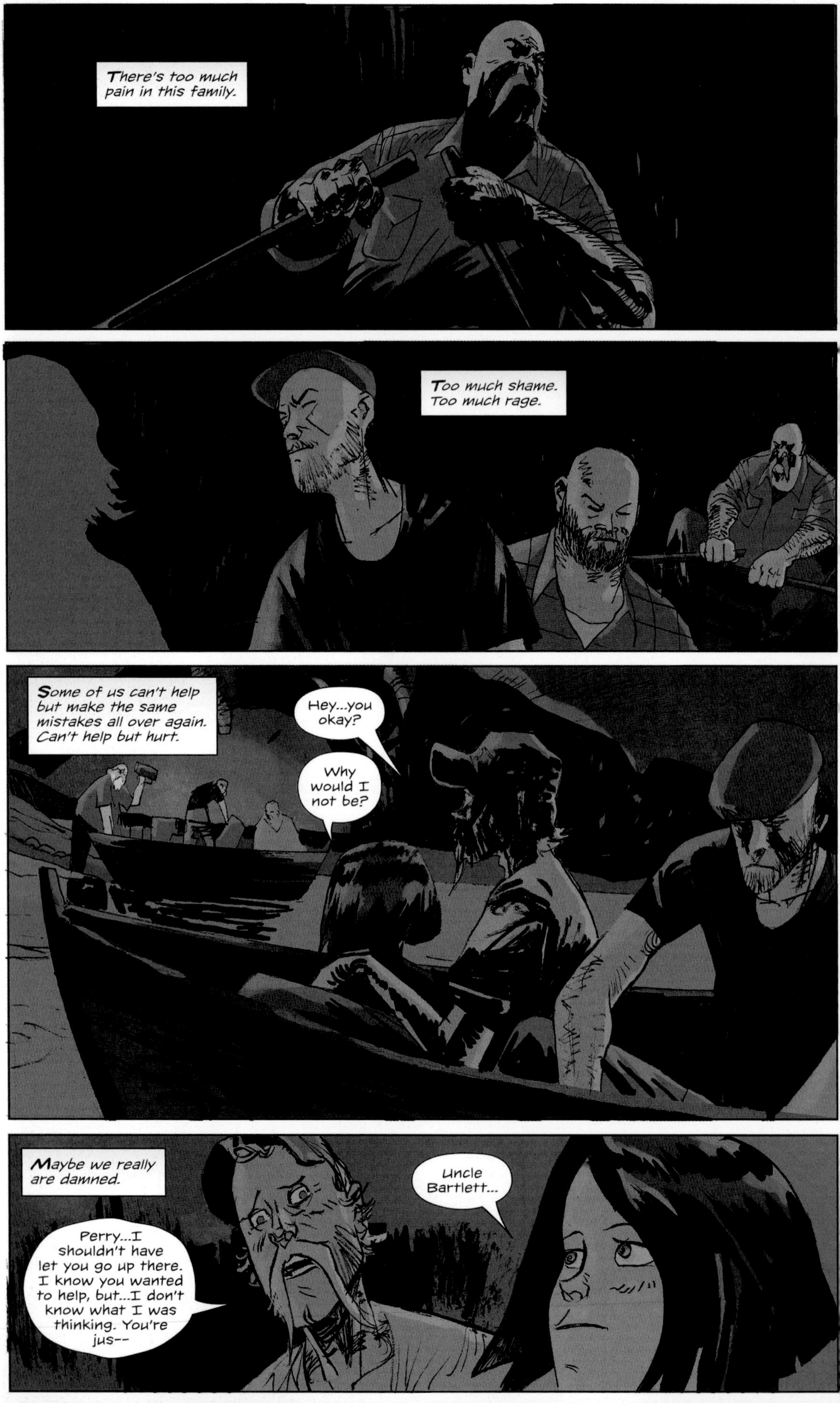
There's too much pain in this family.
Too much shame. Too much rage.
Some of us can't help but make the same mistakes all over again. Can't help but hurt.
Hey...you okay?
Why would I not be?
Maybe we really are damned.
Uncle Bartlett...
Perry...I shouldn't have let you go up there. I know you wanted to help, but...I don't know what I was thinking. You're jus--

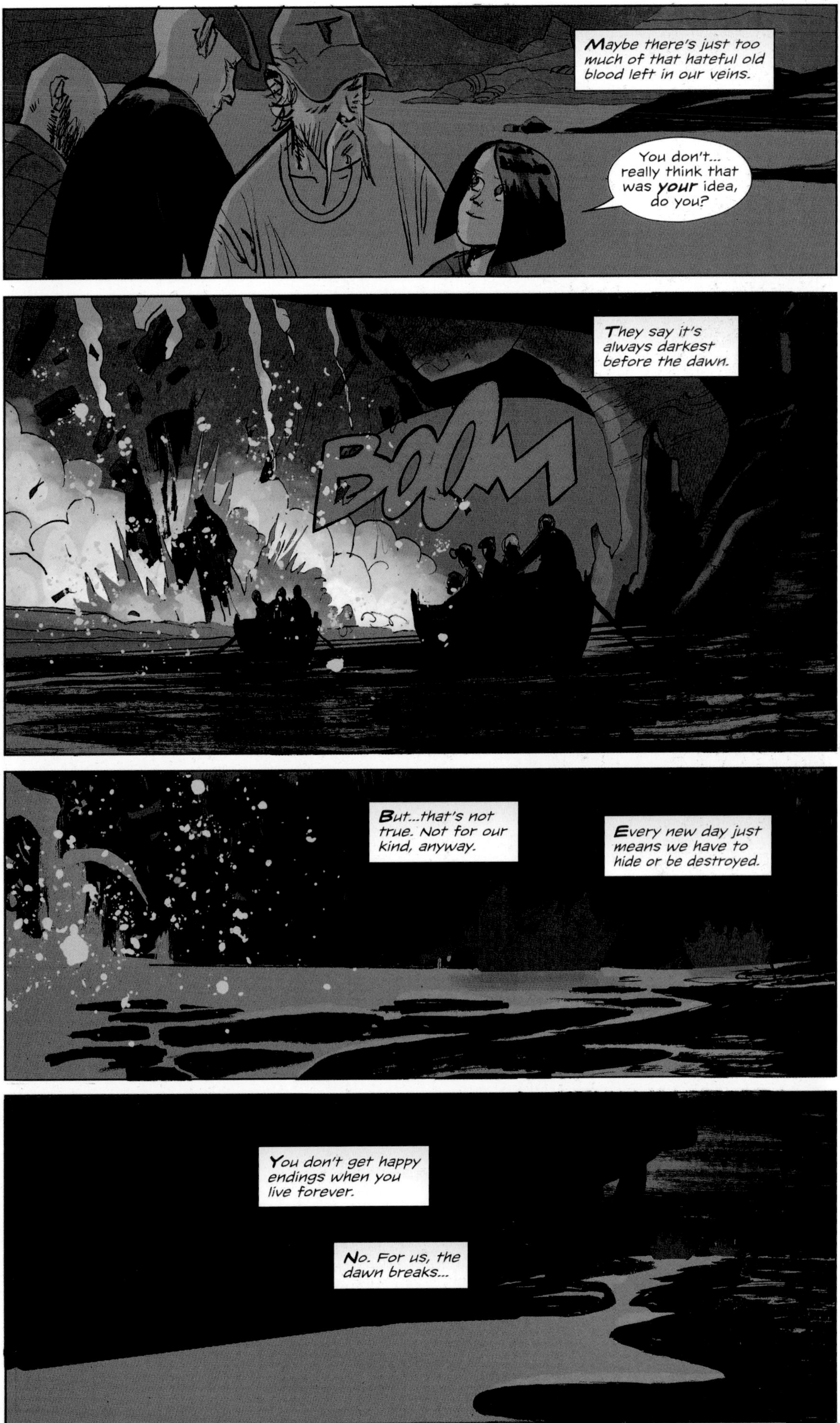
Maybe there's just too much of that hateful old blood left in our veins.
You don't... really think that was your idea, do you?
They say it's always darkest before the dawn.
BOOM
But...that's not true. Not for our kind, anyway.
Every new day just means we have to hide or be destroyed.
You don't get happy endings when you live forever.
No. For us, the dawn breaks...

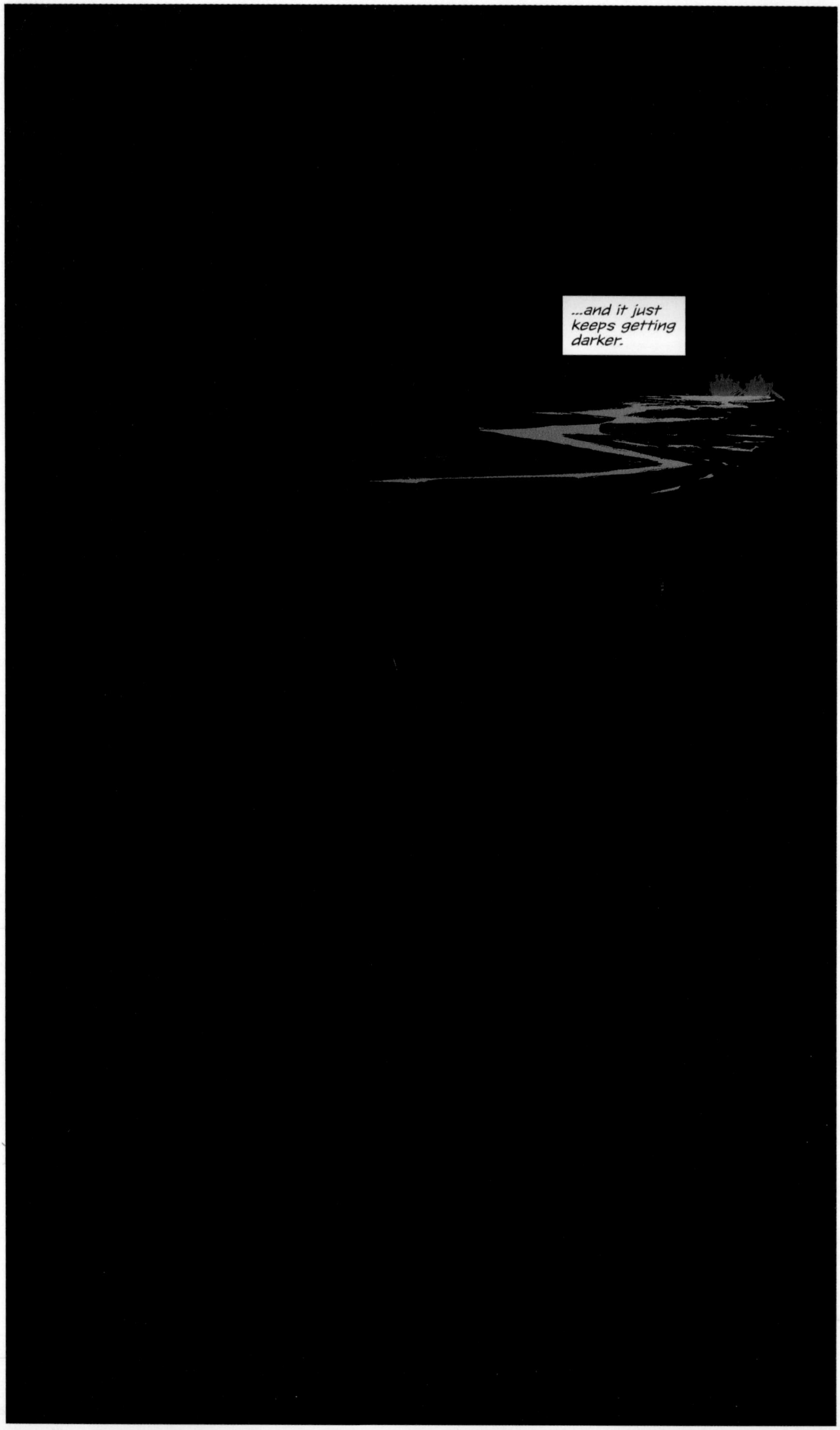
...and it just keeps getting darker.

To be continued...

"You don't get happy endings...

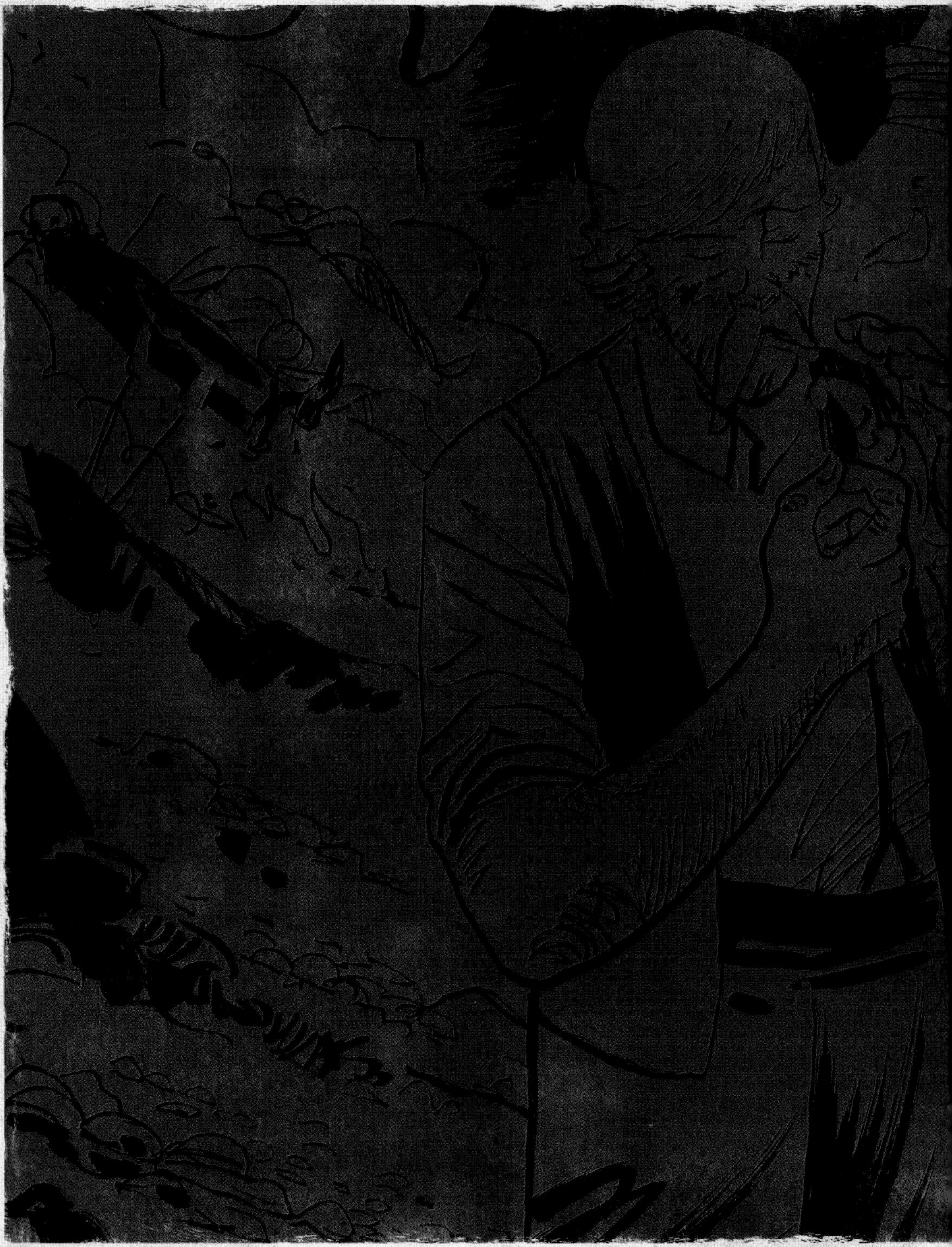

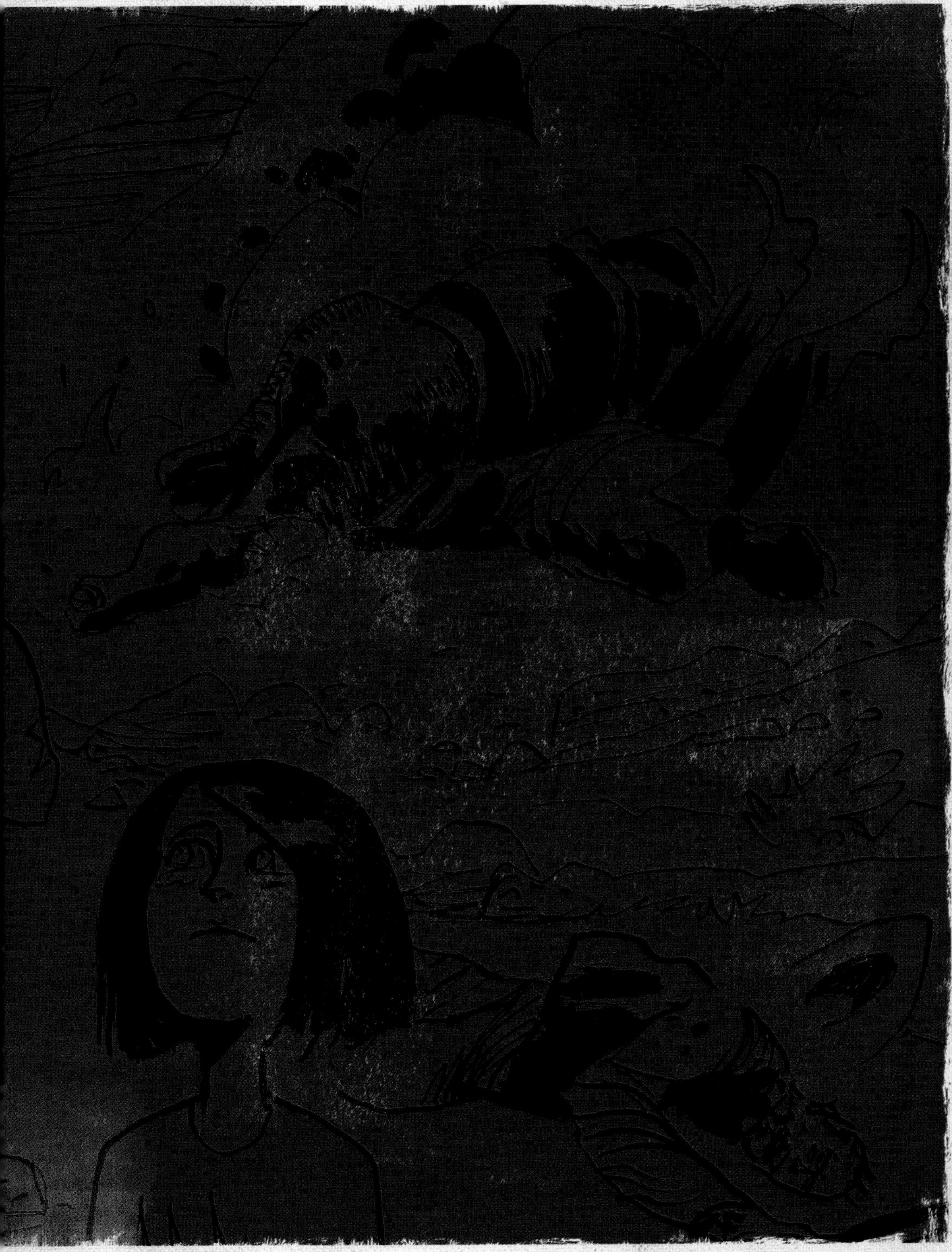

when you live forever."

FOR MORE TALES FROM *ROBERT KIRKMAN* AND *SKYBOUND*

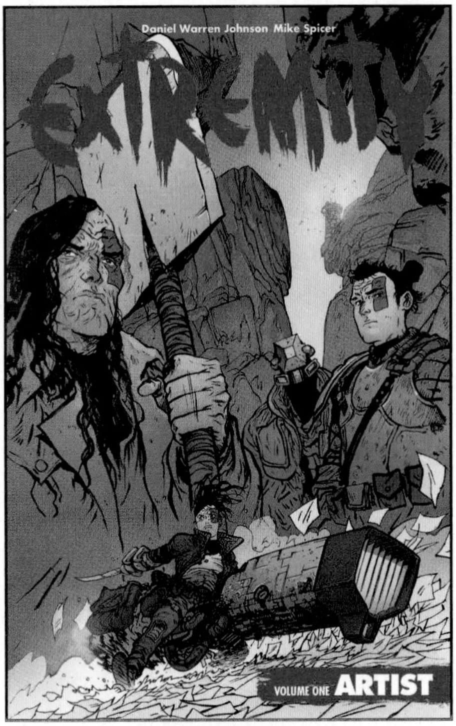
Daniel Warren Johnson Mike Spicer
EXTREMITY
VOLUME ONE ARTIST

VOL. 1: ARTIST TP
ISBN: 978-1-5343-0242-6
$16.99

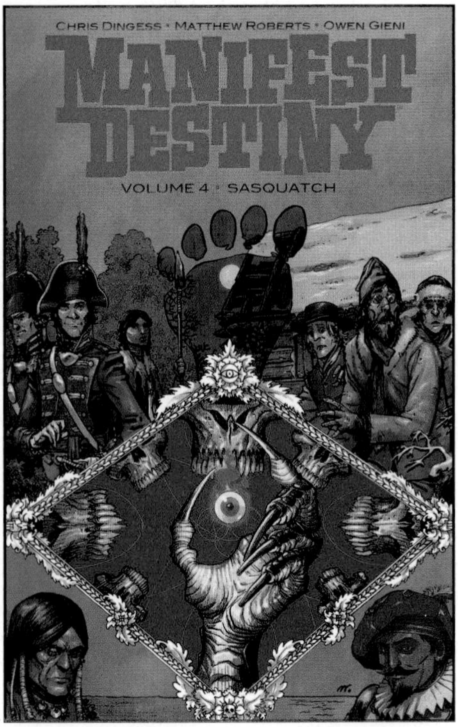
CHRIS DINGESS • MATTHEW ROBERTS • OWEN GIENI
MANIFEST DESTINY
VOLUME 4 • SASQUATCH

VOL. 1: FLORA & FAUNA TP
ISBN: 978-1-60706-982-9
$9.99

VOL. 2: AMPHIBIA & INSECTA TP
ISBN: 978-1-63215-052-3
$14.99

VOL. 3: CHIROPTERA & CARNIFORMAVES TP
ISBN: 978-1-63215-397-5
$14.99

VOL. 4: SASQUATCH TP
ISBN: 978-1-63215-890-1
$14.99

VOL. 5: MNEMOPHOBIA & CHRONOPHOBIA TP
ISBN: 978-1-5343-0230-3
$9.99

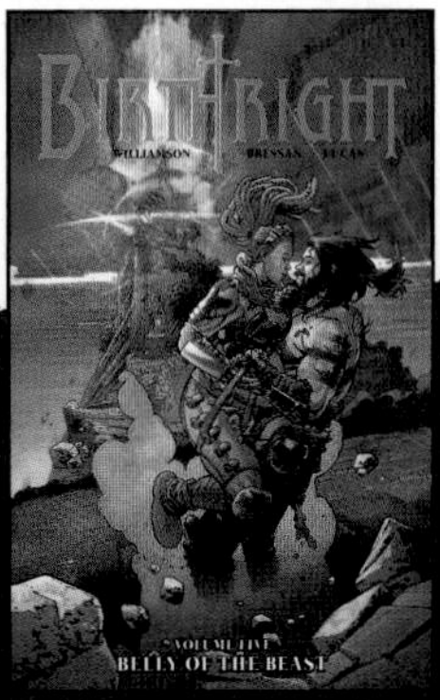
BIRTHRIGHT
WILLIAMSON BRESSAN LUCAS
VOLUME FIVE
BELLY OF THE BEAST

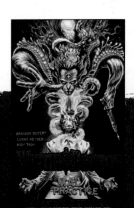

VOL. 1: HOMECOMING TP
ISBN: 978-1-63215-231-2
$9.99

VOL. 2: CALL TO ADVENTURE TP
ISBN: 978-1-63215-446-0
$12.99

VOL. 3: ALLIES AND ENEMIES TP
ISBN: 978-1-63215-683-9
$12.99

VOL. 4: FAMILY HISTORY TP
ISBN: 978-1-63215-871-0
$12.99

VOL. 5: BELLY OF THE BEAST TP
ISBN: 978-1-53430-218-1
$12.99

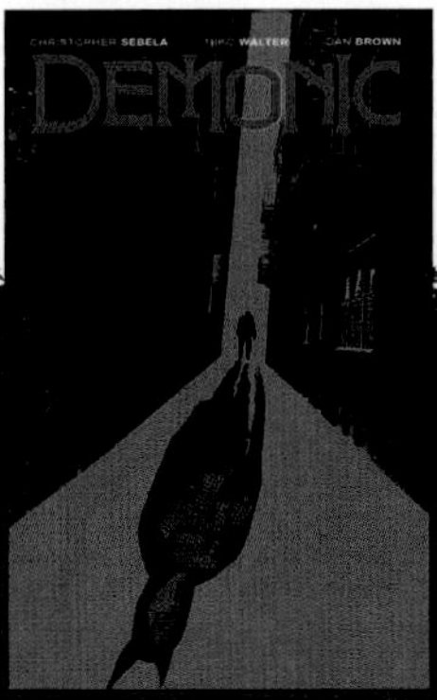
DEMONIC

COMPLETE COLLECTION
ISBN: 978-1-5343-0057-6
$14.99

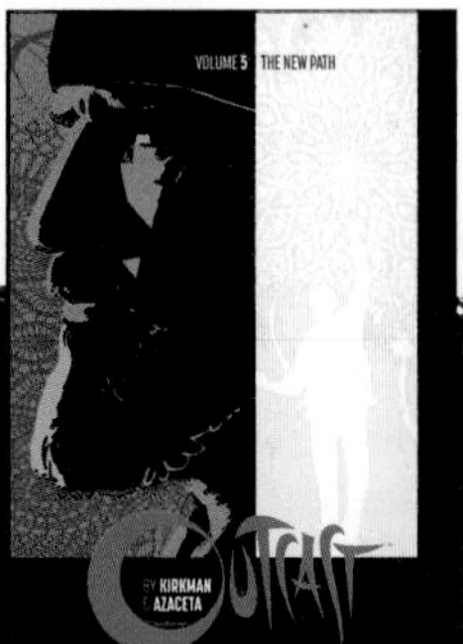
VOLUME 5 THE NEW PATH
BY KIRKMAN AZACETA
OUTCAST

VOL. 1: A DARKNESS SURROUNDS HIM TP
ISBN: 978-1-63215-053-0
$9.99

VOL. 2: A VAST AND UNENDING RUIN TP
ISBN: 978-1-63215-448-4
$14.99

VOL. 3: THIS LITTLE LIGHT TP
ISBN: 978-1-63215-693-8
$14.99

VOL. 4: UNDER DEVIL'S WING TP
ISBN: 978-1-5343-0050-7
$14.99

VOL. 5: THE NEW PATH TP
ISBN: 978-1-5343-0249-5
$16.99

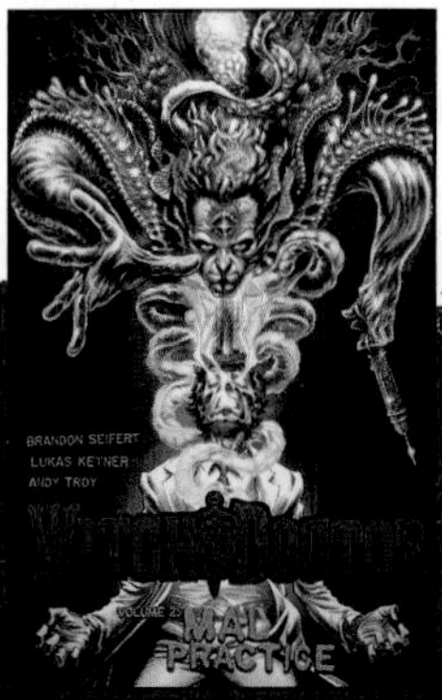
BRANDON SEIFERT
LUKAS KETNER
ANDY TROY
MAL PRACTICE

VOL. 1: UNDER THE KNIFE TP
ISBN: 978-1-60706-441-1
$12.99

VOL. 2: MAL PRACTICE TP
ISBN: 978-1-60706-693-4
$14.99